SIX CONVICTS
FOR
BOTANY BAY

David C. Lawton

Published by

MELROSE
BOOKS

An Imprint of Melrose Press Limited
St Thomas Place, Ely
Cambridgeshire
CB7 4GG, UK
www.melrosebooks.com

FIRST EDITION

Copyright © David C. Lawton 2010

The Author asserts his moral right to
be identified as the author of this work

Cover designed by Jeremy Kay

ISBN 978 1 907040 40 5

Printed and bound in Great Britain by:
CPI Antony Rowe, Chippenham, Wiltshire

This book is dedicated to all those people, known or unknown whom I have met in my passage of life, many of which have given me the inspiration to set down in words my experiences. This especially so to my wife Jean, who has stood beside me for over fifty years.

CONTENTS

FOREWORD

THIS NOVEL IS A TOTAL WORK OF fiction except where specific mention is made of a factual event.

No official English police force existed at the time this story opens in 1796. (The first was founded in 1829 by the parliamentarian Sir Robert Peel.) The law up to then was administered by local constables, sheriffs, magistrates and judges appointed by the Crown. A person could be hanged for physical assault, theft, poaching, highway robbery and of course murder. It was a rather wild and lawless period of British history due in part to the abject poverty which prevailed among the common masses leading naturally to crime both petty and major. In many cases it was pointless for a judge to impose a fine because the culprit had no means of paying therefore prison was the only answer. This resulted in overcrowding of almost all jails.

As a way of dealing with the vast number of incarcerated criminals the government introduced a system of transportation to Australia of both male and female convicts in 1788. The penal colony was located at Botany Bay near Port Jackson, later to be renamed Sydney. Thousands of both young and old were transported, some for very minor offences indeed. Conditions aboard the ships could only be described as appalling, as a result of which many never survived the long voyage. Those who did usually arrived in very poor physical condition but were put to work immediately. Males farmed and performed manual labour to develop Port Jackson and other areas while females were employed mainly as domestic servants. It was not uncommon for younger women to arrive pregnant, having given themselves to sailors aboard the ships in return for small favours. Upon completion of their sentences many chose to remain in the country and some made a great success of their new-found freedom.

Transportation continued for sixty-nine years with the final batch of convicts being shipped in 1857. The system was finally abolished in 1868. For an accurate insight of a convict's existence aboard the ships and a brief description of life in Botany Bay the non-fiction work: *The Floating Brothel* by Siân Rees is highly recommended.

This is a fictitious story of six transported female convicts, who by a unique twist of fate had freedom returned to four of them.

The facts concerning King George III's madness are true. He finally regained his faculties in March 1789 and reigned until his death in 1820.

By necessity many characters in this novel appear more eloquent than they normally would have been for the period in which I write. Education for the average citizen was very minimal and in many cases totally non-existent. It is also worthy of note, and without disrespect, that women in those days were far more robust than the average female of today. They had to be because countless thousands had to live by their wits alone, in today's vernacular they were 'streetwise'. In most families of very modest means the wife had to suffer a birth without anaesthetics. Frequently their children were treated no better than slaves and forced to work long, arduous hours, performing household duties with no labour-saving devices at all. A washday for an average family could take five to six hours and usually in cold water. Some families because of poverty simply cast unwanted children out on the street where they were forced to become either thieves or prostitutes or they died.

Naturally there were also many hundreds of families in England who had amassed great wealth either by fair means or foul. Generally families of affluence exploited those they employed, treating them little better than slaves. On the other hand it must be admitted many families did treat their servants with kindness, respect and civility although they were the exception rather than the rule.

It should also be borne in mind that communications generally in the eighteenth century were governed by the speed of horses on land and ships at sea. A letter to Australia therefore could take six months or longer to deliver. The telegraph was yet to be invented.

PART ONE

CAUSES AND CRIMES

LIMEHOUSE – LONDON 1796

CHAPTER 1

ASURLY REPRESENTATIVE OF THE EAST INDIA DOCKYARD stood on the doorstep of twenty-three Grundy Street with his greasy cap in hand, telling Vera Farrow that her husband Sam had been crushed to death under a crate of farming machinery destined for South Africa.

The blousy woman merely sniffed, hitched up her copious bosom and said, "So bloody what!"

Hovering nervously in the background was Vera's daughter Catherine who appeared unemotional although inwardly she was buoyed by the news in the hopes that her father's death would mean a release from the many years of physical and mental abuse she had been subjected to since a very early age. Many times it had been said by her father and mother she was an unwelcome addition to the family, a sexual mistake. As a result of this she had been forced to perform almost all the household tasks during the day and on into the night while her parents were out drinking beer, gin and cheap whisky at one of the many dockside taverns. Such socializing and child abuse was not uncommon in the Limehouse district which was a very rough neighbourhood indeed.

Catherine heard her mother asking the man how much money she could expect in settlement as a result of the accident.

"I'm sorry, Vera lass, but all you'll get is what Sam had earned up to the time the crate fell on him. According to the yard manager he was half drunk and had rigged the load himself. Lucky nobody else was under it. You'll get what's owing on Friday. Sorry, lass."

He dropped his head, replaced his greasy cap and left.

"What's to become of us, Mama?" Catherine asked after her mother had kicked the ill-fitting street door closed.

"The bloody poorhouse if we're not very careful. I'll have to get a job as I can't rely on you to work outside. All you're fit for is bloody housework and you don't do a good job of that. If you must know we'll hardly have enough to pay the rent which is due in two weeks. Go pour me a big gin, I need to sit and think."

Like she always did, Catherine obeyed.

* * *

Next afternoon another man arrived from the dockyard with a few coins in a brown paper bag. Sam's fellow workers had held a collection but like him they existed on the fringes of poverty so were unable to donate much, plus Sam wasn't too popular among his workmates due to his excessive drinking. They knew the money he outlaid for beer, gin and whisky would have been better spent on his family; but don't dare tell Sam that or you could expect a fist on the chin. Residents of Grundy Street had also managed to scrape together just under two shillings but even then there wasn't enough for another week's rent. And the church couldn't be expected to help out financially, they gave compassion and prayers in great abundance, sadly little money.

Half sotted with gin, Vera threw the paper bag to one side and stared at her daughter with that look which always scared Catherine. It usually meant she was going to get a clip across the ear or be beaten again with her father's leather razor strop. She shied away as her mother said, "There's only one thing for it, we need money so I'll have to start selling my only asset around the taverns. There's many that want me and now your dad is gone they can have me, provided they pay first."

"Is that a wise thing to do, Mama?"

"Of course it is, you stupid bugger, otherwise we'll find ourselves and our miserable bits of furniture out on the street. Do you want that?"

"No, Mama."

"Then make me a pot of tea while I get changed."

Catherine watched her stagger upstairs knowing her wretched life was going to continue. In fact it could be even worse from now on. She went to the small kitchen alcove, filled the kettle and put it over the cooker flame before spooning some tea leaves into the pot. Then she went to the rocking chair by the fireplace, sat down and began to cry.

* * *

So Vera Farrow started going out almost every night to one of the many local taverns, trying to solicit a customer who was willing to pay for what she had to offer. Her main business came from sailors home after a voyage where they had been deprived of female company for too long. Occasionally there was the odd dockyard worker who had won a bit of money on the horses.

"Buy me a goblet of gin and we'll kiss on a bench behind the curtains," was her usual opening proposal before adding, "It's sixpence extra to feel my tits. A shilling to feel lower down. If you want entry it's a florin and we'll do it in the backyard."

The backyard was where all the other tavern tarts did their tricks. They would ruffle their skirts and petticoats up and let the client poke them. Their pleasure was usually faked as all they wanted was the money. Easy money provided they were careful not to get pregnant.

Most nights Vera returned home drunk and usually with a man on her arm. If Catherine was still up she would be sent to her dingy, damp room. Once there she had socks to darn or frayed hems of skirts to repair. While sewing she listened to the creaks of her mother's bed and, although somewhat naïve, she had a good idea what they were doing as one night she had spied through a crack in the doorframe. All she saw was the naked bottom of a man pumping away between her mother's parted legs.

One night she was caught spying and while being held across the man's knee her mother laid ten hefty strokes across her bare bottom with the leather strop while shouting, "If I ever catch you spying on me again, Catherine Farrow, I'll chain you up in the cellar for a month. And it's no use blubbering like that, you're lucky I don't send you out on the streets to sell yourself, but nobody wants a halfwit!"

And so it went on night after night, man after man.

In the morning the man had gone but Vera remained in bed and gave Catherine her instructions.

"After getting my breakfast make the beds, then do the laundry and hang it out. When it's dry do the ironing. Make sure my red lace-up blouse is ready for tonight, the men like it. After that bring a bucket of coal up from the cellar then clean the hen coop and rabbit hutch out, and the house had better be spick and span when I get up or you'll be feeling the strop again."

For the attractive nineteen-year-old it was a nightmare without a visible end. All she could hope for was her mother reforming although that didn't seem very likely. She couldn't run away as there was nowhere to go, not even to relations because the only aunt she knew had moved up north over three years ago. She was ailing then and had probably died by now.

* * *

Much to Catherine's dismay things got steadily worse. Only six months after her father's tragic death Vera married again, to one of those who had become a regular client. Patrick O'Grady was a beefy stevedore who worked at the same dockyard as her late father. Like his new wife Patrick enjoyed his pints of ale chased down with rum. Vera was also introduced to opium, which came in on ships from the East. Together they puffed themselves into a fantasy world and usually ended up passing out.

Patrick did seem to have more money though, and once or twice after Catherine had ironed his best trousers and shirt she was rewarded with a few pence to buy a packet of sweets at a local shop which seemed to sell everything except the thing she desired most, someone to love her.

Despite her new husband Vera continued to abuse Catherine both physically and mentally. "Your real father was too soft with you, my girl. Well, he's dead now and I want a good time before I'm too old. Your new dad can do that for me. Do you understand what I'm saying, girl?"

"Yes, Mama."

"Good. Now heat us a bowl of soup before we go to the tavern. And remember to bank the fire so it's warm when we get back."

And so it went on, month after month. Catherine Farrow was a slave in her own home and she knew of nobody to turn to, even the local constables wouldn't interfere, they never did. If she ran away they would bring her back to face a mother and stepfather who thought a good thrashing solved all problems. Tears were her only companion and on cold winter nights she simply shivered with only a single blanket for cover.

* * *

Once though, when her mother was helping a woman two streets away deliver her seventh child Patrick had shown a little tenderness and gave Catherine a tour round the docks where he worked.

"Where do all those wonderful sailing ships go, Patrick?" she asked, looking across the river, for to her they represented a certain magic in that they sailed to mysterious places while she had to remain at home in Limehouse.

"They sail all over the world, lass," Patrick replied while placing an arm across her broad shoulders. "Wonderful places, so I'm told, where it's hot all year round and the sea is warm and clean. India is one place ships go with their cargos of machinery and usually come back with a cargo of tea and silks. Aye, it's a fine life to be afloat feeling an ocean breeze in your face. You'd colour up nicely in no time."

"I'm pale, Patrick, because I'm never allowed out." She shielded her eyes against the bright sun. "And what are those two ships without masts or sails anchored in the middle of the river?"

"They're abandoned warships called hulks where they keep convicts before shipping them to a prison colony in Australia. It's called transportation. See that ship with its sails set? It'll be sailing shortly with almost three hundred convicts both young and old in its hold. They'll suffer terribly while at sea and many will die on the way. They're the lucky ones as I've been told the prison colony is a frightful place where the masters are guards who wield long leather whips. Anyway that's none of our worry, we'll never be going there."

"Isn't it cruel to whip prisoners, Patrick?"

"That it may be so, lass, but the convicts did wrong and have to pay the penalty. Our government said so and King George agreed."

"Where's Australia, Patrick?"

"On the other side of the world, lass. Too far for the likes of you and me to imagine."

"Do they send women criminals to Australia as well?"

"So I believe, some no older than twelve. Now enough of this doom and gloom, my girl. Seeing as your mother's off doing maternity favours, I'm going to buy you a tankard of ale. Ever had one?"

"No, I haven't, Mama wouldn't let me. In fact she doesn't give me much, Patrick, well, you must have noticed the way I'm treated."

"Aye, but I can't do much about it, lass, it's a parent's right. My mother treated me bad and I never knew my dad. Now come on, there's a new tavern recently opened called The Grapes,[1] it's become the most popular drinking spot round the docks. It's not far and you'll enjoy their ale."

They set off down the cobbled street lined with identical narrow terraced houses with front doors which let out directly onto the street. Catherine knew behind the flimsy doors lay poverty, misery and hunger. But if the wife complained she was sure to get slapped around and end up with a fat lip or a bleeding nose. Limehouse was a rough district, that was why so-called peace officers patrolled in pairs. At closing time drunks staggered wildly, oblivious to robbers who had their eyes on

---

1   The Grapes was mentioned in Charles Dickens's novel, *Our Mutual Friend.*

them. Even gangs of girls were ready to pounce and strip a man of his clothes for the few pennies the rags would bring.

* * *

Inside The Grapes the atmosphere was dense with smoke and the smell of strong ale was almost too overpowering for Catherine. Through the haze she could see half-sotted men with long, unruly greasy hair and watery eyes staring at her, for with her long flaxen tresses which fell easily around her broad shoulders she was eye-catching. There were only two other women in the place, puffing on small clay pipes and flaunting generous amounts of their large breasts. She knew her mother would know them. A small man with a hump back and limp was replacing burnt-out candles while supping a huge tankard of ale.

As Patrick steered Catherine towards a small table it became obvious he was well known. One half-drunk patron said, "Got another new girl, have we, Patrick? She's pretty. Wouldn't mind givin' her a stiff one miself."

"Watch your tongue, Archie, or you'll get yourself a smash in the gob. If you must know she's Catherine, the new wife's daughter, but I'll grant you there's beauty in her. Make some lad a fine wife she will, to be sure. And with those ample hips she'll bear him good offspring. I'm to buy the lass her first ale." He looked at the buxom bar lady who had a thin cheroot dangling from a large loose mouth. "Better make it just a half-pint for the lass, Hilda. I'll have my usual tankard."

"Right you are, Patrick. I knew Vera had a charmer but it's the first time I've seen the lass, she must have been hiding her. Pity, she brightens the place up more than all you miserable buggers who do nothin' but shift ale, smoke and fart."

There was good-natured laughter. Nearly all the patrons were hard-working dockyard workers whose only pleasures lay in cheap beer and tumbles with the wife or ladies of the street if they could afford one. They were also exploited by the dockyard bosses but if they caused trouble it was out on the streets without prospects. Once word got around you were a slacker on the job, don't expect to be taken on by another yard. Most English dockyards were crawling with brainless brawny men looking for work. All the job required was sheer brute strength although it yielded slightly more money than picking pockets. Plus such crimes could lead to one of the hulks out in the Thames where the final destination was Australia.

Catherine sat on a three-legged stool at the small table, aware at least twenty pairs of hungry eyes ogled her. Her temples pounded, knowing the men were imagining what lay below her thin skirt and lace-up blouse. She glanced down casually, hoping her hardening nipples weren't showing, for as the day was so hot she hadn't bothered wearing a full petticoat.

Hilda, the bar lady, set a small pewter tankard of beer down and Patrick told her to take a sip. She did which caused her to cough and splutter, much to the amusement of the patrons.

"Don't be sick, lass, else Hilda will make you lick it up!" one wit shouted.

This raised more raucous laughter.

She took another sip, then another while watching Patrick drink the full contents of his tankard without stopping. Hilda brought him another. He'd drunk four by the time Catherine finished hers and she felt dizzy. Patrick told her to have another because he was going to.

"I really don't feel like another, Patrick. Sorry."

He glowered at her with a ferocious look she'd never seen before. "Don't dare refuse having a drink with me, lass, when I'm buying or you'll be feeling my belt across your arse when we get home. Understand?"

"I don't think I like ale, Patrick."

"Then 'ave a gin, that's what your mother drinks. She likes it so you should too." He looked at the bar. "Hilda, give Catherine a gin, seems she has no taste for ale."

"One gin coming up."

As she always did Catherine felt sick when smelling it but after Patrick's threat she didn't dare not take a sip. All the men watched as she slowly gulped some of the foul liquid. Twice she almost threw it all back up.

Just then a gaudily dressed woman with thick blood-red lips walked into the bar, came straight over and kissed Patrick on the forehead. Catherine couldn't help noticing her breasts which almost popped out of the bright green dress so tightly drawn it even emphasized the outlines of her ribcage. She licked her lips and asked Patrick who his company was.

"The new wife's daughter Catherine, ain't she pretty? Catherine, this is Eunice Wilson, an ex-friend, one I knew before me an' your ma spliced up. I'll 'ave another tankard if you're payin', Eunice, and a gin for Catherine ..."

"Please not another, Patrick!" she shouted loudly. If Catherine had a fault it was her flash temper. She stood up and in a shrill voice said, "I don't want another, Patrick, I don't like the filthy stuff and if you wouldn't mind I wish to be taken home!"

"That's it, lass, you tell 'im!" somebody sitting within the gloom shouted.

Patrick's eyes blazed as he grabbed her bare arm and twisted it. "You'll drink, lass, when I say so. Understand?"

"I want to go home."

"When I'm good and ready. You got to learn to live, lass, just like Eunice. Now sit yourself back down and have another. Trouble with you is you don't know when you're well off." He turned to face Eunice. "How's business these days?"

"Slow. Most sailors want younger than me. They'd like Catherine."

"She ain't like that, Eunice, not yet anyway. She's got a bad temper but she's pure. In any case, if anybody's to 'ave her it'll be me." He looked to the bar. "Hilda, two more gins and another beer for me."

"Who's payin'?"

"Put it on the slate, I gets paid tomorrow."

"Just till tomorrow, mind."

By now Catherine felt flushed all over and was beginning to wish she'd never taken Patrick up on his offer. Since they'd entered the pub he'd become a different man, a cruel streak had emerged. He glared at her like a demon, a man to be scared of. And although she was not too wise about the outside world she was fairly sure Eunice was one of those women who sold her body.

It took some doing but she managed to finish the next gin despite it causing her head to reel. Patrick downed yet another ale and announced he was going to spend a few minutes outside with Eunice. With her head spinning she watched them leave, suspecting Eunice was going to have her skirt lifted in the backyard privy. Then a kindly looking, fairly well-dressed man approached the table, took her hand and said, ."I'd watch out for Patrick, lass. He's not nice when full of ale as he is now. Just heed what I say and be careful. You upset him speaking the way you did just now."

"I'll be careful. Thank you."

Catherine Farrow didn't realise it then but that day was to affect the remainder of her life.

* * *

Finally Patrick returned and finished his ale. Catherine noticed he staggered, causing some of the other patrons to laugh. When she stood up he grasped her arm.

"Take me 'ome, lass."

Once outside, the hot humid air hit them causing Catherine's head to spin and she too began to stagger.

Patrick laughed. "You'd better learn to carry your drink better than that, lass."

"I can't hold your weight, Patrick, please let go of me."

"If I do I'll fall, then you'll be in real trouble, especially when I tell your ma. This is my best suit."

From somewhere she managed to find the strength and luckily Grundy Street wasn't too far. Catherine noticed many other drunks, one actually rolled in the gutter while a child wearing nothing but a long vest and big boots kicked him repeatedly as another cut a small leather sack away from his belt. Then they ran away with their loot. He yelled after them but was unable to get up.

"Shouldn't we help him?" Catherine asked.

"No bloody way, lass. Help him and he'll say it was us who robbed 'im. Just you get me 'ome and laid on the bed."

Finally they arrived at the narrow house she called home. The door wasn't locked and they staggered inside. There was no sign of her mother so it was assumed she was still with the woman delivering her child.

Somehow or other Catherine managed to steer Patrick through the small living room and up the narrow staircase. He hit his head on the door frame as they entered the bedroom, causing him to slur many swear words. With a great effort she laid him on the unmade bed but wasn't prepared for what came next.

Patrick pulled her towards him and thrust a hand up her blouse until it lay over one of her breasts which he then squeezed. This caused Catherine to yelp in pain as tears formed.

"Stop that screaming, lass. Never had a titty felt before? Well, your mother likes it and you're going to. Let's have a look at 'em."

"No, Patrick, please don't make me. You're drunk. Mama wouldn't like it."

"Mama ain't goin' to know, is she? Now unless you want to feel my belt across your arse get that blouse off and show me your titties."

She was terrified now but knew even in his state he was still capable of hurting her a great deal. She knelt over his legs and slowly drew her blouse off. Both his hands came up and began grovelling her breasts. She started to sob deeply, this was the nightmare she'd feared coming for some time.

"Please, Patrick, I beg don't do this. It hurts. Ouch, ouch!"

Now he was squeezing both nipples at once which caused her to fall back. The next minute he was kneeling over her fumbling in his trousers and she gasped when he produced that which she knew he put inside her mother.

"Your mother ain't 'ere, lass, so I want you to stroke it like she does. Don't claim not to know how, we've seen your eye at the gap in the door frame."

He forced one of her sweaty hands on to it. She closed her tear-filled eyes while gently grasping the hard object as he worked himself slowly backward and forward. Finally he emitted a gasp as she sensed a warm substance on her chest. Then through a blur of tears she saw him fall back as he said, "Don't dare mention this to your ma else I'll make your life a bloody misery and lock you in the hen coop. Understand?"

"Yes."

"Good. Now bugger off while I have a sleep, but 'ave some sausages and a pot of tea ready for when I wake up."

He was snoring even before the bedroom door was closed. In the living room she sat on the rocking chair and inspected her bruised breasts. He had hurt her, but for a few seconds at least she'd also experienced a slightly pleasant sensation in her nipples. However these thoughts were soon quelled, knowing and fearing he would be doing it again. Her body was not meant for such a big man. Should she tell her mother? was the main question on her mind. But that wouldn't be today unless the baby arrived early. Of course she could go to the house and tell her what Patrick had done but then thoughts of his thick belt striking her put paid to that idea. And in any case her mother may side with him. And next door she knew Mister Peck was just the same when he'd had a few. They said he even caned his wife and kids which caused Catherine to wonder if all dockyard workers were the same. She trembled in the chair, looking down at the threadbare mat in front of the small fireplace, hoping Patrick wouldn't wake up too quickly.

* * *

Unfortunately for Catherine things got progressively worse. Patrick was now forcing himself into her every time her mother was out earning a few extra coppers at various taverns.

After a month of these terrifying assaults her body was badly bruised so she felt compelled to tell her mother. Her reaction shocked Catherine to the core.

"So bloody what, girl. He's a hard worker and deserves a little pleasure in life. We support you, and what do we get in return? Well, I'll tell you, almost sod all. You're a lazy bastard. You don't clean the house properly, stuff you wash is still half soiled when it's done and you don't bring any money in. You should count yourself lucky you're fed and have clothes on your back. There's many a lass in Limehouse who'd give half a crown to wear clothes like yours, think on that. So if I hear one more complaint about Patrick it's out on the street you go, and see

where that lands you. Now get the dishes done and scour the sink before Patrick
gets home. Do you hear, girl?"

"I hear, Mama, but I can't take too much more. Patrick hurts me."

"And I'll be hurtin' you too, my lass. Now start earning your keep and after the
dishes you can tidy the place up, Patrick likes things shipshape after lugging cargo
on and off ships for fourteen hours a day."

"But he'll be drunk again, Mama... Ouch!"

She had received a crack across her right ear. This brought tears to her eyes as
she went to the small sink in the kitchen to start on the pile of dirty dishes plus her
hands were already sore after doing the laundry in cold water.

* * *

Her heart skipped a beat when she heard the door open and Patrick staggering in.
Vera helped him to the bedroom and took off his filthy clothes. Then she kissed him
and began the arousal by rubbing her hand between his parted legs.

Catherine could hear the moans of drunken passion as the bed springs creaked.
What made it worse was knowing Patrick would want her next while her mother
watched. She seemed to enjoy looking on while her only daughter was being
ravished by a brutal drunk. Later she may get a little rest when they went out to The
Grapes or some other cheap tavern.

"Catherine, get yourself in here," she heard her mother yell. "And you know
what Patrick wants first."

Catherine knew Patrick desired her mouth, and not on his lips. Usually it made
her sick but they simply laughed as she retched into a chamber pot beside the bed.

Finally Patrick was finished. He and her mother dressed to go out drinking
again. Catherine virtually stumbled to her own small room where she fell across the
lumpy bed, clutching herself because Patrick had been violent tonight. And what
was worse, she knew there would be more when he returned.

* * *

Unfortunately for Catherine there was little respite. Endless hours of housework
followed by enforced bedroom visits with her drunken stepfather. Her world had
become one of utter blackness, a bottomless pit of hopelessness, futility, misery,
despair and brutality.

For about a week now she'd been mentally formulating a drastic plan. To her it seemed obvious the only way out was to injure Patrick in such a way he was incapable of abusing her. It would be easy with a sharp kitchen knife when he was too drunk to realise what was going on. Once the deed was done she could report herself to the constable station and ask the law to take pity on her. After all, her body carried the bruises of abuse. Tonight seemed an ideal time. It was Saturday, Patrick and her mother would be drunker than usual as there was no dock work on Sunday. With all the hard work they made her do she was very strong and felt confident her plan would work provided she kept her nerve. If Patrick screamed it wouldn't matter because the neighbours on both sides were used to such outbursts and they never interfered. In fact raised voices and sounds of fighting were commonplace on almost any street in Limehouse. Parents had to vent their anger and frustrations somewhere and what better way than to take it out on their defenceless children.

Many times in her abject misery Catherine had thought if they banned ale, gin, rum and whisky there would be fewer abuses, but dockyard taverns were guaranteed sources of income for the owners, and loose women like Eunice Wilson made a fairly decent living entertaining clients in the backyard or at their lodgings. Some nights they could make five shillings or more. Naturally they didn't last too long in the business as many contracted that dreaded disease carried by most seamen returning from voyages to the East. Eunice Wilson was lucky, she'd lasted longer than most. And that was another thing Catherine was beginning to fear, being sent out herself to earn more spending money for her mother and Patrick. She had resolved to kill herself before that happened. However tonight it may all end when her parents arrived home drunk.

After they'd left for The Grapes she did all the chores her mother had left for her to do. When finished she took numerous deep breaths before taking the sharp carving knife out of the kitchen drawer, she stuck it down the waistband of her skirt and covered the handle with her slack blouse. The knife tip prodded her left thigh but that couldn't be helped. Then she sat in the rocking chair to wait and hoped her nerves held, they had to, there would be no second chance. After the deed was done she'd turn herself in and hope for mercy at the station on the East India Dock Road. After all, what she was going to do was in self-defence of further abuse. To calm herself she poured a small goblet of whisky.

As she sipped her mind kept going over and over again what she would do to Patrick before he started assailing her body. She also hoped it would make her mother finally realise how determined she was and that she would finally start treating her with some respect.

* * *

Her mother was first through the door and once inside she tripped on the hem of her heavy dress and fell flat on the floor where she lay giggling stupidly. Patrick simply laughed as he steadied himself against the door frame.

"Catherine, get me to the bloody bedroom and fast."

She went to him, wiping her clammy hands while trying not to show the concealed weapon. Patrick's arm was taken and she guided him towards the staircase. He coughed and spluttered all the way up and staggered on the small landing but she managed to steer him to the open bedroom door. She'd made the bed and laid him on it.

"Want me to remove your shirt and pants, Patrick?"

"Course, lass, then I want to taste those lips of yours around me. You know how I enjoy that. Get it done before I drop off to sleep."

By now Catherine's heart was beating rapidly while struggling to get his shirt off without revealing she had the knife. Finally it was done and the loose pants were easy after she'd pulled his boots off. As usual she knelt on the bed, gently grasped his manhood and told him to close his eyes. Oblivious to any danger, he did.

She'd rehearsed removing the long carving knife and drew it out easily. Then with all her strength she drew the razor-sharp blade across the erect organ before jabbing the point between his thighs. As blood spurted everywhere he gasped and shouted, "Vera... help me, the bitch has stabb—"

His head slumped to one side. Catherine knew he'd fainted. As she stood up to survey Patrick's injury her mother staggered into the room.

"What the hell have you done, child?"

"Made him useless to you and every other woman including me, Mama."

"You stupid bugger, I may be pissed but I can still wallop the hell out of you and, mark my words, I'll see you flogged outside Newgate[2] for this."

With that she ran at her daughter but Catherine easily sidestepped the sotted woman and saw the heavy ceramic chamber pot under the bed. Swiftly she bent

---

2   A notorious London prison where hundreds were confined under deplorable conditions.

and picked it up just as her mother was mounting a second charge. With years of pent-up hatred and emotion Catherine swung the heavy pot and caught her a solid blow across the right temple. She fell like a stone and lay still. Catherine knew she was out cold but still in a rage she kicked her three or four times in the ribs. Then trembling like a leaf she went to her room where fresh, clean clothes awaited, hoping neither recovered consciousness while she changed and left.

Once in fresh clothes she ran down the steep stairs quickly and just before leaving she saw the goblet of whisky with a little remaining. It was grabbed and the contents gulped down. It made her cough and splutter but she felt a sense of great relief now the job was finally done. The easy part was reporting it.

As she headed for the door the realisation began to set in. What if the constables didn't believe her actions were fully justified? What if they looked upon her as a mad woman? They could lock her up in Newgate along with all the other crazy convicts and there the guards would do exactly what Patrick had done. Then a vision of the naked Patrick appeared at the bottom of the stairs, clutching himself with blood still dripping through his fingers.

"Why did you do this, Catherine? You know I really loved you. I didn't deserve this. You are destined for hell, my girl. Three-headed dogs will devour you ..."

"Noooooooo!" she screamed loudly. "You abused and used me, now it's over, I'm free, free of you and my mother. The constables will believe me and take pity. My beautiful body has been released from your torments, Patrick. You brought it upon yourself."

Realising all this was just her imagination she took a very deep breath, went to the door and walked out into Grundy Street.

* * * * *

Chapter 2

D ESPITE IT BEING ALMOST MIDNIGHT THERE WERE still scores of people bustling one way or another, some staggering with uncertainty while trying to avoid horse droppings, street vendors and begging urchins. Despite their poverty people always managed to find a few coppers for an ale or a gin, especially on a Saturday night. The churches just wished they could attract as many people into their houses of God as the public houses. But if it came down to a choice between the Almighty or a beer, the ale won almost every time. Even faithful Catholics drank although not before taking Mass and confessing their sins, absolving them until next Saturday.

People stared at this lone young woman as if knowing what she'd done. Her guilty conscience was intensified by their faces which seemed almost ghostly from the eerie yellow light cast by gas lamps. And three times she'd had to look around to make sure the footsteps behind were not those of her mother or Patrick. It was a humid night causing sweat to run between the valley of her breasts to gather at the skirt waistband which seemed to become tighter with each step she took. She was thankful her choice of skirt had been the loose-fitting one because something tighter would have made walking swiftly very difficult. The whisky had made her thirsty so she was almost tempted to take a sip of water from a horse trough. The constable station had never seemed this far before.

Then there it was at the corner of Cotton Street. There was a carriage standing outside with its horse eating from a nose bag. Two children, who should have been in bed at this hour, sat on a wall as if waiting for somebody to be released. They both stared at this young woman who looked distressed.

There were six steps up to the main door which to Catherine seemed like scaling a mountain. Inside it was fairly cool and reeked of floor polish. Directly ahead was a high solid oak counter with a gaunt-looking man sitting behind it. At least Catherine assumed he was sitting as she could only see his buttoned-up jacket.

His severe face was illuminated from either side by two oil lamps. In the fashion of the day he sported thick mutton chop whiskers but no beard. Never had her heart pounded so much as she looked up at him but she was so scared words wouldn't form.

Seeing her distressed state he took the initiative. "Well, lass, what is it? You look all in."

"Please, sir, I've stabbed my stepfather and laid my mother out."

He smirked and stroked his whiskers. "Have you now. That was a silly thing to do, wasn't it?" He leaned forward slightly, letting his eyes scan her up and down. "I can smell whisky on you from here, lass, so are you sure you're not just saying all this to get a free bowl of soup? We get many who do, especially on a Saturday night."

She took a deep breath. "No, sir, honestly I really did those things."

"And where might we find your parents?"

"Where I live ..."

"Where's that?"

"Twenty-three Grundy Street. They were in the bedroom when I did it, I don't know where they are now."

He wrote something down, stroked his whiskers again and said as if still not believing her, "And where did you stab your stepfather?"

"In the bedroom, like I said."

He wagged a huge finger at her. "Don't get cocky with me, girl, or you'll be feeling our strap across your arse. I meant in what part of the body did you stab him?"

"Between the legs."

"I see. And how did you lay your mother out?"

"With a chamber pot."

"Did the pot break?"

"I don't remember."

"I see. And why did you do these things?"

"My stepfather did things to me which he shouldn't while my mother watched. They also beat me, I've got bruises to prove it."

"That may be so, lass, but you shouldn't be taking the law into your own hands. You should have reported it to us. Anyway you'd better give me your name and age."

"Catherine Farrow. I'm almost twenty, according to my mother."

His pencil point was licked before notes were taken. Finally he looked up.

"Alright, lass, for now I'll believe you. I'll send a couple of constables round to the house, but if they find nothing you can look forward to spending a few weeks in one of our cells and they ain't nice plus the rats and cockroaches enjoy plump lasses. Do you understand that?"

"Yes, sir, but I'm not lying. I couldn't take any more of their cruelty."

"We'll see. If it's the truth you'll be up before a magistrate on Monday morning for assault."

She was shocked at hearing the words magistrate and assault. "But, sir, I thought you'd take pity on me."

"Pity is not up to me, lass. That's for the magistrate or a judge to decide."

There was a large handbell on the counter beside him. He rang it, causing Catherine to jump. Shortly two gigantic constables entered the room through a door to her left. The situation was explained but before they went to investigate she was to be taken to a cell. One grabbed her wrist with a hand bigger than Patrick's even. She was dragged away.

Now the smell was different. That of an outhouse which hadn't been cleaned in a month at least. Then down a short cobbled corridor to a solid door which the other constable had to unlock first with an enormous key. This was the cell area, causing Catherine to gasp. The area was cold, the smell terrible. Human smell and that of open-flame gas lamps which provided the only illumination. The flames flickered in the draught as the heavy door slammed shut behind them. In the gloom to her right, behind closely spaced bars, were at least a dozen unshaven evil-looking men with almost blood-red eyes which stared at her like she was a ghost. To her left was an identical cell except with women in it. Some wore nothing but a flimsy, dirty shift. One was bloodstained.

"Been picked up for selling that little bit of hairy space between your legs, have you, deary?" one said, causing the others to laugh.

The jailer who held Catherine's wrist told her to shut up. By now they'd almost reached the far end where there were very narrow cells on both sides. Catherine was roughly pushed into one and the heavy barred gate pulled shut and locked. The two constables left.

There was no bed, just some damp-looking straw on the cobbled floor. At the end was a wooden bucket with a lid on it. Catherine knew it was a slop pail. She'd heard Patrick talk about such things on ships which came into the docks.

"What you in for, lass?" A female voice asked out of the gloom.

Standing near the bars Catherine could just see the woman, who had unnatural red hair. "I attacked my stepfather with a knife and knocked my mother out."

"Why?"

"Because they were very cruel to me. Especially my stepfather. He did me while my mother watched."

"You realise using a knife could mean the hangman?" a gruff male voice said.

"I'm hoping the magistrate will take pity on me."

"Pity, lass, that's a laugh. Magistrates don't show pity for the likes of us. Now if you was a toff and had money to pay a bribe, the chances are you'd be let off with a small fine. Have you got money, lass?"

"No, of course not."

"Then there's a good chance you'll swing."

"Oh, please don't say things like that!" she screamed before dropping to her knees, crying.

One of the women seemed to take pity. "Cheer up, deary. They may show a bit of mercy and only give you a few years in Newgate. Or you could even be shipped off to Australia where they need child-bearing women. Either way it'll be rough but it's better than that short drop through a trapdoor at the end of which is blackness forever. My dad knows. He was hung last year and my brother the year before that."

Catherine shivered both from cold and fright on the damp cobbles. She remembered Patrick showing her that ship which was due to sail to a penal colony. Then she heard the main door open and her heart skipped a beat. But it seemed they hadn't come for her.

"Sorry, Tom," she heard one of the jailers say, "we've just been told you're off to Newgate to await a trial."

"Fucking hell. All I did was give the bastard a black eye."

"Plus you kneed him in his privates, so he said, and we did have a witness. You must learn to curb your temper, especially when full of ale. Now come on and don't struggle, it'll only make things worse."

Catherine licked her dry lips and wished she could get a drink of water, at least at home she could do that. I didn't realise it was going to be like this, she thought to herself. Men and women in the same cell area. I thought England was more civilized than that. Obviously I was wrong.

She lay down on the straw and wrapped her arms around herself for comfort while wondering if the constables were at the house yet and had seen what she'd done. Gradually she began to realise the enormity of her actions. An assault the constable had said but surely it couldn't result in losing her own life, dangling on the end of a rope. I'm too young to die, she thought while starting to shiver again. I just hope and pray I'm stood before a kind magistrate who'll take pity on me for the suffering I've been put through. Perhaps they can find Eunice Wilson to speak on my behalf. I did tell her the things Patrick and my own mother made me do. Now I must try to sleep, time passes faster that way and at least Patrick won't be calling for me.

Her troubled eyes closed as she curled up into a ball, still shivering.

* * *

Both hardened constables looked down at Patrick who was moaning deeply, wallowing in a pool of his own blood. Vera Farrow, who had a large bruise on her left cheek, was cradling his head. They knew Patrick O'Grady was a rough cut because he'd caused many disturbances while drunk and had twice been kept in the cells overnight. They also knew how Vera Farrow earned money in the taverns although they usually turned a blind eye, knowing she was almost destitute after her first husband was killed. However they didn't know she and Patrick were abusing her daughter.

"It looks like you urgently need a doctor, sir," Albert, the senior constable, said.

"Of course he does," Vera snapped. "So do I. The bitch must have kicked me 'cause my ribs ache like hell. He won't die, will he?"

"I don't know, madam. It looks a real mess to me. We have your daughter down at the station saying she did it. Did she?"

"Yes, she bloody well did. The girl's mad and needs putting away for life. And to think all I've done for her."

Just then Patrick retched and was violently sick.

Albert dispatched the other constable to get a doctor. Vera was asked to get him a drink of water and a cloth and wipe his face. In obvious agony she hobbled out of the stinking room.

Albert looked down at the victim. "Your stepdaughter says you sexually abused her, sir. Is that true?"

"I never touched her... Oh dear God, it hurts."

"Yes, sir, I imagine it does. If you hadn't been abusing her, why did she slash you like that?"

"The girl's mad like my wife said."

Just then Vera arrived with a large goblet of water and a rag. She sat by Patrick and gradually poured some into his mouth. After a few gulps he fainted; she screamed, "He's not dead, is he!"

"I'd not imagine so, madam. He seems a strong lad although by the looks of that injury I hope you're not expecting him to give you another child."

"Of course not. I didn't even want Catherine with my first husband. What will you charge her with?"

"Grievous assault would be my guess."

"Do they still flog people for such crimes?"

"I don't think so. Not females at least."

"Pity. She deserves a few strokes laid across her back."

Albert pulled a puzzled frown. "You would wish the lass flogged, madam? But she's your own daughter."

"Not any more she ain't. She's not welcome in this house ever again."

Albert was speechless. He had a daughter himself and could not imagine her mother saying things like Vera had just said. He was beginning to feel sorry for Catherine but it wasn't him who administered the law. Judges did that. Then he heard footsteps on the stairs.

Doctor Horace Packard entered and looked at the victim whom he knew vaguely, having attended many accidents at the docks. Albert thought he saw a glimmer of a smile on the doctor's face.

As the doctor began to inspect the slashed victim, Albert asked Vera to come downstairs and make a statement so he could write it up.

Three quarters of an hour later Patrick was all bandaged up and ready to be taken to the hospital where a closer inspection could be made. Doctor Packard would take him in his carriage. Vera's bruised ribs had been wrapped in a long piece of cloth. It didn't appear any were broken but she'd been told they would be sore for a few days.

They left and the constables returned to the station in their hansom cab, taking Vera's statement, the knife and the chamber pot with them as evidence.

* * *

Back at the station Albert explained everything to the Chief Constable Henry Random although he was careful not to voice an opinion. The chief didn't like that, he was the one who reasoned a case logically. When Albert was finished he was asked to bring the lass before him.

Catherine stood before the bench, trembling with fright and cold as the forbidding-looking chief questioned her. She could see the chamber pot on his bench but not the knife. The chief leaned forward slightly to start his questioning.

"Do you still admit to this assault on Patrick O'Grady and hitting your mother Vera Farrow with a chamber pot? Tell the truth, lass."

"Yes, sir."

"Did you kick her as well? A Doctor Horace Packard said her ribs were badly bruised."

"Yes, sir, I did, just to get back for all the times she's hit me."

"And you are claiming physical abuse as your reason?"

"Yes, sir. I've got bruises."

"Then I'll have a lady come in to inspect you. Your own bruises won't alter the fact that you'll be charged with assault using a knife and using your feet as weapons. However the bruises may affect your sentencing. We're going to keep you here until Monday. Then you'll be taken to Bow Street for a hearing before a magistrate. Have you anything else to say?"

"They'll not hang me, will they, sir?"

"That's not for me to say, lass. You did wrong and will just have to accept what the magistrate and judge decide. Now go with the constable."

As she walked in front of the constable he couldn't see her lips quivering or feel how her legs were shaking. In fact she was almost at the point of collapse. The passage began to spin as she was taken back to the cell and once again locked in. Now she needed a pee.

The lid was removed from the slop bucket. After hoisting the loose folds of her skirt she squatted over it and let go. The others must have heard her as one man said, "Don't do the other, lass. The smell's bad enough as it is."

"So what's to happen?" one of the women asked after she saw Catherine stand up.

"I'm to be taken before a magistrate on Monday morning, charged with assault."

"Are you scared?"

"Course I am. I never considered it would go this far or that they could hang me."

"Aye, the noose is the worst part. When they drop you it's all over. I know, I've watched up at Tyburn. Most victims piss themselves as the noose tightens, some even mess themselves."

"Please, please!" Catherine shouted. "It's bad enough to know what I may face, I don't want to hear details."

She sank to her knees then lay down knowing sleep would not come easily. Thoughts of a noose around her neck came to mind. She remembered a few years ago after dropping four plates on the hard kitchen floor and breaking three of them she was throttled by her mother. The pressure was so intense she almost passed out; as it was, her throat was sore for at least a week. To make matters worse, when her father arrived home he gave her a dozen strokes with the razor strop, claiming the plates represented almost a month's pay.

While lying in the gloom she saw two of the women kissing each other with their hands up each other's skirts. Then a guard entered and they were told to stop. If they didn't he'd get the cane out.

"They're a bloody pair of harlots," one of the men shouted, "they deserve to be thrashed!"

Harlot was a word Catherine had not heard before but she assumed it meant two women going together.

When the guard appeared at the bars of her cell he stared down with what looked like pity.

"You're a bloody fool, girl. Taking revenge like that just ain't worth it. You had a future, not now. Monday you'll find out. Shortly a woman will be coming to inspect your body, try to rest until she does."

She watched him leave before resting her back against the damp wall and bringing her knees up under her chin.

"That was a daft thing you did, lass," she heard one of the men say. "You should have just run away from home."

"Where would I have run to?"

"There's many a gentleman toff in the West End who'd take you in for a month or so if you obliged him in bed. He may even have bought you some clothes and perhaps give some spending money. And through 'im you may have met others. I know many a young lass who lives like a lady now. You females are lucky, you 'ave what men want. If you do happen to get off that's what I'd do. Lie with a rich man and take what he's got. If you don't enjoy it, fake it, he won't know the difference. It ain't a bad life, mark my words." He stopped talking because Catherine had screamed.

"Oh no!" A rat had just run out of the straw and scurried past her down the cobbles towards the door. That caused her to shiver again. I've been a fool, she thought. At least after Patrick had finished with me I had a bed and a blanket to lie on and once or twice when he wasn't too drunk I got a kind of thrill but I couldn't let Patrick know. Now though with tears running down her pale cheeks she realised the deed was done and she was going to pay for it in one way or another. Even a few years in prison would be better than death. Anything to save her life. Then when released she could look up Eunice Wilson and they could live together. Eunice knew how to look after herself.

With these thoughts and despite the sound of water dripping somewhere and knowing there was vermin in the straw, she lay on it. Sleep had to come.

* * *

She awoke with a start when hearing the cell door being unlocked.

"Is it morning already?" she asked.

"No, lass. There's a lady here come to look your body over. Now stand by the back wall and undress. Don't try anything funny or I'll put you down a pit full of slimy water till it's time to go to court. Understand?"

"Yes, sir."

"Good. Hold your hands out."

Trembling like a leaf she watched as a small middle-aged, ashen-faced lady, dressed in all black including her gloves and bonnet, appeared and stepped into the cell carrying a lantern. She didn't speak but the constable did.

"Right, lass, get your clothes off, and I mean everything."

Slowly she began to remove her clothes sweating and shivering at the same time, aware the constable and the woman had their eyes on her. Nervously she let her slip fall to the cobbles before easing the pantaloons over her hips until they fell to her ankles. Her shoes and knee-high stockings were last. Her temples pounded. It seemed like the constable's eyes would pop out as he scanned her nakedness up and down until coming to rest on that tuft of corn-coloured hair centred between her quivering thighs.

"Spread your legs, lass, and put your hands behind your head so the lady can inspect you," the constable said.

She obeyed and her stomach churned as the woman stepped forward holding the lantern so it illuminated her trembling body. Then she crouched and closely inspected between her legs. Finally she stood up and told her to turn round. She felt the lamp's heat on her bottom before being told to face the front again. After one last look the woman walked out of the cell.

"Right, lass, you can get dressed again," the constable said while staring at the rounded mounds of her breasts.

She trembled while putting her clothes back on. Would the woman confirm she'd been abused or simply say she saw no signs. After pulling up her stockings and stepping into her shoes the constable left and locked the cell.

"Did the inspection make that thing between your legs twitch?" the raspy voice of a man in the other cell asked.

"No, it did not. I was truly embarrassed if you must know. Now please be quiet, I want to sleep."

"A week or so from now you may get to sleep forever, dear," one of the women said, causing the others to laugh.

Catherine ignored that as she lay on the straw hoping sleep would come although knowing it wouldn't. While planning the attack she hadn't imagined it would be anything like this. Maybe it might have been better to explore things a little more thoroughly before she carried out the act. Perhaps she should have consulted Eunice Wilson, she would have known what to do. She may even have helped because Patrick was rough with her too when he had her against the wall in The Grape's backyard.

But it was too late now, the deed had been done.

* * * * *

CHAPTER 3

C ATHERINE AWOKE TO THE RATTLE OF KEYS as her cell door was being unlocked by a burly, heavily whiskered constable she had not seen before. His voice boomed.

"On your feet, lass. You're on your way to Bow Street. Just wash your face in that bucket of water then follow me. Remember, when stood before the magistrate there's to be no talking unless he asks you a question. If he does, answer him honestly, he'll know if you're lying. These men are used to types like you. Now hurry up, we haven't got all day and magistrates are impatient."

She quickly washed her face and pushed a few strands of matted hair out of her eyes. With that done she was handcuffed. On her way through the cell block all the men and women wished her luck. Unfortunately she didn't feel quite so confident.

The wait after being inspected by the woman in black had been some of the worst hours in her entire life. Every time she heard the door to the cell area being opened her stomach lurched, wondering if one of the evil-eyed constables was coming to assault her. Luckily that hadn't happened. Usually it was a drunk or a tavern tart being put in one of the communal cells to await a hearing. Nevertheless she never felt really safe even behind the locked gate.

* * *

Her transport to Bow Street was a small black carriage drawn by a single horse with its driver already sitting at the reins. Four men smoking pipes and a group of children watched from across the street as she was jabbed in the back to mount the three steps. Being handcuffed it was difficult so the constable pushed on her bottom. Inside it seemed like an oven as she sat on the narrow slatted bench. Already sweat had formed on her brow and belly which ached both from hunger and trepidation. The door slammed shut, plunging her into near darkness. She heard bolts being drawn seconds before there was a crack of a whip as the cab lurched forward. Her eyes gazed blankly at the opposite side, knowing beyond it were London streets where men, women and children walked freely. She was not free and was on her way to face a magistrate. Despite the manacles' weight she lifted her hands to bury her face in them.

* * *

There were four other women in the holding cell. All had been told to sit still and await their turn by the constable who looked like he could wrestle a bear and win. He told them they could talk if they kept their voices down. Almost directly above their heads the magistrate sat in judgement.

Catherine's keen eyes surveyed the other prisoners, one of which looked to be about her own age. As they sat almost next to each other Catherine whispered her name.

The woman replied in a lilting whisper, "I'm Emily Kilpatrick and I wish to hell I'd never come to this godforsaken city which smells worse than a cow's arse."

"Where are you from?" Catherine asked.

"Ireland, north of Belfast, where I was treated like a bloody slave. My dad signed me over to work for a heartless man who kept me toiling in his fields from dawn to dusk for very little pay and hardly any food. After work he made me lie with him and open my legs so after a month I decided to run off. A man at the docks offered to pay my passage across to England if I shared myself with him. I knew what he meant but anything was better than what I was leaving behind. Then a month after he'd had enough of me I was forced to entertain his friends first then people I never knew. I do know they paid my so-called benefactor a lot more than he paid me. I also know he robbed them while they were with me. This went on for about three months before I was arrested and charged with the theft of a fob watch off a so-called client. I knew it was my so-called benefactor who stole it but the law officers believed him not me. So here I am, and I say fuck."

Catherine wanted to hold her hand for mutual comfort but she didn't dare with the constable watching. She saw a certain hardness in Emily with her straight black hair shrouding an oval face with a generous mouth and nice teeth. Catherine realised Emily's life since coming from Ireland had been one of mistreatment similar to her own.

One of the other prisoners was just about to give her name when a man entered the cell and pointed at her. "Barbara Henshaw, you're next. Look sharp, the magistrate is in a bad mood today because he's got a headache."

Barbara stood up and said, "Well, I ain't in too good a mood myself if you must know."

With that remark the constable on guard gave her a smart clip across the ear. "One more word like that, lass, after you're done with the magistrate we'll hang you from a hook by your handcuffs for a few hours. In here women get treated just the same as men. Now get moving."

Both Catherine and Emily cringed as Barbara was quickly escorted out. It was obvious they could expect little or no compassion.

The one sitting across from Catherine forced a half-smile. "I'm Lydie Denner. I bashed in an aristocratic lady's face with a shovel after she accused me of stealing her jewellery. I do admit they caught me with a couple of small pieces but there was no cause for her to set two bloody great dogs on me. I've still got fang marks on both legs. The one who put me up to the theft weren't even charged. They pick on women they do, tain't fair."

"That's enough talking," the constable said. "Now sit still and wait."

"Ain't we going to get fed?" asked the one sitting next to Lydie.

The constable looked at his list then glared at her. "Mary Campbell, ain't it? Well, getting fed is the least of your worries. I see on the list you drowned the twin babies born to your sister, ain't that so?"

"Yes, because she didn't want 'em, Constable. I just helped her out, that's all, she was too poor to keep the kids and the father had buggered off. They won't string me up, will they?"

"Who's to know? Anyway like I said, shut up or I'll make sure you're all stood on the gibbet. The hangman likes pretty necks and the crowd enjoys seeing a skirt dropping through the trapdoor."

They sat there in stunned silence, each with their own thoughts and worries. Catherine wondered what state Patrick was in. She hoped agony as he'd caused her enough. Then her eyes caught those of the constable staring at her so she lowered her head, knowing he was having unclean thoughts. It had been the same in The Grapes when Patrick took her there. All the younger men looked at her through their glass-bottomed tankards, imagining her with no clothes on. Even Hilda had said how pretty she was and would make some man a comfy wife. And with the right man she could have. However the harsh reality of the moment quickly returned when she heard her name being called.

In a daze she followed the constable up a steep flight of stone steps where at the top her nose sensed perfume and burning oil lamps. Then it was up an open set of wooden steps to emerge in the prisoner's box. She was told to face the magistrate and reminded not to talk unless he asked a question. He sat behind a huge bench at a higher elevation than herself. For what seemed an eternity his narrowed eyes stared at her as if she was an animal up for auction. His face was one of the severest she'd ever seen, gaunt and unsmiling. A man incapable of mercy or compassion. And at day's end he was free to return home, sit down to a fine meal, drink vintage wine and would probably have a mistress to satisfy him in bed. Catherine saw the contrast. Him on the one hand applying the law, her on the other having to accept it. There was nobody to represent her. The head constable at the station had told her there was no need, she'd already admitted her guilt.

To her left a lean old man wearing a well-worn, shiny frock coat said, "Are you Catherine Farrow?"

"Yes, sir," she stammered.

He looked up at the magistrate. "My lord, Henry Random, the chief constable for the Limehouse district, has investigated the armed assault on the stepfather and mother of the accused. He is now prepared to present his report."

Catherine watched as the constable walked into a stand beside the judges' bench. He was sworn to tell the truth and then glanced at Catherine before beginning.

"My lord, late last Saturday evening Catherine Farrow walked into my watch station and admitted stabbing her stepfather in his private areas and striking her mother with a heavy chamber pot. We have the kitchen knife and pot as evidence. Later my men discovered the accused had also kicked her mother in the ribs several times. Doctor Horace Packard was brought to the house and he had Patrick O'Grady taken to hospital. The man is still there, I believe. Doctor Packard is present, sir, to confirm what I have said."

"Yes, we will hear the doctor, Constable, but first I'd like to know if the accused gave a reason for her actions."

"Yes, sir. She claimed physical and sexual abuse by both parents."

The magistrate glared directly at Catherine. "You realise, woman, it is not your place to extract revenge upon anybody, especially parents. There are people like Chief Constable Henry Random to investigate such incidents. So why did you take it upon yourself to commit these violent crimes?"

"At the time I thought they were necessary, sir."

He emitted a sinister laugh. "At the time, I like that, Farrow. However such vicious actions are never necessary, child. Explain to me in your own words why you did it."

She went on to describe her life as one of drudgery, all the housework she was forced to perform or expect beatings from her parents who drank far too much. Then came even more mistreatment when her mother remarried after her first husband was killed in a dockyard accident. This time to a brutish Irishman who made her perform degrading acts while her mother watched. She concluded by saying her life was one of terror for almost every hour of the day. She wasn't even safe when tucked up in her own bed.

The magistrate stroked his chin and pursed a pair of thin, mean lips while rubbing his eyes as if smoke was getting in them. Finally after what seemed an eternity to Catherine he spoke.

"There are societies who take in abused children, Farrow, yet you chose to act upon your own initiative. Why?"

"I wasn't aware there were such places, sir."

"Ignorance is no excuse. However that is as it may be, the deed is done. Did you think in the morning all this would have been a bad dream?"

"No, sir."

"Exactly, Farrow. Now from all accounts a person lies in hospital with severe injuries and your own mother with bruised ribs. It would seem to me, Farrow, you are not a fit person to be free on the streets. Have you had any education?"

"Only what I've managed to learn myself, sir. My mother gave me too many household jobs, there wasn't time for school."

"I see. Are you a God-fearing woman?"

"No, sir, not really. My mother didn't attend church, claiming God had never done anything for her so why should she worship him. Yet when she took the strap to me it was God's way. I never did understand that."

Others sitting in the hot courtroom laughed when she said this and silence had to be called for.

The magistrate's expression became even sterner. "God, my child, in his own way has control over all things. Anyway we are not here to discuss religion but to assess your brutal actions." He paused and looked at Chief Constable Random who still stood in the witness box. "The accused has claimed physical abuse, Constable. Is there any evidence of this?"

"Yes, sir. As usual in such cases I summoned Clara Thornton of the Rights for Women Movement to inspect the girl's body. She's present now to give evidence at your discretion, sir."

"Oh, very well. Bailiff, have Clara Thornton take the witness box and swear her in. But be quick because my headache is becoming worse by the minute, in fact I'd like another glass of water. Bailiff, have a clerk attend to it."

"Yes, my lord." Then Catherine watched as Clara slowly entered the witness box. Her outfit was the identical one she wore when inspecting her. But clothes didn't matter, at least Clara represented a small hope.

Clara swore to tell the truth as the magistrate stared at her before opening. "I believe you inspected the body of the accused."

"I did indeed, sir."

"Is that her on the stand?"

"Yes, sir."

"Was the prisoner in a state of complete undress during your inspection?"

"Yes, sir, she was."

"And what were your observations?"

"There was evidence of bruising on both arms and the inner upper thighs. I also observed recent teeth marks on her neck and breasts plus her lower lip appeared to be swollen. This I imagine was caused by enforced kissing. There were also marks on her bottom which would indicate to me some form of strap had been applied. I observed no other injuries."

The magistrate scratched the nape of his neck before speaking. Catherine anxiously awaited what he would say.

"And in your opinion, madam, could these bruises have been made by a person or persons forcing themselves upon the accused?"

"Almost definitely, sir. I have seen far worse cases but I'm in no doubt the bruising was the result of an assault upon the girl's body."

"Is it possible they could have been self-inflicted?"

"No, sir, especially the teeth marks."

"I thank you, madam. You have been most helpful and are excused."

Catherine trembled, wondering what the magistrate's reaction would be. He watched the witness leave then took a fresh glass of water from a spotty-faced clerk before looking back at the accused.

"Well, Farrow, from the evidence of Clara Thornton it seems you may have been mistreated although in my opinion not unduly. I would now like to hear from Doctor Packard."

He took a sip of water while the portly doctor took the witness stand and was sworn to tell the truth before being asked the condition of Patrick O'Grady.

"I found the wounds inflicted were of a nature to render the man impotent and I suspect he will suffer pain on a continuing basis."

"Yes, yes, yes, Doctor. Do you consider the wounds life-threatening now or in the future?"

"No, sir. The victim will survive but he will have difficulty passing urine and he has lost one testicle."

"So am I to assume, Doctor, you would consider this a serious crime of assault?"

"Well, she did use a sharp knife, sir."

"I see. Thank you, Doctor. What about the mother, Vera Farrow?"

"She'll be alright, sir, although she may suffer headaches for a week or so due to being hit with the chamber pot."

"Ah yes, headaches. I know them well, Doctor. However you may step down."

Doctor Packard looked at Catherine before stepping down. His expression seemed to say he pitied her.

And on the stand Catherine trembled visibly despite the doctor confirming Patrick would not die. However hearing her crime was being considered serious gave her cause to worry.

Reality returned when she heard the magistrate speak.

"Well, Farrow, you have heard the evidence just as I have. I would strongly suggest you start believing in God and controlling your obviously violent nature. I like to think we live in a civilized country yet you seem to prefer taking the law into your own hands. This we cannot have. However, in your favour, whatever abuse you suffered will be taken into consideration when making my report to the district judge. Until then you will remain in custody. Take her away."

As the constable took her arm she breathed a small sigh of relief. At least her actions were under consideration. For the moment her fate lay in the hands of those who had to apply the law as it was written. She knew that waiting to hear the verdict would seem like an eternity. At the bottom of the steps Emily Kilpatrick stood waiting to go up.

"How did it go?" she asked in her lilting Irish.

She was jabbed in the ribcage. "Keep your mouth shut, lass, and get up them stairs."

Catherine was led through a huge door reinforced with flat steel bars and down two flights of narrow stone steps to enter into another cell area which felt damp, smelled musty and from somewhere she could hear water dripping. In the gloom all she could see were rows of narrow doors with small square openings at eye level in them. No cell bars here. Four doors down, one was thrown open but before being pushed inside the guard removed her handcuffs which eased the rubbing on her chafed wrists.

It took a while for her eyes to become accustomed to the gloom. When they did she saw the cell was nothing but a space. No bunk, not even straw on the cobbled floor. There was a slop bucket minus a lid, luckily at the moment it was empty. She jumped as the cell door slammed behind her and was locked. Now, apart from a glow through the small eye level opening in the door, she was in darkness. Carefully she eased her back down the rough stone wall and sat with her knees tucked up under her chin. A ghostly wind howled down the corridor and in the distance somebody was screaming to be set free. She shivered and bit her lower lip.

If she had realised such conditions as these existed it may have been wiser to have second thoughts about her actions. Compared to this place the small house on Grundy Street was a palace and at least she had a bed and a blanket. Now she would have to suffer alone for an indefinite amount of time. Her fate now lay in the hands of one man, a judge. She wondered if he believed in God and had she ruined her own chances by admitting she did not?

* * *

Sometime later she was wondering what had become of the others who had been brought up before the magistrate. Lydie Denner, the sultry one who spoke with an unfamiliar, slightly lilting accent as if either her mother or father had not been English. Then there was Barbara Henshaw, an emaciated-looking woman with closely cropped streaky hair, like it had been cut with a pair of sheep shears. Dressed as she was in an all-black, tight dress which contrasted greatly with her starkly white, taut-skinned face and intense dark-brown eyes she exuded an evil countenance, almost that of a witch.

Suddenly Catherine's thoughts were interrupted when she heard a tapping on the wall against which her back rested. She turned to face it and asked who it was in a whisper.

"Emily Kilpatrick. Is that you, Catherine?"

"Yes. How did you get on?"

"The magistrate is going to report my case to a judge."

"Same with me. We should wish each other luck."

"There is no luck in this world, Catherine. Life is what you make it but it looks like we've buggered ours up."

"Well, it's too late now. What about the others, how did they get on?"

"No idea."

"Someday we may know, Emily. Now I'm going to try and rest. I got hardly any sleep yesterday."

"Same with me. We may meet again."

As she was trying to settle herself Catherine was startled by that shrill scream again, pleading for freedom. A deep, loud voice told it to shut up. It didn't. There was another scream, a thud, then silence. Catherine quickly realised she was in a world of half-mad criminals. Her own actions had brought this nightmare about and perhaps in retrospect she had overstepped the bounds of common decency although it was nice knowing Patrick would have difficulty peeing. That thought alone brought a smile to her face.

* * *

Catherine's assault on Patrick and her mother was on everybody's lips in The Grapes. Nearly all the regular customers felt sorry for the lass because they knew what Patrick O'Grady was like and in fact some thought he had turned Vera Farrow into a demon since marrying her. Patrick had never been liked but because of his enormous strength people showed him respect, especially when he'd been drinking. Hilda, the bar lady, didn't care for him although he was good for bar profits and that was all the owners were interested in.

After she heard Catherine was being held in prison for the assault Eunice Wilson stood up at the bar counter and asked if anybody thought something could be done for her. One patron, who claimed to be a writer, stood up and asked to speak. Hilda told him to go ahead.

He removed a tall top hat and clutched the very wide lapels of his grey jacket before speaking.

"I'm not a man of the law although I do know those who administer it are a different breed to us commoners. They value their own lives while thinking nothing of ours. Most of you here live and breathe constant poverty while they exist in luxury. You work like slaves so they can reap the profits. Patrick O'Grady worked his soul out in the dockyard only to receive coppers for his weekly toil while city merchants became rich on the goods he handled. From what I've heard he was also a cruel man and many wished him dead. Catherine Farrow did the next best thing by wounding him, now sadly she languishes in a stinking cell but I don't think there's much we can do until her judgement day arrives. Then we can mount a protest outside the Old Bailey pleading for clemency. Nothing is ever achieved by inaction so I'm prepared to mount a protest on the lass's behalf. Who's with me?"

"A tankard of ale for all who agree with Mister Snekcid!" Hilda shouted.

Every hand in the pub went up, even those who had no idea who Catherine Farrow was. Of course the offer of free ale helped them make their decision. Hilda drew the ales with her usual dexterity and Eunice served them around. The toast was to Catherine Farrow and the hopes she wasn't given a too severe sentence.

Many said they would help with the protest if somebody could make up the placards. The unknown man promised to write some slogans, mount them up on poles and deliver them to Hilda in the morning.

It seemed this was not the first protest rally he'd organized on behalf of a single person; however he did admit this could be the most important if it reduced Catherine's sentence. He was asked his opinion but said there was little logic in the way the law worked. It seemed much depended on your status. If you were rich, had influence and could afford somebody skilled in presenting your case the chances were you'd get away with it. Even bribes were not out of the question. Those applying the law sometimes flaunted it themselves.

He knew of a rich landowner in Essex who had thrashed a stable lad almost to death because he'd let a favourite horse out of its barn. The owner was fined half a crown. No thought was given to the lad who would be crippled for life. It also seemed Mister Snekcid could quote incidents like this until daybreak if asked to do so. Even his own priority in life was writing about the impoverished, uneducated masses who lived in dire hardship while the gentry exploited them.

Eunice asked Mister Snekcid if he could represent Catherine.

"I'm sorry, my dear, unfortunately it's out of the question. In the first place I'm not a lawyer, and secondly Catherine has already admitted her guilt so the judge is not obliged to hear pleas. Our only chance is the protest. I'm sorry."

"Aren't we all," Hilda said before offering every patron another ale.

Later she was to tell Eunice her generosity would eventually pay dividends by bringing customers back, plus the tavern owner could well afford it. She knew he kept at least four mistresses and owned his own coach and horses.

* * *

Of course times were not quite so jolly for Catherine or Emily Kilpatrick. At six this morning they'd been given a small bowl of thick gruel, a cob of stale bread and a mug of water for their breakfast. The surly guard said it wasn't worth giving them a lot to eat as they could be dead the day after being brought before the judge. In fact three cells down a man was to swing in the morning and his only crime had been to steal six chickens.

Catherine complained of stomach cramps to the guard before he closed the cell door. He told her to exercise by what he called running on the spot. She told him it was her week when a woman bled and could he let her have a rag. He told her to rip a piece off her petticoat and warned if she made a mess in the cell she'd have to clean it up. She followed his advice.

With nothing at all to do she sat on the damp cell floor. Her life at home had always been active because she was kept busy for most of the day. The laundry took at least six hours and many a time after it had been hung out to dry it became soiled again with soot which belched from untold numbers of chimney pots. Frequently she was forced to wash many items again despite her hands being chapped almost raw. And if Patrick's one and only best white shirt wasn't gleaming and ironed perfectly she could expect to feel his thick belt across some portion of her body.

She realised now these events at home had slowly been sowing the seeds of her drastic action until she could take it no longer. Although Patrick could be kind at times his fits of rage were commonplace and she was the one to suffer either from his belt or a slap from one of his large hands. Occasionally her mother received a beating as well, this usually after he returned from the docks sotted with drink. It was a fairly common practice for some workers to bring a bottle of rum or gin into work with them and hide it from the foremen. All this of course had been told to the magistrate and she knew scribes had written everything down. However if she had heard what Mister Snekcid had to say about the truly biased English system of law and justice her despondent mood would have been lower still.

The chill made her shiver but now her hands were free she could at least cross them across her chest and cling to her shoulders. Her blouse gaped slightly so in the gloom she looked down at the swell of her breasts, thinking no man may ever look upon their beauty again or a child suckle milk from the nipples. Her nineteen years of life had been well and truly wasted.

* * *

As barely anybody at The Grapes could write legibly Mister Snekcid had agreed he would pay for a signwriter to make up four placards, all depicting in one way or another why Catherine Farrow should only receive a minimum sentence for her crimes. He hoped they would do the trick although knowing there were no guarantees. Men of stature were rarely influenced by pleas from the poor. And yet for thousands of Londoners acts of crime were their only way of making an income. Women had their bodily endowments to sell, generally men did not.

Eunice Wilson was so taken by Mister Snekcid's generosity she offered him herself free of charge. He refused, citing it was against all his doctrines to take advantage of the misfortunes of others. He did however give her a florin for the kindly thought. She was truly grateful and kissed his whiskered cheeks.

Once the placards were complete Mister Snekcid said he would try to find out the date when Catherine was to be brought before the judge for sentencing. On that day the marchers would have to be at the Old Bailey very early so the judge was sure to see them as he arrived. The mysterious Mister Snekcid also warned them they stood the chance of being arrested for creating a disturbance. If so he promised to bail them out and pay any fines levied.

Of course Catherine was totally unaware of all this activity on her behalf and was beginning to wish the day of sentencing would come quickly because every hour in her damp, cold cell seemed like a day. Plus she didn't know whether it was day or night and the guard refused to say. All he ever said was, "Don't wish your life away, lass, your day will come all too soon. If you're to die the hangman will pull a lever so you drop a few feet and it'll be over. You may not even hear the crowd cheer, take my word for it though, they always do."

It was obvious the guard had no respect for his fellow human beings. Catherine imagined it must take a special type of person to become a prison guard. Ones which revelled in the misery of others, especially those who could possibly be facing death.

* * *

Just by the look on the guard's face Catherine knew the day had arrived to hear the judge's verdict. If further silent evidence was required it was in the pair of heavy handcuffs he carried. Earlier she'd been served a bowl of hot gruel and a cob of bread. She had even been allowed to wash her hands and face, her first since standing before the magistrate.

Without being told she stood up and presented her wrists, knowing today may dictate her entire future. Despite what the magistrate had said she had not prayed, this in the belief that God couldn't come to a person just because they had nowhere else to turn. He hadn't come when they were desperate for money after her first father died. And he certainly didn't intervene when she was gasping for breath under the weight of Patrick's body.

"Come on," the burly guard growled.

Her stomach churned as she followed him past the row of cells. She cast a quick glance at the door of Emily Kilpatrick's cell and wondered if she was to hear her verdict today as well.

* * *

Outside in the street protest marchers from The Grapes were walking up and down the damp cobbles in front of the Old Bailey alleyway, to the left of which was the notorious Newgate Prison in which untold numbers existed in squalor and half starved to death. Many in there were simply forgotten and more than a few young girls were bloated with child. Their offspring would never know their father who in all probability was one of the guards or another inmate.

Ten minutes ago Mister Snekcid had wished the group well before leaving to sit in the court.

All the women marchers walked barefoot, wearing black aprons and bonnets symbolizing their poverty. Few men had shown up as they had to be at work, those that did wore cloth caps and ragged dark suits which at some point in time would have been new. All the scene lacked was a brass band playing a dirge.

Eunice Wilson carried one placard which read:

CATHERINE FARROW
IS NOT THE GUILTY PERSON
HER PARENTS ARE
SHOW THE GIRL MERCY
SHE DOES NOT DESERVE PRISON

A brawny man with a limp carried another:

DON'T TAKE THE LIFE
OF ONE SO YOUNG
CATHERINE FARROW DESERVES BETTER

Hilda, the bar lady, bore another:

CATHERINE FARROW
DESERVES TO BE SHOWN MERCY
BECAUSE HER PARENTS NEVER DID
IN THE NAME OF GOD GIVE IT TO HER

And a final one read:

PROVE THERE IS JUSTICE
IN ENGLAND FOR A COMMONER
SET CATHERINE FARROW FREE
ALL SHE DID WAS ACT IN HER OWN DEFENCE

Two constables carrying black ebony truncheons escorted the marchers although it seemed they were not to make any arrests provided the protest didn't become violent like so many did.

Quite a crowd had gathered with some siding with Catherine, others with the law. Two very severe-looking women, dressed in all black with huge bonnets covering almost all their faces, knelt at the curb praying. Scruffy half-naked children wandered around, begging a few coppers from those who looked like they at least had some money. Usually all they got was a glare or a clip across the ear. The children swore and moved on, hoping somebody would press a coin into their dirty palm.

Now people began to point as an elegant hansom cab drawn by a magnificent shiny black horse rounded the corner. In it was Harcourt Longman, one of the London circuit judges. There was no doubting he saw at least two of the placards before his carriage passed through the short passageway which led to the private courtyard.

* * *

Of course the very nervous Catherine had no idea a protest on her behalf was in progress as she waited nervously in a holding cell below the courtroom. This time she was totally alone, without even the reassuring smile of Emily Kilpatrick. And even now memories of Emily's melancholy face had faded somewhat.

Although she didn't know it her mother had hobbled into court, anxious to see what befell her daughter. Her face was drawn and haggard due to still-aching ribs and sitting at home with Patrick who moaned almost constantly and screeched every time he took a pee. Patrick had said it was her duty as a wife to tend him but she wasn't so sure. Now he wasn't capable of giving her what she desired most in life and obviously he couldn't work so once again she would be forced to become the breadwinner although her pitch wouldn't be at The Grapes this time. There she was despised. Catherine had become the hero.

Mister Snekcid was taking his seat in the public gallery among other spectators and the men of the newspapers who were keen to hear the verdict. An appointment with the hangman would be the ideal outcome as an execution sold more copy. They had heard the Farrow girl was very attractive with a good figure and long golden tresses framing her pleasant face. These features were also good for sales. Normally those who stood in the prisoner's stand were surly brutes and usually little better than animals. One man sitting next to Mister Snekcid held a large pad and a stick of charcoal ready to sketch this girl who had taken out violent revenge on her stepfather and put the boot to her mother.

Those in the street outside continued to circulate in the hopes their protest would do some good. They were all aware of course Catherine may have to serve many years in prison and there were some who considered death was a better option. Catherine wasn't the average hardened type and she would be taken advantage of by her fellow female inmates, some of whom would lust for her body. Even the guards would simply look on, watching the girl receiving more abuse than Patrick O'Grady or her mother ever gave.

In his chambers the sixty-eight-year-old judge was asking his dresser if he had seen the protest outside.

"Yes, I did, my lord. It certainly seems this Farrow woman has her supporters, but why, don't ask me. I heard the assault on her stepfather was particularly vicious."

"It certainly was, Claude, the girl must be little better than a wild animal although those protestors seem to think otherwise. I do know women are becoming an ever increasing problem in our society, a pestilence, a blight. It is a good thing our government had the good sense to approve transportation for criminals otherwise we would have nowhere to put them. Oh, I suppose we could send them out into the countryside, even to Scotland, but it's far better shipping them to Australia. At least out there they're well out of our hair."

"Indeed, sir. In my opinion females are fit for naught except bearing children."

"I agree. However there was a time, Claude, when I enjoyed going through the motions of impregnating my seeds in a comely wench although lately the ability has left me. Now I enjoy a really good brandy as my nightcap. Hurry yourself, Claude, and help me on with my wig and robe so I may deliver judgement in this case. And I believe there are another four to follow Farrow."

"Indeed, my lord. One Emily Kilpatrick, a Barbara Henshaw, a Lydie Denner and the one who drowned her sister's twin babies, Mary Campbell."

While the vivid red robe was being placed across his shoulders Judge Longman stroked his smooth chin with a thumb and forefinger and asked his man a question.

"You consider me to be a fair judge don't you, Claude?"

"Why of course, sir. Why ever do you ask?"

"Last evening three very senior members of King George's inner court visited me quite unexpectedly in my apartments. They said their instructions had come directly from His Majesty's council and putting it very simply, Claude, I was told that, excluding Mary Campbell, the other four females I'm about to sentence today should be transported for at least a minimum of twelve years. I know you're not aware of the technical or legal aspects of the cases but in each the preliminary magistrate's reports indicated the defendants may have been somewhat justified in the actions they took. And in fairness I had to agree. That being the case I would have handed down sentences ranging between eight and ten years. Now this royal directive has placed me in a deep quandary. Do I answer to my conscience, my monarch or my God? What do you think? And please believe me, Claude, I will value your opinion."

"As you say, my lord, a quandary. Do you know the reason why these instructions have been given?"

"No. Naturally I did ask but was told it was a private and personal matter concerning the king. Further than that they refused to elaborate other than hinting that if I cooperated I could be honoured with a title at a future date."

"Well, my lord, if it were up to me I'd comply with the king's request. Not to do so could be detrimental to your own future. Let us not forget now George is recovered from his illness he once again wields absolute power."

"Yes, Claude, your point is well taken. The king must have a very good reason for this most unusual request and when all is said and done the accused are the low life of our society anyway. They will not be missed, I'm sure."

He shrugged his shoulders and asked Claude to hurry as he was due at the races by three this afternoon. Then his club was holding a dinner for a new member of the Law Society. A William Grenville, a man with high prospects and political ambitions. With another shrug Claude was asked to inform the court clerk that he was about to take his seat and have the Farrow woman brought up.

* * *

"On your feet, Farrow, it's time to go up," the constable guarding her said after hearing a bell ring.

Once standing everything began to reel before her eyes. This was it, her day of judgement. She ran trembling fingers through her matted hair which hadn't been washed since before the attack on Patrick and her mother. Yet her hair was of little consequence, she wasn't in court because of her looks.

On the stairs she was prodded with the official's truncheon for climbing too slowly. He didn't want to upset the judge who was well noted for his irritability towards prisoner guards. To him they were brainless idiots who couldn't hold down a proper job, and such was his lofty and noble status nobody dare argue with him. A central criminal court judge was a law unto himself and rarely if ever questioned.

In a daze Catherine entered the prisoner's box, facing the high bench where the judge would sit. She peered left and right through the gloom at the sea of faces. She saw numerous scribes seated ready with their quills to record the proceedings and of course the judgement. Oil lamps and candles burned and flickered as her nostrils inhaled the pungent smell of scent used by all those who wished to hide their bodily odours. To her right was the public gallery although she wasn't aware one of those sitting there was hoping she may be spared. Then her keen eyes set upon her mother which caused her temples to pound. She looked away rapidly, seeing her only returned sad memories.

Seconds later everybody was told to stand up, Judge Harcourt Longman was about to enter. Catherine watched him walk slowly to his very high-backed crimson chair. His gaunt face was shrouded in a tightly woven grey wig and his grizzled facial expression forewarned Catherine that her chances of leniency were very slim. He bowed and sat down. Everybody else followed suit and a deathly silence fell over the court. Only the judge himself was aware who the two men standing in the shadows were.

A man wearing a frock coat stood up at one of the tables, looked Catherine directly in the eye and asked, "Are you Catherine Farrow of twenty-three Grundy Street, Limehouse?"

"Yes, sir."

"Are you aware why you stand before Judge Longman today?"

"Yes, sir."

"And do you still admit to the vicious assault upon your stepfather and mother?"

"Yes, sir, I do."

"Have you anything further to say before judgement is passed?"

"Only that my actions were necessary because eventually I think my parents would have either driven me to madness or killed me. I had no alternative."

Well said, Catherine, Mister Snekcid thought. At least she was a woman of strong conviction and unusually eloquent for types like her.

The man sat down and everybody looked at the judge who was about to deliver his verdict. As he always did he cleared his throat first.

"Catherine Farrow, you are little more than a child but chose to mount a vicious attack upon those who clothed and fed you. I have carefully read the magistrate's report and your reasons for committing this crime. However abuse by parents does not give you the right to extract revenge by using what could have been a deadly weapon. I'm sure up and down our country children suffer equal torment but they do not commit acts such as yours because of it. Do you understand what I'm saying, child?"

"Yes, sir. But it wasn't you who suffered, it was me."

There were murmurs around the court at her reply and silence had to be called for. Judge Harcourt coughed and continued, "Your suffering is beside the point, my girl, and don't get cocky with me. I have been informed your stepfather will survive the attack so luckily for you we don't have a case for premeditated murder. In your favour and from the evidence given I shall consider the assault upon your mother with the chamber pot as one of self-defence; however kicking her while on the floor was not. That was an attack with malicious intent. In my considered opinion you committed a grievous bodily crime upon your guardians who by and large are law-abiding citizens, therefore I must deem you are not fit to mingle with ordinary people and your punishment must reflect that. However it may surprise you to know I have weighed this case very carefully and to a certain degree I can appreciate you felt compelled to commit this crime as an avenue of escape from torment. I'm in no doubt your mother and stepfather did not show due consideration and yet as an offspring you should have accepted these conditions, painful as they might have been. In this world we know there are parents who for unknown reasons will mistreat their children, it is an affliction of the society we live in, one which I fear will never be fully eliminated. You, Catherine Farrow, were one of the unlucky ones. However in the opinion of this court two very serious crimes have been committed therefore it is my duty to render punishment. I hereby sentence you to be transported to the penal colony in Botany Bay in Australia for a period of twelve years, and may the Good Lord have mercy upon you. Take her away and see she is properly prepared."

He stood up, bowed and departed. A hum began to develop in the court as officials began refilling oil lamps and replacing candles. The two unidentified spectators smiled and lit cigarettes to await the next sentencing. It would seem Judge Longman had heeded their request of last night. The royal court officials would be very pleased.

"The poor lass," Mister Snekcid said to the person next to him.

"Aye, sir, I agree. I've heard Botany Bay is a hell on earth, riddled with cruelty, corruption and disease of all kinds. The lass would have been better off swinging, believe me."

"Yes, well, the decision has been made."

"Is she a friend of yours, sir?"

"Actually I've never met her in my life. Now I must be off."

"There's four more due up, you know."

"They don't interest me. I bid you good day."

"And to you, sir."

The well-dressed man was allowed to pass.

Catherine's head had almost exploded. Twelve years in Botany Bay and from what Patrick had told her about the penal colony it amounted to a lingering death sentence assuming of course she survived the long voyage. How long that voyage would be she had no idea except Patrick had said it took months. In all her life she had never travelled further than Canning Town, now she was going to be shipped to the other side of the world and probably in chains. She looked up to where her mother had been seated only to see the space was vacant. She had probably left to tell Patrick so they could gloat together. She gasped as her right arm was roughly grabbed from behind by the constable.

"Come on, lass, we've to get you ready for a little voyage."

"I don't think I can walk, sir."

"Well, you'd better 'cause I ain't going to carry you. Now look sharp. There's another due up after the judge has had a cup of tea and a biscuit."

"Who is it?"

She was jabbed in the ribs and told to shut up. Her body began to tremble from head to foot, not having any idea what lay in store for her now only that any possibility of a normal life free of torment was gone for at least twelve years. Perhaps on the ship she could leap overboard and drown. The narrow stairs began to distort as she stood at the top. She wobbled so the guard steadied her as she took each step as if her descent was into the fires of hell.

* * *

As Emily Kilpatrick was taking her place in the prisoner's box, out on the street Mister Snekcid was telling the protesters what sentence had been imposed on Catherine.

"Oh dear God," Eunice Wilson wailed. "The poor lass will never survive and she'll get plenty of what people pay me for. I've heard women at Botany Bay are fair game for any men that want them. I know a sailor who's seen the place, he told me. Is there nothing we can do, Mister Snekcid?"

"No, I'm afraid not. Unfortunately the judge's decision is final, there is no appeal. He made his judgement as he saw the case, not unfortunately from Catherine's point of view. If there is any consolation Catherine looked to be a robust girl so she may well survive the ordeal."

"What happens to her now?" Hilda asked.

"I have no idea. All I can suggest is we pray for her."

"Praying does no good," another said. "My wife fell ill, I prayed on my knees for her recovery but she passed on. I've never prayed since."

Just then two constables appeared out of the alleyway and approached the group.

"Right, you lot, move on. Farrow has been sentenced and your protest did no good. If you don't want us to run you in you'd better be out of our sight in a minute. Now scarper."

With some protestors in tears they moved away after shaking Mister Snekcid's hand. Eunice looked back at the court.

"Goodbye, Catherine, we did all we could for you. Try and come back."

Then with her own life to lead she went in search of a client.

* * *

Downstairs Catherine was shaking like a leaf with tears running down her flushed cheeks. She was strapped tightly in a solid chair with her legs outstretched resting on an anvil, having shackles riveted around her ankles. They had pulled her filthy skirt up above the knees and removed her shoes and stockings. Three guards had admired her shapely legs for a minute or so before beginning the preparations.

Now her face grimaced as the blacksmith knelt to secure a two-and-a-half-foot length of link chain between the shackles. Then began her next indignities. While one guard clipped her toe and fingernails another produced a large pair of shears and proceeded to hack her long flaxen hair off, causing her to sob loudly. Once it had been her pride and joy and whenever possible she combed and brushed it for ten or more minutes every day. Now all those long tresses were being picked up by a guard who said they would make a nice wig for some rich lady.

Her head hung low as they unstrapped her. She was told to stand up and walk to the door.

"What about my shoes?" she asked.

They all laughed.

"It's summer, lass, you don't need 'em. You may get a new pair in Australia, till then it's bare feet. That's it, you're ready for the ship now. Hope you don't get too seasick. They say the roughest part is from here till you're round the bottom of Africa. Now try to walk normally."

As she moved her right foot it seemed to be encased in lead. They laughed as she almost stumbled. Slowly her first steps were taken and the manacles cut into her ankles far worse than the handcuffs. The chain dragged on the cobbles as she hobbled to her cell to await being taken to the ship. The guard wouldn't say when that would be.

In her cell she was given a pewter goblet of water, a large hunk of bread and some strips of cold bacon. She nibbled, realising this would be the pattern of life from now on, accepting whatever they gave her. There would be no choice. She would also have to obey all instructions or face the consequences. Up to this morning there had always been a slim chance of being released with a severe warning or one or two years in Newgate. Now though her fate had been well and truly sealed. Transportation to Australia. She wondered what would happen when her years had been served, would they bring her back to England as a free woman or expect her to pay for the passage? Still, that was in the distant future, she was now almost twenty, in twelve years she'd only be thirty-two, still time to lead some sort of life assuming anybody would accept an ex-convict. Yet now uppermost in her mind was how long would they keep her waiting before being taken to the ship. Or would they transfer her to one of those hulks anchored out in the River Thames that Patrick had told her about. Then those vessels on the river had simply been a part of life which really didn't concern her, now they could become a horrible reality. She also cringed at the thought of being placed alongside men who were sentenced to suffer the same fate as herself.

She suddenly felt sick and threw up all she'd eaten into the slop pail. Her mind and stomach were in a turmoil, this caused by deeds of her own doing. She lowered her aching body to the floor, curled herself into a ball, clutched her shoulders and began to cry.

"It's no use you crying, lass," a gruff voice at the opening in the cell door said. "You dug your own grave by attacking your innocent parents."

"They weren't innocent, they committed crimes against my body."

"Aye, perhaps so, sadly the judge saw it otherwise. Now take my advice and try to get some sleep. Tomorrow you have a very early appointment on a ship called the *Bromley*."

"How long does it take to reach Australia?"

"Six or seven months given good seas, longer if there's little wind. I'm told they allow convicts up on deck for an hour or so each day. You gotta be careful though not to get washed overboard because with those ankle irons you'll sink like a stone. Now like I said, sleep."

"Can I empty my slop pail? I've been sick in it."

"Aye, alright, only don't try any funny stuff. On your feet and stand well back, I've been attacked by mad women before, you know. This place used to be overflowing with 'em before they took most to where you're going."

She picked up the slop bucket and once out of the cell he pointed to a hole in the cobbles. At it the contents were slowly poured down the hole. Then she swilled the pail in a trough. On her way back she saw Emily Kilpatrick being escorted to a cell. Her ankles were in irons also and her short hair was shorter still now.

"Twelve bloody years in Australia the bastard gave me," she said when seeing Catherine. "And all for selling what God gave me. What did you get, Cath ...?"

"That's enough!" the guard shouted as he pushed her roughly into a cell. "You'll have plenty of time to chat when at sea."

"Bastards!" Emily screamed as the cell door slammed shut. "All men are bastards!"

"Aye, lass, that may be so but at least we get to go home at nights. And if you must know, I've a nice comely wife waiting for me. Now I don't want to hear another peep else you'll be shut in a small box till it's time to sail."

Catherine sat on the floor, cradled her chin, took a deep breath and vowed not to cry again. But on looking down to see those irons encircling her ankles, tears began to well in her bloodshot eyes. She had been reduced to a status little better than an animal. In fact she felt sure the coal delivery man's horse had a better life than the one she was about to face.

"Ah well," she sighed to herself. "My life as a convict has well and truly started and I know it will be more severe than the one I was forced to suffer at home. You were a fool, Catherine Farrow, and now you must begin paying. Twelve years, only eight less than I've already lived. Somebody please help me through them."

Sadly for her there was nobody.

* * *

In his chambers Judge Longman was enjoying a goblet of port with the two king's representatives. Hands had already been shaken after his man Claude had been dismissed.

"On behalf of His Majesty, sir, we are to thank you for the judgments you handed down this morning. Your patriotism to king and country has been duly noted and you can be assured rewards will follow."

"For that I'm grateful, gentlemen," Judge Longman replied. "However since I have complied with your requests, may I now ask the reason?"

"Unfortunately not, sir. All we are prepared to say is that it was a just cause on behalf of His Majesty. Now let us say a toast to our monarch."

They each held their goblets high in the air.

"To King George, may his life and health continue to prosper."

The men shook hands again before taking their leave.

Judge Harcourt Longman sat in a comfortable chair, still wondering if he had done the correct thing. Due to his decisions he had condemned four young ladies to a life of hell, one which they didn't truly deserve.

Fifteen minutes later he rang for his man to help him dress for the Ascot races. A life of ease and plenty for him, lives of hardship and manual labour for the ladies.

* * * * *

PART TWO

TRANSPORTATION

CHAPTER 4

CATHERINE WASN'T ASLEEP WHEN THE CELL DOOR opened, in fact she'd hardly slept at all. Throughout the seemingly endless night fearful visions of life on a sailing ship had haunted her with the prospect she may fall overboard. In her distorted vision she imagined the captain wouldn't even bother mounting a search, knowing the ankle chains would have dragged her under to be consumed by a gigantic sea monster even before her body hit the bottom. Patrick O'Grady had told her seawater was salty, she'd never tasted it. Now it seemed very possible.

"Come on," the guard growled. "I don't get off duty till I've got the four of you in the wagon but it ain't prison you're going to. It's the docks where a nice boat awaits. Move yourself, girl."

When on her feet she felt light-headed before realising most of her hair had been shorn off. It was hard work going up the steep steps, having to drag the chain with her plus the manacles cut into the tender skin of her ankles. Once outside in the bright sunshine she saw how filthy her blouse and skirt were which caused her to wonder if there would be a chance to wash them on the ship. A sharp jab in the small of her back with a truncheon brought her out of the brief reverie as she was told to get on the wagon. The door was open and with effort she climbed the three steps to enter what felt like an oven. Barbara Henshaw and Lydie Denner already sat on a narrow slatted seat. She sat opposite them. They smiled weakly and as her eyes became accustomed to the gloom she could see Lydie had a badly bruised lip. The door was slammed shut and locked. No words were exchanged. Each of them were engrossed in their own thoughts. Mainly thoughts of the past as they had no concept of the future.

Some minutes later the door opened again and Emily Kilpatrick climbed in. Her pale face seemed even more ashen as she sat next to Catherine. They rubbed thighs and both women sensed a certain affinity. At least they were not alone.

"Have a nice voyage, ladies," the sarcastic guard said. "If you ever come back bring me an ostrich feather for my cap." He laughed, slammed the door shut and the bolts being drawn sounded like hammers nailing their coffins closed.

The wagon started with a jerk. "Here we go," Emily said. "The first leg of a journey into purgatory."

"If we ever arrive," Lydie Denner muttered above the clip-clop of horses hooves. "I've heard many convicts fall sick and die on the way. Those who do make it are put to work straight away and I expect women like us will be detailed to act as house servants. We may even be sent to serve a former convict. One who has served his or her time and I imagine they'll be the worst to work for as they want to get their own back for all the suffering they were put through. I'm also expecting to be thrown on my back by a guard who'll hoist my skirt and pull my knickers down the moment we arrive. It's the way."

"How do you know all this?" Barbara Henshaw asked.

"Because a year ago I went out with a man who'd just come back from a place they call Port Jackson. He gave me a really good time provided my body was available whenever he wanted it. Then he got me a job in this fancy mansion as a maid to a bitch of a woman. It was him who made me steal the woman's jewellery. If I didn't he'd chuck me out and I had nowhere to go. Unfortunately the miserable old woman caught me in her jewellery box and set the dogs on me. Then two of her labourers dragged me to a well, tied a rope round my wrists and lowered me down until I was up to my chin in water. I was left in there for two days with no food or drink. When they finally pulled me out I had the fever and my man took me home, gave me a bath then took me as I shivered. All the time I could think of nothing else but getting revenge on the old woman.

"Finally my strength returned and I went back to where she lived, stole a shovel and waited for the bitch in the garden, knowing she'd be out picking flowers. When she showed up I bashed her head with the shovel. It was worth it just to see the terrified look on her face as blood ran down it. Naturally I was arrested and pleaded my boyfriend forced me to do it. He told the magistrate he'd done no such thing. In fact I'm sure he bribed the magistrate, anyway here I am, facing fifteen bloody long years."

"I only got twelve," Emily Kilpatrick said.

"So did I," Catherine added. They exchanged smiles although they had no earthly reason to do so.

Barbara Henshaw licked her thin lips. "Perhaps we're all lucky. Remember the one called Mary Campbell who killed her sister's twin babies? Well, the guard told me she's to hang tomorrow so I suppose in a way we're better off."

"Who's to know?" Lydie Denner replied. "We may be lucky and get a considerate captain who'll treat us a bit like human beings on the way. The shipping line gets paid to take us, you know, seventeen pounds seven shillings per convict. A guard told me that after I'd let him kiss me but then he wanted more so I refused. He punched me, that's how I got this fat lip, then he took me anyway. However, like I was saying, we may get a kind captain; on the other hand ours may be a right bastard who'll treat us like shit all the way and feed us pig swill so more money goes in his pocket. One thing's for certain, we won't be able to complain. Convicts have no rights."

"Will they keep us in these handcuffs?" Catherine asked, holding her hands up.

"Who knows? I just hope not," Emily replied. "It's awkward fingering yourself with both hands so close together."

"How can you think of something like that at a time like this?" Barbara asked.

"What else is there? I don't suppose we'll be wined and dined by the crew once we're afloat and I admit I'll miss getting poked now and again."

They all laughed despite knowing there would be little humour in their future lives. Everything fell silent as the wagon lurched this way and that, heading for the docks. People going about their regular businesses stopped and looked for a moment, knowing any carriage heading away from Newgate Prison meant the occupants were either heading for the gallows or Australia.

One young girl who was on the arm of a man said, "In an hour you and me will be clamped together enjoying the nakedness of ourselves while them poor buggers face either a stretched neck or life down in the stinking hold of a ship bound for Botany Bay."

"How do you know?" the man asked.

"Because three years ago my mother was sent there for stealing two shillings off a gent who'd done her but then refused to pay. Which reminds me, I'll want paying before we start. Are we agreed?"

"Yes, I suppose so. How much was it?"

"Five bob and you get the full works. Come on."

They turned away from the prison cart and walked on.

* * *

Somehow Mister Snekcid had learned what time the prison wagon was due at the docks and had told Catherine's friends in The Grapes. Almost all were out now at the dockside awaiting its arrival. They could at least wave to Catherine as she was being taken to the transport ship now lying at anchor in midstream. Since daybreak rowing boats had been ferrying supplies out to the *Bromley*. A dock worker who was a regular client of Eunice Wilson had told her the ship was due to sail tomorrow morning. It seemed two female convicts were already aboard but nobody knew anything about them. In addition to the convicts it carried a cargo of mining equipment plus six passengers who had been charged a lower rate because of the prisoners. Two were women going to join their husbands who had sailed three years previously. It seemed they were to be a surprise. The other four were farmers intending to start sheep ranching on the wide open plains Australia had to offer. Plus the climate was more favourable than in England, or so they had been informed. The farmers were to be dropped off on the west coast of the massive island, at the mouth of the Swan River.

"There's the wagon!" one of the group shouted as it rounded a corner.

They followed it until four burly constables stopped them. It was not unknown for rescue attempts to be made at this point in a prisoner transfer. In fact it was the last possible chance to free a friend. Once aboard ship it wasn't possible to rescue anybody as they were sealed in holds, at least until the ship was well out to sea. After that it was at the captain's discretion if convicts were allowed up on deck. Some did, some didn't, they made their own rules.

The door of the wagon was unlocked and opened. As Emily Kilpatrick was last on she was first off. Not knowing the small crowd was there for Catherine she waved her manacled hands at them while being escorted down a set of steep, slippery steps and helped into a waiting longboat.

Catherine came next and broke into tears when she recognized Hilda and Eunice Wilson. They waved, she returned it and gulped.

"Oh, the poor dear," Hilda said, "she's had most of her beautiful hair cut off."

"I think that's normal," Mister Snekcid told them. "It may seem cruel but actually it helps to keep the convict cooler as the weather gets hotter the further south they travel, plus it gives some protection against itchy head lice."

"Just look at those ankle irons," Eunice said, "they must weigh a ton. Oh, Catherine, why were you so bloody stupid?"

On the steps Catherine looked back to get her last sight of friendly faces. She raised her shackled hands and heard Eunice shout, "I'll be here when you return,

Catherine my love, see if I'm not!" Then she turned away, fell into Mister Snekcid's arms and burst into tears.

"We did all we could, Eunice," he told her, "and I'm sure Catherine appreciated us being here. Now let's go back to The Grapes and I'll buy you a large gin."

"I'll not refuse that, sir. Then I'd very much like to cuddle up to you, if you know what I mean."

"We'll see about that. In fact I'd like to question you on life in Limehouse generally as I intend to write about it and hope to sell the story to a newspaper or a book publisher. I'll pay for any information you or anybody else gives me. What do you say to that?"

"I'd be honoured, sir."

She waved one final time at the rowing boat which was just pulling away from the jetty. Unfortunately Catherine didn't see her as she was facing the *Bromley*, her home at sea for at least the next six months. It looks such a small vessel to be sailing all that way, she thought. Lydie Denner had said it was over twelve thousand miles to Australia. To someone who had never travelled more than a few miles in her entire life, Catherine could not even begin to imagine such a distance. In her troubled mind, as the boat cut easily through the water, it almost seemed as if she was passing through a void from one life into the next. Her first life had not been pleasant and she knew the next would be no better, in fact it could be far worse. Sadly it was too late to have regrets.

Although the day was hot Catherine shivered as the longboat touched the *Bromley*'s side where hardened sailors looked down on them from the ship's rail. Some faces showed pity, others lust at the thought women would be aboard and already mental images were being created of them, especially her with the golden head of cropped hair. Emily saw a person who looked no more than a lad holding a telescope to his eye and he wasn't looking at the two oarsmen. Catherine could see no way to get aboard but it soon became evident.

A thick rope with a hook on the end was lowered and Emily Kilpatrick was told to hold her wrists out. In silence she did so and the hook was put over the centre links of her handcuffs. Seconds later she was being hauled up, rotating slowly. Once she was level with an opening in the deck rail rough hands pulled her in. She was taken away as the rope was relowered.

Catherine knew she was next and presented her wrists, not wanting to incur anybody's wrath so early in her sentence. Now she trembled as her arms were drawn upward and then stretched taut as her full weight was taken up on them. She gasped when the metal handcuffs cut into both wrists as her ribcage was forced tightly against the skin, making breathing difficult as she rotated slowly so the dockside came into view with people watching the action. Free people, she thought. Then she too was grabbed by rough hands and pulled onto the deck in time to see Emily being lowered through a deck hatch in front of the foremast and she wasn't smiling. Across the deck from her Catherine was surprised to see a number of sheep, hens and rabbits in separate pens but she was quickly jolted back into reality by a loud barking voice telling her to get over here right sharp.

Beside the hatch stood a severe-looking, clean-shaven uniformed man holding an open book. A sailor gave Catherine a sharp jab in the ribs and told her to move. With as much speed as possible she shuffled across the deck towards the very forward part of the ship where the man stood. He grasped her chin between thumb and forefinger.

"Name?" he snapped.

"Catherine Farrow."

He slapped her face. "It's sir to you, lass, remember that. All the ship's officers are to be called sir. This is the only time you'll be warned. Now I'll ask again. Name?"

"Catherine Farrow, sir," she stammered with her eyes watering.

"That's better." He made a note in his book. "For your information, Farrow, my name is Pimm, I'm first mate of this vessel, only the captain outranks me, remember that also. There's those aboard who say I'm a bastard, well, I'll not deny it. Cause any trouble and you'll find yourself at the mainmast having the cat-o'-nine-tails laid across your back. Know what the cat is, do you?"

"I think a whip, sir."

"Aye, a whip. Nine leather tails which slice flesh to shreds. Him at the rail over there, watching barrels of salt being put aboard, is Mister Malone, the ship's bosun. It's him who lays the strokes and, believe me, he doesn't care who his victim is. Now you'll be lowered into the convict hold just as you were brought aboard. When you land on the deck, release the hook so we can lower the next down. Think you can do that?"

"Yes, sir."

"Good. Once we're under sail and out in the channel Captain Stricker may give permission to remove your handcuffs but the ankle bracelets stay. For you convicts it won't be an enjoyable voyage but you're lucky not to be swinging on the end of a rope. You and the other five may as well be cattle for all we care. Once in the hold find yourself a spot and sit down. Now hold your wrists out to be lowered."

She did and took a deep breath as another hook appeared before her eyes. A seaman attached it to her handcuffs and once again she was hauled up and lowered through the hatch opening which wasn't much wider than her hips. Down one side were coarse-looking ladder rungs which she imagined would be difficult to climb wearing handcuffs.

It was gloomy, hot and smelly as the dangling chain hit the deck first, then her bare feet. As instructed she released the hook before seeing Emily leaning against what must have been the base of a ship's mast. She remembered it had three. Hanging from the mast was an oil lantern which gave a minimum of illumination. Among other things she could smell tar.

As her eyes became more accustomed to the gloom she saw there were two others sitting with knees drawn up and resting their backs against rough wooden planking which was angled slightly. One of them looked to be younger than herself, the other a few years older. Catherine nodded her head at them but they didn't respond. Perhaps talking was forbidden? She asked if it was in a whisper.

The elder of the two women answered. "We're not supposed to talk until everybody is aboard so take my advice and shut up. Him up there is a bastard, he's already punched me in the gut for not calling him sir."

Catherine went over to them and sat down next to the younger one whose closely cropped hair seemed to be a dark reddish, almost rusty colour. Her sweaty face with full pouting pink lips conveyed nothing except utter sadness. Even her grey-green eyes stared blankly ahead almost as if she was blind. Yet in the face Catherine could imagine a livelier character as if at some time she'd been much happier. Then the hold became darker still as another pair of dirty bare feet appeared through the hatch. They belonged to Lydie Denner. And shortly after her Barbara Henshaw arrived. Moments later a grille was placed over the hatch opening so the sunlight was broken up into four dust-filled beams which did little more than illuminate the shaft itself. They heard bolts being drawn before the voice of First Mate Pimm boomed down.

"Right, you lot down there can talk but keep it quiet. You'll all be getting something to eat and drink in about an hour. After that there'll be nothing until we set sail tomorrow morning. You'll also get a blanket, look after it well because another won't be issued."

"He said he was a bastard and I just know he will be," Emily Kilpatrick said while lifting the front of her blouse to wipe her sweaty face. The others couldn't help staring at the white bare flesh of her belly. Then they all looked up when hearing Mister Pimm's voice again.

"Attention, all hands. Captain Stricker coming aboard, attend your stations." This order was followed by a rapid scampering of feet.

"I'll bet he comes aboard in a lot better style than we did," Lydie Denner said before casting her glance at the two strangers to ask who they were.

"I'm Sophie Hart," the older of the two replied. "And if you must know I've been sentenced to spend the rest of my natural life in that shit hole of a prison colony. Plus I'm to be confined and shackled in a solitary cell at the end of every day for six full months."

"What was your crime?" Emily asked.

"I kidnapped the son of a politician and held him for the ransom of five thousand quid. A deal was made but when I went to collect my money in a park six constables were waiting. At the station house they all had me before I was even charged. That's it and, just between us girls, I may chuck myself overboard once we're at sea because life won't hold anything for me."

"You shouldn't do that," Catherine said. "A friend of mine who worked in a tavern said things always got better. Now I'm down here and admit there doesn't seem much hope but I've vowed to try and survive."

"What's your name?" Sophie asked as she stood up and flexed her long slender arms. She was also tall as her cropped hair brushed the overhead timbers.

Catherine gave her name and the three others added theirs.

"Yes, well, as I was saying," Sophie continued, "what hope do we have? Up there on deck there's that bloody first mate who's just dying for one of us to step out of line so he can order the bosun to flay us. And even if we all behave we'll be treated no better than pigs. Then there's the seamen, all they'll want is to get themselves stuck into us and I'll lay odds the captain will turn a blind eye. You see the upper crust just don't care, I know, I've lain with enough. And this poor little thing," she turned and looked down at the younger girl still sitting beside Catherine. "Well, you tell 'em why you're here, Ann."

Before speaking her eyes scanned the newcomers as if for the first time.

"My name is Ann Lingos, I'm eighteen and my story is almost too weird to believe. Sophie didn't at first but I convinced her while we were in Newgate Prison awaiting a trial, a trial which never came in my case because I'm an illegitimate daughter of King George the Third. At least I think that's the reason. My mother only told me who my father was on her deathbed earlier this year. I'd often wondered why there was never a regular man around the house or where my mother got money to clothe and feed me because she didn't work regularly. Then of course I realised after she passed on the king was paying her to keep quiet about the affair. A couple of months after her death I thought the king owed me something so taking a chance I tried to get an audience with him at Kew."

"I heard the king had gone barmy in the head," Barbara Henshaw interrupted.

Ann nodded her head and said, "He had been mad but was cured.[3] Anyway as I was saying, I tried to see the king but got no further than a very nasty man who wanted to know my reasons for an audience. Of course I refused to say and was escorted off the property by four royal guards. This annoyed me as I still felt the king owed me something so I sought the advice of a cobbler friend of my mother's. He advised me to see a man of law. I did and quickly discovered that was a big mistake. The lawyer must have been a true royalist for the next day I was arrested on a charge of something called sedition where they said I was inciting a rebellion against the king. I was taken to Newgate Prison and threatened with torture if I didn't confess, they even showed me some hideous instruments which scared me so I promised not to say anything. Even that didn't satisfy them so they put me in chains and threw me in a small, cold cell with nothing but some damp straw on the cobbled floor. Eventually I was brought before a very smartly dressed gent wearing an all-black suit and a white wig. He told me I was to be shipped to a penal colony in Australia for the rest of my life and that I should count myself lucky I wasn't to be executed. A prison guard who felt sorry for me said it had been arranged to ship me out very quickly before anybody at home noticed I was missing. That was less than a week ago. That's my story and I wish now I'd kept my big mouth shut."

"What a dreadful tale," Emily Kilpatrick said. "I thought I'd been hard done by but your case is worse, Ann, and I'm truly sorry for you. It proves what lengths our royalty will go to when they want to silence a commoner."

"Remember, Emily, I do have royal blood in me so I'm not exactly a commoner. Every night I spend a few moments wishing a great evil will befall our king. Something like going mad again and rotting in the same hell he's condemned me to. I also dream of the day when I can extract revenge but I know it'll never come unless a miracle happens."

"I don't think we can expect miracles, Ann," Catherine replied while standing up to look around the space which was to be her home for at least half a year.

---

3   King George III did suffer a bout of madness which his doctors seemed unable to cure. A Doctor Willis was finally brought in who eventually cured the monarch. This was in March 1789, seven years prior to the commencement of this story.

There was a flat space of perhaps six feet before it started to taper towards the front of the ship. Thick reinforcing beams ran across the space making access almost impossible although it looked like a person could squeeze under them if they wished to lie there. To the right was what looked like a narrow bench with a hole in its centre. Directly above her head was the shaft which they would have to enter and exit by, there didn't appear to be any other. About four feet downward of the shaft rose the large-diameter mast which continued down below deck level. If it was a deck? She imagined the area they occupied would usually be used for carrying cargo, except on this voyage the consignment was human. Beyond the mast was about another five feet of space before it was walled off with more solid timbers running across the full width of the ship which her mind estimated to be twice the width of the living room at home. A room she may never see again. She looked around in the gloom at the creaking timbers despite the ship still lying at anchor. And aloft there was the constant patter of feet on the deck and the shouting of orders. Below her feet she could hear water slopping about.

This was a world foreign to her as of course it was to her fellow travellers although Emily had said she sailed across from Ireland. That island across the sea where Patrick came from. She shook her head and looked down at Ann Lingos whose eyes still gazed blankly ahead, hardly blinking as she leaned her back against the slightly angled side timbers. The bottoms of her feet were dirty and there were obvious cuts on them. As her skirt was drawn up above the knees it exposed a pair of sturdy legs although it was difficult to see any form of her upper body as she wore a very slack, short-sleeved red cotton blouse. With her closely cropped hair and understandable sullen expression Ann still managed to emit a certain quality which seemed to radiate from within. A person obviously with royal blood in her veins although she was not of high breeding herself. Nevertheless a person who would make a man's heart beat more rapidly if they met on the street or in a tavern. It was an allure some women were blessed with while the majority were simply members of the common downtrodden masses. Ann's manner of speech wasn't that of a commoner, nor was it aristocratic although certainly not of the farmyard or dockyard either. Catherine didn't want to interfere but she felt compelled to make friends with the girl because an innate sense was telling her some sort of affinity could develop between them. She didn't know quite what but the thought alone made her temples pulse slightly faster.

As she made her way over to Ann, taking care to duck below the low beams which braced the mast, she heard Emily sigh and sit herself down.

"God, it's hot down here, it's like being stuck inside a bloody haystack."

"Stuck in hell more like," Barbara Henshaw replied and Lydie Denner agreed. Catherine sat down beside Ann and was surprised to see Emily unlacing her sweat-stained blouse completely. The others stared almost in disbelief as her breasts became exposed. Catherine bit down on her lower lip, this was the first time in her entire life she'd seen the upper figure of a woman other than her mother. Perhaps later she might have the courage to do the same, but not now. Maybe tonight when the others were asleep or when the lantern ran out of oil.

"It may not be too wise to expose yourself like that, Emily," Sophie Hart told her. "If any of the sailors see you they could take it as a message you're a very loose woman."

"Who's to say I'm not? You don't know it but the man who helped me get across from Ireland made me entertain men yet they paid him. He also robbed them while they shagged me. Then we robbed a toff who brought the law in. Me and my benefactor, as he called himself, got charged with robbery and me for prostitution as well. I got twelve years and I just know I'll be forced to give freely in the prison colony." She looked at Catherine. "Earlier you said things always got better, well, I hope so because they can't get much worse, can they? Pigs live better than we will. I'll say this though, if a sailor up there wants that little part of me I'm available. I do know how to give a man a good time."

"Don't be a bloody fool, Emily," Lydie advised. "If the captain or that first mate found out you're sure to get whipped and I've been told that's not very nice."

"Well, I need a pee," Barbara Henshaw suddenly said. "Being surrounded by water has that effect on me. Where do we go, Sophie?"

"To that narrow bench up front. You'll have to crouch and sit over the small hole. What you deliver goes somewhere below the deck which must be a slop area. It's easy to go now although I don't know what it'll be like in a rough sea."

In the gloom they all watched Barbara go to the back, hoist her skirt and squat. They heard the stream.

"It is hot down here," Catherine said, trying to find a not too dirty piece of skirt to wipe her face. "I'm wearing a slip under my blouse and skirt, do you think it will be alright to remove it?"

"I'd ask somebody first," Sophie advised.

Catherine took what sounded like good advice before deciding to lie down on the hard deck beside Ann Lingos. For a moment they stared at each other as if looking for solace. Finally Ann whispered, "I think I'm going to like you, Catherine. You seem just a little different to the others and speak better. Were you once happy?"

"Yes, when I was a very little girl. My original father took me out for walks when he wasn't working in the dockyard or getting drunk. Then as I grew my parents made me do all the housework while they went out to taverns. They spent more of their money on ale and gin than they did on me. I was lucky to get a new dress every five years."

"People like us will never have any money, Catherine," Ann replied while licking her dry lips. "The aristocrats and royalty keep it all for themselves, that's why they have power. I realise now it was foolish of me trying to get anything from the king, in fact I imagine he'd forgotten all about me, don't forget I happened over eighteen years ago. I stood no chance."

"Didn't your mother leave any money?"

"No. She earned some mending people's clothes but everything else just seemed to be paid for. We lived in a very small cottage although I never saw a landlord or anybody like that. And once every month a cart arrived carrying some food and bottles of wine. Now of course I know who sent it."

"In other words they were payments to your mother for keeping her mouth shut about who your father was."

"I suppose so. Unfortunately everything stopped when she died and I was told to leave the cottage by some men I'd never seen before."

"Where did you move to?"

"I remembered the cobbler friend of my mother's, Henry Lastman, who was a shoemaker to the king. I went to him and although he had a lodger in his upstairs spare room he let me sleep on his shop floor. I even liked the smell of his raw shoe leather. Like I've already said, it was Henry who advised me to see a man of the law. I did and that was the last I saw of Henry or his shoe shop. I imagine he was worried stiff but there wasn't much a man like him could do. He wasn't rich but did have what he called a steady income as the king paid him fairly and I knew his footwear was of high quality because he made me a pair of shoes. After I was arrested a prison guard stole them, saying they'd fit his wife. Now I have nothing, not even a friend unless you'll be one, Catherine? Will you?"

"Of course I will."

"Please kiss me."

Catherine looked surprised for a moment before raising herself up on an elbow to peer down into the girl's sad face with those penetrating greyish-green eyes. Her full pale lips trembled slightly and she was obviously scared of what the future held. Gradually she lowered her own face until their lips met softly. Immediately she sensed a great tenderness and sweetness, not at all like those kisses Patrick forced on her as he thrust his tongue deeply into her mouth. Catherine slowly ran her tongue over Ann's lips causing the mouth to open slightly.

Gradually Catherine came to realise this was an entirely new experience kissing somebody of her own sex. Ann's lips were not like her mother's when long ago she had kissed her goodnight. Now though those kisses seemed very distant memories. Her temples began to pulse when the tip of Ann's tongue made contact with her own. She also sensed a slight reaction within her sex. It was wonderful. Sadly however the idyll came to an abrupt end when sunlight flooded down the shaft. She looked up and saw the grille had been removed. There was the face of a young boy at it, the one with the telescope she'd seen when being hoisted aboard.

"Stay clear, you poxy convicts. I'm going to lower a box down with six blankets and some food in it. There's also a flagon of water which you have to share. Make it last as you'll not get more until after we sail. Do you hear me, convicts?"

"Yes, we hear you, little boy," Sophie replied. "We may be convicts but there's no need to treat us like dirt."

"You are dirt, Mister Pimm said so. We carry two other women, both elegant ladies, so you lot just watch your step or I won't lower the box down."

"What's your name?" Emily asked, trying to ease the moment.

"Albert, Albert Brooks, and one day I'll be a ship's officer like Mister Pimm. Now stand clear, the box is coming down. Empty it so I can haul it back up."

"Thank you, Albert," Emily said. "I think we should become friends, don't you? It's a long way to Australia."

"We're not to be friends with convicts, captain's orders. He told us you may try to overrun the ship. Anyway that's the last you'll see of me until we sail. And once underway try not to be seasick as it wrenches the stomach and smells awful."

The box landed between them. After the coarse blankets had been removed there were some cobs of fresh-smelling bread, slices of fatty meat, some thick hunks of cheese and an earthenware corked jug which obviously contained water. The box was quickly unloaded as instructed and Albert pulled it back up before replacing the grille, casting them in semi-gloom again.

"I suggest we ration ourselves equally," Sophie Hart said as if she'd been adopted as their leader just because she was first down the hold. "Once that's done it's up to the individual how fast they eat their portion. Remember, we won't get anything else until after we sail."

"I agree with Sophie," Barbara Henshaw said as she returned from yet another pee. "As for myself, I'm not going to eat anything now as my stomach feels quite queasy."

"But we haven't even moved," Lydie observed.

"Well, I still feel sick. I'm going to lie down after I've had a sip of water."

There had been no mugs in the food box so she uncorked the jug and took a short sip.

"Bah, it tastes salty." She retched and Catherine, who was closest, shied back in case she was actually sick. Her clothes were messy enough as it was.

After Barbara had lain down they each took equal portions of the food and began nibbling. The bread was fresh but they all assumed as the voyage progressed the food would get worse. Catherine knew because Patrick had told her many convicts were forced to eat rats and mice just to stay alive. The thought had disgusted her then, it sickened her now because it may become a reality. She started to chew her meat.

After that and with nothing to do they each took a blanket from the pile and lay on them. Luckily it wasn't cold although Emily did refasten her blouse.

Catherine lay beside Ann Lingos again as she felt truly sorry for the girl. It wasn't her fault who she'd been born to and she hadn't committed any crime, except perhaps stupidity for even expecting to get anything from such a powerful person as the King of England. That was bribery and nobody got away with it. Ann was perhaps lucky she still had her life although after they arrived in Botany Bay she may wish otherwise. In fact they all may feel that way. Life was difficult for a woman as it was and they all sensed life in the remote prison colony had to be a hundred times worse. Catherine sighed deeply, resigning herself to the fact that Australia was at the very least six months in the future. Much could happen in that time.

Ann was lying on her side sobbing. Catherine stroked her shorn hair but there wasn't much else she could do. She looked back at Barbara who was retching again into the slop hole but she couldn't do anything for her either. Then again, why should she? To survive she must look after herself first with Ann Lingos perhaps coming second.

* * * * *

CHAPTER 5

U P ON DECK THERE WAS MUCH SHOUTING, clamouring and general noise. One voice could be plainly heard above all others. It was that of the first mate, Hector Pimm.

"Hoist the mainsail and be sharp about it. Bosun, be ready to fly the forward sheets. Raise the anchor and, helmsman, steer a course into the mid-stream current."

"Aye, aye, sir, mid-stream it is."

There was lots of creaking and the sound of ropes running through pulley blocks as sails were hoisted. In the convict hold they all heard canvas flapping and cracking as the sails caught the wind. They were underway. None of them had any idea of the time or date, not that it mattered, their schedule was being governed for them. They were also unaware that on the dockside a few patrons from The Grapes had gathered to wave and watch the ship leave.

Eunice Wilson was in tears. She had come to like Catherine Farrow, now she might never see her beautiful face again. She raised her arms and shouted for all to hear, "It is the twenty-first day of August in the year seventeen ninety-six and my good friend Catherine Farrow is being transported to Botany Bay in Australia, there to serve a twelve-year sentence for simply defending herself against cruel parents. I shall remember this day forever. Good luck and goodbye, my friend, and may God preserve you!"

Everybody waved as the *Bromley* slowly gained headway. Obviously Catherine did not see them. Nor did she see her mother watching from behind a pile of crates on the jetty waiting to be loaded on another vessel. There was a man with her, stroking her long hair.

"Lie with me tonight, Vera, and we can go places."

"I have a sick husband, you know."

"I have a sick wife. I say bugger them both. Do you agree?"

"Aye, bugger them, Idris. Have you a place where we can live?"

"In Cardiff which is far from here. I've got money, we can take a coach."

Vera took one last look at the *Bromley* as it headed downstream, leaving a small wake behind. There were no tears in her eyes. Her daughter was gone and to hell with Patrick.

"Come on, Idris, let's go. I'll just need to pack a bag."

Eunice Wilson and Hilda were returning to The Grapes when they saw Vera Farrow walking away with a strange man on her arm. They both felt an urge to kill the dreadful woman but knowing the consequences they continued on their way. The slut wasn't worth it.

* * * * *

CHAPTER 6

A T TYBURN HILL MARY CAMPBELL WAS NEXT in line to be hanged. She had already heard the crowd cheer three times as two robbers and a murderer had made the final six-foot journey of their lives.

Many spectators felt sorry for young Mary as she climbed the scaffold steps. Yet she had drowned two of her sister's babies who were not even old enough to know what life was. Her appeal to Judge Harcourt Longman that her sentence be repealed to life in prison had been rejected. When hearing this she fainted but it had no effect on the judge. He didn't consider Mary deserved any form of compassion. Nothing had driven her to kill except the simple request from her sister. She could have refused but didn't, therefore she had to pay the ultimate penalty. Death.

Mary licked a pair of thin, almost bloodless lips as the noose was placed around her slender neck with the thirteen turns of the slip knot running up and across the left ear. She had refused a final prayer so without further ceremony the hangman pulled the lever and watched the young girl drop like a stone through the trapdoor. Those near enough heard a crack and saw the eyes bulge as her head snapped to one side. The body bounced and rotated slowly and was left until they were sure all life had departed. Then it was taken down to be buried in an unmarked grave.

Mary was the last that day and people began to disperse. Ladies of the streets still touted business, knowing many men were aroused by the sight of death. Sooner or later a few would realise their pockets had been picked yet that wouldn't stop them coming for the next hangings. It was free entertainment and to stand there full of life while death came to the victim was a pleasure indeed. This spectacle was only surpassed by watching somebody being flogged because the process took longer and most victims screamed for a short while at least.

* * * * *

CHAPTER 7

UNBEKNOWN TO THE CONVICTS STILL COOPED UP in the hold, which was beginning to smell terribly, the *Bromley* was making steady progress down the Thames Estuary where it would eventually enter the North Sea before heading for the English Channel, then south to the Cape of Good Hope before swinging east to enter the Southern Ocean sailing directly towards Australia. However that was a long time in the future for the convicts who were already gasping and retching from the smell.

Albert Brooks, the cheeky deck lad, had told them that below their feet was the bilge where all bodily discharges went. Eventually it would be pumped out but not for a while yet. They'd all used the slop hole once or twice, Barbara Henshaw six times. Above they could hear the constant movement of feet, both shod and unshod. Emily had deduced that directly over their heads were the crew's quarters and above that the main deck.

They'd all lost track of time and just wished they could be up on deck for a breath of fresh air because very little filtered through the grille. Despite still being handcuffed all except Barbara had slackened their blouses off or rolled them up, allowing some air to get at their sweaty bodies. Barbara's black dress buttoned up at the back so Lydie had undone them for her and slipped the dress off her shoulders, leaving just the shift covering her lean upper body which seemed to lack any sort of figure. These exposures had been a revelation to Catherine, seeing her fellow inmates in various states of undress. She'd even overcome her own modesty and removed her petticoat.

* * *

Captain Stricker was entertaining the six passengers in his aft cabin. They were all drinking port wine and had cheese pieces to nibble on. He had been asked about the treatment of his convict charges.

"I'm duty bound to allow them up on deck at certain times although they will be kept forward, well out of your way. I intend having a white line painted across the deck which they must not cross. If you see any one of them doing so report it to Mister Pimm immediately. The offender will be confined below for two days at least and I can assure you their hold is very hot, cramped and does not smell the sweetest."

"Are they dangerous, Captain?" the gaunt Alice Edwards asked.

"All convicts are dangerous, Mrs Edwards, however, as you may know, all are shackled at the ankles, this measure severely restricts their movements. Normally convicts are not shackled but since we carry you passengers the penal authorities thought it wise, as did the ship's owners."

"I observed they were handcuffed as well," Silas Martin, one of the prospective sheep farmers, said.

"Presently they are but I intend to remove these once we enter open waters. This so they can steady themselves when we encounter rough seas which I can assure you we will."

"Why are there only six convicts, Captain? It seems a very small number. I had heard it is usual to ship hundreds at a time," Tom Stevens, another farmer, commented.

Captain Stricker stroked his clean-shaven chin. "That is usually the case, Tom, unfortunately I'm duty bound not to give a reason why we only carry six so please don't press me." Only he knew it was to ensure Ann Lingos didn't travel alone.

The burly farmer nodded and took another sip of his drink. He would have preferred beer but it hadn't been offered. Next time he intended to ask.

"Do you intend to be soft with the convicts?" Clare Hamlyn asked while allowing the captain to pour herself and Alice Edwards more wine.

"Definitely not," Captain Stricker replied to the rather severe-looking twenty-eight-year-old who by her very tone seemed a stuffy, snobbish sort of person. "If any of the convicts step out of line, Mrs Hamlyn, they will be punished appropriately. On the other hand it is required of me to ensure they get a proper meal each day and are allowed exercise time on deck. I shall also assign them specific duties such as cleaning out the officers' and your cabins plus performing laundry and galley tasks. They will also be required to clean out the sheep pens, hen and rabbit hutches."

"I hope they will keep themselves clean as well, Captain, as I'm well aware what these lower classes are like. Some need to be physically stripped and thrown in a tub before they'll wash their grubby flesh. I know because I've witnessed it being done myself." It was Clare Hamlyn making the observation which confirmed the captain's opinion of her.

"They will be encouraged to wash, Mrs Hamlyn, but you must remember they are not people of your social standards. And let us not forget they are all facing a very harsh life once we arrive at Botany Bay. They may have no inclinations about their own cleanliness. However I or one of my officers will do all we can to ensure they keep themselves reasonably clean."

"Will we be able to wash in fresh water, Captain?" Bob Jones asked.

"That is a very good question, Bob, and I'm glad you brought it up. As you may appreciate, water is a very precious commodity aboard any ship so I'm afraid washing in it must be limited to once a week. The convicts will be required to wash in salt water all the time. So with this in mind I must ask you all here and now to conserve water and treat it almost like this fine wine we are drinking. While we're sailing down the coast of Africa there are a few ports we shall call into and refill our water tanks but once we depart Cape Town there is virtually nothing until we arrive in the western waters of Australia."

The two women looked at each other, realising now the privations they must travel under despite knowing they were getting the voyage at a bargain rate. Also it would be a very pleasant surprise for their husbands when they arrived at Port Jackson. The two men had no idea they were coming.

Just then the ship's cook, Fred Pankhurst, entered the cabin carrying a large silver platter with a roast of beef on it. Behind him came Albert Brooks, the deck lad, with a large steaming tureen containing potatoes and an assortment of vegetables. They were set on the captain's table and plates were laid out.

"Eat, ladies and gentlemen," Captain Stricker said as more wine was poured. "The food may not always be this good. In fact if we hit really rough weather our diets will consist of dry bread and biscuits."

"Will it get very rough, Captain?" Alice Edwards asked with a look of concern on her rather pale face.

"I can almost guarantee it through the Bay of Biscay, Mrs Edwards, it cannot be avoided. With good winds though we'll get through in a day or so. Once we have rounded South Africa we can expect constant swells in the Southern Ocean; however I intend heading slightly north-east into the Indian Ocean where it will be warmer and free of icebergs which tend to drift up from Antarctica where quite a few ships have been lost due to floating ice. Now, how are you all finding your accommodation?"

Clare Hamlyn answered for herself and Alice Edwards. "Adequate, Captain, we cannot say more."

They shared a cabin fitted with upper and lower bunk beds and one small porthole. There was a slop pail which a member of the crew emptied regularly. The four would-be sheep farmers had to tolerate a cabin only slightly larger than the females and two were required to sleep in hammocks which had to be slung every night. They had agreed last night to alternate their sleeping arrangements. However these men were hardy types, used to roughing it, and knew the benefits they would be reaping later upon arrival in western Australia. They had all been told there were vast fortunes to be made from sheep farming and England was a prime market for both meat and wool.

Charles Bower looked around the cabin and realised even the captain didn't have a great deal of space and was surprised when told he slept in a hammock. When he boarded two days ago he'd been shown around the ship by Hector Pimm. At first sight the crews' quarters seemed almost impossibly low and cramped with hammocks having to be shared because there were always sailors on duty. At least their quarters were more airy than the convicts' as they were located on what Pimm had called the orlop deck, which was the lowest and just above the bilges. It was difficult for Charles to imagine six women having to exist under such tight conditions for over half a year despite the time they were up on deck. He'd asked Pimm if the captain would permit any of his crew to socialize with the convicts.

"I don't imagine so, Mister Bower, knowing sexual contact with the lower classes could lead to complications such as disease or pregnancies. There could also be problems with fighting between crew members as there were only six females among at least twenty-five men."

In the short time he'd known Captain Stricker it was his impression the man was fair but strict, one who abided by all the rules and regulations dictated by maritime law. A man who strove to make his company some profits. He knew the shipping line was paid to transport convicts under a government contract.

Now as more wine was being poured the lively Silas Martin asked if they could expect any entertainment during the voyage.

For the first time they all saw a smile crease Captain Stricker's sharply featured, usually stern face. "Well, I wouldn't call it great entertainment, Silas, although we do have a crew member who plays the concertina fairly well and another who can blow a tune on a tin whistle so we may have a few sing-songs. Do you play an instrument?"

"I have tickled the ivories in my local tavern. I can also play the harmonica, which I've brought with me incidentally. I'd be willing to demonstrate when we get properly settled and into warmer climates. A sing-song under tropical stars sounds quite appealing to me."

"I'll bear that in mind, Silas. I'm sure our passengers and the crew would enjoy the diversion. Boredom at sea is commonplace when we're making easy sailing. In a storm it's all hands to work stations as I'm sure you'll see." He looked at the brass clock on the cabin wall. "Now you must excuse me, ladies and gentlemen, as I must check our progress with my first mate and the helmsman. You may remain here and help yourselves to more meat and wine, we do carry plenty. And of course as you have seen, we carry twenty-five sheep which will be slaughtered as required. Plus with the hens we have a daily supply of eggs and from the rabbits a pie now and again."

They watched him go and the two ladies stood up to look out of the rear windows. Many seagulls flew above the *Bromley*'s wake, probably hoping for morsels to be thrown to them by members of the galley. The women also noted the north and south banks of the river were now further apart. It was assumed they were almost in the open sea and for now it excited them. This was the first time either of them had sailed, it also meant as every hour ticked by on the ship's clock they were a mile or so nearer to the husbands they hadn't seen for almost four years. Their occasional letters had indicated both men had found prosperity on the large island. They just hoped they hadn't found other women as well for they had heard gossip that some Australian women were quite wild and free with their bodies. Even transportees had entered into relationships, both with ship's crew members and other convicts. Australia needed a population no matter how it was achieved. And when a child was delivered to a convict the young mite was innocent, for a while at least.

Up on the quarterdeck Captain Stricker was looking through his telescope at the estuary opening. Ahead was another ship obviously making faster headway although that didn't concern him. He knew they carried more sail than the *Bromley* which in heavy weather could be a detriment. After folding his telescope he asked Wilf Malone, his trusted bosun, if there had been any trouble with the convicts.

"No, sir. At the moment they seem settled although one seems to have been sick once or twice. That one who was first aboard seems to be tending her."

"Ah yes, Wilf, that'll be Sophie Hart, she did seem to be a motherly type despite her crime."

"Kidnapping a politician's lad, wasn't it, sir?"

"Exactly so, Wilf, rather stupid if you ask me. It was obvious she'd get caught. However the convicts' crimes are no concern of mine, all I have to do is deliver them in reasonable good health. How are the crew reacting to the fact they're female?"

"I've heard a few say they wouldn't mind giving the girls a little stick, if you know what I mean, but I've warned them to steer clear. Which reminds me, are we going to let them up on deck? They should get some fresh air, as you know it's hot and very cramped down in the orlop."

"Once we're in the channel I intend having their handcuffs removed. We'll do that up on deck. At the same time I'll read them the riot act, as it were, and make it clear what they can and can't do. Oh and while I remember, have a white line painted across the deck just in front of their hatch entry. I'll tell them it's out of bounds beyond it. If any of them cross it they'll be confined below for a few days, that should be enough incentive."

"Are we going to detail them to any duties, Captain?" Hector Pimm asked.

"Definitely. I'm sure even convicts won't object being put to some work." He turned to face the first mate. "I'll leave you to allot tasks, Mister Pimm. I suggest one is detailed to clean my cabin, another yours and perhaps another for the two ladies' cabin. I'm not sure about the farmers, they may try to get amorous."

The trio laughed.

"I don't know who we should warn, sir, the convicts or the men," the thirty-five-year-old bosun said with a smile creasing his ruddy, friendly face.

"Well, for the moment, Wilf, there's no need to warn anybody, the girls stay below. Make sure they get fed though, I don't want to lose any of them. Remember we're only paid for those who arrive in the colony and are able to walk off the ship by themselves even if they have to paddle ashore."

"Aye, aye, Captain, I'll see to it right away."

* * *

Emily Kilpatrick held her stomach. "Are they never going to feed us again? This is worse than Ireland where starvation was a way of life, a potato a day if you were lucky, luckier still if it was cooked."

"We'll get fed, Emily," Sophie Hart replied while easing her position against a rough hull timber for about the tenth time.

Barbara Henshaw sat up and stretched her long scrawny arms. "Well, I hope food comes soon, Sophie, as I've retched my stomach empty."

Catherine, who was folding up Ann's petticoat to use as a pillow, looked round. "I don't think Ann will be wanting much, she's feeling quite ill. I don't suppose it's any use asking for something."

"Not a chance," Emily replied. "In fact I'd be surprised if they carry anything for seasickness except perhaps rum and you can be sure we won't get any of that."

Catherine looked at Ann's ashen face, placed her hand under the blouse and began rubbing the soft stomach gently. Suddenly Ann flinched and said, "Ouch!"

Catherine asked what was the matter.

"One of your fingernails caught the underside of my right breast. It was just the shock, it didn't really hurt."

"I'm sorry, I'll be more careful."

Then as if in answer to their prayers the hatch cover was removed and they all heard the voice of Albert, the deck lad.

"Watch out, I'm lowering the box of food and a pail filled with drinking water. Empty the box as before."

What they didn't know was the meat and cheese were leftovers from the fare Captain Stricker and the passengers had been eating in his cabin. Even if they had known, the food would still have been accepted. They were only into the second day of their voyage heading into years of confinement, realising their right of choice had been lost the moment their sentence was pronounced. Captain Stricker could even have them tossed overboard and nobody would care. Only a handful thought of them in England, the rest either didn't know and those who did were not about to lose any sleep over their fates. England was well rid of them, let Australia do the taming. Even Vera Farrow hadn't spared a thought for her only daughter since she watched her being hauled aboard the boat. Vera was being well entertained by the Welshman as they travelled by coach to Cardiff. Even her second husband Patrick had been forgotten.

Ann Lingos looked at Catherine chewing on a piece of fatty meat and was physically sick down her sweat-stained blouse. From above they all heard Albert laugh.

"Just you lot wait till we hit the Bay of Biscay. The hold will be swilling with your retchings. I know, I've seen it with male convicts who were all tougher than you lot."

Emily Kilpatrick looked up and shouted, "Why don't you piss off, you little piece of snot!"

"I could have you flogged for saying that, woman. In fact I'll report it to the bosun, let him decide what to do. Now keep clear, I'm pulling the box up."

After the hatch grille had been replaced and bolted Emily said, "I'll throttle the little bastard before this voyage is over, believe me I will even if it means taking a few strokes of the cat. It'll be worth it."

"Don't say things like that, Emily," Lydie Denner told her. "I have no wish to watch anybody being flogged. I once saw a man in some stocks outside Cardiff taking fifty strokes from the sheriff and his back was cut to ribbons. Now let me eat in peace." She selected another small slice of the beef.

In fact they all sat in silence chewing slowly, trying to enjoy their meagre meal. Catherine made sure some was left for Ann as she felt really sorry for the eighteen-year-old. If anybody had been treated badly by the so-called law it was her. However there was another reason for her remorse, she had enjoyed rubbing the girl's stomach and when her sickness had passed she intended to rub it again and perhaps probe a little higher to caress the small firm breasts. Even with Patrick in one of his infrequent gentler moments she had enjoyed having her own fondled.

Sheepishly Albert approached the bosun. "One of the convicts, I think Kilpatrick, sir, told me to piss off and called me a little piece of snot."

"She must have had a reason, lad. What did you say to her?"

"I just told them they'd be retching their guts up when we entered the Bay of Biscay."

Wilf scowled and grabbed the lad's ear. "Look, lad, they may be criminals and I'm sure they all feel bad so don't you go making things worse. Understand?"

"I was just hoping, sir, you'd have her strung up to take a few strokes."

"Listen, Brooks, it'll be you at the mast if you're not careful. I'm not saying we should show them the same respect as our passengers, then again there's no need to treat them like cattle. Now start polishing the compass. You know the captain likes to see it gleaming."

"Yes, sir. Sorry, sir."

As he walked to get some polish and a rag Albert began planning his revenge on that loud-mouthed Irish woman.

* * *

As the *Bromley* left the Thames estuary and entered the North Sea they encountered heavy seas causing the ship to pitch and yaw in all directions. Barbara Henshaw screamed while clinging to the mast-support timbers for all she was worth. In fact they had all sought something to clasp as the ship creaked and heeled under the strain. The wind howled as waves broke against the hull timbers with such force that seawater began to seep through the caulking and slop around the hold. Catherine had tried to stand up but was unable to hold her balance and fell over Sophie.

"We'll all be drowned down here!" Lydie Denner screamed, loud enough for all to hear.

"No, we won't," Emily replied. "The water will drain away. It was the same when I came across the Irish Sea which seemed rougher than it is now. I'm no expert but I think the waves are a result of washing off the land. It'll calm down soon, I'm sure."

"Well, I hope so because my stomach's feeling sickly now," Catherine said while rubbing Ann's stomach but with the pitching she was finding it difficult especially with handcuffs on. She saw Sophie Hart crawling to the slop hole and bending over it.

"Bring it up, Sophie, it's better that way!" Emily, who seemed impervious to seasickness, shouted. Still above the wind and crashing waves there were loud sounds of retching.

Things were not much better in the female passengers' cabin. Both women lay on their bunks, holding hands to aching stomachs. The ship's doctor Rodney Mountjoy had been called to attend them.

Before sailing Doctor Mountjoy had lodged his opposition to the *Bromley* carrying passengers in addition to convicts as there were bound to be clashes of cultures. The ship owners, on the other hand, had made it clear that the six convicts filled the hold which otherwise may have had to remain empty. The doctor of course had not been made aware that one of the convicts was being removed from England under a royal decree concerning her birthright. It had also been emphasized that females were in demand in the colony if for no other reason than bearing children which had been the policy since the first fleet sailed. So the decision was left with Doctor Mountjoy, either sail under the conditions outlined or find another ship. This would have caused him to lose face with his family who had a long tradition of providing medical services at sea. Reluctantly he agreed. Now he was trying to be pleasant with the ladies Edwards and Hamlyn.

"I'm sorry, ladies, there isn't much I can do for the most common malady afloat. Seasickness is suffered by almost everybody including ship's captains. Strong or weak people succumb to the motion caused by tides which we cannot control. One thing which may ease your situation is to eat an apple. I have brought one with me and strongly suggest you try and eat at least part of it."

He produced the fruit from his frock coat pocket, cut it in half and handed a piece to each woman. He helped them sit up and cut Alice's half in half again. She bit into it and chewed vigorously. Clare Hamlyn started to nibble like a hamster.

"Will we grow out of this sickness as the voyage progresses?" Alice asked through thin trembling lips.

"Yes, I imagine so, the body quickly becomes attuned to the motion. A ship such as this almost never sails on a perfectly even keel nor will the sea be calm as a mill pond, unless we hit the doldrums which lie much further south. However until somebody invents a better method of travel between land masses we're stuck with ships such as this which I add is of the most modern design. Now apart from your present discomfort, how is everything else?"

The two women looked at each other before Clare answered.

"Generally we are very pleased, Doctor, except this cabin as you can see is a little cramped."

"Everything is cramped aboard ship, ladies. Even I have to share a cabin with the second mate. And if it's any consolation the hold containing the convicts is little larger than this cabin and there are six of them."

Clare Hamlyn tutted. "They are convicted criminals, Doctor Mountjoy, and cannot expect comfort. I imagine though they have more comfort than in Newgate Prison where I'm told convicts are packed like sardines. I just hope they are not granted any favours and in my opinion they should remain in their hold for the entire voyage."

"Captain Stricker is the only person aboard who dictates how the convicts are treated, madam. Now if you will excuse me, I have to attend two of our male passengers. I suggest you make every effort to finish the apples, I can't guarantee results but they certainly won't make your conditions any worse and once we enter the English Channel it should be smoother. Then you can go on deck and get a good breath of fresh air. Good day to you for now."

"He's actually quite nice," Clare said once the door had closed.

"Yes, and he can't be that old," Alice added. "I wonder what prompts a good-looking man like him to isolate himself from society generally. I mean being a doctor he could have the choice of almost any female he desires."

Clare Hamlyn smiled. "Perhaps he prefers his own type, Alice. I believe it is not uncommon and don't forget aboard a ship there are no newspaper men to print a scandal."

"He may even be intimate with the second mate, he said they shared a cabin. And do you know, my stomach is feeling slightly better after this apple."

"So is mine."

* * *

"Hold her steady to the wind, Mister Crawford, don't forget we've got delicate females aboard!" Hector Pimm shouted sarcastically to the helmsman above the howling wind.

Victor Crawford smiled. "To which females do you refer, sir, the ones in irons or the married pair?"

"Actually, Victor, the convicts seem a much hardier lot, all except Ann Lingos, the rather frail-looking one." He frowned and licked his lips. "You know there's something strange, even mysterious about her, Victor. The captain showed me the records of the other five convicts but not hers. And by the looks of her fingernails they've been treated by a manicurist, at least until she was arrested. Still, in her own way she is attractive and carries that air of one who's had at least a little education. Not like Emily Kilpatrick, she's a hardy Irish commoner if I ever saw one. Got the voice of a fishmonger's wife. Worked on her back she did until getting nabbed for theft from her customers. I'll bet her opening is like that of a female elephant." He came closer to the helmsman. "Just between you and me, Victor, I intend to probe a little deeper into Ann Lingos. She's hiding something, I sense it. She may well have been a mistress to somebody fairly high up in society, in which case she'll be well versed in the art of pleasing a man, especially with that well-formed mouth. We'll just have to see. Are there any of the convicts you fancy?"

"Actually there is, sir. Catherine Farrow. Well built, and from her bulges out front she'd be comfy to lie on. Stabbed one of her parents, didn't she?"

"Indeed she did, Victor, tried to slice her stepfather's cock off so the report says."

The helmsman laughed heartily. "I'll bet that hurt."

"Unimaginably, I expect. Anyway if you wish when I assign duties I could put Farrow down to clean your cabin. I'm sure the bosun would turn a blind eye."

"Thank you, sir, I'd like that. I may end up with a slap across the cheek but you never know until making the attempt."

"No, you don't. Just be sure she's not carrying a sharp knife."

They both laughed before Pimm warned Victor not to let the captain hear of this discussion.

"My mouth's sealed tighter than a clam, sir. Seems the weather is clearing ahead, shall I take her further offshore to catch the stronger winds?"

"Aye, do that, Victor. Course two degrees off due south. I'm going to inspect the cargo. That's pretty heavy machinery we carry, in rough weather like this it could easily break free if the tethers aren't inspected regularly."

* * *

"It's getting calmer, I can sense it," Emily said as she stood up to get a drink of water from the pail which had slopped much of its contents.

Sophie Hart and Lydie Denner also stood up while being careful not to crack their heads on the overhead beams. They each took deep breaths and looked up at the slatted hatch opening through which they could see blue sky and wispy clouds. The storm had passed but both knew they would encounter many more before arriving in Australia.

"How do you feel now?" Catherine asked Ann while wiping her hands across the girl's forehead.

"Much better and thank you for showing me such kindness. I didn't expect anybody would bother about me."

"We have to stick together, Ann, beside which I've come to like you. I've never had a gentleman friend, will you be my lady friend?"

Ann smiled. "Of course I will. Now please kiss me."

Flushed with a feeling of utter bliss, Catherine bent forward and lightly kissed the girl's lips. The others watched but didn't comment. They knew this voyage was the lull before the real rigours of their sentences commenced, when they would face long hours of unpaid labour and goodness knows what else.

Through blue-green waters the *Bromley* sailed on. The rigging creaked as a moderate wind filled the sails while up aloft sailors set more canvas.

* * * * *

CHAPTER 8

THE *BROMLEY* WAS NOW IN THE STRAIT of Dover, sailing through calm seas, so Captain Stricker had decided it was time to allow the convicts up on deck to brief them on what lay ahead. Albert Brooks, the deck lad, had just removed the hatch cover and stood aside so First Mate Pimm could shout his instructions down.

"Down there, convicts, heed what I say! You will be hauled up on deck one at a time. When the hook arrives slip it around your handcuffs and prepare to be lifted. When you arrive move forward of the hatch and stand facing aft, that is the back to those unfamiliar to nautical terms. Once on deck stand perfectly still to await Captain Stricker who is going to say a few words. There is to be no talking. The hook is coming down now."

Two seamen lowered it and Emily Kilpatrick stood ready to be the first up. Her face grimaced slightly as the steel handcuffs cut into her wrists yet it was worth it to be heading into fresh air. Like all the others her clothing was stained in sweat and dirty from the floorboards but with no washing facilities there was nothing they could do.

All six passengers and some of the ship's crew watched from their stations as Emily's stretched arms appeared, then her partially shaved head and the remainder of her lean body. This was the first time they had seen any of the convicts. Alice Edwards felt somewhat sorry for the lass when she saw the wide iron clamps around her ankles and the chain separating them.

A seaman pulled Emily over and released the hook once her feet had landed on the deck. She shuffled forward to a point indicated in front of the hatch opening and took some deep breaths while eyeing one or two bare-chested seamen and the bulges in their pants, knowing what lay behind. One by one all the convicts were brought up with Ann Lingos coming last. Hector Pimm gave her a weak smile as she walked into place. They all stood in a line looking about them, seeing first the sheep pen, then the hen and rabbit hutches before looking left to see land. They had no idea what part of England it was except the high cliffs were white as chalk. Catherine closed her eyes to create a memory.

Then they all averted their gaze as Captain Algernon Stricker appeared out of a central hatchway and stood facing them. The convicts made their own assessments of him. Sophie thought his facial features were a little too severe, a man perhaps who smiled rather too infrequently. To Lydie Denner he was smaller than she'd imagined a ship's captain to be although he looked strong. Catherine saw him as a man who was firm but fair, showing no favouritism, what the book said he would comply. For a moment he concentrated his gaze on Ann Lingos, knowing he was the only one aboard who knew the true reason for her being here. In his own opinion she hadn't received fair justice yet his orders were to sail her and the others to Australia and that was exactly what he intended to do. He licked his salty lips before speaking.

"Obviously I cannot welcome you convicts aboard and I know you are not happy being here. However that is because of your own criminal actions which are no concern of mine. I'm paid to run this ship and ensure the safety of our passengers and crew, even surprisingly you convicts. I also know your conditions down in the hold are far from elegant, that again cannot be helped. I will say this though for what it's worth, your conditions are better than on a ship which only carries transportees. In their holds convicts have to sit shoulder to shoulder with barely room to stretch their legs. Due to their closeness disease runs rampant and many convicts die unpleasantly during the voyage. I don't know what your personal hygiene habits were previously but to avoid disease upon this vessel I insist you all wash regularly. A trough of salt water and soap will be provided on deck. As you are all females, at certain times a privacy canvas will be slung across the deck so you may remove such items of clothing for washing as you deem fit. I advise though treat your clothing with respect as no others will be provided. I also require that you wash your hair regularly to prevent head lice which are a very common affliction aboard ship. Limes will be issued once every other day, these will prevent scurvy. This I should point out equally applies to all passengers and crew so everybody arrives at our destinations in good health." He looked back at the convicts. "As a small measure of benevolence your handcuffs will be removed after I have finished speaking with you. This will help your situation both above and below decks in rough weather. In addition to being assigned certain duties you will all be allowed up on deck to stretch your limbs at times to be determined as the weather dictates. You will notice a white line has been painted across the deck in front of the hatch, you must remain behind it at all times unless being escorted to one of your duties. Break this rule and you will be confined in the hold for three days. Now we are fully at sea and as laid down by the penal authorities you will receive at least one hot meal per day provided the weather is suitable. I have been informed some of you have been seasick, unfortunately there is little we can do about it. Most people get used to the ship's motion in a very short time, you are no different in this respect. If you are interested to know, our anticipated time of arrival at the penal colony is late February or early March next year. Australia will be in its summer season so you won't have to suffer through an English winter." He paused for laughter. Unfortunately there wasn't any. None of the convicts cared if they never reached their final destination for they had nothing at all to look forward to except cruelty and hardship.

Undaunted by the convicts' lack of response, Captain Stricker continued, "While it is my intention to treat you all like human beings make no mistake you will be severely punished for any misbehaviour in any form whatsoever. Despite you all being female I shall have no hesitation to have the cat-o'-nine-tails applied should it become necessary. And I advise you now the lash is not a pleasant experience as one or two of my crew members will attest. I think that is all I have to say except to advise you again to heed what I have said. Are there any questions?"

Sophie Hart held both arms up. "Does our time on this ship count as part of our sentence, Captain?"

"Yes, it does. Your terms began the moment we set sail. It is registered in the ship's log. Anybody else?"

"What about our female cycles, Captain?" Emily Kilpatrick asked.

"I will ensure rags are provided, that is until we run out. All I can say is wash what you use frequently. However I shall ensure more are obtained at our ports of call. I now hand you over to Mister Pimm who will detail your duties. Following that your handcuffs will be removed but not the ankle restraints, I'm afraid. This order was decreed by our government not myself." He turned and gestured the first mate to take over as he returned to his cabin.

Hector Pimm stepped forward and removed a sheet of paper from an inner pocket.

"Before detailing your duties let me just say I concur with everything Captain Stricker has said. Act in a normal manner and all will be well. Break any shipboard rules and watch out for me or our bosun." He then glanced at his notes. "Here are your assigned duties. Lydie Denner will clean Captain Stricker's cabin at a time convenient to him. Ann Lingos is assigned my cabin. Catherine Farrow the helmsman's and bosun's. Emily Kilpatrick Doctor Rodney Mountjoy and the second mate's. Barbara Henshaw shall look after the female passenger quarters and finally Sophie Hart will be responsible for the male passenger cabin. All these duties I add will be at the convenience of the cabin occupants. You will be called when you are required so be ready to comply. I also warn all of you now not to steal anything. Captain Stricker has decreed the penalty for a proven theft shall be eleven lashes so heed my warning. Naturally you are all required to keep your own hold clean and tidy and remember regular inspections will be held. You may also be co-opted to assist our chef Mister Pankhurst in the galley plus there will be the sheep pens and hutches to keep clean. Finally just let me say you are all fortunate to be sailing under Captain Stricker for he is a fair master with an honourable record. The bosun will now remove your handcuffs. With this done you will be able to use the shaft ladder to access or leave your hold. Grip the rungs tightly as you go up or down, your leg chain should not be a hindrance. After your handcuffs have been removed, by the grace of Captain Stricker you are all permitted to remain on deck for two hours but remember not to proceed beyond the white line."

All six convicts eagerly held their wrists out for the removal of the manacles. At least now they wouldn't have to suffer chafed wrists. As each convict was released they walked towards the ship's starboard rail to gaze for perhaps the last time at their home country.

"Would the captain actually order a female to be flogged?" Alice Edwards asked Clare Hamlyn, her cabin partner.

"I imagine he means what he says, Alice, we shall just have to wait and see. Is it your desire to witness such an event?"

"I once saw a young maiden being caned in public for stealing a hen. It was sickening and yet it did arouse both my husband and myself and later we made wonderful love."

"Yes, I know. Such events have that effect on people. I'm told in certain private London clubs they employ and pay women to accept punishments. Our so-called upper classes are not quite so puritanical as people imagine. Anyway I think I'm going for a lie-down, my stomach is still a little queasy."

"I'll join you. Mine is the same."

"So what do you think of our captain?" Emily asked Sophie Hart who stood beside her at the rail.

"Alright, I suppose, yet I think he's a man to be wary of. He means what he says and will not be tolerant. His main concern is delivering live bodies, not dead ones."

"What about our assigned duties?" Lydie Denner broke in. "You heard I was detailed the captain's cabin and I imagine he'll be fussy over everything. Why he even keeps his fingernails filed and polished and his body reeks of scent. I could smell it from where I stood."

"We all could, Lydie. It's alright with me so long as we get fed and are allowed up on deck at least once a day. I don't think we can ask for more."

Emily stuck a hand up her blouse and scratched. "I think I've already got some form of lice on me, I itch like crazy."

"We all will in time, Emily," Catherine told her. "Some days my stepfather came home from the docks riddled with fleas if he'd been working in a ship's hold. He would stand naked in a tin bath while my mother washed him down with cold water. When she'd finished the water was alive with the horrible little things. It made me itch just looking at them. Once he'd dried himself he took me upstairs, made me remove my pantaloons before laying me on the bed and poking his thing into me. It hurt but he wasn't concerned, to him I was just a toy, a live toy. Sometimes he even called me his little lamb."

"All men are the same, Catherine," Barbara Henshaw told her. "Bastards every one of them. They treat women like pieces of meat before going out drinking and treat them worse when they get back. You should see how bruised and battered my mother was some mornings. That was why I left home and joined this gang of highway robbers. I simply wanted a more adventurous life with plenty of money. It was good for a couple of years, strong men whenever I wanted them and we lived very well off the proceeds of our robberies. I had expensive rings on all my fingers and jewels in my hair. I felt like a queen. Then we were nabbed."

"How did you get caught?" Ann Lingos asked while licking her salty lips.

"Our leader said it was a set-up. We waylaid a coach which turned out to be full of constables and a sheriff. We stood no chance. The three men were knocked senseless and handcuffed to a coach wheel before each constable took a turn with me. Six bloody big brutes and they weren't gentle. At my so-called hearing I told the magistrate what they'd done but all he said was, can I prove it. Of course I couldn't although it must have had some effect because I got twelve years while all the men were sentenced to be hanged. They probably have been by now."

"So are you glad to have survived?" Emily asked.

"For the moment, yes." She shrugged her shoulders. "On the other hand who knows what will happen when we arrive? We may all find we'd have been better off dead."

"Please don't talk of death, Barbara," Ann Lingos appealed. "The very thought sends shivers up my spine. I watched my mother die and it wasn't pretty. Towards the end she was in great pain. Just before her last gasp she told me to beware of diseases men carried in their sex organ."

"It's syphilis," the down-to-earth Emily Kilpatrick told them. "Most men who go with loose women get it."

"Good God, Emily, have you got it?" an alarmed Sophie Hart asked.

"No bloody way, Sophie. I was careful. I smoked heavily in those days and the tar left on my fingers burnt the man when I grasped his cock. That told me he had the disease so I chucked him out unless he just wanted to feel me. That was alright."

"Tell me, Emily, did you ever suck a man?" Lydie asked.

"Oh yes, if I knew he was clean."

"And did you ever permit a man to give you tongue down there?" It was Lydie again.

"Yes, if he could afford to. I charged triple for that and always demanded the money in advance." She paused and then whispered, "That little snot of a deck lad is staring at us. I've a good mind to report him to Captain Stricker. The lad needs a good thrashing."

"I don't think complaining would be wise, Emily," Sophie Hart advised. "Remember what we are. I'd imagine the captain would stand by any of his crew in preference to us. Anyway the lad is going below now. They must have stairs to their deck level which I think is above ours."

"It must be almost time for us all to go below again," Lydie said. "But until we're told I'm going to wash my hands and face before gulping some sea air. They say it's good for you and healthy."

She headed for the small lead-lined trough of water as Barbara laughed before saying, "Why bother about our health when we'll all get the pox once we step off this ship. Anyway for now I intend to enjoy our view of the coastline so I can recall it when in the penal colony."

They all saw the evil-looking Second Mate Felix Bloom approaching and knew they were going to be ordered below. However they all felt refreshed and in the calmer sea their stomachs felt easier, for the time being at least.

As predicted Felix Bloom told them all to get below. He did warn them to be careful going down the ladder with their ankle chains dragging.

"We'd not object to you removing them," Emily told him and for it received a menacing glare and a warning not to speak to him like that again otherwise she'd be up before Captain Stricker and he didn't take kindly to lippy convicts.

His look scared Ann Lingos, especially with that long scar running down his left cheek. She knew as females they were all vulnerable and being the youngest she feared they may single her out for treatment which wasn't quite legal. When she was fourteen and developing breasts she had been warned by her mother to be wary of all men as many were after only two things. Feeling her breasts was one, putting themselves inside her was the other. Then she hadn't considered it possible, now as a convict it was entirely probable and to resist would be futile. Felix Bloom looked like he could crack a man's skull with one blow. She must be very careful.

Sophie was first down the ladder followed by Catherine. The rungs were rough and dug into the soles of her feet which were still slightly tender from having to walk everywhere barefooted. The weight of her dangling chain didn't help either. However she made the deck without incident. She saw Ann Lingos ready to come down so stood at the ladder's base in case the girl slipped. In doing so she got an unusual view of this girl she was becoming enchanted with. All she could see were Ann's legs yet that desire swept her to kiss those soft lips again and that thought clouded everything else from her mind. It was a sensation she had rarely experienced before. Apart from her mother's the only other lips she'd tasted were her father's and Patrick's and they were both unpleasant plus their breath usually reeked of onions which both used to eat raw. Now in the harshness of her situation she was experiencing tenderness and feeling in the form of a girl she had only known for a few days.

Ann smiled while stepping away from the ladder to let Lydie come down. Catherine took her delicate hand and together they walked the very short distance to their regular place beside one of the hull-bracing timbers behind the mast. It was an area which didn't actually offer much privacy from their fellow convicts although it did prevent someone seeing them from the entrance hatch. As they lay down on the unyielding boards Ann smiled.

"You know, Catherine, my face really tingles."

"So does mine, it must be the sea air. And to think people live by the sea all the time. It must be nice."

"They perhaps paddle in the sea while we are cooped up in this small hold, sweating and worrying about our futures."

"Unfortunately we have no control of the future, Ann. A woman told me that in a tavern my stepfather took me to. How does your stomach feel now?"

"Much better but I'd still like you to rub it. Would you?"

"Of course. Lie down flat."

After she had done so Catherine worked the slack blouse up to expose her belly and the undercurve of both breasts. She stroked the smooth flesh gently and saw Ann's lips begin to tremble slightly.

"Go a little higher please, Catherine, lay a hand on one of my breasts. I used to enjoy doing it myself but your hand will feel nicer, I'm sure."

Catherine needed no encouragement and without handcuffs it was so much easier. Her heart started to beat rapidly when sensing a nipple hardening against her sweaty palm. Ann is so gentle, so unlike that animal Patrick O'Grady, Catherine thought as her temples pulsed. She continued to rotate her hand for many beautiful moments before going up to kiss Ann's moist lips. And this time mouths opened and hard tongues began to invisibly explore their hot inner depths. Catherine sensed Emily and Barbara were looking but she didn't care. Down in this gloomy hold they still had partial freedom when in six months there would be nothing except hard work and cruel taskmasters. They could even be separated, never to see each other again when male guards, which she imagined would be animals like Patrick O'Grady, claimed them as unwilling mistresses.

As they continued to kiss, Ann took Catherine's hand and once again laid it on her stomach. "Kiss me again, Catherine."

As they gently kissed, Catherine moved her hand down until it met the resistance of Ann's skirt band. Ann responded by contracting her stomach slightly, allowing Catherine's fingers to pass so they encountered the soft matt of hairs.

"Oh, Catherine, that is so very wonderful. My entire body is throbbing, oh yes …" Then she simply gasped as her legs stiffened.

Suddenly they had both been transported into a different world. A magical one, not that of a sailing ship bound for hell. They lay there oblivious to all as the *Bromley* rocked slightly with the sea motion and their internal passions ascended to heights neither had ever attained before. They sweated, they trembled, their young bodies quivered in perfect harmony embroiled within the unity of themselves. And still oblivious to their fellow convicts they lay staring into each other's eyes, knowing amid all their discomforts and worries about what the future may hold they were rapidly falling in love.

When they finally parted the others simply smiled. Sophie Hart knew what had transpired because a similar event had taken place in her own life before the girl was forcefully removed from her. Barbara Henshaw wasn't quite sure what had happened because all her experiences had been with men. The man was supposed to do what Catherine and Ann had done to each other. And yet she had seen in both their faces looks of total contentment and the sounds they emitted were genuine expressions of extreme pleasure.

Suddenly their idyll came to an abrupt end when Ann's name and Emily's were called to report on deck immediately. Quickly Ann rearranged her blouse and skirt and followed Emily up the ladder. At the top they were met by the second mate.

"Lingos, you're to give the first mate's cabin a thorough dusting. The same for you, Kilpatrick, in my cabin and be careful not to touch any of the doctor's instruments. He'll know if anything has been moved. Follow me."

They both followed the odious man across the deck to enter a narrow passageway into the cabin areas. At the appropriate doors a seaman gave them a piece of rag to use as a duster. They were to give him a shout when finished. He warned them not to return to their hold alone, those were Captain Stricker's orders.

Once inside the first mate's cabin Ann was surprised to see Mister Pimm standing at a slightly inclined board on which were charts, a pair of dividers, some rulers, a magnifying glass plus a number of well-sharpened pencils standing in a pewter tankard. His head almost touched the overhead beams and to Ann he looked formidable.

"You look scared, lass. Are you?"

"Not actually scared, sir, apprehensive may better describe my feelings."

"Those could almost be the words of an educated lady, Lingos, not a condemned convict. Were you perhaps once a lady before turning to crime?"

She realised he was probing her and wondered if he knew the true story of who she was. Whatever his motives she answered his question.

"No, sir, I was never a lady but my mother did give me lessons in the correct use of words. She herself was self-taught and hoped I could do better for myself. Unfortunately things didn't work out too well."

"What was your crime?"

"I tried to bribe a very influential gentleman, sir. He had me charged and I was sentenced to spend the rest of my natural life in Botany Bay."

"Who was this influential gentleman?"

"I was warned not to say, sir. If I did, I was to be executed immediately along with the person I told. I believe the captain carries such orders."

He frowned. "Yes, I see. In any case it's obvious to me, Lingos, you're somewhat different to the other convicts and I must admit to finding you quite attractive with a pleasing personality. Have you had many relationships with men?"

"Just one, sir, though only for a week or so. My mother fell very ill so I had to look after her. We couldn't afford either a nurse or a doctor."

"I see. Has your maidenhead been broken?"

"I don't know what that word means, sir."

"Did the man you went with ever attempt to interfere with your more private areas? I think you know what I mean."

"No, of course not, sir." She assumed a shocked expression as thoughts of Catherine's finger came to mind.

"Then you are intact, Lingos. Would you enjoy a relationship with a man?"

"I'm honestly not sure, sir."

He ran a stubby finger down her right cheek causing her to shy away. "Don't be scared, lass, I mean you no harm. However if you could find yourself attracted to me, I may be able to arrange small favours. Do you understand my meaning?"

"Not really, sir."

"Oh, I think you do, Lingos. It's my feeling you're not so naïve as you appear." He withdrew a pocket watch, opened it and looked. "Unfortunately I must leave now for a meeting with Captain Stricker and the second mate, however I have enjoyed our short conversation. Think about what I have said and we'll continue it at another time over a goblet of port. Would you like that?"

"Yes, sir."

"Good. Now get on with your dusting and be careful not to disturb anything on my chart table. Remember to clean the window as well. You'll find a jug of water behind that curtain. When I return I shall carry out an inspection and for your own sake I hope to find everything shipshape, as we say."

With that he snapped his watch closed and left.

She looked around and decided to start dusting the bookshelves, taking care not to disturb the books themselves although they too bore evidence of dust. As she worked Pimm's conversation began to give her concern. Many of his references had been of a sexual nature which raised the possibility that he intended trying to ravish her, knowing sailors generally were deprived of female company while at sea. Silently she questioned herself why Pimm would pick on her? She didn't consider herself as a worldly type like Emily or Sophie and her breasts were small compared to theirs. Perhaps it was because of her young age? What compounded her thoughts was this new relationship between herself and Catherine. Never in her entire life had she been aroused by another female but her tender kisses had caused her head to spin and those final internal sensations almost caused her heart to stop beating. She just hoped there was more to come. With these thoughts it occurred to her that transportation had given herself and Catherine something which may be precious to them both, that was time. Time to love, time to enjoy the bliss of each other despite the privations, the cramped space, the smells coming up from the bilge, the body sores and the meagre rations, until they finally arrived at their destination. Then what? The answer to that lies in the future, she thought as she continued dusting. The work was not hard, she'd had to do worse at home.

In Doctor Mountjoy's and the second mate's cabin Emily Kilpatrick had a larger area to clean and the place was thick with dust as if it hadn't been touched since they sailed. This condition seemed strange to Emily as she always thought a doctor wanted everything spotless. Even some of his crude instruments looked like they hadn't been washed since they were last used. In fact two iron knives still appeared to have blood on them. She wondered who he had treated? Certainly it wasn't any of the convicts. Perhaps one of the passengers, or of course it could have been a crew member? Perhaps they were like that even before they sailed?

After wetting her cloth she started to clean the window and saw another vessel sailing in the opposite direction. She assumed its destination was London. The crew would be looking forward to many nights ashore where they could visit the taverns and frolic with ladies who enjoyed being entertained. Ladies who were free and at liberty to do whatever they pleased.

"God, what a bloody fool I was," she muttered to herself while looking down at her shackled ankles. "I could have been drinking rum myself now, sitting on the knee of a man who was going to give me a good time. Alas, my keeper was greedy. What the clients paid wasn't enough, he had to rob them. I also know the man was keeping more money for himself despite the fact it was my body being used. He lived in an elegant apartment while I had a squatty room rampant with cockroaches and other vermin. Now aboard this ship I've got filth again except there are no men lining up at the door, in fact I wish there were. I can't imagine six months or more of this. You could always chuck yourself overboard, Emily Kilpatrick, only remember in death there is nothing, it is final. At least I have some kind of life and perhaps Lydie or Barbara would like to share their bodies with me. It seems Ann and Catherine have hit it off and I wish them happiness while it lasts for all good things must come to an end."

She started polishing the window rapidly after hearing the cabin door opening.

"Who were you talking to, Kilpatrick?" Doctor Mountjoy asked.

"Myself, Doctor, I do it frequently. It's not wrong is it?"

"No, I suppose not. Are you nearly finished? I have some notes to write up."

"Just this window, sir. It was really grimy."

"I know. The entire ship is grimy. I feel sorry for our two female passengers. For a cheap voyage they have inherited filth."

"And what about us convicts, sir, if you don't mind me saying?"

"You've got what you deserve. You'll find out once we arrive at Botany Bay."

"Is it so terrible, sir?"

"Worse than you can ever imagine. You may think conditions are bad aboard this ship, well, it's a quality inn compared to Botany Bay. Everybody lives in utter squalor and are made to work fourteen hours a day on one meal. You may be detailed to work as a servant and be lucky to get a compassionate person, or it could be one who treats you badly, it's just the luck of the draw. Some female convicts are made to work in the fields, raising crops for the community. I'll advise you now never try to do anything stupid like running away because you'll be caught and brought back. Then it's the whipping frame followed by solitary confinement for months and the guards are the worst type of humanity you could imagine. Now enough of that. How many years did you get?"

"Twelve."

"You'll be lucky to survive ..." He paused and coughed. "I'm sorry I said that, my dear, I apologize. Would you like a pear?"

"Is there a price to pay?"

He smiled. "No, of course not. Not all men have sex on their minds when with a woman. I'm not a womanizer, quite the reverse actually. Now have a pear before returning to the hold."

"Very well then."

He removed one from a drawer. She took it and bit out a large chunk as if somebody would steal it. Juice ran down both sides of her mouth so she licked it off. It was soon finished, core and all. The stalk was handed to the doctor as she asked him if he'd like her to wash his instruments.

"If you wouldn't mind, my dear. Be careful with the knives, they're very sharp, you know."

While carefully washing each item she sensed they all had a friend in Doctor Mountjoy.

Then with her work finished the second mate was called. He also collected Ann Lingos and they were escorted back to the hold and climbed down the ladder. Albert, the deck lad, had replaced the grille before Ann's feet touched the deck.

"They're scared we'll escape," Barbara Henshaw said tongue in cheek.

Then of course Ann and Emily were questioned about their first duties. They related everything except Emily didn't mention the pear. She did say however it was her impression Doctor Mountjoy preferred men to women.

"It's not uncommon among seamen," Sophie Hart replied without hesitation.

Ann looked to Catherine for an explanation. "Like us, Ann, he enjoys the company of a person of his own sex."

Ann smiled and they kissed.

* * *

Everybody was dozing when they heard Albert shouting down the hatch that he was going to lower their food. He also added sarcastically it was the last they'll get until tomorrow.

Emily wanted to reply but restrained herself. Even though Albert was the lowest-ranking person on the ship he had more standing than them.

Their food was a mushy stew mixture in a large iron pot. With it came a round loaf of bread, six wooden bowls and spoons. As usual it was water to drink.

Sophie ladled the mixture out equally while Emily broke the bread. Then they all adopted cross-legged positions and began to eat. At least it was hot and quite spicy.

"I wonder if the senior crew and passengers get the same?" Barbara Henshaw questioned anybody.

"I expect so," Lydie replied, "they'll also get wine to wash it down."

"God, what I'd do for a goblet of wine now," Sophie said. "I used to drink lots during the day. They said it was better for you than water ..."

She was interrupted by a shrill scream from Lydie. "A rat just ran under my skirt! Let's try and catch it, I'll not sleep till we do."

"We should shout for help," Sophie advised. "One rat means there's more and I know rat bites can be nasty." She looked up and shouted, "We need help down here, there's at least one rat!"

Moments later the bosun's face appeared at the hatch. "I'll send the ship's rat catcher down. Stand by."

They all waited to see who would come. The rat catcher turned out to be a tabby cat which was dropped down the shaft but as with all cats it landed squarely on all fours and at once scampered off in search of its prey. It was difficult for them to see under the beams towards the front but they did hear a pounce and a squeak. They assumed the rat was being devoured. The cat must have been as hungry as themselves.

Ann shuddered. "I just hope we don't get many more of the horrible creatures, they scare me to death. How do they get aboard?"

The seeming know-all Sophie Hart answered. "They swim out from the docks and climb up the mooring ropes. Eventually our four-legged friend will catch them all. We just have to hope they haven't bred aboard or we may be overrun with the horrors. At least everybody on the ship will have to suffer them. Rats don't know the difference between law-abiding citizens and convicts. Anyway let's finish our food; like Albert said, we'll get nothing else today."

They all continued eating and most put some of the bread aside for later. After that and with nothing at all to do they lay down to try and sleep although with the rat still on their minds it wouldn't come easily. Catherine didn't even feel like making love again although she did snuggle up close to Ann, knowing in themselves they had found an uneasy solace.

They listened to the continuous creaking of the ship's timbers and the flapping of sails. They were reassuring sounds as the *Bromley* made good headway down the English Channel, heading towards rougher seas and everybody aboard knew the Bay of Biscay was still to come. Even a seasoned seaman like Captain Stricker was not looking forward to crossing some of the most turbulent waters in the world. If the weather was severe he had given orders that all passengers and convicts would be confined to the relative safety of their quarters, knowing it was not uncommon for somebody to be swept overboard. A crewman was an acceptable loss, a passenger wasn't, not even if they were convicts.

They all noticed it at once, the oil lamp flickered and went out. Sophie took it upon herself again to shout up and inform anybody who was within earshot. Shortly a thin rope came down and the lamp was tied to it. Within half an hour it was returned burning brightly. Emily hung it on its hook and they all resumed reclined positions, trying to get comfortable on the hard, unyielding boards. Some lay on their blanket, others used it to cover themselves. Above them was the almost constant tramping of feet as sailors went about their duties. They also heard raucous laughter.

"It'll be a joke about us," Barbara said. "I'll bet every man up there has imagined getting stuck into us."

"Any one of them are welcome to visit me," Emily replied.

"Amen to that," Lydie added in her twangy accent which she had explained was Welsh. Her father was a coal miner and her mother took washing in to earn a few extra coppers.

Ann snuggled up to Catherine and whispered, "You prefer me to men, don't you?"

"Yes, my dear, I do. Let us kiss."

In the gloom their lips met softly so they became oblivious to all other sounds.

* * * * *

CHAPTER 9

T HE *BROMLEY* WAS ABOUT TO PASS ABOUT thirty miles west of the island of Ushant which to mariners represented the northerly tip of the Bay of Biscay. Passengers and convicts alike had been warned once again the crossing could be rough and windy because of tidal swirls from the bay itself. Yet once across they had been promised smoother sailing and warmer weather as they progressed down the west coast of Portugal before the massive continent of Africa loomed. Captain Stricker had suggested the convicts should take advantage of the sights to build memories because once they were in the penal colony recollections could be an important factor of their lives. Only Catherine and Ann Lingos were impressed.

Life generally aboard had become routine with the passengers idling their time either gazing at the coastline, playing cards or being entertained by crew members who thought they could dance jigs to music supplied by a concertina and Silas Martin's harmonica. Of course eating had become a way to pass a couple of hours. And once further south they had been told meals could be taken on the open deck. For the convicts it had been days of performing their assigned duties, doing their own and others' laundry, cleaning out the animal pens and idling the times between as best they could. Emily and Lydie had also been detailed to help the chef Fred Pankhurst in the galley. Their work consisted mainly of scouring pots and pans in addition to peeling potatoes and washing other vegetables. As a reward Fred let them help themselves to biscuits provided they ate them before returning to their quarters. Yet while at work time passed much quicker than idly sitting about in the hold. All their bottoms were sore from contact with the hard unrelenting timbers. Their blankets managed to stave off chills at night but even folded they made poor cushions.

Ann Lingos had been flattered by First Mate Pimm each time she was detailed to clean his cabin which usually consisted of dusting, making up his bunk and cleaning the window. Once a week she'd had to get down on her hands and knees to scrub the floor and apply polish. To her this was the hardest work of all especially if Pimm stood watching and peering down her slack blouse. Catherine had tried to tighten it yet it always seemed to sag slightly. If Pimm wasn't in the cabin she always studied his maps which detailed the ship's daily progress although she was ignorant of the coastline. Once he'd given her a small goblet of wine after she'd finished her duties, hoping perhaps she might succumb to his subliminal hints. She hadn't of course because her affection for Catherine was growing daily. It was always a relief when she was dismissed and escorted back to the hold so she and Catherine could simply talk of happier times, cuddle and kiss. Of course they had to be careful not to be seen by a crew member but as darkness fell in the hold they could exchange affections fairly easily. In these they managed to attain almost unimaginable heights of pleasure by very simple touches to those bodily areas they had found most responsive. Ann called these moments voyages of mutual discovery.

It wasn't always physical between them though, sometimes they made imaginary plans as if they were free citizens. Like the type of house they would live in and would it be in the city or the country. They would have horses and dogs, things which had been denied in their normal lives. However knowing their times together were limited they both had a desire to get the most out of their somewhat unique relationship by physical contact which stimulated them both.

After they parted to take a breath Ann usually had something coy to say. "We may be heading for hell, Catherine, until then let us linger in our own private heaven until dropping anchor in Botany Bay."

This budding relationship however was making things difficult for Catherine during her cleaning duties. If the bosun Wilf Malone wasn't in the cabin the helmsman Victor Crawford would try to bribe her with food and drink if she'd allow him to kiss and fondle her. She refused, assuming it would not stop there. And if she did succumb to these advances she was concerned Captain Stricker may find out and have her punished. Victor had promised on his word the captain would never hear of what transpired within the privacy of his cabin. Unfortunately Catherine wasn't totally convinced, knowing men frequently boasted about their achievements with members of the opposite sex. She'd heard men in The Grapes bragging to their drinking friends what this or that girl had done to them out in the backyard. Others complimented a girl on her looks so she may lift her skirt for a few minutes and surprisingly these ploys sometimes worked. Of course in those dark days Catherine was always safe from any advances because she was with Patrick O'Grady and nobody dare challenge him.

Now it was a senior crew member making a proposition to her. So far she had refused every offer although the situation was becoming more tense with each cabin visit. She and Ann had talked it over and mutually agreed it would be alright to let Victor kiss her on the promise it wouldn't go any further. Now of course with the Bay of Biscay looming they might not be required to perform any cabin cleaning duties for a few days, this according to Captain Stricker.

As for the captain himself Lydie Denner had found him to be a meticulous person in every respect as she dusted and scrubbed his cabin along with polishing the brassware. It was a demanding duty and she had to be very careful to replace everything exactly as it was or receive a rebuke. There was a Bible and a prayer book on the shelves along with all manner of technical books on sailing including knot tying. He had shown her just how many knots were used aboard a ship and how many yards of rope were used to support the sails and to secure cargo both on deck and in the hold. One thing she had discovered, the *Bromley* carried no navigator, Captain Stricker performed that duty himself. Usually when she arrived in the cabin and the captain was still there he would ask if she would like to say a prayer with him, reasoning it may cleanse her soul.

"No thank you, Captain, unfortunately I'm beyond cleansing," she would reply. "I battered an old woman and am paying dearly for it. I do not believe in redemption because the judge who sentenced me said there was no such thing and I believed him. I'm sorry but that is how I feel. My life had been good when I was a child until my father began seeing me as more than a daughter so I ran away from home. From there my life became a misery, one which I brought on myself so please just let me get on with my work."

"Oh, very well."

She sensed he felt sorry for her.

Barbara Henshaw was finding it difficult working for the two female passengers because both were very fussy and treated her with utter disdain. She was also sure they went out of their way to make things untidy so she had more work to do. They had also accused her of using their brushes and combs when they weren't present. She denied it of course and said if they had positive proof it should be reported to Captain Stricker. Knowing she had called their bluff they simply warned her to be very careful. Of the two, Clare Hamlyn was by far the snobbiest, even loathsome as if she carried a hatred for everybody below her own station in life.

Barbara had met snobs like Clare before, almost every town and village she visited had them. Usually the local squire and his wife were persons to be cautious of because they truly believed such people as themselves were above the law and could treat anybody in whatever manner they pleased. Almost every squire she knew commanded and demanded attention wherever he went and thought it was their God-given right to take any lass who took their fancy. Unfortunately most lasses were too scared to refuse as their parents usually worked for the man. Whenever possible Barbara and her gang tried to rob these overly rich landlords for even if they didn't carry money they and their wives were frequently bedecked with jewellery.

Barbara, being a realist, accepted her lot with the two women and their obvious pettiness which caused her to wonder just what type of husbands they were going out to meet. From what Lydie Denner had told her about Australia it didn't seem the sort of country two pampered English women should be going to. Australia's climate was hot and dusty with very little civilization. Barbara knew if Alice and Clare were expecting the London social scene they were in for a very rude awakening.

Unlike Barbara, Sophie Hart was getting along famously with the four male passengers and they had even offered employment when her time was served. It almost broke her heart when she had to tell them her sentence was for life which meant just that. It would therefore be in their best interests to simply forget about her when they reached their destination.

As a measure of kindness after her duties were complete she was given a goblet of rum and a thin cigar. This on the firm understanding she didn't mention it to any of her colleagues or members of the crew otherwise trouble might erupt as Captain Stricker had made it clear the convicts were not to be shown any favours. Even he was stretching the limits of his mandate by allowing them to remain up on deck far longer than the authorities had laid down. Despite this it still meant they had to spend at least fourteen hours out of twenty-four in the stuffy hold with virtually nothing to do except talk, eat their meagre daily rations and try to sleep.

The long hours did give Ann and Catherine time to continue developing their relationship by exchanging life experiences which in Ann's case were pleasant up to the moment of her mother's death. Then the cloud of doom descended very rapidly. Catherine's life had of course been much sadder from the age of eight on. Simply one of almost constant toil with the added physical abuse if everything wasn't perfect when her parents returned from the tavern. Finally it became too much when her mother remarried Patrick O'Grady which ultimately led to assaulting them both. At times she did wonder if her stepfather had recovered but she held no remorse.

Naturally these somewhat sad verbal sessions terminated in them making love although they rarely lasted longer than fifteen minutes as their manacles impeded much movement and they had to be careful not to injure each other. However seeing these amorous activities and hearing the outpourings of emotion Emily and Sophie Hart had started petting each other.

Captain Stricker had suspected such exchanges would arise when Clifford Prosser, the *Bromley*'s owner, told him he had reached a lucrative financial agreement with a fairly senior government official to convey six female convicts to the colony in Botany Bay. It was at this meeting when the captain was given the short history of Ann Lingos. He also had to swear on the Bible never to relate Ann's story or who her father was. When he asked why there were only five other convicts he was told they were fill-ins on the sound reasoning that transporting Ann Lingos by herself would have raised many eyebrows within the shipping community, especially if the newspapers got hold of it. So he accepted the six females, anticipating relationships would develop. He knew such associations were fairly common in prisons so it logically followed the hold of a ship would be no different. He was also worldly enough to know women making love with their own kind were not likely to cause trouble. On the other hand captains of ships transporting perhaps two to three hundred desperate men and a handful of women knew trouble would erupt sooner or later, it was human nature. Additionally the convicts had little to lose and a large percentage were at the stage where they didn't care if they lived or died.

Of course Captain Stricker could be strict himself if any serious incident occurred because once at sea he was the unquestioned master. It was accepted that rank and file crew members did not have impeccable qualifications and they themselves were quite capable of causing trouble especially if the food started to go rotten. Yet by and large the *Bromley* had a happy crew and so far at least the meat hadn't developed maggots and the hens were still laying. Still much could change as the voyage progressed.

* * * * *

CHAPTER 10

APTAIN STRICKER HAD BEEN CORRECT, THEY HAD sailed less than forty miles south into the Bay of Biscay when strong winds and very heavy seas were encountered. Passengers were ordered to their cabins and convicts to the hold. Two strong seamen were detailed to man the helm and many sails were taken down and securely tied.

In their hold the convicts clung to anything they could find as the ship pitched and yawed in all directions. They could hear the seas crashing against the bulwarks and frequently gigantic waves broke over the deck, much of which poured through the hatch grille, drenching those directly below. And even above the howling wind the convicts' screams could be heard as they slithered across the wet boards until part of the structure or one of their own stopped them abruptly.

Barbara Henshaw suffered a cut lip. Emily Kilpatrick bruised her right shoulder and Lydie Denner was sure two of her toes were broken. Catherine and Ann clung to each other for dear life and together they slid into Sophie Hart who grasped the mast base with both hands.

Above they could hear Captain Stricker and First Mate Pimm barking instructions to watch this, secure that, reef in another sail. The sheep and hens too were getting drenched each time a wave broke over the bow, spewing a fine cold spray in all directions. Nevertheless the *Bromley* gallantly sailed up mountainous waves only to crash sharply into the trough beyond. This made their footing very difficult as the deck angles changed constantly. Seamen manning the sails had tied ropes around their waists and secured them to spars to prevent them being washed overboard. Yet conditions like this were simply another hazard for men at sea, nobody was immune. The sea was master.

Alice Edwards hadn't dared climb into her top bunk for fear of being thrown out. Instead she sat on a floor mat, gripping the bolted-down chest of drawers. Clare

Hamlyn lay on her bunk, clinging to both sides with white knuckles matching her ashen face and twice she had been overcome with seasickness.

"This can't last much longer!" she screamed, not aware it could possibly go on for days yet. On the other hand the wind could die down and relatively calm seas return in a matter of an hour. The Bay was like that. A raging monster one moment, placid as a village pond the next.

In the men's cabin Silas Martin and the brawny Bob Jones were actually enjoying the event as they peered out of their solitary porthole, seeing first a wall of salt water approaching then nothing but grey sky as the ship rolled, heeled and creaked under the strain. The other two men were kneeling on the floor trying to restrain their heaving stomachs but without success. The convicts didn't know it yet but when calmer seas did arrive they would all have a lot of cleaning up to do.

Captain Stricker knew all he could ask his helmsmen to do was keep the bows into the waves as best they could. Head on contact with the massive swell was far safer than a broadside. And the captain didn't shirk his duties either as at certain critical times he added an extra hand to the wheel. Naturally every man on deck was soaked to the skin but the body could be dried off. A foundered ship meant disaster with every man and woman being consigned without ceremony to the deep, cold Atlantic Ocean. Captain Stricker silently thanked the builders of his vessel who had constructed a stout ship. He also had to hope the ropes securing their heavy cargo held. If they snapped the machinery could shift and break through the bulwarks in which case the *Bromley* would surely be lost.

"Try and kiss me goodbye," Ann shouted in Catherine's ear. "I don't think the ship is going to survive through this storm!"

Holding onto one of the steel brackets securing the forward mast, she stroked a finger down Ann's soaking wet face for another bitterly cold shower of salt water had just drenched them all. Above the sounds of the raging seas she yelled, "We'll make it, my love, have no fear. For the first time in my life I've found true love and I know it just cannot end like this."

Except for Eunice Wilson she had never known or had experience with another female except her heartless mother so she had no way of comparing Ann with anybody else. It didn't matter, Ann was the sweetest, most sensitive girl imaginable. When clasped together they transported themselves into realms of rapture neither could have imagined six weeks ago. As they made love it seemed as if their blood was boiling which in turn made their temples pulse in unison until that final conclusive moment arrived, galvanizing them both. These sensations had been a puzzle to them upon their first discovery and were still somewhat of a mystery now.

This caused Catherine to wonder if it had been fate which had drawn them together. If so it was a unique occurrence.

Their circumstances couldn't have been more divergent. Ann born to a woman who had given her body freely to King George III for some anonymous reward. Then after her mother died she rather foolishly commenced an action which it was hoped would end in being given some form of financial recognition from her father. As it was, those loyal to their king and country had effectively stifled the young, somewhat naïve girl by arranging her transportation to Australia for life. Their consciences would be clear because all it took was a signature on a sheet of official parchment and the king need never know. For Ann this meant being cast into the unfamiliar world of the criminal and that of shipment to possibly one of the harshest prison environments in the world. Once landed she would face further officials who thrived on making miserable existences even more so, in fact unbearable.

Outwardly Ann appeared to be of slight build but as Catherine had discovered when they embraced she was physically strong. Yet from what she had heard from her fellow convicts it was doubtful Ann would be able to endure the rigors of colony life for the remainder of her days. King George's reputation was safe, Ann Lingos's future wasn't.

Catherine knew she had brought about her own misfortunes by committing those violent assaults on her stepfather and mother. That wasn't fate because she had planned the event, fate was to come later in this bizarre situation. Judge Harcourt Longman didn't know when sentencing Catherine to transportation that a similar penalty had already been secretly imposed upon Ann Lingos despite her total innocence. Therefore neither party could possibly know they would be aboard the same ship. Thus it had to be fate which brought them together, albeit in chains, nevertheless they had met. That first kiss they exchanged was to be their foundation of a loving relationship. They both knew a harrowing destiny awaited them in Australia but they also knew their arrival was months away so in the meantime they had time to enjoy each other. They were not being cruelly treated and were given enough to eat each day to keep them alive which couldn't be said for many who still enjoyed their freedom. And during long periods down in the hold love could be made despite their fetters. Catherine realised it was not an ideal situation but she could be buried by now if the judge had decreed she must hang. In life there is always hope, in death there is nothing.

Despite their soaking wet clothing and being pitched to and fro Catherine cradled Ann in her arms as best she could. In fact at times they found it impossible to maintain their grasp on each other. Yet they came together again, knowing this couldn't last forever.

In fact if there was a common thought factor aboard the *Bromley* from the captain down it was that the tempest would abate. And the sooner the better for all concerned.

* * *

Unfortunately for all aboard the heavy weather and mountainous seas persisted for another two agonizing days. Captain Stricker had even considered sailing nearer the French coast although from his blurred telescopic sightings the weather didn't look any better so he elected to continue on his present heading.

With seawater constantly sweeping the decks it had become impossible for Fred Pankhurst, the ship's cook, to keep his oven fires alight so he was unable to prepare any warm meals or even bake bread. All he could offer in the way of food was cheese and hard tack biscuits. This had to suffice for crew, passengers and convicts alike and everybody received equal rations much to the chagrin of Clare Hamlyn who thought the convicts deserved lesser portions. They were probably half starved at home, so why not aboard ship? Making matters worse she had been told by Hector Pimm that many chickens had perished in the constant deluges so she wouldn't be getting many more eggs for breakfast until they arrived at the island of Tenerife, their first scheduled stop to replenish supplies.

In the convict hold about four inches of greasy, smelly water slopped about. Bailing buckets had been lowered down on a regular basis which achieved just one thing, they kept the water from rising. Captain Stricker had considered bringing all six convicts up on deck but there was nowhere to put them. Even soaking wet they were safer down there.

Then finally and very suddenly the weather broke and a most welcome sun emerged from behind the clouds, causing everybody aboard to breathe a collective sigh of relief. Captain Stricker also broke tradition by excusing the convicts duty for two days and allowing them up on deck to dry out their clothing. Each woman was supplied with a blanket to wear and a length of rope to secure it around their waists.

So while sailors pumped out the hold, the women wrung out their clothing and hung them on lines to dry in the warm sun. Doctor Mountjoy had gone around rubbing cream into cuts and bruises although nobody had sustained a serious injury. Lydie Denner's toes were not broken, simply bruised. They were even served a hot meal on deck and for once smiles replaced sadly strained faces. For the moment this life wasn't at all bad. As they lay on the deck sunning themselves they all became the objects of lusty seamen's glances and it didn't take much imagination to know what thoughts lurked in every man's mind. The *Bromley*'s sailors had rarely seen such expanses of bare shoulders, arms and portions of legs. It was just a pity Captain Stricker had forbidden physical contact.

Clare Hamlyn taunted the convicts from the poop deck. "Cover yourselves up, sluts, you are not living in the gutter here or selling yourselves in grotty taverns. Mrs Edwards and myself strive to be decent, so should you."

Emily took a chance and rebuked her. "I don't suppose anybody has seen any portion of your feeble body, madam, not even your husband, I suspect. I pity him."

The bosun heard this and was amused so he decided not to take any action because secretly he agreed with the convict.

Among the sailors they would have voted Catherine Farrow and Ann Lingos as the most appealing. Lingos especially for she had that strangely alluring quality about her which Catherine had seen almost from the first moment their eyes met. And now her face had become slightly suntanned she looked more irresistible, even bewitching. Captain Stricker could have told his crewmen about her birthright but of course he didn't. That was just between him, his masters in London, members of the king's court and of course Ann herself. If she had decided to tell her fellow convicts, that was her business.

Still irked by Emily's reply Clare Hamlyn lodged an official complaint with the captain. It seemed to herself and Alice Edwards the convicts were receiving better treatment than themselves. In his cabin they were asked to sit down.

"Your complaint is duly noted, ladies, and will be entered in the ship's log. When we call in at Tenerife you may lodge your complaint again to the British Commissioner if that is your desire. However I shall also note the convicts suffered far greater privations in their hold than you did in your cabin. For over three days they have existed in four or five inches of water which made it very difficult for them to sleep, if indeed they were able to get any."

"We appreciate that, Captain," Clare replied, "but now in addition you have excused them their appointed cleaning duties and our cabin is in a mess, as you may well imagine. Is it your intent to maintain these charitable attitudes all the way to our destination?"

"Of course not, ladies, and normal shipboard routine will return as promised the day after tomorrow. I can also assure you that should any convict utter further disparaging remarks about either of you the offender will be punished to the full level of my authority. I truly hope that satisfies you and the remainder of our voyage can be conducted in harmony."

"Yes, Captain, we both hope so," Clare replied, wondering if their protest had been worth the effort.

As a measure of compensation they were both offered a goblet of the captain's high-quality red wine so the atmosphere became more relaxed as they chatted about other things with emphasis on the truly foul weather. Of course Captain Stricker tactfully didn't mention they could encounter equally bad weather once they entered the Southern Ocean after leaving Cape Town.

* * *

A few hours later as rain seemed a distinct possibility First Mate Pimm instructed all the convicts to gather their drying clothes and take them below before they got soaked again.

As Sophie began to take her skirt off the line she asked Pimm if they were now required to hand in the blankets they had been given as substitutes while their clothes were drying.

"Keep them for the moment, I'll check with the captain when he's free. Also remember the day after tomorrow you will all return to your normal duties." He pointed at Ann Lingos. "You, girl, will report to my cabin at the usual time. I warn you now there is much cleaning to do as the spray from the bay crossing has left many salty deposits. And need I say heaven help you if things don't come up to my rigid standards which you are well familiar with now, or at least you ought to be. I assume you understand. Do you?"

"Yes, sir, I do."

"Good. A little hard work will stand you in good stead when we reach Botany Bay for there your assigned tasks will be far more arduous. Do you understand what I mean by arduous?"

"Yes, sir, I do."

Both she and Catherine saw Pimm's brow crease as if questioning how an eighteen-year-old convict could be familiar with such a word. He knew most of the crew would have no idea what it meant, in fact they had limited vocabularies. This usually amounted to acknowledging their captain's directives, ordering a drink in a tavern or asking a tart how much she wanted for a few minutes in the backyard.

So once again Ann Lingos became a question mark in the first mate's mind plus each time he saw her the more infatuated he became. He'd seen and entertained many women who were more beautiful and yet there was that certain aura about the girl which stirred him both mentally and physically. He couldn't pinpoint exactly what, just a combination of many things such as her sensuous lips which blended perfectly with the oval face, shrouded as it would normally have been with long russet hair. Now with her body draped in the blanket her square shoulders and full arms were revealed. He had also noticed how her breasts thrust themselves against the grey blanket. All in all Ann Lingos exuded an air of mystery. Had they met in a private club he would almost certainly have asked her to join him for a drink. From there things would progress naturally until he made a proposal that she join him at his lodgings for a more private drink. Once in his rooms, following flattery and numerous glasses of champagne, she would have been asked to expose her upper body for him so he may feast his eyes on those assets which made her feminine. In her inebriated state a refusal would have been virtually impossible. Following compliments, kisses, fondling and more champagne, she would be asked to remove everything. In all probability she would after all he was not unattractive and by all appearances he was a man of means. Once in a state of complete nakedness he would gaze upon the youthful supple body before asking her to recline on the bed while he undressed. Moments later a fusing of their bodies was inevitable. Following mutual satisfactions, more champagne would be consumed before she was invited to kneel between his legs and savour that which confirmed his masculinity. It was all possible.

Pimm now licked his lips while watching Ann and Catherine walk towards the hatch which led down to their hold. It irked him that Farrow was much closer to Lingos than himself. He was also inflamed that when in the hold they would caress each other while permitting their fingers to blindly explore the privacy of themselves. In fact he dreamt about Ann fondling him almost every night until he attained a very private conclusion.

Actually his imagination was not far off the mark. Once in the hold and in their semi-private retreat behind the foremast base, Catherine and Ann kissed with their usual intensity. And as they were still attired in the wrap-round blankets they were able to run their hands across the bare skin of their backs.

As they sank to the floor Ann said, "I'm forming an intense dislike for Mister Pimm. There was no need for him to say what he did up on deck."

"He's just exerting his authority, my dear. Men like to do that. My stepfather was the same with both me and my mother, me more so unfortunately. If he'd been drinking I could expect to feel his belt across either my back or bottom at least once before he demanded my body first, then my mother's."

"Why would he strike you?"

"Dominance. Oh, of course there was always some excuse like the cabbage I'd cooked was soggy or the potatoes too mushy. He never understood how I could not avoid such things. They'd go out to the tavern and promise to be back by a certain time and for me to have the meal ready, which I usually did. Sometimes though they were an hour and a half late. How could I possibly not spoil a meal when that happened. Sometimes I think they did it on purpose just for an excuse to beat me. At least now I've escaped that."

"Yes, although we may face much worse in Botany Bay, my love. We've already heard they whip people there. I cannot begin to imagine what the pain would be like."

"I know. That is why we must make the most of our time now. Let us kiss."

"Willingly."

Emily Kilpatrick and Barbara Henshaw watched them kiss for a moment before lying down to try and recoup some of the sleep they had missed while crossing the Bay. Although the passage had brought them nearer to their destination they were all glad it was over. All were silently thankful the *Bromley* itself had survived for in their hearts none of them wanted to die despite what they faced in Australia.

* * * * *

CHAPTER 11

C LAD IN THEIR NORMAL CLOTHING ONCE AGAIN, the convicts began to assume their regular assignments. Of course they all expected a heavier workload as the cabins hadn't been cleaned properly since entering the Bay. Working, however, meant they weren't cooped up in their hold which had now developed a more putrid odour due to the stench rising up from the bilge and the increase in temperature since they had entered slightly warmer climates. In an effort to keep themselves cooler and reduce sweating, they had all stopped wearing underclothing.

Of all the convicts Barbara Henshaw perhaps had the worst duty in having to clean the female passengers' cabin. They had done nothing since entering the Bay of Biscay and when Barbara was allowed in she mentally compared it to a pigsty. It smelled terrible and soiled clothing was strewn everywhere. Clare Hamlyn told her that when the cabin was thoroughly clean she would have to wash all their clothes except the ones they wore. Unfortunately for Barbara she knew to refuse would mean some form of punishment, as if her duty wasn't punishment enough.

When Ann Lingos entered First Mate Pimm's cabin she found him shaving but was told to continue anyway. This embarrassed her somewhat to be in the presence of a man who was undressed down to his waist. By the look in his eyes and the smell of his breath it seemed obvious he'd been drinking despite the early hour and for a brief moment their gazes met.

"What are you staring at, woman? Haven't you seen the bare chest of a man before?"

"No, sir."

"I find that very hard to believe, Lingos. In fact I'd imagine you've seen a great deal more of a man than what I'm displaying now. Is that not so?"

"No, sir, it is not. In fact I have never been with a man who was undressed."

"I think you're a bloody liar. I'll bet the hands of many men have groped and sucked those little titties which lie below your blouse. Tell the truth now."

"It's not true, sir. I'm pure."

He laughed loudly while wiping his lathered face on a towel.

"Ann Lingos, in my opinion you're about as pure as a tavern whore, a convicted slut. I know you don't wear pantaloons or a petticoat beneath that skirt, so why don't you lean against my chart table and raise it so I can look at your pretty legs and what lies between. Go on, girl, or I'll have you suspended upside down from one of the spars with your legs widely parted so every member of the crew can see what you've got."

She shied back in terror. He advanced and forced her bottom against the sharp edge of the table so tightly she began to struggle and flay her arms at him. One hand knocked over his pewter tankard containing the sharpened pencils. She grabbed one and to protect herself against further assault stabbed him in the ear with all her strength. He sank to the floor moaning and holding a hand over the bleeding organ.

As blood seeped through his fingers she screamed for help. It came in the form of Second Mate Felix Bloom with Doctor Mountjoy close behind. He knelt at the inert figure and immediately stuffed a handkerchief into the ear before looking up.

"Get help to take him to my cabin, Mister Bloom, and see the captain is informed. We have a very serious case here."

"What about her, sir?" Felix asked, pointing at Ann who was cowering in the corner with her arms crossed across her shoulders, trembling like a leaf.

"She's not going anywhere. Do as I ask quickly, minutes may count."

Felix dashed out just as Catherine, who had heard the commotion, was peering in the cabin door. She asked Ann what had happened.

"He was drunk and tried to assault me."

Just then two burly seamen brushed passed Catherine and picked the unconscious body up. Doctor Mountjoy told them to take him to his cabin and lay him on the treatment table. After they had cleared the doorway Felix Bloom entered and grasped Ann's right arm.

"I'd say you're in serious trouble, my girl. Come on, we're off to see Captain Stricker."

She was dragged roughly past Catherine, Lydie and other crewmen who had gathered to see what was happening. Tears welled in Catherine's eyes as the bosun ordered all the convicts back to their hold where they were to remain until further notice.

Once they were all down the ladder Albert Brooks replaced the grille and bolted it. He also shouted, "I'd say Lingos is in a whole pile of shit! You'd better start praying for her as she's sure to swing from a yardarm."

Fighting tears, Catherine was trying to explain what Ann had done. The problem was she didn't know the full story, only that it was something involving the first mate.

For a seeming eternity Captain Stricker stared at Ann after Felix Bloom had given his description of the event. Finally he spoke.

"Tell me your version, lass, and I want the truth."

Through nervous lips Ann explained. "Mister Pimm seemed at least a little drunk, sir. He first made comment about my breasts before telling me to lift my skirt so he could see my legs and what lay between them. Then he pushed me against his map table which scared me so I grabbed one of his pencils and stabbed him."

"Had you perhaps encouraged him?"

"No, sir. I had noticed though that whenever I entered his cabin to clean it he looked at me with lust in his eyes. He also made references that I was different to the other convicts. Well, you know why."

"Yes, I see. And you say Mister Pimm was drunk."

"I smelled rum on his breath, sir."

"Even so early in the morning?"

She simply shrugged her quivering shoulders.

Captain Stricker sat back in his chair and steepled his fingers under a stubbly chin.

"You realise, child, attacking a senior officer of this ship is a very serious offence indeed. If Mister Pimm dies I shall have no alternative but to execute you. Should he live, well, that decision can be left until we know better of the outcome. For the moment though you will be confined in the convict hold." He looked at the second mate. "Mister Bloom, I'd like you to assume the duties of first mate until we know better of Mister Pimm's condition. Think you can handle it?"

"Oh yes, sir. I guarantee you'll have no complaints."

"Good. Now see the prisoner is returned to the hold and have Doctor Mountjoy report to me."

"Yes, sir. Come on, woman."

Again Ann's arm was roughly grasped and it hurt but she managed to suppress a cry of pain. Once down in the hold she fell into Catherine's arms and began sobbing deeply.

"If Pimm dies I'll be hung, Catherine."

"Then we must all hope he doesn't. Tell me what happened."

They all listened as the terror-stricken girl gave her story in-between sobs.

"Did the pencil penetrate deeply?" Catherine asked.

"I've no idea. I was inflamed with rage and just stabbed him. I may be a convict but he had no right ordering me to expose myself."

"Pimm may have been in the wrong, Ann," Sophie told her. "Alas, everything is on his side. As you well know, convicts have no rights."

"Assuming Pimm lives, what will her punishment be?" Lydie Denner asked anybody.

Nobody was sure exactly except Barbara Henshaw seemed to think Captain Stricker would issue his own punishment and that would end the matter.

Catherine feared if Pimm didn't die her lover would be flogged but didn't say so. Inwardly she cringed at the thought of lashes landing across Ann's graceful back. Once in The Grapes tavern she'd seen a sailor display his back after he'd received sixty lashes for hitting the ship's bosun. Although three months had elapsed since the flogging his back was almost completely covered with ugly gashes created by the nine leather tails. Now in the tavern with a large tankard of ale in his mighty hand he could laugh about it and many female customers were allowed to run their fingers through the scars. That was fine for a strong man like him but Ann was no beefy sailor and could well die if the captain ordered too many strokes.

It was obvious nobody wanted to upset Ann more than she already was so they dropped the subject.

As Barbara started to relate how dirty and untidy the female passengers' quarters had been Doctor Mountjoy entered Captain Stricker's cabin and was asked to sit down. The obvious question was asked.

"Will Pimm live or die, Rodney?"

"At this moment, Captain, I can't even hazard a guess. The pencil definitely punctured the eardrum. It might even have penetrated deeper into the brain, an area we doctors know very little about, I myself almost nothing. It may have affected him mentally although it's difficult to say at the moment. I'm almost certain though Pimm will be deaf in that ear forever. I should also point out, just for the record, I have never had a case like this before therefore it would be my advice to drop Mister Pimm off at a convenient port where he may receive more expert treatment. You could promote Felix Bloom, he's a competent man."

Captain Stricker mused for a long moment while sipping his wine. "I take your points, Rodney, and as a matter of fact I have already asked Bloom to assume the first mate's duties. God, it was a stupid thing the girl did. She said Pimm was drunk. Was he in a habit of drinking so early in the morning?"

"I think he did take a couple of early tots to start him on his day although I've never seen him drunk. If you ask me, he was infatuated with the Lingos girl."

"Yes, I got that impression as well. I remember shortly after we sailed he questioned me about her and said she seemed slightly different to the average convict. More refined shall we say, as if she'd had a better upbringing. And even I must admit the girl is attractive in her own way. However that is by the way. Whatever the reasons a man of Pimm's status should never have immoral thoughts about any convicts, male or female. Our function is simply to deliver them to Botany Bay, from there they become somebody else's problem. Anyway we stray off the point. I believe you said it would be your recommendation to drop Pimm off at a convenient port."

"Yes, I did, Captain. Even if he survives, being aboard a pitching and tossing ship is no place for a very sick man. Ashore he will receive better treatment, I'm sure of that."

"Yes, I'm inclined to agree, Rodney, and I value your advice."

He turned in his chair and consulted a large world map mounted on the wall. He stood up to take a closer look and made some measurements. Finally he turned back and resumed his chair.

"We could call in at Lisbon, by a quick estimation it's only three days' sail from our present position. Do you know what medical facilities are like there?"

"Not really, although I imagine there will be a couple of competent doctors in the city. They could initially treat Pimm and then perhaps have him taken overland to Calais and get a ship to Dover from there. At least the man would have half a chance, that is if an infection doesn't set in from the pencil point. If it does I wouldn't hold much hope for his survival."

"Which means his assailant would be a murderess."

The doctor licked his lips. "Thankfully that's your decision, Captain. Of course if we do drop him off in Lisbon and have sailed again we wouldn't know his fate, not for a while anyway. There is one other thing I must point out and I know this from experience. Any doctor we hire in Lisbon would require some form of payment in advance. Do you carry sufficient funds?"

"Oh yes, in bullion. Our esteemed owners look upon gold as an international currency. I assume doctors would accept such?"

"Of course. Gold is good anywhere. Now assuming Pimm lives, what are your intentions regarding the Lingos girl?"

"Above all else order and discipline must be maintained on this vessel and it will be. That being the case and despite her sex she will be flogged. You know full well that is the prescribed punishment for an attack upon a senior officer."

"Yes of course. As I recall, one hundred lashes are called for. I may be out of place saying so but in my humble opinion I honestly don't think the lass could endure that many. I've even witnessed men dying before a hundred have been laid."

"I'm aware of that and will take it into account when and if I have to assess her punishment. Strangely I would have thought Lingos to be the most placid of the convicts. It must have been an impulse reaction. When will you know Pimm's fate?"

"By this evening, one way or the other, he's a strong man. Now I should be getting back to him. I thank you for the wine." He stood up.

"And I thank you, Rodney, for your valued advice. I shall now set my course for Lisbon."

* * *

Even on a ship the size of the *Bromley* everybody aboard was aware of the incident within fifteen minutes. It would be true to say many of the crew were pleased about what the young convict had done to the first mate although they wouldn't have dared do it themselves, being too scared of the consequences. Even Alice Edwards detested the man because he had made suggestions of a sexual nature towards her. She had of course rebuffed him but was in no doubt he would try again before they dropped anchor for the final time in Australia. He appeared to be a man who considered all females fair game. With Ann Lingos it seemed he'd met his match. Now of course Alice feared for Ann's future. If Hector Pimm died Captain Stricker would have no option but to hang her. If he survived, the girl would almost certainly be flogged or some other harsh penalty applied. Whichever way it went, the girl's future was not bright.

Clare Hamlyn had volunteered to act as a nurse for Doctor Mountjoy and was in his cabin now, bathing Pimm's ear which was clotted with blood. Occasionally she dabbed his forehead with a damp cloth. The man himself was still unconscious although some colour had returned to his cheeks which she knew was an encouraging sign. On the other hand, blood running from the patient's nose was a bad omen. Yet even the doctor had admitted he was beyond his depth in this case. Usually shipboard occurrences were cuts, sprains, broken bones, stomach ailments, head lice or bad teeth which needed pulling. All these were easily treated but not a pierced eardrum caused by a sharp pencil.

Captain Stricker had announced that due to the incident he was heading for the Port of Lisbon in Portugal some three days ahead. They would restock the ship there instead of calling into Tenerife as intended. He did not anticipate their stay would be very long but if any of the passengers wished to go ashore to purchase private items they were quite welcome to do so. Naturally the convicts would not be permitted to leave the ship.

Ann Lingos was worried she might be taken ashore and either driven or sailed back to London to face a trial. Catherine was broken-hearted and could not imagine her life now without Ann. In the depths of their combined miseries they had found a certain peace and tranquillity. She also found it ironic that it had taken her almost twenty years to find love, now she could be deprived of it in less than a month. If Pimm died so would Ann. If he lived Ann's future still remained uncertain. Albert, the deck lad, had not helped matters either when he yelled down into the hold an hour or so ago.

"Ann Lingos may find herself tethered at the mast having the cat laid across her skinny back which will be blood red when Mister Malone has finished. You can be sure I'll be watching."

"Shut up, you little piece of vermin!" Emily Kilpatrick had shouted back up.

He simply laughed. Of all aboard the *Bromley* he was becoming the most hated and there were at least five women down in the hold who were scheming to injure him in some way.

Ann was shaking like a leaf in Catherine's arms, dreading the next twenty-four hours. All her life she'd been a little impetuous but had never done anything so rash as stabbing anybody.

"Perhaps, Catherine, I should have simply complied with his requests," she stammered with her face buried in her lover's bosom. "He may not have done me any real harm, just touched me a little."

"We both know it wouldn't have ended there, Ann. He would have wanted more and more until you were forced to perform vile acts like I was on my stepfather. Men are like that, they are never satisfied. A woman to them is an object for making love to or having a baby, little else. There is nothing we can do. The keys to our future lie in Captain Stricker's hands, who fortunately seems to be a fair man. Now kiss me, my love, and for now let us quell our fears."

Lydie Denner shed a tear when she saw their lips come together. It was a cruel world, unfortunately a man's world. Ann Lingos would suffer for what she had done despite it being the act of an insensitive man which caused her to do what she did.

* * *

There had been nervous tension all night aboard the *Bromley*. Word had filtered out from the doctor's cabin that Pimm had regained consciousness yet he was still in a state of shock and running a fever. Doctor Mountjoy had elected not to make any statement on his health until morning.

Captain Stricker had accepted his advice and late last night, to cover all contingencies, he had spoken to the bosun.

"This is a terrible affair for us all, Wilf, sadly one we have to face. If Pimm dies Ann Lingos must forfeit her own life, if he survives you'll have to flog the girl, there are no alternatives. You do realise this, I hope?"

"Yes, sir, I do."

"And you will have no qualms the subject is female?"

"No, sir. It will grieve me naturally but I know it's my duty."

"Well said, Wilf. If it is to be lashes they must be laid in the prescribed manner, there must be no holding back because of her sex. You understand that?"

"Yes, sir. They will be laid exactly as I would to a crewman."

"Then let us leave it at that for now. You are dismissed."

"Thank you, sir."

In a morose mood Wilf left the cabin, went to his own and poured a tankard full of rum. He would not relish performing this act, if indeed it was required.

* * *

The new day arrived all too quickly for the convicts. It was an unusually calm, hot, sunny day with the *Bromley* slowly making headway in a slack wind. The sails were barely filled and water lapped casually against the hull as if they too knew of the tense onboard situation. Crew members stood idly around as Doctor Mountjoy entered the captain's cabin. His face looked tired and drawn, having slept little last night.

Captain Stricker came straight to the point. "Well, Doctor, what do you report?"

"Mister Pimm will live, sir. Sadly, as I predicted, he has lost all hearing in the left ear. However his fever lessened overnight and this morning he was able to ingest a weak soup specially prepared by cook."

"I see. That is good news. With Pimm's recovery, do we still head for Lisbon or continue on?"

"No, I still think it's wise to let him off where I'm sure he'll receive more skilful attention than I can give. He'll be weak for some time, and won't a lack of hearing affect his ability to perform his duties?"

"Yes, of course it will, Rodney. I shall continue on to Lisbon."

"And what of the Lingos girl, sir?"

"I have thought very deeply about her, Rodney. She has to be punished of course but as you said yesterday I don't think her body could endure a hundred strokes. With this in mind and considering her sex, I shall order the bosun to lay twenty-five. I also ask that you attend her during the punishment and after it is over." He rang a handbell which was on his chart table.

Felix Bloom, the acting first mate, appeared.

"Mister Bloom, have the convict Ann Lingos brought before me instantly. Then advise Mister Malone to break out the lash and assemble the crew and convicts to witness punishment. In case of trouble have the convicts handcuffed, also have the Master at Arms stand by with four armed men."

"Aye, aye, sir, right away. What about the passengers, do they witness as well?"

"That is up to themselves, Mister Bloom. But if they do I don't want to hear any outcries of emotion. Tell them that."

"Aye, aye, sir."

After he had gone Captain Stricker poured two goblets of wine and knowing the conditions why Ann Lingos was aboard he said, "You know, Rodney, there have been numerous occasions where I have had cause to order a flogging. In all honesty though, I have no stomach for this one."

"I appreciate your sentiments, Captain. It has to be done though."

"Yes, of course you're correct. Now sup up and we'll proceed."

* * *

It was natural for Ann and Catherine to have spent a restless night knowing it may be their last together. They had made love gently, appreciating the tenderness of their lips and the sensations their caresses brought. Neither had known times like these and they both hoped at the bottom of their hearts the beautiful relationship wasn't about to end abruptly.

Catherine sensed Ann lurch when she heard her name being called.

"The convict Ann Lingos will come topside immediately to be brought before Captain Stricker. Make it sharp, girl."

With tears in her eyes she kissed Catherine. "Wish me luck, my love, and if I'm not to return I thank you for giving me yourself and filling my heart with memorable moments of happiness."

"You will return to me, Ann, I know it. A love such as ours cannot terminate like this. Whatever happens, I shall be praying."

She was cut off with the booming voice of Felix Bloom telling her to look lively.

In a semi-daze Ann stood up and shakily began walking towards the shaft. She didn't hear her fellow convicts wishing her luck although they imagined she wasn't going to get any.

After Felix Bloom had delivered Ann to Captain Stricker's cabin he returned to the hatch and instructed the remaining convicts to come up on deck. Under the captain's command they were to witness punishment and there must be no talking or expressions of emotion.

Captain Stricker stared sternly at Ann whose lower lip trembled visibly.

"Well, Lingos, it appears First Mate Pimm will live, therefore your life will not be forfeit. Unfortunately and despite the circumstances you assaulted a senior officer of this vessel. For this the prescribed punishment is that the offender must receive one hundred strokes of the cat-o'-nine-tails." He paused for a moment to let what he had said to sink in.

"I see you cringe, Lingos, and well you should. Despite Mister Pimm's actions there was no justification in stabbing the man in his ear leaving him half deaf, added to which there may be further complications of which we are not yet aware. The proper thing to do would have been shout out for help and let others take whatever action they thought necessary. However you foolishly took the law into your own hands, an act which has caused me to have you flogged. Despite company orders and in due consideration of your sex I have deemed you shall only receive twenty-five strokes for which you must count yourself lucky. There are many captains who would have seen the full punishment applied regardless. The flogging will commence immediately. It is required the lashes are laid across bare flesh but to save embarrassment at the mast and so your blouse is not ruined I shall permit you to remove it here and drape a blanket around yourself until you have been secured." He handed her a blanket.

Captain Stricker and Doctor Mountjoy turned their backs as Ann nervously removed her blouse and let it drop to the floor. She noticed the upper redness of both breasts, knowing they had been caused by Catherine's kisses. Now as she draped the blanket around her she wondered if those lips would ever kiss her again. It had come as some relief that she was only going to receive twenty-five strokes yet she wondered if her body could even withstand that many.

Captain Stricker and the doctor turned round and for a second looked sadly at her sweat-covered face and quivering shoulders before the captain secured the blanket with a clip.

Outside on the deck the convicts had been handcuffed and stood in a line facing the central main mast. Two burly crew members stood on either end of their line, holding loaded muskets ready to quell any trouble which might arise. Each convict now realised what Ann's punishment was to be but didn't know how many strokes. Catherine had already accepted the fact it was going to be a fearsome and painful ordeal for them both. She knew what strokes across the back felt like, having received many from her father and more recently Patrick. All she could hope for was Ann surviving her ordeal. She had to otherwise her own life would not be worth living. If Ann died so would she in one way or another.

Above the convicts all passengers and crew members had assembled to watch on the poop deck. Albert Brooks stood at the front with First Mate Pimm sitting on a chair beside him. He had a thick bloodstained bandage wrapped numerous times around his head.

"The bitch deserves all she's going to get," Clare Hamlyn whispered to Alice Edwards.

Hearts began to beat faster as two crewmen appeared, each carrying a length of rope. They were accompanied by the bosun who carried a fairly long rectangular box which he set down on the deck to the right of the mast. It was obvious to all what the box contained.

Then Ann was brought out of the rear hatchway by Felix Bloom and another.

Catherine saw fear in her eyes and her own heart began to beat faster as Ann was held facing the mast while two crewmen tied one end of the ropes around her slender wrists. Then the free ends were threaded through an iron ring fastened to the rear of the mast at a height well above Ann's head. The ropes were pulled drawing the arms up with them until her upper body was forced against the radius of the mast before the ropes were tied off to a hook. She looked up at her splayed arms, gulped and bit her lower lip.

Behind and above them the convicts heard Captain Stricker's voice.

"The convict you see tethered at the mast committed a very serious offence by severely wounding the ship's first mate. Because of that I have instructed the bosun to lay twenty-five strokes. Please proceed with the punishment, Mister Malone, after Doctor Mountjoy has removed the blanket."

"Aye, aye, Captain."

As the doctor unclipped and pulled the blanket away there were gasps as Ann's starkly white back became fully exposed with beads of sweat tracing trails down it. Those standing further to the side could see the distinct outlines of her ribcage and the rounded mounds of her breasts pressing against the mast. Catherine saw her back muscles beginning to twitch as if they had already anticipated what was about to happen.

With obvious sadness in his eyes the bosun removed his jacket and rolled up his sleeves before removing the whip from its box. It had a fairly short stubby handle to which were attached the nine two-feet-long leather tails. A few crewmen watching knew what it felt like. As the bosun measured the tails to Ann's back she turned her head and looked almost directly at Catherine as if to say, 'Pray for me'.

Catherine whispered to herself, "May whoever dictates our lives, my love, let him now give you the strength to endure this ordeal. When it is over I shall be waiting."

Then after the bosun drew the whip back there came a distinct swoosh as the cruel lashes travelled through the humid air to land diagonally with a sharp crack across Ann's back, forcing her chest against the unrelenting wooden mast.

Catherine bit her lower lip and closed her eyes when she saw her lover's head snap up and her mouth tighten from the impact and shock her body had undergone. When her eyes opened she saw a series of weals had formed which were already filling with blood. But the next stroke was on its way to land slightly lower down so the tips cracked around the ribcage, causing Ann to twist her body slightly within the unrelenting tethers.

"Catherine, somebody, help me!" Ann screamed as the next cutting stroke landed, causing her delicate fingers to curl into fists before opening again.

On the poop deck Alice Edwards bit down on her lip as the punishment continued, leaving thin rivers of blood running down the victim's back to be trapped in the waistband of her skirt. The lean body squirmed in agony as her head rolled from side to side with streams of tears running down her distressed face. Her mouth gaped widely open as screams emerged when subsequent strokes cut gashes across her already bloody back. Suddenly her eyes began to bulge and then close as she finally sagged so her full weight was taken up totally on her arms.

Captain Stricker raised a finger at Doctor Mountjoy who stood on the lower level beside the lined convicts. He removed a small bottle from a jacket pocket, pulled the cork out, went to the inert victim and ran the bottle under her nose. After a few moments she began to cough, splutter and retch as a stream of thin brown vomit ran from between her bleeding and swollen lips.

"Eleven strokes have been laid," Captain Stricker said, "please continue, Mister Malone."

As the whip was being drawn back Tom Stevens, one of the passengers, asked the captain if the girl hadn't taken enough.

"My orders were for twenty-five strokes, Mister Stevens, and they will all be laid no matter how long it takes. Now please don't interfere again or I will have you taken below. That order applies to all passengers. Now continue with your duty, Mister Malone."

"Aye, sir."

All the convicts were crying and trembling now as one of their own continued to suffer this dreadful punishment. Catherine's head was spinning and her legs felt like rubber but she took a deep breath, bit her lower lip and vowed to remain standing in support of Ann who had no alternative but to endure every cruel stroke, some of which were landing across weals previously inflicted causing blood to splatter in all directions, even up into the short hair. Ann's shrill screams carried across the water as her body twisted within the tethers but all that accomplished was to abrade her wrists further so blood now ran down her extended arms. Even the waistband of her skirt was so saturated with blood it began to run down the material and gather in a pool around her feet.

On the poop deck Hector Pimm smiled as the flogging continued until the victim's screams were reduced to mere moans. He looked across and saw Alice Edwards had fainted. Clare Hamlyn was attending her.

Captain Stricker had just announced the twentieth stroke when Ann passed out again so her body hung limply at the mast with a red froth bubbling from her gaping mouth. The doctor applied more smelling salts and as she recovered consciousness her entire body began to quiver uncontrollably. As he stood aside he knew the girl had entered into a state of deep shock from which she may never fully recover.

Wilf Malone was sweating himself now and he hated to see the state of his victim's back. He'd applied many lashes but always to seamen with skin like leather. As his strokes landed he tried to miss the weals already there. With one stroke to go her body slumped again so he landed the last rapidly, hoping and praying her heart was still beating. The whip was handed to a crewman for him to wash the tails and return the instrument to its box ready for the next victim.

As Ann's inert body was being let down Doctor Mountjoy instructed the crewmen to take her to his cabin where a salving lotion would be applied. There was little else he could do.

"Are you satisfied now, Mister Pimm?" Captain Stricker asked the injured first mate.

"Not really, sir, I'd expected her to be given the full hundred strokes. I should report you for dereliction of your duty."

"I did my duty as I saw fit, Pimm. You and I know this may have affected the lass mentally for the remainder of her life, such as it is. Yet if you wish to report me, by all means do so. I showed a little compassion and don't forget the girl claimed you were drunk, drunk on duty ,I may add, as you had the watch. If I were you, Pimm, I'd hold my tongue and count yourself lucky you're not dead."

Catherine had overheard Captain Stricker say Ann may be affected mentally. This hadn't occurred to her although now seeing her lover's body still trembling uncontrollably with her arms slung across the shoulders of the crewmen it seemed logical. She had seen a face in a similar state of shock once before when witnessing a young woman who had been hit and trampled on by a bolting horse drawing a hansom cab. She didn't know what became of the woman although she could easily recall the vacant gaze of her eyes as others went to help. Then her mind was snapped back to reality when one of the armed guards ordered all the convicts back to their hold. They all began to walk slowly forward with drooped heads, dragging their leg chains with them. Nobody spoke, it had affected them deeply and silent prayers were being said for Ann.

At the hatch Albert, the deck lad, stood watching as their handcuffs were removed. Barbara Henshaw had been first so she stepped on the ladder, shaking like a leaf, and as usual the cheeky lad had a comment.

"See what happens when you attack a crew member. Who's going to be next, I wonder? It's still a long way to Australia." He laughed.

"Haven't you any heart at all?" Lydie Denner said while stepping on the first rung of the ladder.

"No heart for you women, each and every one of you are pig slime. Now look sharp as I still have to get my breakfast. You scum may get fed later."

Once they were all below Emily Kilpatrick threatened once again to kill the little bastard before they reached Australia. Sophie Hart warned her to be careful. Nobody wanted to witness another event like this morning.

After a few moments Catherine wondered aloud if Ann would recover from her ordeal. Nobody was sure. They all sat on the floor and except for some slight creaking and water lapping against the *Bromley*'s hull all was silent.

Ann had been laid face down on the padded table in Doctor Mountjoy's small anteroom adjacent to his cabin. He had applied some foul-smelling ointment to her lacerated back before laying a cotton cloth soaked in seawater over the wounds. It had been a good sign to him that she had winced and cried out in pain when he spread the ointment.

Her head was laid to one side with a cloth under her mouth to absorb the saliva and thin vomit which still trickled from between her bloody lips, the lower of which had swelled considerably. Another good sign to the doctor had been her fluttering eyelids. And before she was turned on her face a sounding device had been placed under her left breast. Although the heartbeats were weak and irregular he was fairly sure she would survive.

Her arms hung limply down either side of the table as the doctor now applied some ointment to the abrasions around her wrists. Every now and again her young body twitched as another spasm of pain flashed through it. This was a common reaction with anybody who had been flogged. Every ship's doctor knew it was the central nervous system responding to the shock it had been subjected to.

There was a knock on the cabin door. Whoever it was asked to come in. It was Captain Stricker to ask about Ann's condition.

"You'll not have to perform a burial, Captain, I'm happy to say. She's a strong lass. I just hope there's been no damage to her spinal column. We won't know that until she's walking again."

"When will that be?" the captain asked while looking at Ann's ashen face rather than the bloodstained cloth on her back.

"She may be able to walk tomorrow, Captain. Hard to say really and I don't want to rush her. She may be a convict but she's also a human being and it's my duty as a man of the medical profession to see she gets the best treatment possible. You understand?"

"Yes of course, Doctor, and I do appreciate your sentiments. Is there anything else you can do for her?"

"A few sips of brandy wouldn't harm."

"I'll instruct the new first mate to bring you a bottle."

"So you'll be promoting Bloom, will you?"

"I already have, I told him following the flogging. He's been around Pimm long enough to know what's wanted of him. I know he's not popular with some of the men but we do need a man who can give orders and ensure they are obeyed. I'm now going to my cabin and will write up a report of this incident so I can have it sent by coach back to company headquarters after we arrive in Lisbon."

"When will that be?"

"About dusk the day after tomorrow, all being well. The winds are light but favourable. We'll obviously be unexpected so I'll anchor offshore overnight then go in a dinghy to the dock at first light to make the arrangements. I'll expect you to have Pimm and his possessions ready to ship him ashore. He wasn't pleased when

I told him but I can't run this ship carrying a half-deaf officer. You'll need to write up a medical report and suggestions for his care en route back to England."

"Yes, I'll do that, Captain. Ah look, the girl's eyes are opening. It might be a good idea to get me that brandy."

"I'll do it right away. And thank you, Rodney, for all you've done."

"My duty, Captain, nothing more."

After hands had been shaken and with the captain departed, the doctor went to Ann and wiped some saliva from her lips.

"How do you feel, lass?"

"Terrible. I ache all over and I have a dreadful headache."

"It's to be expected, you took a terrible punishment. There's some brandy coming, that may make you feel a little better."

"Where am I?"

"In the medical room next to my cabin. Lie still, you've lots of pain to endure yet."

"Why, isn't my punishment complete?"

"Yes, but the feeling in your back hasn't fully returned. When it does you can expect more anguish over the next few days. I'll mix you a potion which will relieve some of the pain for a while at least. Naturally I shall ask the captain to excuse you duties. Now lie very still, I'm going to remove a soaked cloth off your back and put another in its place. There isn't much more I can do. Grip the sides of the table tightly."

She did as he began to slowly peel the cloth off, causing her to scream loudly as pieces of skin came with it.

In the hold Catherine's head suddenly shot up when she heard the scream. "That was Ann, I know it. What are they doing to the poor girl now?"

"I think it may be the doctor treating her, Catherine," Sophie Hart replied. "Try to relax. The screams are a good sign, they mean your lover still lives."

"And I hope, Sophie, she'll still be my lover when she's brought back. You cannot imagine the loving feeling which exists between us. I never imagined such a thing was possible. We only thought loving sentiments were possible between a man and a woman."

"I've heard of female to female relationships before," Barbara Henshaw told her. "I once knew a gang of all-female robbers who stole nothing except valuable church pieces. There were six of them and I know they made love with each other. They held wild parties in a forest somewhere up north, so I'm told, before they were captured in a trap set by the Church."

"What happened to them?" Emily asked.

"Four were hanged and two were transported like us because they gave evidence against their friends."

"How long ago was this?" Lydie asked.

"About three years."

"Then we may meet them in the penal colony," Lydie replied.

"We may. By now though I think they'll have been forced to accept men which I know won't be a pleasure for them. I mean, how can it be!"

Lydie looked at Catherine. "You realise the same might happen to you and Ann?"

"Yes, of course I do. Despite that we'll have had some time together, and who knows how things will work out? It sounds like Ann is quiet again now, I hope she's alright."

In the gloomy, hot, reeking hold the others simply nodded.

Actually Ann was being given a sip of brandy by Doctor Mountjoy. Since this was the strongest liquid she'd ingested since being arrested it made her cough and splutter, causing some of the weals to start bleeding again. Slowly the doctor poured more into her mouth and this time she was able to swallow. For the first time since stabbing Pimm she was able to smile and thanked the doctor. More of the fiery liquid was administered before being asked if she felt like sitting up.

"I'll try, Doctor."

Her face grimaced as the doctor helped. "Here, drink this, lass, it's a painkilling potion. It doesn't taste too nice but it works."

While she was unconscious he'd mixed a concoction of laudanum and opium with pure alcohol. It was handed to her. Her delicate hands trembled almost uncontrollably as she drank the potent liquid through tightly drawn lips. She began to gasp deeply, fighting for breath with her eyes opening and closing rapidly as shooting pains shot through her young body.

Doctor Mountjoy took the goblet and laid her back down again, knowing her recovery would take time. He gritted his teeth, sensing a great animosity towards Hector Pimm who by his cruel lust caused this girl's distress. The man was supposed to be a gentleman when in fact he was nothing more than a bully who deserved to be flogged himself.

While Doctor Mountjoy was treating his patient Clare Hamlyn had gone to see Captain Stricker, requesting to see the doctor because she'd developed a headache.

"I'm afraid at the moment the doctor is otherwise engaged, Mrs Hamlyn. Sorry."

"I suppose with that brat of a convict who was flogged."

"I cannot deny it, madam."

"Really, Captain Stricker, this is almost beyond reason. I suffer a severe headache and require something from the doctor only to be told he's engaged. Is it your shipping line's policy to give preferential treatment to a criminal rather than a paying passenger?"

"The convict has suffered greatly, madam, far worse than you could ever imagine. And for the record, as captain of this vessel I'm at liberty to handle matters as I see fit. Now why don't you sit down and take a goblet of port with me. I'm sure that will alleviate any ill feelings you may have."

"Oh, alright. I do insist though my complaint is recorded in your log, including your refusal to let me see the doctor."

"It will be done, madam. And if you or your companion Mrs Edwards wish to leave my ship in Lisbon you are quite welcome to do so. You may be able to catch another more luxurious vessel sailing to Port Jackson. However there could be a long wait and it will obviously cost you more money. Let me know if that is your wish and I will reimburse you one third of your passage fee. Now shall we have that drink?"

"Yes."

He poured as she contemplated. She knew neither herself nor Alice could afford to pay for another vessel or even wait for one in a foreign port. Both were anxious to rejoin their husbands and savour once again married life. And when all was said and done life aboard wasn't too bad and the food was passable. She also knew Captain Stricker had called her bluff once again, aware he was well within his rights to treat the injured convict.

They both drank up and had another. As the captain continued writing his report she returned to her cabin feeling slightly light-headed.

Ann was feeling a little better despite the fact full sensation had not returned to her back but the brandy and painkiller had brought some ease. In fact she felt very warm and quite dizzy. She did not refuse another drink and this time Doctor Mountjoy decided to join her.

He was pleased and inwardly felt quite relieved he wouldn't have a seriously ill convict on his hands all the way to Australia. As he looked at Ann now and despite the bruised lips, deeply bloodshot eyes and pallid face he saw something of the dynamic young lady which had obviously raised Hector Pimm's sexual urges to the point where he had been driven to assault her. Sadly for him she did not succumb to his advances. She retaliated and had rendered him totally deaf in one ear, it also cost her a back which would carry scars forever. There were also five other women down in the hold heading for very uncertain futures and if any one of them attacked an official at Botany Bay similar to Ann Lingos's onslaught they would be cast in solitary for at least half a year and their backs would be in far worse shape than Ann's. The colony governor Edgar Boag was not a man of compassion like Captain Stricker. In fact he was known as the Beast of Botany Bay.

* * *

Down in the hold Catherine was becoming increasingly worried, in fact they all were. Ann had not been returned among them and it was now dark outside. The last any of them had seen of her was being carried away unconscious to Doctor Mountjoy's treatment room. They had heard her screams but had no idea what caused them.

"Perhaps they have a special lock-up for wrongdoers," Emily had suggested a while ago and Sophie agreed.

Catherine had visions of Ann securely clad in handcuffs, cramped in a space not much larger than a kitchen cupboard. It would also be located within the bilge area where she could easily be overcome with the poisonous gases which accumulated down there. They experienced the gases themselves which at times caused them to retch. Fortunately after the Bay of Biscay crewmen had vented the ship so at the moment it wasn't too bad.

"Can they hang a person for attacking a ship's officer?" Barbara Henshaw questioned.

"Perhaps," Sophie replied, "but surely they wouldn't flog the person first."

"Who knows, at sea there may be different sets of rules," Emily replied, trying to avoid Catherine's eyes.

"Please, please," Catherine cried out, "can't we talk about something else? I may have lost the only person in the world who I ever loved." Then she turned over and cried into her hands.

The others looked at her, feeling truly sorry. They were all convicted criminals but a certain camaraderie had developed between them since they sailed. Acquired friendships were perhaps the only thing the authorities couldn't take away from a convict.

* * *

By mid morning of the following day Ann was able to stand up and take a few steps although they were agonizing, especially as she had the added weight of the ankle manacles and chain to drag with her. Doctor Mountjoy saw the extreme anguish on her face, unfortunately she couldn't remain in his treatment room any longer. Captain Stricker had instructed she was to be returned to the convict hold without delay, he had shown the girl far more compassion than he would to a crewman who had received similar treatment. Yet within his heart he felt sympathy for the lass, knowing the truth about her past. A conspiracy by the monarch himself had led indirectly to this unfortunate incident aboard his ship.

Doctor Mountjoy broke the news to Ann gently.

"Captain Stricker has given orders you are to be returned to the convict hold immediately. Before you leave I will apply more ointment and place another soaked cloth on your back and tie it in place before replacing your blouse. I also advise that once the cloth dries out it is soaked again in salt water, it will help to fend off infection. Tomorrow we are calling in to the port of Lisbon to drop First Mate Pimm off. After we sail I shall inspect your back again to ensure the weals haven't festered. Now sit on the table."

He watched as she did so but didn't help. She grimaced and began to cry when the old bloodstained cloth was peeled off. As the ointment was applied she gasped audibly and knotted her slender fingers. However when the new cloth was laid on it brought a little relief. There were two lengths of twine attached to the top which the doctor tied under her chin. Then very carefully he helped her on with the blouse which fortunately was very slack. As a final gesture the doctor poured her a goblet of brandy which she supped greedily.

Two crewmen were summoned to assist in returning her to the hold.

"I hope you recover fully, Lingos," Doctor Mountjoy said with obvious compassion.

"Thank you, Doctor, for what you've done," Ann replied weakly as the crewmen took her sore arms.

Most of the passengers saw her being walked slowly across the deck.

"She's lucky to be alive," Clare Hamlyn said to Silas Martin, one of the sheep farmers.

The pleasant-faced, clean-shaven man looked at her with narrowed eyes. "You would wish such treatment of a young woman, Mrs Hamlyn? That surprises me. She could have been your daughter."

"No daughter of mine would dare attack a superior, Silas. If I have children I intend to be very strict with them. My father took a cane to me from time to time if I misbehaved and it did teach me a lesson. I'm a faithful wife now of course and eager to be reunited with my dear husband who is forging a new life for us."

"I hope he meets with success, Mrs Hamlyn."

"Oh, he will, I know it. He's in construction, you know, building stone structures of high quality. Edifices which Australia will be proud of for centuries to come. I foresee the day when the Hamlyns will be one of the premier Australian families. Oh look, the convict is being helped into the hatch."

Silas Martin turned to look in the direction of the hatch, glad he had nothing at all to do with the callous and obviously snobbish woman. He saw Ann's face contort in pain as her arms were raised so she could be lowered into the hatch opening. One hand was released and she grasped a rung of the ladder. Barbara climbed up the ladder and guided Ann's feet on to the rungs as each step was taken carefully. Her face was sweat stained when her feet finally hit the deck and Catherine was waiting to embrace her.

"Welcome back, my love. I've missed you."

"I've missed you too. Now I need to lie down."

Catherine carefully walked her the short distance to their space behind the mast where four blankets had been laid out. Once lying face down, Catherine knelt beside her.

"Oh, my love, you can't believe how happy I am to see you again. Tell me, how do you feel?"

"Not good naturally, I ache terribly and pains still shoot through me but Doctor Mountjoy was very kind and gentle. He advised it would be better for the whip marks to heal if I went without my blouse, something to do with fresh air. He also said to resoak the cloth on my back once it dries out. Somehow or other we must get a bucket of salt water."

"I'll yell for somebody to get us one," Lydie Denner said as Emily helped Catherine remove the blouse.

Albert Brook's head appeared in the hatch opening and Lydie explained to him what they wanted. He laughed.

"Can't the lass take a few strokes without wanting treatment? You women are weaker than a pile of cow shit. Anyway I'll ask the new first mate and don't go away," he added sarcastically.

Emily Kilpatrick fumed again while patting Ann's sweaty brow as they removed her blouse. They were all appalled at her bruised breasts which had been forced against the mast when the strokes landed. Ann began to tremble uncontrollably again as they laid her down. They could all see the still damp cloth on her back was stained with blood.

Because her eyes were closed Ann didn't see Catherine crying. Seeing her lover like this was causing her far more grief than when the man came to announce her real father had been killed at the docks. An urge swept her to kiss Ann's swollen lips yet she refrained, knowing the body must remain untouched.

A shout from the grille announced Albert had a pail of water. They were to stand clear so he could lower it down. Sophie unhooked it and took it to Ann's side. Ann was asleep so Catherine thought this was a good chance to remove the cloth and rinse it out.

Lydie was forced to hold a hand over her mouth at the dreadful sight of Ann's back when it became fully revealed. Even where the lashes hadn't struck the flesh was badly bruised. Sophie rinsed the cloth out two or three times before soaking it thoroughly again and gently laying it over the scarred flesh. It didn't need retying. Ann's eyes had fluttered but she still slept. Emily suggested removing the girl's skirt which was also stained with blood. Catherine rejected the idea as it might disturb Ann. They could wash it later when they were permitted up on deck again.

Emily simply nodded as Catherine sat cross-legged beside Ann, stroking the matted hair around the nape of her neck. Religion had never been a part of her life but she silently prayed now for Ann's full recovery. She imagined no woman had ever paid such a great price for simply defending herself against an evil man who outranked her in both position and strength. Of course she wasn't aware yet that Captain Stricker was heading towards Lisbon where Hector Pimm would be put ashore and returned to England, perhaps not in shame although certainly deaf in one ear and maybe with a guilty conscience.

"Come back to me, my love," Catherine softly whispered as the others sat or lay around mournfully. A pall of even greater depression had fallen over the hold.

Outside dusk was falling rapidly as Captain Stricker viewed the flickering lights of Lisbon through his telescope. He ordered all sails to be dropped, the anchor deployed and lanterns lit as he didn't want to be taken as an enemy man-o'-war. He knew Spain was not too far south, the country Sir Francis Drake had defeated on the high seas in 1588.

* * * * *

CHAPTER 12

ALL SIX PASSENGERS STOOD ON THE POOP deck gazing at the Port of Lisbon as
the *Bromley* slowly sailed through the narrow entrance into the harbour
with all sails reefed except the foremast jibs. They were being watched
by four sailors in a cutter which had been dispatched to see who and what this
mystery ship was. If necessary a dinghy had been slung ready to take Captain
Stricker ashore.

Quite by chance the *Bromley* carried a topsail man named Eduardo Vicosa
who was Portuguese by birth, so prompted by Captain Stricker he related their
intentions to an officious-looking military man standing at the cutter's prow. By his
uniform it seemed obvious he was the harbour master.

Eduardo had been told to say they came in peace, wishing to drop off a senior
crew member who had been seriously injured during their crossing of the Bay of
Biscay. It was their intention to have him returned to London with all possible haste
so he may be treated. Words of reply were shouted up to Eduardo who translated
for his captain.

"Captain Jarez Beira understands about our man, Captain. Also he would like
to know what we carry, what is our ultimate destination and are we aware there will
be harbour charges?"

"Tell him we carry mining equipment destined for Port Jackson in Australia
and six important passengers, two female and four male. You may also tell him we
wish to reprovision the ship, fill the fresh-water tanks and that I'm aware of and
expect to pay harbour costs."

"What about the convicts, sir?"

"There is no need to announce them, Vicosa. Just tell Captain Beira what I
have said."

"Aye, sir."

More exchanges were made until finally Captain Beira threw up a salute to Captain Stricker and said in passable English, "Welcome to Lisbon, Captain. Please anchor where I show you as no dockside spaces are available."

Captain Stricker gestured his agreement. In fact he preferred to anchor off the quay as there would be less prying eyes to worry about. The *Bromley* drifted to a spot indicated by Captain Beira and the anchor was dropped.

"I wonder where we are?" Barbara Henshaw asked after hearing the anchor splash.

"Lisbon," Ann muttered through her thick lips.

Catherine turned sharply and asked how she knew.

"Doctor Mountjoy told me. They're dropping First Mate Pimm off and having him sent back to England."

"And bloody good riddance," Emily replied, rubbing her hands together in glee.

Of course now Ann had found her voice they all gathered round to express their relief and ask how she really felt. Amid the noises up on deck Ann mumbled her reply.

"I don't feel too bad after the sleep," she glanced with one eye at Catherine, "but I don't feel up to making love." She forced a smile and asked Catherine how her back really looked.

"Not so good at this moment, my love. It will improve though, won't it, girls?"

Almost in unison everybody said it would although Lydie Denner had reservations. She knew scars such as those rarely healed fully but as a person's back was usually covered up to the neck it really didn't matter. Only aristocratic ladies or street tarts would dare to wear a dress which fully exposed their backs.

Then from above they all heard Wilf Malone order the boat to be lowered. There followed lots of creaking of blocks and tackle as it descended to the calm water littered with flotsam, as of course it was in almost every harbour in the world.

Captain Stricker was in the boat along with his new first mate and their interpreter Eduardo Vicosa. Two crewmen would row. Captain Stricker was very pleased he had a man aboard who actually spoke the local language although once ashore he had expected to find somebody who spoke passable English.

As he stepped on the dock Captain Stricker and Captain Jarez Beira met physically and shook hands warmly. As it appeared that Captain Beira spoke English reasonably well First Mate Bloom was introduced before the request was made to allow passengers ashore to do some shopping. This was agreed. It was also settled that Felix Bloom would supervise provisioning of the *Bromley* along with the chef Fred Pankhurst. Edward Vicosa seemed upset when told he could to return to the ship after being told his valuable translation service would be noted in the log.

Captain Beira agreed to help all he could and asked Captain Stricker if the injured man could walk.

"Oh yes. The injury is in his ear, he accidentally got spiked. I did not wish him to continue on as my doctor doesn't know the full extent of his internal injuries."

"Yes, I see, Captain. We should perhaps visit the British consul here and let him arrange to have your man given safe passage back to England."

"I would appreciate that, Captain Beira. What is the consul's name? Perhaps we have met."

"Lawrence Carlyle. A man of fifty-five years, so I believe. He is very pleasant, we meet occasionally on harbour business, also socially. I also know he enjoys a brandy, as I myself do when the occasion permits. Have you met him?"

"No, I don't think so, the name doesn't register. Then of course we have so many consuls scattered around the world."

Felix Bloom who stood slightly behind his superior had to smirk at Captain Stricker's remark. It was a little bit of one-upmanship at Great Britain's status in so many countries over which the Union Jack flew.

It didn't appear Captain Beira caught the inference as he said, "Then you must meet the consul without delay, Captain, I will escort you to his residence myself." He clicked his fingers to summon a chaise which stood ready. This arrival of a British sea captain was a feather in his cap. Normally Lisbon was bypassed in favour of the Canary Islands where many of the local women were willing to share themselves with visiting seamen in the hopes a marriage may result. The women were also a welcome relief for rampant sailors who had been living on memories for weeks, sometimes months.

Captain Stricker turned to Felix Bloom and instructed him to oversee the passengers once they landed. If they carried no money or gold he was to record all purchases and settlement would be made before they sailed again. Felix was also warned to be on the lookout for cheats and pickpockets. As for crew members they should be careful not to associate with dockside ladies who would probably be riddled with disease. The captain stressed he didn't want to continue on with pox running out of control aboard the *Bromley*.

Felix promised to be helpful, realising this was a big step up for him. Promotions such as his were very rare at sea plus he and Pimm had never really been friendly. For two voyages now Felix had envied Pimm's status and especially the way he flaunted it.

Captain Stricker climbed in the chaise with Jarez Beira who instructed the driver with a flourishing wave of his hand to make for the consul's residence.

* * *

"Stand out of the way, you slimy lot, I'm lowering another pail of water," Albert Brooks said after removing the hatch grille. When it landed Barbara Henshaw asked if they would be allowed up on deck today.

"No way, Lisbon is not for criminals. Just get yourselves washed, I can smell you from up here."

"And we can smell you from down here," Emily replied.

"You'd better watch your tongue, woman. If I report what you just said to the bosun we'd be witnessing another session at the mast. Just get your scabby bodies washed."

With that the grille was replaced, leaving a partial view of the main mast with seamen still furling sails. And beyond the canvas an azure-blue sky could be seen.

Catherine was the first to take a turn at the pail after she'd removed her blouse. Two days ago they'd been given a block of hard carbolic soap so she rubbed her upper body with it now. With salt water it produced hardly any suds but she did feel slightly cleaner. Finally her soiled skirt was raised to wash between her legs. The blouse was replaced before she returned to Ann who still lay on her stomach. The exposed cheek was kissed. Ann smiled weakly and said, "That felt nice, Catherine, thank you. I do feel better today and haven't had too many shooting pains. How is my back?"

"It's looking much better, my love. The weals are healing and luckily none have festered."

"That's good. Doctor Mountjoy said that was his main worry." She licked her still swollen lower lip which gave Catherine an idea.

Some of her own saliva was raised, put on her finger tip and wiped over Ann's lips. "I could lie down beside you and lick your lips if you feel up to it. Do you?"

"Yes, I think so."

Catherine got beside her, being careful not to touch the back. She inched her face forward and began to gently lick the lips as a cat may lap milk.

"It feels nice," Ann said as she turned her face slightly upward and opened her mouth.

Catherine took the hint and poked her tongue into the warm opening to feel the tip of her lover's tongue. It felt so good knowing Ann was gradually returning to her normal self. Soon now she imagined they would be able to make proper love again. A tribute to the girl's fortitude.

The others watched, happy in the knowledge one of their number had survived a terrible ordeal and by all appearances it had not affected her mentally.

* * *

The British consul's residence was located at Collares, high on the cliff, offering a magnificent view of the Atlantic Ocean with frothy surf rolling up the white sand.

Captain Stricker took in the vista from the patterned mosaic-tiled terrace while savouring a glass of locally made port wine. With him stood the consul Lawrence Carlyle and his daughter Isabelle. It seemed Lawrence's wife Clara was in London tending an ailing sister. Following introductions and taking a drink himself Captain Jarez Beira had returned to his harbour duties full of his own importance having served an English sea captain.

Captain Stricker had explained the reason for his surprise visit and for Hector Pimm's benefit he had distorted the truth slightly. It had simply been reported as one of those dreadful accidents which sometimes occur in rough seas. A boom had splintered while they were passing through the Bay of Biscay and a sharp section had pierced the first mate's ear. As his report to the company in London was officially sealed with wax there was no way the consul could discover the actual course of events leading up to Pimm's deafness. Plus no mention of the convicts had to be made.

"So now you wish me to arrange a swift passage back to England for your injured mate," Lawrence Carlyle said while watching his glass being refilled by a liveried servant.

"With your kind cooperation, sir, yes. The man is suffering severe headaches and loses his sense of balance at times. My doctor cannot say whether these are temporary afflictions or will be permanent. With my voyage being of lengthy duration I didn't want to subject Mister Pimm to the rigors it entails. It was perhaps fortunate the accident occurred when it did. If it had happened somewhere in the Southern Ocean my man might well have died before he could receive expert treatment."

"Yes of course, Captain Stricker, you did the correct thing and may be assured Mister Pimm will have a comfortable transport to Calais and a sea passage across the Channel. Making arrangements will be a slight change in the somewhat mundane life we live here although it does have its compensations. Ideal weather for one thing and this rather good wine of which there is an abundance." He turned slightly to look at his daughter. "Isabelle is involved quite deeply with a local vineyard and gives her own ideas for blending. It also keeps her out of trouble, doesn't it, my dear?"

"Quite so, Father, but I'm sure the good captain doesn't want to hear about these things."

"Oh, I do, Miss Carlyle, and please call me Algernon. The name is a family tradition dating back quite a few generations."

"Are you married?" asked the attractive woman whom Algernon estimated to be in her late twenties.

"Oh no. A sailor's life and that of marriage don't mix, I'm afraid. I spend more time on the quarterdeck of my vessel than I would on a veranda at home although there are times when I wish for a slightly livelier social life than the one we lead at sea. Still a person cannot have it all ways."

Isabelle smiled, displaying a set of the whitest teeth Algernon had ever seen except perhaps those of Ann Lingos. After licking her full ruby-red lips she said, "There are times, Algernon, when I sit here looking at passing ships, wishing I was on one. To me ships open up the world. Oh and by the way, please call me Isabelle, I'm sure Father will not object."

"Of course not, my dear. Perhaps if we were in London it would be different but here everything is so informal. Now I assume, Algernon, you will join us for supper and perhaps stay the night. I shall make the arrangements for Mister Pimm so you will know his situation before sailing again. Do I have your acceptance?"

"How can I refuse, sir. You are most kind."

"That's settled then." He rang a handbell and a servant appeared. He was asked to ride into town and return with Alberto Novas. The servant bowed and left. Then the slightly overweight, well-tanned consul explained the man he had sent for owned a fleet of coaches which operated throughout Portugal and Spain so it would be no problem for him to go further north into France. It was suggested a fully qualified travelling nurse be retained for the journey plus an armed guard as the coastal road was a favourite hunting ground for highway robbers.

Captain Stricker totally agreed. He had no taste for what Pimm had done but he didn't want to see the man harmed further.

Lawrence asked how payment would be made.

"I assume gold will be acceptable."

"Oh, I'm sure it will be. Not a country in the world refuses the metal, it is an international currency. I keep a supply here and if you wish I can make payment for you and bill your company. We'll probably get a more favourable price that way. The merchants all respect me and my office so we enjoy generous discounts. Now perhaps another drink before we prepare for supper. What say you?"

"I'd be pleased to, Lawrence. I must admit when sailing into the harbour I never expected such royal treatment."

"It is a pleasure to have the company of an Englishman, Captain. We get so few here. Naturally I entertain many locals although most are, how shall I say, not up to our intellectual level. It is especially hard for Isabelle. I've tried inducing her to return to London where the social scene is far more active but she prefers to remain here with me, don't you, my dear?"

"Of course, Father, especially with Mother away. Do you carry anything or anybody of importance on your ship, Captain?"

He accepted his refreshed drink before replying. "Not really, Isabelle. Our main cargo is mining equipment destined for the Australian outback, as I believe the locals call it. We also carry six passengers, two of whom are female who are joining their husbands in Port Jackson. The other four are lusty, ambitious farmers intending to get into the sheep-rearing business in western Australia. They claim wool is fetching higher prices every year."

"Indeed it is, Algernon," Lawrence replied. "Just as wine is here. Portugal exports thousands of gallons every year, not all of which is the quality we drink now of course. Some of it, I hazard to say, may be quite deadly if consumed in quantity. The locals seem to enjoy it though plus the Spaniards who will drink most anything."

Algernon laughed. "I do know dockside taverns in London make huge profits out of wine which is little more than vinegar, and there are numerous deaths. However let us talk of lighter subjects, death is so morbid, don't you think?"

"It is, Captain," Isabelle said sharply, "although it is worth remembering death is an element in life which we must all face sooner or later. Perhaps you know Lisbon was almost totally destroyed by an earthquake on the first day of November in the year seventeen fifty-five. Untold numbers perished under collapsed buildings and in the many fires which erupted. Entire families were lost in the carnage and I pray to God such a catastrophe doesn't occur again. In certain areas of the city, buildings are still under reconstruction ..."[4]

"Isabelle also has strong feelings on another subject, don't you, my dear?" Lawrence Carlyle cut in.

---

4   This earthquake was a factual event on the date stated.

"Yes, I certainly do." She looked directly at Captain Stricker with an expression of grief on her usually pleasant face. "What I refer to, Captain, is the transportation to Australia of female convicts. From what I hear from the occasional ship which calls in here they travel under appalling conditions, crammed tightly together in rat-infested holds and are fed barely enough to sustain them. I also hear many of the younger women are invited to become playmates of crew members. Then once landed, these same women are encouraged to become pregnant as a way of increasing the population. In my own humble opinion, Captain, God never intended women to become production factories. I also think it a bad idea to found a new country from the wombs of convicts. What are your views?"

For a moment Captain Stricker wondered if she was aware the *Bromley* carried convicts. He considered it very unlikely and replied, "All I can say, Isabelle, is that transportation was adopted by our government as a way of curbing overcrowding in the prisons, which I believe had reached epic proportions when the first batches of convicts were shipped. As to your personal sentiments regarding females, we must remember they are equally capable of committing violent crimes as men. On using them to breed, I have no opinion other than to say their offspring are not considered criminals. I imagine in time transportation will be abolished, until then certain ships will be required to perform this duty. I'm sorry if my answer offends you."

The consul stepped in. "I think this conversation has gone far enough. I know your views on transportation, Isabelle, but as Captain Stricker has said, at this point in our history it is necessary. Shipping convicts might not be the most honourable mission in the world but somebody has to do it just as coal has to be mined. Whatever way we look at it, for better or worse convicts are seeding a population of what we may call a new world. A world unfortunately which I know little about. However let us drink up and prepare for supper."

Isabelle bowed before the two men. "It is as you say, Father, and I do apologize to you, Captain. It was not my place to criticise your profession."

Captain Stricker bowed and accepted the apology before Isabelle led him to where he may wash before eating. Naturally in his mind were the six convicts in the *Bromley*'s hold, especially the Lingos woman. If Isabelle were to discover he carried convicts she would probably have him forcefully evicted from the villa as he imagined she had a fair amount of influence over her father, especially when his wife was away.

* * *

Aboard the *Bromley* in the swelteringly hot hold the convicts were moaning and all except Barbara had removed their blouses in an effort to keep cool. Barbara's dress top hung about her waist as usual yet her lean body still glistened with sweat as of course did the others. While the ship was underway there was always a slight breeze coming down the hatch. At anchor the air was stagnant.

"We may be criminals but I don't think the captain should subject us to conditions like this," Emily Kilpatrick was saying while mopping her brow and chest on part of her skirt which wasn't soiled.

"What can we do?" Lydie Denner asked anybody.

"Bloody nothing, that's what!" Barbara Henshaw snapped. "If we raise any objections we'll be confined down here for two or three days at least, mark my words." She stood up to get a sip of water and cracked her head on a low beam. "Oh shit, this is a bloody hell on earth."

"Captain Stricker is not all bad, I'm sure," Catherine said from beside Ann who still lay on her stomach. "Perhaps if one of us requested a little more deck time he'd agree. I'd be willing to do the asking and take the consequences if he thinks I'm being too pushy."

"Don't take the risk, Catherine," Ann mumbled, "I know what that lash feels like and I wouldn't wish it on my worst enemy."

"Not even King George?" Sophie Hart asked.

Ann forced a smile. "Him, yes. Then I'd like to see a dog chew off that thing which dangles between his legs. If that had happened earlier in his life I'd not be here now."

They all laughed at Ann's wit and then looked up as they heard Albert Brooks asking what they found so funny.

"The little brat has been spying on us again," Emily whispered before telling the odious boy they needed more fresh water as their pail was empty.

"I'll get you some. Wait."

They were amazed the lad was going to do as asked. Only moments later a deluge of seawater came through the grille, drenching Emily and Lydie who were directly underneath. Albert laughed loudly. "Want more water, girls? There's plenty out there in the harbour."

"No thank you, Albert," Barbara replied.

Unbeknown to Albert the bosun had seen and heard the exchange but he said nothing while continuing to watch two seamen varnishing the deck rail as a trio buffed deck planks while another four men were caulking joints. Seamen had to be kept busy, even in port. Another pair had started to replace the rudder ropes as they had taken a beating during the Bay of Biscay crossing. Soon though all working parties knew it would be their turn to go ashore for a while, that was unless the skipper returned and ordered them to set sail again. They didn't know it but this was unlikely to happen as Captain Stricker was outlining his terms for returning Pimm to England with the coach master Alberto Novas on the consul's sunny terrace.

"I want the very best for my man, Alberto, and that includes good food and comfort. He still suffers piercing headaches and periods of dizziness, you know."

"He will get all you have asked for, Captain Stricker, including a nurse. It is my pleasure and honour to serve the British."

"That is good, Alberto. When can you be ready to leave?"

"By nine tomorrow morning if that is agreeable to you."

"It suits me fine. I will have Mister Pimm on the dock by eight thirty."

The two men stood up and shook hands. Both were pleased with the business conducted. Captain Stricker had ensured a comfortable return to London for Hector Pimm and Alberto Novas would make a tidy profit for as he had said in his broken English, "My company is not the cheapest in Portugal, Captain, but my service is first class all the way. I guarantee satisfaction and I think your esteemed consul will endorse that."

Lawrence Carlyle nodded his head. "It is a fact, Captain Stricker, the Novas coach line provide an excellent and speedy service. We use it frequently."

Isabelle Carlyle arrived on the terrace to announce supper was ready to be served just as Alberto was leaving. The meal would be roast beef in honour of Captain Stricker. Isabelle had changed into a formal, fully off-the-shoulder satin dress which emphasized her full figure to perfection. Lawrence had chosen to remain in his day clothes in deference to Captain Stricker who only had what he arrived in. Naturally he had no idea he was to be so well treated. Yet it was obvious the Carlyles enjoyed some fresh company, especially one who took pleasure in a quality port wine and had a good command of the language.

Many decanters of wine, both white and red, were set at the dinner table which a waiter poured as a cold cucumber soup was served by another.

"This soup, Algernon, sets the palate off perfectly for the beef to follow," Lawrence said, obviously proud of the service.

Actually the captain hated cucumbers because they gave him indigestion; however on this occasion he refrained from comment. And in actual fact the soup didn't taste too bad at all when washed down with the quality port.

The usual small talk ensued as the meal progressed such as: How was London before he sailed?

"Actually, Lawrence, the weather has been unusually hot this year, especially June and July."

"We enjoy such weather almost year round, Algernon, and believe me it can get monotonous, especially at Christmas. However to change the subject, we hear on the grapevine King George's mental health has improved thanks to a certain Doctor Willis. I do believe though there are still factions trying to oust the king and bring the Prince of Wales in as a regent. How do you see this situation?"

"From what I've heard the Prime Minister opposes any such moves and will do all in his power to see it doesn't happen. The young Mister Pitt and his senior staff run the country anyway. George is merely a figurehead whose main function is approving expenditure and granting titles."

"I have heard, Captain," Isabelle added, "that in his earlier days the king dallied and frolicked with many young women and in fact made some of them pregnant. Have you heard that?"

"I'm afraid I know nothing of these stories, Isabelle."

He knew of course it was true, as one of the king's offspring was in the convict hold of the *Bromley* at this very moment. He was saved further discussion on the subject when the waiter offered him more beef. Two thick, generous slices were served as his wine glass was being refilled yet again. The food wasn't this good on the *Bromley* and for once he was drinking rather more than he did aboard ship. It wasn't good to let the crew see a drunken captain as they may take advantage when a situation arose where they felt entitled to something which the master had refused. Severe rationing was one example or holding back on their rum allocation. Many a mutiny had arisen because of these factors.

Finally the three of them were fully satisfied and Lawrence suggested he and Algernon retire to the lounge for a brandy and a cigar which had been shipped specially from an island named Cuba. A refusal was out of the question.

"So you enjoy life at sea, do you, Algernon?" Lawrence asked once they were seated, holding large brandy snifters and puffing on long thick cigars.

"It is as Isabelle said earlier, Lawrence, the sea opens up the world as no other method can, that is of course until we learn to fly."

"Ah, I fear man will never do that, he's too heavy. Why look at me, almost fourteen stone, a weight my doctor gives me hell about when I get a check-up. I do enjoy life though, as I do my position of course and one day there may be an accolade for me, assuming of course King George doesn't go daft again and has to be locked up in the Tower."

"I'll drink to that, Lawrence, the knighthood I mean."

Glasses were raised and toasts said.

"When will you arrive in Australia?" Lawrence asked next.

"All being well late February next year, perhaps early March, it all depends on the winds and seas. We were due to replenish our supplies in Tenerife but with Pimm's condition I thought it better we called in here. He will stand a much better chance of recovery by returning home."

"You fear for the man's life then?"

"Yes, a little. My doctor also has his concerns, you see we know so little about the inside of a person's head. I know some men who can take any amount of blows to the skull and have no effects, while others can be laid out by a simple tap. The head is one of life's great mysteries, at least it is to me."

"Many others share your views, Algernon, and I'm one of them. Now drink up so we may have another before retiring. I know you have a busy day tomorrow. I shall ask a servant to give you an early call."

"Thank you, Lawrence, however it won't be necessary. A captain must have the ability to wake up at almost any hour of the day or night and if you want the truth I'll find it difficult sleeping tonight, it's always the same on my first night ashore. You see, a ship is always in motion even at anchor and there is no such thing as a steady bed although I prefer a hammock."

"I take your point, Algernon. The reverse is true for me."

The genial consul got up and poured two more very large measures. As he accepted his the captain already felt slightly dizzy.

It was over an hour later when the pair agreed to retire for the night. Algernon was surprised when he entered the guest bedroom to see a nightshirt had been laid out for him. He peered out of the window which overlooked the harbour below and could see the *Bromley* sitting in the glass-like water which carried the moon's reflection. He thought here was peace and tranquillity yet on the ship he knew Ann Lingos would still be tormented by her badly bruised back. He wished he could do something for her but she was a registered convict and he had a position to uphold.

Once in bed he relaxed back under the dim but steady glow of an oil lamp and considered which life was the better. His at sea or the consul's? Lawrence Carlyle's life had a constant while his own did not. Almost every minute of the day was different at sea. He was just about to extinguish the lamp when the door slowly opened to reveal the silhouette of Isabelle standing in it.

"I thought you may enjoy some company, Captain. If I'm not welcome please say so."

"No, please come in, Isabelle."

She wore what appeared to be a very flimsy turquoise nightdress of a flowing material, probably eastern in origin. Captain Stricker's reaction was most natural for a healthy man who had been deprived of female company since the night before he sailed. To him Isabelle could have been a dream although it was plainly obvious she was pure flesh and blood.

She peeled the bed sheet back before slipping the nightdress off her shoulders so it floated rather than fell to the floor. Her body was a golden brown as she got on the bed beside him. Her full ruby lips found his as she ran a delicate hand down his body to probe under the nightshirt where it located what she expected.

"It seems you are very well prepared, Captain. Well, so am I. Please reduce yourself to a similar state as myself then do your duty."

As he drew the nightshirt off she rolled on her back and parted her long legs widely as he came over the flawless body. There was no need for him to move, she did all the work and in moments they had both attained ecstatic conclusions. She throbbed. He throbbed.

Following another lingering open-mouthed kiss, she said, "I thank you, Captain Stricker, you are certainly a man of men. I believe they say ships pass in the night, well, I'm very glad yours tarried for a while. Thank you again. Now I must go."

She gave him one more kiss, got off the bed, slipped her nightdress back on and left without a further word. It was an interlude he had never anticipated but one to be remembered for a long time as he sailed on towards Australia, and nobody aboard the *Bromley* would ever know. He did wonder though how many men she entertained in this fashion and did her father know? Perhaps he did but in all things he was diplomatic.

* * *

In the steaming-hot hold Catherine was once again replacing the cloth on Ann's back. It did look slightly better and tomorrow if they were allowed up on deck she would insist Ann exercised a little. With the cloth in place Catherine lay beside her and kissed the exposed cheek.

"Thank you, Catherine, for acting like a mother. You are the kindest person I have known except for my own mother. Now she's gone so there is just you and me. I love you."

"And I love you, Ann. In whatever time we still have together let us forge memories, ones of love not cruelty and hate. Now try to sleep and remember I'm beside you."

Ann's eyes closed and Catherine began to cry. Life is so cruel, she thought. I have found true love and it could be too late. I have never accepted the existence of God but if there is one I beg now that we are permitted to have a longer and happier life than the one we face.

As her own eyes closed, up on deck a bell sounded to change the watch.

* * *

Captain Stricker was being rowed out to the *Bromley* by ten the following morning. He was a little behind schedule, having lingered over breakfast with the Carlyles. Following that he was driven back to the harbour to settle the fees and provisioning costs. It pleased him though to see his new first mate had the sense to take on board plenty of fruit in addition to more rabbits and laying chickens. Sheep though were not available. He had also been introduced to Catriona Vigo who was to be Hector Pimm's nurse for the return journey to London. The coach driver Enrico Douro had introduced himself with a polite bow followed by a handshake. Both seemed able and efficient.

Once aboard Captain Stricker was welcomed by the bosun and new first mate. He was informed the replacement rudder ropes were finished and repairs to sails should be complete by noon. His two senior men were thanked and told they should prepare the ship for sailing at three. He then went to Hector Pimm's cabin where he found the man sipping brandy while Doctor Mountjoy applied a fresh bandage around his head. His face was still very ashen and both hands trembled visibly.

Perhaps these are signs of things to come, the captain thought although he really had no idea. The head was perhaps the most important part of a person's anatomy and yet so little was known about it. Even the King of England had suffered delusions of the mind, but he had been cured, or so it was said.

Hector's travel arrangements were explained and that he could expect a comfortable journey back to London under the care of a nurse who would travel with him. There would also be an armed guard as insurance against bandits. Financially everything had been arranged with the consul. Pimm was handed the captain's sealed report which he was to deliver to company headquarters once he arrived. If he wasn't in a fit state to do so he must get the nurse or the coach driver to do it, they had been paid enough.

"Is it a favourable report, Captain?" Pimm asked.

"It relates events exactly as they happened, Hector, nothing more, nothing less. It will be up to the company managing director what action he chooses to take. You may get another ship or you may not. In any event I wish you luck and in all honesty I wish this incident had never occurred. I was forced to discipline a girl who is heading for further punishment. However these things are now in the past. Now I must leave to supervise preparing the ship to sail, we will not speak again. Goodbye."

Hands were not shaken and the captain departed.

"He's too soft and compassionate to command a ship, Rodney," Pimm said to the doctor once the cabin door had closed.

"He does his duty as he sees fit, Hector, you can't blame him for that and I know for a fact this is a far happier ship than some I've sailed on. The lash might keep men in line but it rarely gains respect."

"There has to be discipline, Rodney, the lass asked for it. She was a vamp, a harlot fit only for spreading her legs for any man who had sufficient funds to pay. Many a time as she cleaned my cabin the skinny whore bent down, causing her blouse to gape so I may see the formation of her breasts. I as a normal healthy man reacted, and what did she do? Took a pencil to my ear. My only regret is leaving this ship knowing she still lives."

Doctor Mountjoy removed a pocket watch and consulted it. "It's time for you to go up top, Hector. I do hope you recover although I fear your hearing may never return. I did all I could."

"Yes, and I appreciate it. That I still live is an endorsement to your skill. Thank you."

He stood up rather unsteadily and asked that the deck lad be sent for to carry his personal effects. This was quickly done.

Albert picked up the two canvas bags, pulled a face and said, "Christ, sir, what have you got in here, cannonballs?"

"Show some respect, you little runt," Hector replied as a last rebuke aboard the *Bromley*.

Willing hands helped him into the bosun's chair to be lowered down to the waiting longboat and more hands helped him aboard and guided him to the stern seat. There were no waves of farewell, nobody was really sad to see him go, not even the passengers.

After inspecting the replaced rudder-control ropes, Captain Stricker used his telescope to look up the hill where he knew the consul's residence lay and wondered what Isabelle would be doing. Probably preening her body for another midnight visit to one of her father's guests. Like she had said, ships which pass in the night.

With a sigh he turned his attention to studying the harbour opening through which his ship would shortly pass.

* * *

In the convict hold they could hear the distinct sounds of pulley blocks and tackle as sails were being hoisted.

"They're getting ready to sail again," Sophie Hart said from atop the ladder which she had scaled to get a breath of air and a look through the grille at the sails being hoisted by swarthy men.

"Let's hope the buggers give us some deck time and perhaps let us have a good rinse down," Barbara Henshaw added. "My crotch is sore from sweating."

Lydie Denner laughed. "Are you sure you haven't been fingering yourself in private, Barbara?"

"So what if I have. Up there are more than twenty men and I'm denied every single one."

"I'm sure you'll get more men than you want when we arrive at Botany Bay."

"That may be so but I'll put up one hell of a fight first."

"I wouldn't," Emily said, "they'll only make it worse and I don't imagine anybody would care if somebody killed you."

"We all may be better off dead," Lydie mumbled as she licked her parched lips while scratching her midriff.

Catherine smiled at this good-natured bantering as she continued to stroke Ann's hair which had grown noticeably since they sailed. In fact everybody's had and she wondered if they would get it cut again. Short hair certainly was better in this hot weather and she knew from hearing sailors talking it would only get hotter. Then hair became forgotten when Ann's hand came up in search of her lover's.

"I think by tomorrow I may be able to tolerate lying on my back, then we can kiss properly again."

Catherine kissed the sweaty palm and smiled.

* * *

"Haul in the anchor!" shouted the First Mate Felix Bloom.

The *Bromley* once again sprang to life as the orders were executed with efficiency. The breeze was slack although the vast expanse of canvas soon filled and the ship gradually began to move towards the open sea once again. Captain

Stricker waved to Captain Jarez Beira who he could see standing on the dock. For him and the passengers it had been a pleasant twenty-four-hour layover.

Alice Edwards and Clare Hamlyn had purchased new dresses and a parasol each. The four would-be sheep farmers had bought caps and shirts, they had also supped a good quantity of a locally brewed ale. Silas Martin and Bob Jones, the Welshman, had bought pipes which they now smoked as the *Bromley* headed for the harbour opening.

Down in the convict hold everybody was glad air had started to circulate and each hoped Captain Stricker would permit them up on deck once they were on the open sea again. And despite the fact that as every hour elapsed they were closer to Botany Bay being up on deck was quite pleasant, especially gazing at the foreign lands they passed.

Once clear of the harbour bar Felix Bloom ordered full sail as the ship was brought about to a south by south-westerly heading which would eventually take them past the islands of Madeira and later the Canaries, then on round the bulge of West Africa. Following that there would be the ceremonies as they crossed the equator. He wondered if the captain would involve the convicts. Once that imaginary line had been crossed it would be due south to the Cape of Good Hope by which time they would have been at sea for ninety days. Unknown to the convicts they would be halfway to their final destination.

Captain Stricker scanned the horizon with his telescope before checking the clock and compass. He was satisfied with their heading and was just about to retire to his cabin when the bosun asked him if he could have a private word.

"If it's about the convicts being confined to their hold for the past two days, Wilf, I'm well aware of it and will be issuing orders shortly."

"No, sir, it's not that, another matter not relating to the convicts. I've informed the first mate and he suggested I talk to you."

"Then let's go to my cabin."

Once seated Wilf related what he'd seen while the captain was ashore.

"One of the convicts, sir, I don't know which one, told Albert, the deck lad, they needed more fresh water down in the hold as they'd drunk all in the pail because of the heat. I saw Albert get a large pail, lower it over the side and fill it. Then he went to the hatch grille, poured the contents over whoever stood below and laughed. Now I appreciate they're convicts, sir, and have done wrong but to my way of thinking they don't deserve treatment like that, especially from the lowest-ranking person on the ship. At the time I didn't take any action, thinking you should be informed first."

"You did the right thing, Wilf, and I agree the lad was completely out of place. I'm also aware this is not the first incident. If memory serves me, we took him on at the request of his father who's a first mate himself on a ship sailing regularly to the Americas. The father was keen to have his son work his way through the ranks but didn't want him on his own ship for obvious reasons. So do you think Albert needs taking down a peg or two?"

"Yes, sir, I do. For his own benefit as well. We both know it's not good developing a cocky attitude at such an early age."

"I agree, Wilf. Refresh my memory, how old is the lad?"

"Sixteen, nearly seventeen I believe."

"Then seventeen strokes across the backside with the knotted rope should bring him down to earth. Arrange it for tomorrow when the convicts are on deck. It's too late today. Thank you for bringing this to my attention, Wilf, you did the right thing. And while we're about it, I'm going to allow the convicts on deck for six hours tomorrow. They all deserve some fresh air. How's the Lingos girl?"

"Seems she's talking, sir, and in a better frame of mind. We have to assume she's over the worst."

"That's good. I'll get Doctor Mountjoy to take a look at her back in the morning. Now why don't we enjoy a goblet of port, some good stuff the British consul gave me."

"I'd enjoy that, sir. Thank you."

Captain Stricker poured while asking the bosun if he agreed with dropping Hector Pimm off.

"Yes, sir, I do. The man carried a very mean streak for those below his own station. Oh, I realise there have to be ones giving orders just as there have to be people taking them. Every ship needs a captain as much as it needs a bosun. You are my superior and I accept that just as I hope you respect the role I play."

"I do indeed, Wilf. Whether on land or sea it all boils down to teamwork. Now if you'll excuse me, I have to bring my log up to date and there's much to enter."

Wilf finished his drink and left feeling better for the way things had gone.

* * *

"God, I wish that creaking would stop," Barbara Henshaw said to nobody in particular.

She was referring to the constant grating sounds the hull timbers made as the ship heaved due to tidal motions. Of course Barbara was not to know these sounds indicated the flexibility of the ship's structural construction which prevented it breaking apart, especially in very heavy seas. Barbara wasn't the first to have complained. They all had at one time or another, especially when they were trying to sleep. Their enforced idleness, the discomfort, the stench plus a variety of noises had frayed their nerves to the point where the slightest occurrence caused tempers to rise. Only thoughts of what punishments would be levied actually stopped them coming to blows.

"It's no bloody wonder mutinies occur on ships," Emily had said an hour ago to which there was general agreement.

"It also looks like we're not going to be allowed up on deck again today," Lydie Denner added as she drew her legs up to rest her chin on them.

"It has been a little better since we got underway though," Emily replied while mopping her brow on one of the blankets. I can't imagine what it'll be like when we're in the Indian Ocean."

"It'll be bloody murder, believe me," Barbara told them.

"At this moment I wouldn't mind just getting fed," Sophie said. "That porridge we got this morning seemed like it was yesterday's and I'm sure that boiled egg was bad."

"The captain's back on board now so we'll get fed, I just feel it," Catherine replied while continuing to fan Ann's face with part of a blanket. Of them all Catherine's frame of mind was the happiest because some colour had returned to Ann's cheeks and her lip swellings had gone down.

Then from above they all heard the cocky voice of Albert telling them to watch out as he was lowering the food box. They watched it descend and as usual it was dropped the final few inches, spilling much of the soup bowl's contents. Albert laughed as he said, "Eat well, bitches."

Emily seethed as usual and once again threatened to kill the little sod.

"Once we get up on deck again, if ever, we should report this to the bosun or first mate," Sophie said as she handed the bowls around. "We may be criminals but the shipping line is getting paid to take us to Australia so we shouldn't have to suffer a little prick like him. If you'll all back me up I'll tell somebody, believe me." She looked around in the gloom and asked if they all agreed.

They did. Even Ann Lingos held her hand up before wiping a finger across Catherine's dry lips. Catherine responded by doing the same and they both sensed that urge rising where they needed the closeness of each other again.

"Tomorrow," Ann whispered.

* * * * *

CHAPTER 13

I T WAS BOWLS OF THIN GRUEL AGAIN for breakfast along with hot cocoa and thick slices of dry bread. For once the box landed softly on the deck floor. Then instead of a snide remark by Albert they heard Felix Bloom's booming voice.

"Captain Stricker has instructed me to tell you girls that once your cleaning duties are finished for today you'll all be permitted to stay up on deck for six hours. A tarpaulin will be strung across your portion of the deck so you may wash yourselves and your clothes in privacy. Unfortunately it will be salt water but it's better than nothing. All I can say is don't abuse this privilege."

"We won't, and thank you!" Sophie shouted up. "What about Ann Lingos, Mister Bloom? She's still not fit enough to perform any sort of work."

"She's excused. One of you will have to do my cabin. I don't care who."

"I'll do it," Lydie volunteered after the first mate had gone. "The captain's cabin can't be too bad as I gave it a good going over before we docked in Lisbon and we know he spent the night ashore."

In highly elated moods they set about eating their food and drinking the cocoa after dipping their bread in it. They all began to feel slightly human again, realising they were not entirely forgotten.

When they were finished Albert removed the hatch grille.

After Catherine had helped Ann on with her blouse she and Lydie assisted her to the ladder's base. Emily had already gone up to help their comrade climb out of the hatch. Still in anguish Catherine watched her lover take each rung carefully and was ready in case she faltered. She didn't but was quite breathless when stepping on the deck with her eyes watering. Emily helped her to the port rail where she sat on a large coil of rope.

Slowly the others emerged and left to perform their duties under the watchful eye of the bosun. Many of the crew simply stood and watched with some no doubt having thoughts of what they'd like to do to any one of them. Yet they had all been warned not to touch. Captain Stricker might have control over their actions but he couldn't repress their thoughts.

Ann sat on the rope, holding on to the rail and looking between the supports at the distant coastline. Of course she hadn't any idea her view was the Strait of Gibraltar which gave entrance to the Mediterranean Sea, at the eastern end of which was biblical country. Then her keen gaze was diverted to a group of dolphins which swam beside the ship, occasionally leaping out of the water playfully.

They're free while I'm not, she thought as her back began to twitch having suddenly become exposed to the hot sun. She couldn't see it but her blouse was becoming bloodstained where some of the weals had cracked open. She turned away from looking at the sea and saw Doctor Mountjoy approaching.

"How do you feel this morning, my dear?"

"My back is beginning to hurt. I think it's the sun."

"Yes, it may be. Come with me to my cabin, I'll smear some ointment on a new cloth."

She walked gingerly, grimacing slightly at almost every step. Sailors doing various duties felt sorry for her. For most she was the first woman they had ever seen flogged. Of course it was her own fault but if Captain Stricker had ordered the full amount of strokes she wouldn't be walking the deck now. Her grave would have been the Atlantic Ocean, sewn inside a canvas sheet.

In the doctor's cabin Emily Kilpatrick was just finishing her dusting. She was asked to carefully remove Ann's blouse while Doctor Mountjoy applied some ointment to a cloth. Emily cringed again at seeing the scars as Ann lay on the table. She winced as the cold cloth was laid over her back then in some discomfort she sat up so the cloth could be tied. After taking a few deep breaths she admitted feeling slightly better. Doctor Mountjoy advised against exposing her back to the sun.

Emily took her hand and once on the aft deck they were slowly escorted by a bearded seaman to the area assigned to the convicts, ahead of the forward mast. As the privacy tarpaulin had yet to be hung in place all the other convicts either walked slowly around their portion of deck or leaned on the rail, looking at the dolphins or the seagulls which seemed to be constant companions of ships at sea. Lydie actually wondered if their caws meant anything to them and if they did, what were they saying? She also wondered if they knew these women with their ankles clad in iron bands were wrongdoers and on their way to a prison colony which according to Captain Stricker lay very far to the east. She licked her salty lips and smiled at Catherine and Ann as they walked to an area of deck shielded from the sun by the foresails. Ann sat on another coil of rope and clasped both hands around her knees.

Suddenly everybody heard Albert screaming at the top of his voice. "I'll promise not to do it again, sir, on my honour! I'm sorry!"

All the convicts smiled when they saw the obnoxious deck lad being dragged kicking and screaming to the port deck rail. His upper body was bent over it before his arms were pulled out to either side and tied securely.

Captain Stricker and First Mate Bloom appeared up on the quarterdeck along with the bosun who held a two-foot length of knotted rope.

Captain Stricker spoke. "Albert Brooks, you have been observed by certain crew members showing undue disrespect to the convicts. It is not your place to make their situation any worse than it is, I'm the only person with authority to do that should it become necessary. Therefore you are to be punished. You will be spared the lash but I have instructed the bosun to lay seventeen strokes with the knotted rope. Please proceed, Mister Malone."

"No! please, sir!" Albert screamed again as he saw the bosun coming down the steps, drawing the rope through his left hand.

"I'm going to enjoy this," Emily said. "Perhaps now the little brat will treat us like human beings, at the very least we are still that."

"I hope the bosun lays it on hard," Barbara Henshaw said, rubbing her hands together in glee.

By now the bosun had removed his jacket, rolled up his sleeves, drawn the rope back and brought it swiftly across his body so it landed squarely across Albert's bottom. Another was quickly laid.

Squeals similar to those of a pig having its throat cut filled the morning air as the lad kicked, struggled and sobbed with each subsequent stroke. "Stop it please, sir! I'm truly sorry, honest... Aaaaah!"

"Take it like a man, lad," the sweating bosun said as another vicious stroke landed.

Blood could now be seen seeping through the coarse cloth of Albert's trousers. Catherine noticed Ann was not watching but the rest relished seeing Albert suffering. Since sailing he had made their miserable lives even more so by his taunting and deliberate unnecessary acts of sheer spite.

Finally it was over and Albert released. He fell to his knees, sobbing and holding his bottom. Everybody hoped he'd learned his lesson and all the convicts secretly admired Captain Stricker for the action he'd taken. There were many captains who would have allowed crew members to do whatever they wished with female convicts, knowing they had nobody to complain to. Captain Stricker was at least human. Even Ann Lingos couldn't blame him for having her flogged, she had brought that on herself by assaulting the *Bromley*'s second most senior officer.

While the moaning lad crawled away four crewmen began rigging up the tarpaulin to give the convicts their privacy. Another two men filled pails of water from over the side and poured them into the wooden trough so the women could wash their sweaty bodies. Once the trough was full the sailors retired and all except Ann removed their blouses to begin soaping themselves. When their upper halves were clean most hoisted their skirts to wash their legs and the area between.

"It feels so nice to be a little cleaner," Lydie said. "Now I'm going to lie down and soak up some of this wonderful warm sun. It's never this hot in England."

"I've heard it's hotter still in Australia," Emily told nobody in particular as she lay down and stretched her arms above her head, remoulding both breasts to mere mounds. She sighed. "Ah, if only I could have a man on top of me now life would be ideal."

"Just try to imagine one," Sophie told her while shaking her short hair to rid it of water.

Catherine was the last to finish and suggested Ann remove her skirt so the accumulated blood could be washed off. The others agreed and Lydie got up to help. Emily volunteered to get some blankets.

One was given to Ann which she wrapped round her waist as Catherine washed the skirt numerous times so the water was blood red by the time she'd finished. Barbara laid the skirt out on the hot deck to dry while Catherine went to join her lover. They sat holding hands for many minutes before their lips came together softly despite Ann's still slightly thick lower lip.

"Oh, that feels so nice, Ann. Does your back feel better now?"

"Yes, since the doctor put the new cloth on. Tonight we shall kiss and make full love."

"Only if you feel up to it."

"I will."

Through half-closed eyes Lydie watched the pair, feeling slightly jealous they had at least got each other. Having never experienced the lips of another woman she had no concept if it felt any better than a man doing so. She did of course realise from the expressions on their faces it must be nice. This caused her to reflect upon her own life which had been harsh almost from birth. Then when she was old enough she ran away from home only to be exploited by men worse than her father. They made her work for that rich aristocratic bitch who had everything in life she hadn't, wealth, nice clothes, shoes which fitted properly and a beautiful home. She could well afford to lose those pieces of jewellery I took but instead issued instructions to have dogs set on me before her men dumped me down that well. Now Ann has Catherine Farrow while I have nothing. I think before we arrive in Australia I shall kill myself, in death I may find the peace which I have not had in life. Slowly her eyes closed and sleep came.

Down below decks Albert was still sobbing, lying face down in his hammock, hoping for sympathy but getting none. His shipmates knew he deserved the whipping. Never in his life had he experienced such pain and when he returned home his father would be told that Captain Stricker ordered the bosun to lay the rope on him. His fingers gripped the hammock strings as he fought shooting pains which darted through his body.

Alice Edwards and Clare Hamlyn were sitting on the poop deck, eating an orange each from one of the baskets which had been brought aboard while they were in Lisbon. Both were shading their delicate skins with the parasols they'd purchased. Alice looked at the canvas sheet up forward and asked Clare what she thought the convicts were doing behind it.

"Probably performing disgraceful acts upon themselves with their grubby fingers," Clare replied. "Low forms of life do things like that. However once in the penal colony they'll be worked so hard all they'll want to do is sleep when their day is over. And every day of their sentences will be exactly the same. Get up at a certain time, eat a meagre meal before being marched off to work for at least twelve hours. And once finished there will be guards wanting to fill them full of themselves."

"How do you know all this?" Alice asked.

"Hector Pimm told me one afternoon while we were playing cards in his cabin."

"Did he try anything on with you like he's supposed to have done with Ann Lingos?"

"As a matter of fact, yes. We stopped playing cards and, just between us, I did permit him to kiss me. He was a nice man. More may have developed at another time if that horrid girl hadn't attacked him."

Alice frowned. "Didn't you have a guilty conscience letting Pimm do that to you?"

"Yes, for a few moments but my husband was so very far away and I did yearn to feel a man against my body again. I'm only human, you know."

"Would you have eventually let Mister Pimm... well, you know... let him?"

"I may have. After all I'm worldly enough to think my husband will have taken a girl in my absence, it's natural. He may well have paid her but it's still being unfaithful."

"And what will happen if you find upon arrival he's fallen in love with somebody else?"

"I'll take him for every penny he's earned then make my own way. There's plenty of opportunity in Australia, you know, Alice. I'm sure a refined, very active English lady like myself will have no problems finding another man, especially after I've told him I know how to run a home with efficiency and can be very agreeable in bed. Is it not so with yourself?"

"Not quite. In truth I derive very little satisfaction from the sex act, in fact none at all. And would you believe it, Wilfred once tried to stick himself in my mouth. I was almost physically sick and we never came together for weeks. In fact we only did it once again, that was on the evening before he departed for Australia."

"Then why on earth are you joining him, Alice?"

"It's my duty, Clare, after all I am his wife."

"You know what he'll want the moment you're alone together, don't you?"

"Yes, I'm very much aware of that but I do intend to make every effort to enjoy it."

They were interrupted by Captain Stricker appearing on deck to ask if they would like to join him and Doctor Mountjoy for a game of whist at two this afternoon. They both agreed, knowing wine would be available plus it would pass a couple of hours at least.

"Don't you get bored with life at sea, Captain?" Alice asked.

"Sometimes, although there's always something to do. Navigating for one thing, helping Mister Pankhurst, the chef, with his food rationing is another. It's vital at sea to do these things on a daily basis, we cannot simply go to the market and purchase more if stocks run low. Sometimes though we may make an emergency call into a port to reprovision, especially if food has rotted due to extremely hot weather. And as you probably know we restocked our larder in Lisbon, that's why we have oranges which I see you've availed yourselves of. They are a good protection against scurvy. There are grapes as well, you know."

"Yes, we saw a tray of them being carried forward a few moments ago. Were they for the convicts?"

"Yes. We have to try and keep them fit."

"Why bother?" Clare Hamlyn said harshly. "Surely they are the dregs of society."

"What they are, madam, is no concern of mine. My job as I've told you before is to see they reach the penal colony in reasonable health. Now I will bid you both good day and look forward to our card game this afternoon."

They watched him walk towards the helmsman.

"He seemed upset you called the convicts dregs, Clare," Alice said in a whisper.

"Well, in my book they are. If you ask me he's got too much of a soft spot for them. I mean, can you imagine giving them deck privacy so they may flaunt their naked bodies? It would not surprise me at all to find them making love with each other. At home we had two servants who did that, until I caught them at it in their room that is. They were completely naked, you know."

"Good heavens, Clare, what did you do?"

"I had my husband Gordon give them a good thrashing with a riding crop before tossing them out on the street and it was pouring at the time. I wouldn't be at all surprised to discover one of the convicts is taken to the captain's cabin when darkness falls. He isn't married, you know."

"I didn't although it doesn't matter, does it? He's the captain and can do whatever he pleases. Now I think I've had sufficient sun for now and will return to our cabin. Are you coming?"

"Yes, I suppose so."

Lydie turned over to give her back an equal amount of exposure to the sun. Sophie had warned her not to overdo sunning herself as burns could easily occur.

"Who cares," Lydie replied, "I've nothing to look forward to, or my body for that matter. Now if I had a man things might be different."

"There's always hope for something, Lydie," Catherine told her. "I came aboard with nothing and found love with Ann. For the moment we are both content, aren't we, Ann?"

"Of course."

Barbara sat up. "I was once in a village where two like you were stripped naked, tied behind the sheriff's horse and dragged out of town."

"Oh, come on, girls," Sophie said, "our situation is bad enough as it is. Don't let's start fighting and arguing between ourselves or the captain may not let us on deck again and I for one would hate that to happen."

"And me," Emily added. "Just lay off them, Barbara, they harm nobody, let them be happy, for a while anyway." Then she took one or two grapes off the tray, put them in her mouth and sucked.

Both Catherine and Ann smiled, knowing despite everything they were among friends. And for them tonight could not come soon enough.

* * *

After warning the convicts he was about to enter and giving them time to make themselves somewhat presentable Albert moved part of their canvas privacy curtain to one side and passed through, carrying the tray on which their food was usually lowered into the hold. On it were pewter plates with slices of rabbit and boiled carrots on them. The tray was carefully set down before Albert straightened up and said, "Captain Stricker has instructed me to apologize to you for what I've said and done since you came aboard. I do so now and as you saw this morning I was punished very severely. I promise to be a nicer lad from now on."

They all smiled as he left.

"Well, bugger me, I never expected that," Barbara exclaimed. "The next thing we'll be getting asked is to dine with the captain."

Emily laughed as she helped herself to a plate of food. "There's a limit to everything, Barbara, and eating at the captain's table is not one of them."

"Yet it does show he's a man of compassion," Catherine said while handing Ann her plate.

Then except for the constant lapping of water against the hull and sails flapping silence prevailed as the convicts set about eating what they considered a feast up on deck. In actual fact all the passengers were eating on deck as the weather was unusually pleasant. This didn't deter Clare Hamlyn making a comment.

"It seems the non-paying convicts are being served exactly the same food as we are. When we finally arrive at Port Jackson I intend to lodge a complaint. Prisoners should only eat what we leave. That was how we fed our servants at home."

Charles Bower, one of the farmers, made comment. "You know, Mrs Hamlyn, I've never met anybody quite so callous as you. Those young women may be criminals but we have no idea what made them commit their crimes. Perhaps they were driven to it working for people like you."

Looking shocked Clare raised a hand to her brow. "Really, Mister Bower, those remarks were totally uncalled for. I have paid for my passage and as such expect preferential treatment. It's bad enough having to suffer the convicts' smells when they clean our cabin. I shall be obliged if you will refrain from conversing with me again."

"Ladies and gentlemen, can we stop this bickering and act like civilized human beings," Felix Bloom stated firmly as he passed his empty plate to a steward. "We still have a long way to go and I'm sure Captain Stricker will not tolerate much more. You, Mrs Hamlyn, have been a constant cause of friction since we set sail. You were made aware at the outset this vessel was to carry six female convicts. If you were averse you should not have bought passage. Am I making myself clear?"

"Yes, Mister Bloom, you are, very clear. However I still maintain we should receive superior treatment to the convicts."

"You are, madam. You have a comfortable, spacious cabin whereas the convicts have to tolerate an uncomfortable hold in which they can barely stand upright, added to which it is almost the lowest point of this ship and therefore is not always dry, and there are almost constant nauseating odours drifting up from the bilge. In addition they only have the deck to sleep on. If your situation is not up to what you expected I remind you our next port of call is Cape Town, if you wish to disembark there I'm sure Captain Stricker will grant approval. The choice is yours."

Clare stood up with her face beet red. "Well, thank you for your advice, Mister Bloom. I shall now return to my cabin and muse over what has been said today. Obviously my feelings are not those of the majority. However they still stand no matter how radical they may seem to you, sir. In London there are prisons for the types who are enjoying the open air and sunshine at this very moment." She glanced down at Alice Edwards who had not said a single word in these exchanges and asked if she was coming to the cabin.

"I think, Clare, you are well left alone for an hour or so. I shall remain on deck to enjoy the weather."

"So you forsake me as well, do you? Alright, it's no skin off my nose."

They all watched her stomp off, including some of the crew who had overheard most of the conversation and Fred Pankhurst, the chef, made comment to Felix Bloom in a whisper.

"It should be her bound for Botany Bay not those six lasses behind the canvas." He beckoned Albert over. "Go to the cool locker, lad, select six juicy oranges and take them to the convicts."

"Yes, sir, Mister Pankhurst."

Nobody was more surprised than Emily Kilpatrick when Albert shouted from the other side of the canvas he had an orange for each of them. As they'd all removed their blouses again Albert was asked to pass the fruit under the canvas. He did so.

"I wonder what brought this on?" Barbara asked anybody.

"We may never know although I'm not about to question it too deeply," Catherine replied. "It's obvious though the captain is on our side."

"And so he should be," Sophie said. "Except for Ann we were all driven to commit our crimes for one very good reason or another. Of course I realise there have to be punishments but during the trials or hearings judges should consider the facts more carefully and show a little more compassion than they actually do. If I'd been let off I would have started a campaign for the better and fairer treatment of criminals generally and women in particular."

"I'd have joined you," Emily told her.

In fact they all voiced agreement while eating their oranges. Emily was even going to save the peel for later.

"Nobody gave a thought for me," Ann said meekly. "All I asked for were my rights, and see where that got me. We commoners may as well not exist except in places like Botany Bay." She turned to Catherine and started to cry.

Catherine hugged her, feeling more sorry than ever for the girl's plight. She was innocent of any crime, except perhaps being born. She licked Ann's tears away and kissed her.

"Quell those tears, my love. Remember tonight we shall make love."

"We will, Catherine, we will."

The others smiled.

* * *

Captain Stricker had decided to extend the deck time for the convicts by an hour so it was almost dusk when they were ordered back to their dismal hold. Nevertheless they all felt rejuvenated by the warm sun plus the food and fruit. As an added bonus when they arrived below it smelled much fresher because their sweaty bodies had not been present for almost eight hours. The oil lamp had also been refilled. Even Albert was polite when helping them step on the ladder. Yet despite everything else with the restrictions of their leg irons and chains it left no doubts they were still convicts.

They all moved to their normal places which offered little privacy yet they had come to regard the space as their own with each thinking in their own mind theirs was slightly better. Of course the deck was just as hard in any place.

Sophie yawned. "You know all that sun has made me feel quite tired. I'm going to have a sleep."

Barbara and Emily agreed and lay down. Lydie Denner as usual leaned back against the rough hull timbers and closed her eyes but it wasn't to sleep. She continually kept going over in her head the reason for being here and how things could have been so different if she hadn't been caught taking some of her employer's jewels. By now she could have been living in an elegant apartment or house somewhere far away from London with a lover who like herself enjoyed riding horses. Now she rode the Atlantic waves soon to become the Southern Ocean and from there Australia and God knows what?

To ease the stress on her lover's back Catherine lay down first so Ann could come over her. They had both removed their blouses and came together, making total bodily contact. Kissing open mouthed, provided additional stimulation.

When Patrick O'Grady had done this to Catherine she was revolted by it, now it was sweetness itself as she worked her hands slowly up and down both sides of her lover's ribcage, taking care not to touch the still sore back.

Ann looked deeply into her lover's eyes.

"Oh, Catherine, when we make love like this I enter another world which is all pure, wonderful and magic. Now remain where you are and I will take you into this secret world so we may both enjoy its pleasures."

Lydie watched with some jealousy. They had what she had not, companionship. But Ann and Catherine were oblivious of Lydie watching for they were floating in a world where only they existed. They did not hear Barbara snoring or Emily humming a lullaby to herself, or see Sophie Hart lying with her eyes wide open, thinking of much happier times for there had been a few.

Nor did they see sailors up aloft in the rigging making repairs and occasionally looking down to the grilled hatch opening below which lay the six female convicts they were not permitted to touch. And yet up there on the spars they enjoyed an element of privacy not available in their own tightly cramped hold where they were frequently disturbed by those coming off duty or going on. Aloft and almost alone a man could not be blamed for performing an act upon himself with the image of a convict on his mind.

And as night swiftly fell the *Bromley* ploughed steadily southward towards the tip of Africa under a canopy of stars which were light years distant. The wind was favourable, the sails full, impelling the ship at almost maximum speed with one hold containing a cargo of mining equipment and another in which were six female convicts who had no future except one of confinement in a country very few people knew anything about.

* * * * *

CHAPTER 14

T HE CONVICTS AND PASSENGERS ALIKE WATCHED AS a group of seamen rigged a huge canvas between the fore and central masts before stretching it sideways and securing it to the ship's rails so it formed a large trough. Next many buckets were lowered over the side and returned filled with water to be poured into the trough. This filling continued for almost an hour until it contained about three feet of water.

"It has to be a bathing pool," Emily was saying as Felix Bloom appeared at the poop deck rail clad in just his trousers and a white shirt.

"I imagine you're all wondering what these preparations are about so I'll put your minds at rest. Captain Stricker estimates we shall be crossing the imaginary line of the equator at about two this afternoon. Some of you may know there is a ceremony of the mythical sea god Neptune as we cross this line. Captain Stricker will act as King Neptune with myself and the bosun acting as his court. It is maritime tradition that members of a ship's crew who have not crossed the line before were thrown over the side to see if they could keep up with the ship. Some drowned going to what is called Davy Jones' locker, a place where no seaman wishes to go. You may be glad to hear such tactics are not used on this vessel or any other in our line. As a compromise we ask that our male passengers permit members of the crew to submerge them for a few seconds in the pool we have created. I should also mention each participant will be given a beaker of ceremonial rum once they have undergone this ritual. Yes?" He had seen Emily Kilpatrick holding her hand up.

"Will us convicts be permitted to take a dip, sir?"

"I shall have to ask the captain, Kilpatrick. That is all for now. We shall be proceeding shortly."

They watched him leave.

"Well, I'm sure nobody is going to dump me in that foul water after men have been in it," Clare Hamlyn said and for once Alice Edwards agreed with her.

Catherine took Ann's hand. "I don't think you should go in, my dear, not with your back the way it is."

"I agree, but if you want to go ahead I shall enjoy watching. Can you swim?"

"No, of course not."

All the others said they wouldn't mind taking a dunking. In fact Sophie Hart thought she would enjoy it, especially if it was a crew member submerging her.

Ann smiled. "Are you sure it isn't just to get a tot of rum, Sophie?"

"Well, let's put it this way, Ann, I'll not refuse if one is offered."

They all laughed. At least this was something a little different.

* * *

As two o'clock approached a large wooden chair was set up in front of the central mast. Then Captain Stricker appeared wearing a long red dress, a wig which looked like seaweed and carrying a wooden trident. Most of the crew and male passengers whistled as he sat down. Clare Hamlyn scowled and tutted when a barrel of rum was set beside him by one of the crew. Then the bosun and first mate took their places on either side of King Neptune. They too wore rather shabby-looking dresses with their heads draped in seaweed. Fred Pankhurst appeared out of the galley carrying a tray on which were numerous enamel beakers.

King Neptune banged the end of his trident on the deck three times.

"By the ancient lore of the sea this vessel now passes between north and south. I ask our crew members to offer the bodies of those who have not passed this way before to submerge them into the mighty brine. Proceed, men."

All four male passengers must have agreed as they were taken by two crew men each and one by one thrown into the pool fully clothed. Everybody clapped, cheered and laughed. Half a dozen seamen jumped in and pushed their bodies under for a few seconds before releasing them. They all came up coughing, spluttering and laughing. Once they were out each man was given a full beaker of rum. As they sipped King Neptune instructed all crew members who had not crossed the line to be dunked and held submerged for half a minute. This included the lad Albert Brooks who was taken by two seamen and hurled into the water where two others pushed him under and held him there.

"I hope they drown the cheeky little bugger," Emily said so only the convicts could hear.

Albert came up coughing and spluttering and was pushed under again. Everybody laughed as he was finally released to be given his ration of rum.

Captain Stricker then asked if any of the convicts wished to be indoctrinated.

All but Ann stepped forward and they too were dumped without ceremony into the salty water. The crew let out cheers and waved their arms as the women were pushed under just as the men had been although they weren't held there long. Soaking wet they were assisted out and given their ration of rum. They all began to sip the fiery liquid never having expected this most welcome gift. Captain Stricker pointed his trident at Ann and Wilf Malone took a goblet over to her causing the crew to cheer again as she sipped the welcome liquid.

Throughout all these ceremonies Clare Hamlyn had watched wearing a stern expression at what she considered was a barbaric ritual.

King Neptune saw both women and asked them to come and kneel by his throne. Slowly they complied. The king placed a hand on each of their heads and asked them to close their eyes. They did, Mrs Hamlyn somewhat reluctantly. Neither woman was prepared for what came next.

The bosun and first mate handed King Neptune two large eggs which he smashed over each woman's head. "Welcome to the other side of the line," King Neptune said.

Everybody laughed, the convicts more so. The women really didn't know what to do until Alice Edwards joined in the laughter as she wiped the yolk off her forehead. Mrs Hamlyn stood up and stomped away to her cabin to the accompaniment of boos from most crew members. Of them all she was the only one not to have taken the event in the spirit in which it was intended.

The convicts all except Ann stood there dripping wet but knowing their clothing would quickly dry in the hot afternoon sun. They all drank their rum slowly, imagining it would probably be the last they would ever taste.

Now it seemed the thing to do as King Neptune and his court returned to their quarters was for all the crewmen to jump in the pool and splash merrily about. Emily and Sophie wished they could join them although they didn't dare ask. The captain had been very kind and generous as it was. They all sat down on the deck and enjoyed the view of both the West African coastline and of course the men still splashing about.

* * *

All in all it had been a day to remember as the convicts were finally told to return to their hold for the night. They were all tired from being out in the sun so long and the effects of the rum.

Nevertheless Catherine and Ann still had sufficient energy to kiss and cuddle. Actually the taste of their lips and soft caresses rejuvenated them. It would be a while yet before they laid their heads down.

"I suppose it's bloody Cape Town next," Barbara Henshaw said. "One of the crewmen told me this as I resurfaced, and the crafty bugger got a feel of my tits."

"So did the one who dunked me," Sophie added.

Gradually though they all lay down to sleep. It had been a good day. Perhaps the best yet although they knew the worst was yet to come.

* * * * *

CHAPTER 15

A T CAPE TOWN THEY WERE ANCHORED OUT in the bay for twenty days so necessary repairs to sails and recaulking of joints could be carried out. It was also a time to take on as many provisions as possible for the long haul to the western coast of Australia, a distance of over five thousand miles according to Wilf Malone.

Boxes and crates were stored on deck leaving little space to walk about. Even sacks containing non-perishable foodstuffs were piled on top of the hen coops.

As in Lisbon the convicts were not allowed ashore so in addition to gazing at the sights, especially the flat-topped mountain which Wilf told them was called Table Mountain, they helped the sailors revarnishing the decks and sewing the torn canvas. Sophie and Barbara also assisted Fred Pankhurst in the galley, storing food wherever space could be found. They also heard snippets of what the passengers and some of the crew had to say about the South African colony.

They had been greeted with great civility and were treated by the locals like royalty. Of course an English ship was most welcome to expatriates as with it came news of home and the outside world generally. Surprisingly many asked after the health of King George. Most knew he was supposed to have been cured, nevertheless many expected a relapse. Why, it was difficult to know. Obviously there were many staunch supporters of the king although many were opposed to him and were upset about church tithes which increased each year.

Emily had overheard two crewmen talking about the many Dutch people who lived in the colony, some it seemed were cruel taskmasters to the natives by driving them like slaves. On the other hand many seamen returning to the ship talked about the local girls who were willing to give freely of themselves, hoping a marriage may result so they could be taken to that land of plenty they called England. For many of the girls all they would get for their generosity was a child in the belly which unfortunately for them wouldn't be discovered until the *Bromley* had sailed again, a fact the sailors were well aware of.

"Just another place we haven't seen except from the deck rail," Emily had said one day while trying to breathe in the stifling heat.

One minor diversion for the convicts had been the cutting of their toe- and fingernails by Doctor Mountjoy. Unfortunately this was accompanied by the bosun cropping their hair again although he did leave it longer than the cutter in London. Despite the fact it was Wilf Malone who had flogged Ann they all liked him as a person and of all aboard he was by far the most friendly. Although he never said it openly it was fairly obvious he carried a genuine pity for them. Plus he always made sure they had water to drink and seawater to wash in.

One night Emily had claimed Wilf was the sort of man she could have married under normal circumstances. She also had a crude way of putting things.

"I suppose though the nearest I'll come to Wilf is when I perform an act on myself with the image of him in mind. Still, for a few moments I'm in a state of bliss. Then when I open my eyes all I see is you bloody lot and the nightmare of my future returns. Still we've a long way to go yet and God may hand us a miracle."

"God has forsaken us, Emily," Barbara told her. "We're well and truly on our own."

Catherine smiled up at Ann but didn't say anything. As far as she was concerned Ann was her idol.

* * *

Once they departed Cape Town the weather had started to get chilly from winds blowing up from Antarctica but as planned Captain Stricker sailed the *Bromley* further north into the Indian Ocean so they headed almost directly east towards the massive island of Australia and the inlet to the Swan River where the four prospective sheep farmers would be dropped off. They had encountered huge swells but slightly warmer temperatures. However by now all the convicts had become acclimatized and took the rolling and pitching in their stride. Even Catherine and Ann had managed to adapt to the changing angles of the deck as they made love.

One event brought both pleasure and sadness. This was when Captain Stricker announced there was a ship approaching from the opposite direction and when they passed everybody should wave and shout greetings. As it neared it became obvious the vessel was British because it flew the Union Jack. They passed near enough to see its name: *Plymouth*. Sailors lined the deck and up aloft waved their caps, handkerchiefs or just their arms. These actions brought lumps to the convicts' throats when they realised in a couple of months or so the ship would be docking in an English port and those sailors would be home to see wives or girlfriends again and be drinking a few tankards of strong, dark ale.

"Lucky buggers," Barbara said, "wish I was aboard her rather than this flea-ridden hulk. For them freedom, for us captivity."

"Oh, do shut up, you miserable sod," Emily told her. "Just for once can't you smile and at least try to be happy?"

"No, I bloody well can't. In fact I'm going below as I can't stand the sight of seeing other people heading for what I used to call home while I have no future except one of utter misery."

The others watched her leave sobbing as they continued to wave. Catherine put an arm around Ann's waist and whispered, "At least we have each other."

"Yes, and tonight we can make love. Barbara doesn't have that. Now let us get a drink of water."

As they walked to the pail one or two sailors looked at them in sadness, having guessed they were lovers. They also saw Captain Stricker taking one last look at the *Plymouth* through his telescope before going below to enter the event in his log.

* * * * *

CHAPTER 16

W HEN THE *BROMLEY* WAS ABOUT TWENTY DAYS out from the western coast of Australia they ran into a violent storm and all the sails except those on the bowsprit had to be hauled in to prevent them being torn to shreds. One topsail man was lost when he fell off a high horizontal spar to plunge into the surging sea and Davy Jones' locker, from which there was no return.

Unfortunately the storm and high seas persisted for five more days. It became so intense the convicts had to remain in their hold for safety reasons. They were to hear later there had been a spectacular water spout which of course went unseen by them as they were in the hold being swamped with water as it surged over the decks and down the hatch. Once again it was an unnerving time for all aboard.

When the tempest finally abated Captain Stricker held a deck service for the dead man and those convicts who wished were invited to attend. They all elected to in deference to the captain and the fact it brought them out in the fresh air again. During the ceremony they came closer to the passengers than at any time during the voyage. They all noticed Clare Hamlyn sneering down her nose at them but at least Alice Edwards smiled and the four farmers winked.

In his words of compliment to the dead seaman Captain Stricker said such storms were commonplace in these waters and many good men had perished in them. He also warned they could run into others before sailing into Port Jackson. Clare Hamlyn asked a question in her usual abrupt manner.

"How many more days before we reach our destination, Captain? because I am becoming fed up with life aboard this ship."

"In about eighteen days, Mrs Hamlyn, we shall be dropping our four male passengers off and from there I anticipate another forty-two or -three days to Port Jackson. I leave you to do the addition."

Just by his delivery it was obvious he'd had enough of this woman who had complained almost from the moment they sailed. In fact her numerous gripes had become almost a ritual. It was too hot. The food wasn't cooked sufficiently or was overdone. The water was tasting fouler by the day. Salt water washing was affecting her sensitive skin. Her bunk was becoming harder every time she slept in it. Couldn't somebody do something about the stench emerging from the convict hold? In fact crewmen had started making bets on what her next objection would be.

It took all Captain Stricker's willpower to restrain his temper and he certainly couldn't understand why anybody would want to marry such a woman who obviously had some attributes which were not apparent to him. He did know that if such an attitude was maintained in Port Jackson she would be shunned by almost everybody. Of all things he knew Australians were averse to snobs. Those attitudes were better suited to England where class distinction was high on the social agenda especially in London and the larger cities.

By now though the convicts were also getting fed up with their enforced conditions although they realised Captain Stricker was doing his best for them. Most had developed sores of one form or another, either from the effects of the ankle manacles abrading their skin, the burning sun or the lice which now infected their hair and the hold in general. It seemed they had become immune to the daily ration of a lime. Barbara Henshaw had developed a bad boil on her bottom which had to be lanced by Doctor Mountjoy. Her screams as he did so were heard all over the ship. Happily an hour later she was singing his praises because the relief was wonderful. As she put it, "After his knife released all the pus it felt almost equal to the thrill of attaining a sexual completion with a man, although not quite."

Ann Lingos's back was still giving her minor problems. These usually after she woke up to find stiffness had developed at the base of her spine. Catherine massaged the area and within fifteen minutes the aches were usually gone. To Catherine it was a chore of love because following it they usually kissed until breakfast was delivered by Albert, who had now become quite polite. Even so Emily still looked upon him as a little snot who needed a good kick in the balls.

And while they were on deck they all noticed how drawn and tired-looking the crew had become. It was now almost seven months since the *Bromley* had departed London. Catherine imagined some crewmen at least must have had families back at home and were missing them. She also realised the men faced at least another nine months to a year before sailing up the Thames again. Still she and Ann would have preferred that to where they were headed and as each day elapsed they were so many more miles nearer to Botany Bay. In fact with deference to the convicts' feelings Captain Stricker had stopped announcing his estimated daily mileage or date of arrival.

Now as Catherine and Ann made love time factors were never discussed. They simply basked in the beauty of the moment. They were not ideal moments in every respect although they still had each other and that counted for a lot. They might get separated at Botany Bay but for a while at least they would have memories to fall back on.

So a solitary ship named *Bromley* sailed on with six passengers looking forward to stepping ashore so they may start their new lives. Four robust men hoping to make their fortunes from sheep on the west coast. Two married women anxious to be once again reunited with their loved ones. As for the six female convicts they had no future to look forward to except hardship and possible cruelty by people appointed to ensure their sentences were properly served and that they never stepped out of line. If they did the whipping frame awaited.

* * * * *

PART THREE

MIRACLES

Chapter 17

THE *BROMLEY* WAS SAILING ALMOST DUE EAST again, heading for the Great Australian Bight as Captain Stricker had told them after the farmers had been dropped off in the estuary of the Swan River. He had also told them the river was discovered by the Dutch Captain Willem de Vlaming in 1697. At the river's mouth was a settlement which had yet to be officially named.

Unfortunately development of proper docking facilities was presently limited due to an extensive sandbar running across the estuary which restricted access up river to large ships, as a consequence all vessels had to anchor in the bay. From there longboats were used to ferry passengers and whatever cargo the ships carried to growing settlements up river. These longboats were also used to provision the ships for their continuing voyage to Port Jackson or their return journeys to Africa and Europe. It seemed the man in charge of everything ashore was one Hoorn Helderden but he was on a mission inland with his second in command Karl DeGrutt when Captain Stricker arrived at the shipping office to place his provisioning order. However the man left in charge, an educated aborigine, was most anxious to serve an English vessel as so few called in. He willingly provided all the food, kegs of beer, wine and rum at bargain prices. He also had his aboriginal staff clean out and fumigate the bilges plus replenishing the fresh-water tanks.

As they were anchored some distance offshore the convicts had been allowed up on deck but were told to remain fully dressed. Lumps in their throats had formed once again as they watched the four farmers disembark with their luggage. These men were entering this land in freedom and in all probability would make themselves a great deal of money, knowing there were dealers in England willing to buy all the wool they could provide. Each man had waved at the convicts fondly, aware their futures would not be so rosy.

For the convicts it was a time of worry, knowing their next stop would be Botany Bay. Lydie was scared stiff of being molested either by the guards or male convicts. Barbara and Emily didn't seem concerned that they may face similar fates. Sophie of course knew she faced solitary confinement when her working day was done so she expected to be treated roughly. Ann feared the scars across her back would automatically brand her as a troublemaker and she would be singled out for more cruel treatment or a more rigorous working routine. She also worried that the colony head might know of her past and take advantage of the fact in one way or another. Catherine was becoming increasingly worried about how she would be treated which may eventually lead to a total loss of sanity. She had witnessed Ann's punishment and knew she couldn't bear having cutting lashes landing across her own back, to say nothing of her body being violated by some brute of a man or even worse a number of men. Naturally she now regretted the actions taken against her stepfather and mother, a few minutes of revenge had resulted in this. Also of deep concern was the fact she and Ann could get separated, in which case neither would know what was happening to the other. Both were fully aware they couldn't tell whoever was in charge at the penal colony they were deeply in love, or even ask if it would be possible for them to remain together. All they knew of the colony were the snippets Lydie and Doctor Mountjoy had told them. One thing though was very certain, no consideration would be given to the fact they had all been driven to commit their crimes and in Ann's case no crime at all, except perhaps being born. At Botany Bay they would simply be registered criminals and were here to serve their sentences.

As the farmers were being dropped off both Alice Edwards and Clare Hamlyn had expressed a desire to go ashore just to say they had stepped foot on Australian soil. However Captain Stricker had advised against it once he had seen the settlement for himself. He told them this place was not like Lisbon or Cape Town where a semblance of civilization prevailed. He even allowed them to look at the desolate place through his telescope.

Apart from the spacious residences of Hoorn Helderden and his second in command the settlement was nothing more than a conglomeration of poorly constructed huts and thatched aborigine hovels. Only one other building could be classed as having any merit, that was a huge warehouse where incoming and outgoing goods and produce were stored. Most items were for shipment out or restocking the larders of ships such as the *Bromley*. The settlement population seemed to be composed mainly of roughnecks given to much drinking, smoking, chewing tobacco, spitting and gambling when there was no work for them. They also swore almost constantly. Their women were coarse, lacking any social graces, and they too spat even when they were taking a man up against a shed wall. There were no streets as such, just deeply rutted cart tracks fouled with cattle, horse and dog droppings. There were also warnings to beware of poisonous snakes.

In all their years at sea Captain Stricker and Felix Bloom had not seen anything quite so primitive, even on Caribbean islands. Australia was indeed a wild country and the two women could only hope things were slightly more refined in Port Jackson. Still it was a lesson for the pair that they would be entering an environment so very different from England. Yet it had been their choice to come out. Captain Stricker also wondered which would be tamed first, Clare Hamlyn or Australia? Perhaps he would never know as he only intended staying in Port Jackson long enough to discharge the convicts, make repairs, hopefully pick up a cargo, replenish their stores and head back home as fast as the winds could carry them.

* * *

Once they departed the Swan River estuary the convicts fully realised this was the final leg of their long voyage which filled them all with apprehension and foreboding. They had sailed into the New Year of 1797 and in about forty-two days the *Bromley* would be dropping them off at Botany Bay, their home for the full terms of their sentences which for Sophie and Ann meant till the day they took their final breath. Not happy prospects.

Captain Stricker had given the news it was a new year when he graciously allowed them on deck to have a tot of rum as the old year passed into the new. He shook each of their hands and for what it was worth wished them luck. Even Alice Edwards expressed her hope they would not find life too harsh. Naturally, and as expected, Clare Hamlyn remained aloof and only gave them a scowl.

For an hour the convicts were allowed to mingle with the crew although Felix Bloom had made it perfectly clear there was to be no hanky-panky. One of the seamen played lively tunes on a concertina so the convicts danced as best they could with their leg restraints hampering anything except basic foot movements. Catherine and Ann didn't participate which prompted Captain Stricker to ask why.

Ann claimed her back was still causing her some grief while Catherine explained she was experiencing that female monthly malady which gave her stomach pains. They were not pressed after that and the captain suspected once again the only company they desired was their own. When the hour expired all convicts were ordered back to their hold.

Once below and while Catherine and Ann embraced, the others graphically explained what it felt like to have a man pressed against their body again. Emily was sure Wilf Malone had experienced a natural reaction when she danced with him. Lydie said one sailor had fondled her breasts which returned wonderful memories. Barbara and Sophie were not exhilarated with male contact again and although the captain thought he was doing them a favour they considered the hour a waste of time as they were in no mood for celebration.

As Barbara said, "If it had been till morning that would have been different. One crewman I stumbled along with said he would have enjoyed lying with me as he hugged my body to his. I must admit it raised my juices although they rapidly subsided to nothing. I mean what was the point? With eagle-eyed Felix Bloom looking on we didn't dare go further."

Sophie added her bit. "The only real satisfaction I got was dancing with Fred Pankhurst who promised me a meat pie when I was next detailed to help in the galley. I said I'd hold him to it provided the meat wasn't maggot ridden. He told me if there were maggots Mrs Hamlyn would get them. We both laughed at that. I've spent happier New Years though, usually with a man on top of me. Oh, those happy days."

"Well, at least we have each other," Catherine whispered to Ann before their lips met. They intended to celebrate in their own way and like fine wine their exchanges of love and affection had matured to the point where the simplest of kisses sent tremors down their spines. In celebration of the new year they had decided to cast their worries and concerns aside and make love until the new dawn broke.

* * *

The Australian coastline was now plainly visible to those on deck as they sailed eastward parallel with it. In the hold tension was high and tempers were short. Lydie Denner had started to bite her fingernails, something she had never done in her life. Barbara and Emily actually came to blows when Barbara yelled at Ann and Catherine to stop kissing and licking each other like they were a pair of rampant cats. Sophie Hart managed to break up the fight before any of the ship's crew had become aware. Secretly suicide was being contemplated as an alternative to their unknown futures. Up to their arrival at the Swan River the penal colony had always been somewhere far to the east, well beyond the horizon. But as the *Bromley* dropped anchor a foreign-accented voice in a longboat had yelled out for all aboard to hear.

"Welcome to Australia, my friends. May you all find peace and prosperity in this great land which God has blessed. A land I'm now pleased to call home."

"Obviously the bastard doesn't know the ship carries convicts," Barbara shouted. "Well, for myself I'm seriously considering chucking myself over the side when we sail again. No bloody guard, black or white, is going to force himself into me, so there!"

"Drowning isn't an unpleasant way to go," Emily announced. "A sailor told me that as we sailed from Ireland. He said it was a quick, painless death. To me that sounds far better than a slow one, toiling under a hot sun all day on an empty belly."

"Oh, do stop it, Emily!" Sophie shouted. "It may not be all that bad. We thought this voyage was going to be a hell on earth but I think we'd all agree it didn't turn out so. To me at least it has been better than festering in Newgate Prison, suffering rat bites and guards who are nothing more than wild animals. You do what you want, Barbara. Me, I'm staying aboard, beside which I'm on a promise of a meat pie from Fred Pankhurst, don't forget."

Catherine looked at Ann's lovely face which glistened with sweat in the lamplight. "What do you think, my love?"

"I say we must enjoy whatever hours we have left together. I came aboard this ship having nothing. I shall leave it knowing I've spent the most wonderful months of my entire life in the company of a woman I truly love. Kiss me now."

Catherine kissed each of Ann's eyes in turn before they became tightly embraced.

They were still kissing and gently fondling when Barbara stood over them and said, "Make the most of this tranquillity, it won't last much longer."

Catherine looked up. "That was a very cruel thing to say, Barbara. Is there no compassion in you?"

"Not much, I admit, but I am sorry. It made me mad to see those four farmers going ashore free as the wind. I'm jealous, also scared."

"I think we're all somewhat scared, Barbara, although there's nothing we can do. Ann and I intend to stick it out to the end and make the most of our time together."

"Well spoken," Sophie said. "Barbara, leave them be or I'll shove a used rag in your mouth."

"Oh, very well. I'll try to get some sleep."

"I think we all should," Catherine suggested before kissing Ann again.

They made gentle love for another fifteen or so minutes before Ann's eyes began to droop. It had been a long day. Carefully Catherine moved away from Ann's body and drew a blanket over her before draping another around herself.

As her eyes closed thoughts of a sooty and foggy London came to mind. What I would give to be back there now, with Ann of course. No matter what our future may hold, the love we have experienced can never be taken away. We may get separated, perhaps never see each other again but we shall have memories and for those I shall be eternally grateful. We still have time together and must make the most of it. Let us look upon it as a beautiful calm before the storm. Ann and I will not be the first pair of lovers who have been parted and I know for a few days my own mother grieved over the loss of her husband. Then she found a new life, unfortunately it was with a sinful man who between them made my life even more intolerable than it was. I ended that suffering by injuring the man who abused me and was even able to knock my mother out. Unfortunately those who administered the law didn't consider it self-defence, in their eyes I was a wicked, ungrateful young woman who should be put away for a long time. That's why I'm on this ship now. Then an angel entered my life in the form of Ann Lingos, so perhaps there is a God after all? Perhaps God is Ann? I just do not know.

Tears ran down her flushed cheeks as sleep finally overcame her.

* * * * *

CHAPTER 18

ALBERT BROOKS HAD BEEN GIVEN THE RARE privilege of looking through Captain Stricker's telescope at a part of the southern Australian coastline named Brookes Inlet.

"Was it named after any of my ancestors, sir?" Albert asked, looking at the man he admired so much.

"I wouldn't have thought so, son, although you never know. I do know the area is very desolate with not more than a dozen people per hundred square miles, if that, and they will be black not white and quite probably savages. For your information, son, the entire population of Australia doesn't amount to the number of people who live in London. In fact the whole country is a wasteland although for hard workers like the farmers we dropped off it does offer good prospects. I'm told many areas are riddled with pockets of gold which is sought by prospectors from various countries. The problem is they have to dig tons of earth to get perhaps an ounce of the precious metal. However they strive on in the hopes of finding that one nugget which will give them financial security for the rest of their lives. Most will return to their country of origin with their new-found wealth and expect to become instant gentlemen. Of course money doesn't make gentlemen, only birthright and breeding does that. But as I said, Albert, the country is wild and not for the likes of you and me."

"It's no wonder they send convicts here, sir."

"Aye, lad. That was what our lawmakers thought. Those who complete their time at the penal colony are free to settle and work here if that's their desire. Some may even make a success of their lives although they'll always carry the brand of a criminal. Now give me back my telescope and be about your business."

"Yes, sir, but can I ask one further question?"

"Of course."

"Will you really tell my father about how badly I treated the convicts and tasted the knotted rope for doing so?"

"I'll consider that during our return journey. Now get yourself up top and help Mister Vicosa repair that sail which was torn yesterday."

"Yes, sir, and thank you, sir."

Captain Stricker smiled. The lad had been far less cocky since his painful lesson. He looked at the barren landscape through his telescope for a few minutes before a puzzled expression came over his face. Suddenly he didn't like the feel of the weather. The wind had become very slack and the sea was as calm as a millpond. Only once before had he experienced something similar, a doldrum in an area where there shouldn't be one. Then not an hour later they were in one of the fiercest typhoons he had ever witnessed. It near wrecked the vessel. As it was they lost seven good men.

He looked around him and up at the sails, all of which hung limply. Overhead the clouds had formed a strange circular pattern as if being whipped by high winds yet at deck level there was an unreal stillness, as if all surface air had been sucked out.

He cupped a hand to his mouth and shouted up. "Mister Vicosa, what does it feel like aloft?"

"Almost dead, sir. I also see flocks of seagulls flying inland, that's a sure sign we're in for a storm, a big one. And look at those high clouds, sir, I've rarely seen uglier."

"I agree. Set as much sail as we have. I'll send more men up and better send the lad down."

"Aye, sir, straight away."

Captain Stricker turned to the helmsman. "Come about, Mister Crawford, and head for shore, the charts don't show any reefs. With luck we'll make the lee of Brookes Inlet before the storm hits. Where's the first mate?"

"Having breakfast, I do believe, sir."

"You alert him, I'll take the helm."

"Aye, aye, sir."

The sails began to flap a little as the ship came about although by its wake little headway was being made and in the captain's estimation the inlet was at least two miles distant. Felix Bloom reported and was told to assemble all hands on deck and secure anything likely to be washed overboard. Then he could assist with the helm if the storm broke.

The bosun was instructed to prepare the longboats just in case they were needed. When he arrived back on deck Albert was told to quickly alert the female passengers first then have all the convicts assemble on deck.

Shouts of command reverberated in the unnaturally still morning air.

Emily Kilpatrick looked up at the hatch grille and cocked an ear. "There's something afoot, girls. Listen to all those orders being given to set sails and secure everything on deck. I'd say we're in for another storm."

"It can't be, Emily, the sea seems so calm," Catherine said from a kneeling position beside Ann.

"It does feel more muggy than usual," Sophie added as she slipped her blouse on.

"Another storm, that's all we need," Barbara Henshaw moaned. "If the ship sinks we'll go with it, weighed down with these chains. Bloody hell and I was so looking forward to the penal colony."

"Weren't we all," Lydie added dryly as she too slipped her skirt and blouse on.

Catherine and Ann stood up and did the same. Then from above they heard Albert telling them to get up top quickly.

By the sounds of scampering feet on deck they all realised the situation was becoming serious which prompted Emily to scamper up the ladder quick as a monkey. Sophie followed, then Barbara and Lydie with Catherine and Ann close behind. At the top a strong seaman literally pulled them out of the hatch. When they were standing on deck a tarpaulin was flung over the opening and secured with rope.

By now the sails were beginning to fill and all around they could hear an eerie whistling sound as the wind increased in velocity. They saw Alice Edwards and Clare Hamlyn cowering on the poop deck while a seaman tied ropes lined with corks around their waists before they were lowered overboard to the longboats which were being pitched and tossed about like matchwood in the swirling eddies around the ship. Ahead the hazy coastline seemed a very long way off.

Then to the utter amazement of every convict the ship's blacksmith appeared with a heavy hammer, a chisel and a steel plate. He told them to brace themselves as he was going to hack the chains off their anklets. He started with Ann, telling her to lift her skirt while adding it might hurt. Albert held the chisel over the links with both hands.

Ann cried out in pain as the chisel was hit but in two strokes the link was severed. The other went as quickly. Her legs were partially free for the first time in over seven months. Emily came next followed by Barbara, Catherine, Lydie and finally Sophie. They were all crying, firstly from the pain they had endured but also in joy as they had more freedom of movement. It was also apparent that Captain Stricker anticipated the upcoming storm would be the severest they had encountered so far and that was obviously why he had partially freed them. There were still the manacles around their ankles but at least their legs were partially free.

Catherine looked up at the helm to see Felix Bloom and Victor Crawford striving to control the large wheel. Captain Stricker stood at the rail staring first at the sea, then the sky before he saw Catherine looking at him. Despite the dire situation he waved with a free hand. She returned it before putting her arm around Ann's waist.

Unfortunately it wasn't over by far. The wind was becoming more intense by the minute, whipping the sea up so that it was even rougher than when they crossed the Bay of Biscay. Timbers creaked and ropes strained as they never had before. Suddenly the *Bromley* was buffeted to an alarming angle by a huge broadside wall of water, causing everybody to stagger as they desperately tried to find something to cling to. Sophie slithered across the deck only to be stopped by the rail. Catherine saw Emily's arm was bleeding quite badly as she and Ann clung to each other for dear life. Then another wave hit from the opposite side throwing them all back across the deck amid gallons of cold seawater. Lydie saw at least three sailors being washed overboard and their screams could be heard even above the howling wind and crashing waves.

In all his years at sea Captain Stricker had never sailed in such a tempest; as he looked aloft to see the sails being whipped about with some starting to tear in the wind which came from all quarters at once. He knew it was too late to reef them in. Then suddenly the upper foremast snapped with a loud crack. The top half came crashing down, landing where the convicts' privacy canvas had been slung. The water trough was smashed into fragments. Luckily the mast hadn't hit anybody but there was a tangled mess of ropes and sails as another massive wave hit, sweeping completely over the poop deck.

Although nobody could see it, down below in the centre hold heavy iron mining machinery had broken free of the ropes securing them and were sliding about freely as the deck angle altered second by second. Then it began to rain with a severity nobody had experienced before. Sheets of it followed by streaked lightening and thunder. Catherine saw Doctor Mountjoy clinging to a seaman as a giant wave broke over the port side, taking both men with it. The ship's wheel started spinning out of control, sending Victor Crawford and Felix Bloom flying off at a tangent. Both men gripped the port rail for dear life as another wave struck, taking them and Albert into the spuming water. Captain Stricker looked on, realising there was nothing he could do except try and restrain the wheel. Wilf Malone dashed up to help him. Lying on the deck, soaking wet, Catherine gripped Ann even tighter. If they were to die it would be in each other's arms.

The *Bromley* creaked and strained although it was now obvious the sea would eventually win. Suddenly above all other sounds they heard wood splintering below the waterline when a piece of machinery smashed through the hull. As if this wasn't enough to seal the *Bromley*'s fate another mast cracked and came crashing down, landing on top of Barbara and two sailors who were trying to help her. Their struggles continued for a few seconds before all three lay still, covered in blood.

Another giant wave smashed over the ship causing it to tip fully on its side. Those still on board were tossed into the frothy water, bobbing them about like corks out of a bottle as they struggled to keep their heads above the water. One of the longboats floated upside down with no sign of the occupants. Catherine couldn't see Ann but she saw Lydie being hit on the head by a part of the main mast as it swept by, causing the surging sea to become red. The wind screamed, the humans screamed as they struggled desperately in the swirling waters. Sophie saw Clare Hamlyn being thrown out of the longboat as it overturned, catching her right leg as it did so but the cork belt seemed to be keeping her afloat. There was no sign of Alice Edwards, who may have been trapped under the lifeboat, but Sophie knew her only thoughts must be to try and save her own life. This was a situation where it was every person for themselves.

Catherine was gasping for breath, struggling to keep her head above the water when a section of mast hit her shoulder. She grabbed a length of trailing rope and pulled herself up to lie over the mast, being kept level by a cross spar with a piece of sail still attached. She gripped the wood and an iron hook with all her strength, sensing the weight of her soaked clothing and the irons still around her ankles but knowing if the chain had remained she would have been dragged under. As she was carried up on a wave, coughing and spluttering, her keen eyes saw Ann clinging for dear life to a long section of the ship's rail which had been ripped away. From somewhere Sophie's head appeared out of a mountainous wave and she too grabbed the rail but too far away for Ann to render any assistance.

"Help me, help me!" a faint voice cried out. It was Clare Hamlyn, who was being tossed around in the swirling eddies with her eyes agape, looking terrified. Suddenly she disappeared in a spume of spray only to reappear seconds later, waving an arm madly as her cries of anguish were drowned by the howling wind.

Catherine, who still clung desperately to the mast section, saw the bodies of various seamen drift by including Felix Bloom floating head down. He was obviously dead but tied to him was Albert Brooks. He looked to have lost an arm although he seemed to be alive. She tried to grab the lad but failed as parts of the shattered ship now swept past with lengths of rope hanging off them like tentacles of giant squids. An oar from one of the longboats, chairs, pieces of bunks, stools, reinforced chests and the box which their food had been lowered down in floated by, being carried by the force of wind, waves, currents and driving rain. Catherine didn't know how much longer she could hold on as she shivered from both cold and fright. One minute everybody aboard the *Bromley* was secure with a strong vessel beneath them, and now they were all fighting for their lives including Captain Stricker.

Then almost as swiftly as it had arisen the howling wind moderated, the seas gradually calmed and a hazy sun appeared. It was as if a mighty hand had swept the storm away. Catherine's heart began to beat a little faster, realising she may have survived this disaster provided her grip on the mast could be maintained despite a numbness in her hands and feet. She spat out some salt water and with a free hand wiped her mouth then her sore eyes and saw ahead rocky cliffs rising as if out of the sea. She couldn't see a beach but there had to be one, there always was. In a haze she could see swirling sand which the dying wind was still picking up. Yet now just a gentle swell prevailed, washing her towards the shore. Still she didn't dare release her grip, unaware how deep the water was and with her soaked clothing and the iron manacles around her ankles she was bound to be dragged under. She couldn't see Ann and wondered how she was coping. That was if she still lived.

We never had time to say goodbye, she thought to herself while coughing up more salt water.

Catherine had no recollection of time but suddenly the mast and sail came to a halt as it dug into the sand. Now she released her grip to find herself in knee-deep water. Her feet sank in the soft sand as she staggered ashore with her heart and temples pounding like big bass drums. A few feet up on the beach she collapsed, realising her strength wouldn't have lasted much longer and she too would have drowned. Her fingers clawed into the warm dry sand, aware of how very lucky she had been and that it was not her time to die. She turned over and saw fleecy white clouds floating on the high currents of air and in that fleeting second it occurred to her this was not the way she was supposed to land in Australia. Had the storm been a divine intervention by some unknown universal power? A miracle? She may never know but then she sensed movement to her left and looked.

Ann was approaching, wearing nothing but her slightly shredded skirt with a drying mist rising from it as water dripped off her bare shoulders. For a moment Catherine saw something surreal, as if her lover was some kind of semi-naked sea goddess who had induced the storm and then calmed it when she was safe. Then for a brief moment she wondered if she herself was dead and had been reunited with Ann in that nether world where nothing at all existed except eternity. Luckily it was none of these as Ann dropped to her knees and kissed her salt-caked lips.

"Fate has stepped in, my love, and saved us. The *Bromley* is gone, luckily we are not."

"Oh, Ann, it's beyond belief. Do you know if anybody else has survived?"

"Sophie has. She has gone to Emily who was washed up on the beach a few hundred yards away. I saw she had a cut lip and a gash on her right arm but I don't know if she lives. We'll soon see however."

Catherine stood up and seemed to sway. She blinked her eyes as Ann asked what was the matter.

"Nothing really. It's just that I still feel the ship's motion."

"As a matter of fact I do. I suppose it's because we've been so long at sea. Our mental systems have adapted to tidal movements, now they're gone but we still feel them, and don't forget basically we're land creatures. Soon though these sensations will go as our bodies become accustomed to solid unmoving ground again."

Catherine smiled. "You're correct of course but how do you know these things?"

She shrugged her shoulders. "I don't know, my love, I just do. Instinct."

Her eyes scanned around, looking at the rising cliffs. There were depressions where rocks had lain before being blown elsewhere by the whirlwinds. The scrubby grass cliffs seemed torn and dishevelled in many areas but otherwise there seemed little other damage. Not that there was much to ruin anyway, the land looked barren. If the *Bromley* had been much further out to sea it could even have missed the storm completely.

Ann suddenly cast her eyes out to sea and said, "Look."

Catherine followed her arm and saw a body floating at the water's edge on what seemed like a cabin door. There was no doubt it was the bosun Wilf Malone. They both rushed back into the sea and dragged the man ashore. It was an effort getting him above where the tide washed in but they somehow found the strength. Ann slapped his face a few times. Finally he began to cough and splutter and eventually heaved up a frothy white substance which had to be seawater. He sat up and looked around, obviously still slightly dazed. Catherine saw there was a long tear in the left upper trouser leg and the area around it was soaked in blood. She asked if it was alright to remove the trousers so they could look at the wound. He nodded.

Between them they managed to draw the soaking wet trousers off and saw quite a long gash running down his thigh with blood still pulsing from it. He looked and said, "There's a large kerchief in the left pocket. Get it and tie it very tightly around my leg above the gash."

Ann did as requested and Catherine was amazed how quickly she worked. It was as if a different woman had emerged from the sea. She saw Catherine looking and explained.

"I once had to bind a man's leg similar to this after another sliced him with a scythe. I managed to stem the bleeding before some others took him away to see a doctor. I was actually planning to be a nurse when my mother suddenly died. Then I was thrown in prison and, well, you know the rest."

"You've done well on my leg, lass," Wilf said as he coughed again, bringing up more white vomit.

"Do you know what became of Captain Stricker?" Catherine asked while standing up and looking around to see if there were any other survivors.

"The captain remained with his ship, Catherine, and went down with it. We'd shaken hands before I started to assist him on the ship's wheel. However a giant wave washed me overboard. That's how I got this injury when I caught a jagged piece of the ship's rail going over the side. I saw the first mate had grabbed young Albert and tied a rope around them both, Albert couldn't swim, you see. That was the last I saw of them."

"They floated past me," Catherine told him. "I think Mister Bloom was dead but Albert seemed alive although it looked like he'd lost his right arm. Perhaps he still floats somewhere. Ah look, here comes somebody else."

Soon they saw it was Fred Pankhurst, the ship's cook. There didn't appear to be anything wrong with him. He arrived and shook hands with the bosun before hugging Catherine and Ann.

"Well, ladies, it seems the *Bromley*'s voyage has come to a very abrupt end. Are there other survivors?"

"I think Sophie Hart and Emily Kilpatrick," Catherine explained rather breathlessly. "I also saw Mrs Hamlyn still afloat after she'd been thrown from one of the longboats. Mrs Edwards was in it also but I never saw her after the boat tipped. I don't know if there are others."

"I'll take a walk along the beach to see if I can spot anybody else," the chef said. "You two look fit enough to gather in some driftwood floating about at the sea edge. We'll need it to make a fire as it'll get chilly when the sun sets."

"How will we light it?" Ann asked.

"I grabbed a handful of flints from my galley before leaping overboard." Some were removed from his trouser pocket and spread on the sand to dry. Only then did he stare at Ann's upper nakedness so he removed his jacket, took his shirt off and passed it to the girl. "Here, lass, wear my shirt, it ain't right for a young lady to be displaying her chest like that, nice though it may be."

Ann thanked him and put it on. The sleeves extended well beyond her delicate hands so she rolled them up before tucking the shirt's flap into her skirt then thrust her chest out and said, "Now I'm a man."

Fred smiled while replacing his soaking jacket. "Nay, lass, you'll always be a female in my eyes. Men don't bulge in front like you do, not normal men at least."

All four laughed before Fred left to look for others while Catherine and Ann walked back to the sea to collect firewood. At the water's edge they held hands for a moment and lightly kissed.

"It is truly a miracle, Catherine. One minute chained like animals, the next fighting for our very lives in a sea which seemed to boil, now this. A sort of freedom."

"How do you mean, a sort of freedom?"

"Well, in the first place we're a long way from anywhere which for the moment is good, unfortunately we still wear the remainder of our chains. We must try and get rid of them quickly although don't ask me how. Then of course when the *Bromley* doesn't arrive in Botany Bay the prison authorities might send out search parties for us."

"It's a large country to search, Ann. I remember seeing a map of Australia when I was cleaning the helmsman's cabin and as Captain Stricker told us after leaving the Swan River this was a very desolate area we'll be sailing past. Plus nobody will know we're missing until the ship is due to arrive ..." She paused to listen.

Over the breaking waves they could hear a faint cry for help and saw a figure bobbing in the water about fifty yards offshore. One arm was waving frantically.

"It's Mrs Hamlyn," Ann said, shielding her eyes from the glaring sun with a hand. "What can we do? I can't swim."

"We must get Mister Pankhurst. I'll go tell him while you take some wood to the bosun."

Ann started picking up various pieces of splintered wood which had once been the *Bromley*. With an armful she returned to where Wilf lay and told him they'd seen Mrs Hamlyn floating offshore and that Catherine was going to alert Fred Pankhurst. He nodded his approval as she knelt beside his injured leg. She suggested it would be a good idea to wash the blood-soaked kerchief out and asked if seawater was alright.

Wilf smiled. "At the moment, lass, we don't have too much option, do we? Anyway the salt water will do it good." He looked deeply into her eyes and smiled. "It's been said aboard you and Catherine have formed a romantic attachment. Is it true?"

"It is. I hope this doesn't spoil our present relationship, may I call you Wilf?"

"By all means call me Wilf, that's why I was given the name. And as to your relationship with Catherine, it doesn't bother me at all. I'll also let you in on a little secret. We had men aboard the *Bromley* who made love with each other. Many captains wouldn't tolerate such a thing and if they caught anybody at it the offenders could look forward to many more strokes than you took. Captain Stricker was a much more understanding man but you must realise he had to have you punished and I was only carrying out his orders. It's traditional for the bosun to lay the lashes. I hope you don't bear me a grudge."

"At the time I was tethered to that mast, Wilf, I wished you'd drop dead each time a stroke landed but I later realised you were only doing your duty. I bear you no animosity, let us consider ourselves friends."

He smiled. "I thank you, lass, my mind is easier now. I was also glad to see your back's much improved. Dip yourself fully in the ocean while washing my kerchief, it'll do it good."

"I'll do that, Wilf."

She left him and smiled to herself. Making friends with the bosun would be well worthwhile. At the water's edge she looked out but didn't see Clare Hamlyn anywhere. As she washed the kerchief out she hoped the woman hadn't drowned despite her attitude. Before returning to Wilf she waded into the surf up to her waist before lowering her body until the water touched her chin. It did feel good and she vowed to learn to swim.

Returning up the hot sand she saw Fred Pankhurst away to her right pulling a body out of the water with Catherine standing knee-deep, ready to help. The body wore a dress so it could only be Mrs Hamlyn. It was to be hoped this incident had changed her outlook on the convicts. However for the moment there was the injured bosun who needed attention.

She knelt by him to replace the wet kerchief. He grimaced as she pulled it tight but he knew that was the correct thing to do. To him now this slender girl was no longer a convict but one of the survivors of a disaster at sea. He must help them in some way although at this moment he had no idea how.

Fifteen minutes later a reunion of sorts was held when Emily and Sophie joined them. It wasn't a long affair, simply exchanges of kisses before Sophie said Fred and Catherine needed help with Mrs Hamlyn. It seemed she had a badly broken right leg. Sophie volunteered and left. Emily would remain so Ann could bathe and bandage her cut right arm although now it didn't seem too bad or as deep as she had thought. As Emily said, "It's more blood than cut. That comes with being a hot-blooded Irishwoman."

When Sophie arrived at the scene Fred and Catherine were just pulling Mrs Hamlyn out of the water with the cork belt tightly strapped around her slender waist. Her skirt was soaked in blood and soon it was obvious why after they had carefully peeled the soaking material back. Part of her shin bone was sticking through the skin and stocking.

"Best we can do is splint it," Fred Pankhurst said. "It's a great pity Doctor Mountjoy didn't survive, he'd have known what to do. Leg and arm breaks are common on ships."

"I'll collect some strips of driftwood," Catherine told him. "We can rip some lengths of cloth off my skirt to tie them on."

"No, lass, don't do that. Your skirt's tattered enough as it is but it does almost cover those ankle bracelets so if there's any law and order around here it's best they don't see them. There must be some odd lengths of rope floating about. See what you can find."

Catherine nodded and walked towards the sea.

Hearing what Fred had said about keeping the ankle shackles covered pleased Sophie for it meant the man had no intention of turning them in. She glanced around and saw the sheer desolation of this place. Dead ahead lay cliffs with outcroppings of rock and patches of scrub grass. Numerous seagulls hovered around, probably looking for damaged nests and broken eggs. Beyond the cliffs could be anything. Yet it seemed obvious the area must be unpopulated otherwise somebody must have observed the shipwreck by now and come to lend a hand or even loot what was still being washed ashore. She knew that in many English and Scottish coastal towns local residents plundered shipwrecks. Some remote areas even lured ships onto the rocks with false signals especially if they carried valuable cargos.

Fred carefully removed Mrs Hamlyn's stocking then did what he could to push the bone back into place while she was still unconscious. Catherine delivered two lengths of planking and some thick rope. Sophie untwined a few long strands while Fred laid the wood over and below the break and quickly tied them in place.

They all stood up knowing nothing much more could be done for the woman. She was lucky to even be alive.

"I'll have to carry her to the others," Fred said.

"Why don't we have the others come here," Sophie told him. "One place is as good as another."

Catherine volunteered to go and get them while looking out to sea in case she saw any other survivors. Fred asked her to bring the flints when she returned.

* * *

Once they were all grouped together they held a meeting and agreed the first thing to do was light a fire. Secondly they must find a source of fresh water and thirdly food.

"Ironic, isn't it," Fred said. "Here I am, a chef with no food to cook, so we'll have to hunt for some." He looked at the cliff facing them. "There may be wild game beyond that cliff, even snakes."

"Ugh," Sophie said.

"Listen, lass, when that belly of yours starts rumbling you'll eat anything, believe me. I know; I've starved before."

Nobody disagreed, having suffered starvation at one point or other in their lives. Nevertheless they decided a fire was essential. Most of the wood Catherine and Ann had brought up was dry enough to burn so Fred set to work with a pair of flints over a small piece of Mrs Hamlyn's skirt. They sparked but it took twelve attempts to get a flame and very carefully small slivers of wood were placed over it. Everybody cheered as the fire began to kindle. Catherine and Ann volunteered to get more wood while Fred and Sophie decided to go hunting for food and water while there was still some daylight remaining.

Wilf stood up to try and walk only to discover his leg had stiffened making movement difficult but these were not times to be lying around. In fact he more than anybody realised the dire situation they were in. This was no ordinary shipwreck. Among them were four convicts all sentenced to long terms in Botany Bay. For now though, as far as he was concerned, survival was the most important factor they faced and that wasn't going to be easy.

Catherine and Ann stood at the water's edge, sensing the incoming surf running around their still iron-clad feet. They held hands and gazed over the vast expanse of ocean which lay before them.

"I wonder what lies beyond where we can see?" Catherine asked softly.

"I have no idea, my love. Beautiful magical lands perhaps, where all is serene and people like us make love all day long and on into the starlit night. Yet let us both be thankful we're standing here and not still heading for Botany Bay. We've sustained hopelessness and have been given a second chance so at all costs we must make the most of it."

"I'm sure we will. The only person I worry about is Clare Hamlyn and her attitude towards us. When we were anchored at the Swan River while dropping the farmers off Barbara told me she had overheard the dreadful woman saying how much she enjoyed watching you being whipped."

"Then with her we must be careful. She is not one to be trusted and I have no wish to resume our journey to the penal colony clad in chains again."

"If we get the chance, do you think we should try and return to England?"

Ann licked her salty lips while thinking. "I think so even if it's only to right the wrongs done against me, but I could only do that if you accompanied me. A cruel and unjust set of circumstances brought us together and by some mysterious workings of the human body we fell in love. That love must endure, Catherine. One tree doesn't make a forest but two can."

Catherine looked at Ann in amazement. In their almost instant freedom Ann was becoming profound, an emergence from within her very self. Her temples pulsed in the knowledge Ann was all hers and if it hadn't been for their present critical situation she could have laid her on the sand and made love. Instead she simply squeezed the delicate hand and suggested they continue collecting firewood. They both waded in a little deeper and began picking floating fragments which had once been a ship. These were carried up on the beach and they returned for more.

It was then Ann saw something bobbing and tumbling in the waves about twenty feet out. "I think it's a rum cask like the ones the crewmen were given their tot from."

"It may still contain rum. We should try to retrieve it, at least it's something to drink."

"Don't you think it's too far out?"

"No, I don't think so. I'll try to reach it."

"Please be careful, Catherine. I'd hate to lose you."

"If I consider it too dangerous I'll come straight back. You're worth far more to me than a keg of rum."

She began to wade out with the breakers splashing up her front but it seemed the keg was being washed towards her. The water was well above her waist when she reached it. After turning she began pushing it ashore and was surprised how far away Ann looked. Ann started to come towards her and when they met soft kisses were exchanged.

"We must remember this moment," Ann said. "Just you and me totally wet in a vast ocean. Kiss me again."

They did. Their tongues tasted salty but it was the salt of freedom.

"Look at those two," the bosun said to Emily. "Despite our plight they can still find time to kiss."

"It's love, Wilf," Emily replied. "You can kiss me if you wish, or are you averse to the lips of a convict?"

"No, I'm not. In fact I've had an urge to do that ever since you came aboard but of course it was impossible then. Now it isn't, come to me."

She did and their lips met.

"Look at Wilf and Emily kissing down there," Fred Pankhurst said to Sophie who had just joined him at the top of the cliff, slightly out of breath. The climb had been steeper than they imagined and of course Sophie had the additional burden of the iron anklets and bare feet. In fact her soles were bleeding but that was secondary, her freedom meant much more.

Still breathing heavily they took in the view ahead of a slightly undulating scrub grass plain with what looked like a lake in the distance. On its far side there appeared to be a forest.

Fred gripped Sophie's hand. "The lake could be our lifesaver, Sophie, it has to be fresh water and may also contain fish. A seaman's instinct tells me we're going to be alright."

"I sense good omens, Fred, and for a woman whose lips have been deprived for too long; please kiss me."

"It will be a great pleasure. In fact there's been many a night when I've lain in my bunk thinking about you. Thoughts and desire of women are a natural reaction for men at sea, Sophie. You were near but unfortunately untouchable."

"Well, I'm touchable now, Fred. Kiss me if that is still your desire."

"There's nothing I'd enjoy more, Sophie."

He took her in his strong arms and they gently sank to the mossy ground. There was no sound as their lips met. Both bodies were filled with urgency and neither needed to ask what came next.

Finally they both sighed. A shipwreck had given them both what they so much desired despite there being a twelve-year difference in their ages.

Catherine and Ann delivered what firewood they'd collected and laid it around the fire to dry out. Wilf hobbled around, helping and looking sadly at Mrs Hamlyn who had recovered consciousness. Her rather severe face was contorted in pain as she looked at the hastily applied splints. Wilf knew she was going to be a burden to them and it seemed she did too.

"Our situation is not good is it, Mister Malone?"

"No, Mrs Hamlyn, it is not. We may have to make a stretcher to carry you but for the moment you must simply rest. It's a pity I can't give you anything to ease the pain."

"There is something, Wilf," Catherine interjected before mentioning the keg she and Ann had brought ashore.

"Then let's get it," Wilf said as his eyes lit up. "If it contains rum we'll all be able to take a measure."

He hobbled off, almost having to drag his injured leg. Catherine gave him a length of timber which he could use as a walking cane. As they slowly walked away Ann knelt beside Mrs Hamlyn and took her delicate hands.

"You must rest, that will be best for your leg."

"What do you know, girl, you're nothing but a brainless criminal and the moment we see somebody of authority I shall tell them exactly who you all are. You've probably realised it by now that I don't associate myself with sluts. If only my husband were here, he'd know what to do."

"Well, he isn't, is he? So unless you change your very bad attitude I shall suggest to Wilf we leave you here to die of thirst or get devoured by wild animals. It's your choice!"

"We shall see when Mister Pankhurst returns. He'll agree with me."

"I wouldn't be too sure. Things are very different now from what they were aboard the *Bromley*. In case you don't realise it we are all in a fight for survival. This is a wild, desolate country as you can see for yourself."

She stood up and almost kicked some sand over the awful woman's leg. Then she saw Wilf and Catherine returning, pushing the unruly keg over the sand. It wobbled a great deal so she assumed there was liquid in it.

When they arrived Wilf set the keg upright and saw it was tightly corked. They would need Fred's knife to open it.

"Does it contain rum?" Ann asked.

"Almost certainly. The only other thing in there could be cooking oil, but I don't think so. When we get it open the contents must be rationed carefully, it may have to last a long time."

"Surely you don't intend to let the convicts have some, Mister Malone?" Clare said while easing her leg up slightly.

Wilf looked at her with disdain. "Mrs Hamlyn, while we are in this situation I intend to treat everybody as equals, knowing it will take all our combined strength and willpower to get us out of this mess. For all we know this area could be inhabited by savages, even cannibals who eat humans. We have no weapons to defend ourselves should an attack occur and in your condition you're useless to us. Do I make myself clear?"

"Very clear indeed, Mister Malone. However when we emerge from this situation, as you say, I shall be reporting your attitude to your superiors. Is that understood?"

"I hear you, but for the moment my superiors are thousands of miles away so if I may offer a word of advice, revise your odious attitude very quickly otherwise you will be ignored. On the *Bromley* Captain Stricker tolerated your constant complaints and disdain for the convicts; here I don't have to."

With that he turned away and threw some more wood on the fire, causing it to crackle merrily. Ann noted the expression on his face and knew he was fuming internally. She admired him for the stand he'd taken against the obnoxious woman.

To ease the tension somewhat Catherine volunteered to go and get more firewood and Ann said she'd join her.

When they arrived at the sea edge the area was now littered with debris including parts of sails. They both agreed these could be fashioned into crude tents.

"Perhaps," Ann said, "we could sew Mrs Hamlyn up in one and launch her back into the ocean. There she could swear at all the fishes."

Catherine laughed and sensed one of those twinges in her groin. Ann was becoming more vibrant by the minute. It seemed as if the shipwreck had opened a valve within her, releasing emotions which had been latent since receiving her cruel sentence. However there was still much to be done. They may be free in one sense although now they were captives of the land itself.

Side by side they pulled in some of the canvas and laid it out to dry before more driftwood was collected and made into a pile.

* * *

Up on the cliff Fred and Sophie started to look around for signs of animal life. Soon they came across a series of holes which Sophie knew were rabbit burrows. She'd seen enough in the area around the orphanage where she used to live before the village sheriff decided she was mature enough to sample what life was really all about.

From that assault she swiftly matured and realised if she'd been a young woman of breeding and wealth such a thing would never have happened. Therefore it seemed logical for her to make money by any means possible. Two nights later she left the orphanage in the dark of night and hitched a ride to London on the promise the coachman would be rewarded while the horses were being changed. In London she quickly found others in a similar situation as herself, penniless. In a tavern she was picked up by a man who offered money in return for her bodily favours. This she realised was her ticket to wealth if she was careful. It wasn't an ideal life but she knew of no other job which paid so well.

Two months later she was approached by a cocky lad of about sixteen who bragged how much his rich politician father gave him for pocket money. During a drinking lull he also boasted how many women like her he satisfied in a month. If she agreed to take him all ways they could enjoy good times together. Naturally she agreed as it also pleasured her.

She saw him three times after that and on the third a little something extra was added to his after-sex goblet of port. When he passed out he was locked in a very sturdy wardrobe. A day later the father received a ransom note for his son's return. All went well until she went to pick up the money which was supposed to be in the rotted stump of a tree in Hyde Park. The money wasn't there but six hefty constables were. After being taken to the constable station, charged with abduction and put in a cell the arresting constables paid her a visit which wasn't a social call. The next morning she was up before a judge and a week later sentenced to life in Botany Bay, the boy's father having exerted all his political influence.

Now of course the shipwreck had changed her circumstances and given a moderate amount of luck she may stand a chance of returning to a somewhat normal life, perhaps even with Fred.

She and Fred stood over a burrow and in moments a healthy rabbit came running out. Fred lashed out with his boot and managed to stun the animal. He picked it up and broke its neck.

"Rabbit for supper tonight, Sophie my dear. We'll need more than one though. What we need is a couple of hefty cudgels to kill the buggers as they emerge. We could break a couple of branches off that tree. Come on."

She smiled and licked her lips. "I remember on that New Year's night you promised me a meat pie, Fred. Now you can keep that promise. Let's hunt."

Fifteen minutes later they each stood armed and ready over separate holes and waited. They didn't have to wait long. Sophie missed the first rabbit but got the next three. Fred clubbed four more. It seemed the area was rife with the animals as they saw many more scampering around oblivious to the fact hunters were present. All the dead were gathered up and they set off back to join the others.

"We can set snares to catch plenty more," Fred told his new lover as they carefully made their way down the cliff.

Sophie felt happier than she'd been since her arrest. And just to be out in the fresh air was medicine to her. She and her fellow convicts had been cooped up in that hold far too long and the stench still lingered in her memory cells. Now they could see the fire blazing and hastened their pace so Fred could cook their first meal in freedom.

* * *

After Fred had skinned and gutted three of the rabbits they were placed on hastily made spits. Wilf borrowed Fred's knife and carefully opened the rum keg so he wouldn't damage the cork. One problem remained however, they didn't have anything to drink from. Emily came to the rescue, saying she recalled seeing some shells on the beach where she'd drifted ashore.

Catherine and Ann volunteered to get some, aware it would also give them more time to be alone together. It was as Ann had said while gathering firewood, "These are our first moments in total privacy, my love, so we should cherish and remember them."

They kissed after that. Now they walked hand in hand along the warm sand to the point where they thought Emily had come ashore. And there they were, conical shells of various sizes and to test they would hold liquid two were dipped in the ocean. They did and were tossed away. It was then Ann spotted a body floating face down not far from the shore.

They waded out to it and saw it was the deck lad, Albert. He was obviously dead, the poor lad had not seen twenty years of life. And not only did he have an arm missing, his lower leg was gone also. Ann said it looked like it had been bitten off because of the torn skin. Then a little further out they saw a fin darting about and it scared them. Neither knew what it was, only that it could represent death. They quickly waded back to shore, leaving Albert who was being washed about by the waves coming in and receding but they knew he was past all help. Six shells were collected and they made their way back to the others. Earlier they had revelled in their privacy, now they wanted to be among friends with perhaps Mrs Hamlyn being the exception.

Wilf Malone explained the fin was probably that of a shark, one of the deadliest sea creatures. Some were so large they could easily bite a person in half. Catherine and Ann shuddered, they had been quite close to it. Wilf explained that sharks sensed blood and with Albert's severed arm it would have been attracted to the lad. Wilf warned them all to be careful if they ventured into the sea.

Ann vowed never to go in again and said, "I have survived a shipwreck, that's enough for me. Now, Wilf, if I may, I'd like a measure of rum." She glared at Mrs Hamlyn while saying it.

Wilf poured a small measure for each of them. They drank a toast to their good fortune and continued safety.

Moments later Fred announced the rabbits were ready to eat. Mrs Hamlyn was propped up against the rum keg. With fingers it wasn't the most civilized way to eat a meal; however they all enjoyed the meat immensely. Even Mrs Hamlyn said how good it tasted.

Wilf smiled at her. "Now that's a better attitude, Mrs Hamlyn. From now on why don't we all call you Clare. What do you say?"

"Well, alright since we do appear to be in a predicament."

"That's settled then."

While they continued to eat Wilf said he had something important to discuss and would they please listen. Puzzled frowns appeared on foreheads but everybody was in agreement. Before starting he looked studiously at each convict in turn then cleared his throat.

"We are in a situation which may or may not be unique. It would seem I'm the senior survivor of a vessel transporting you four women to a prison colony. Despite our present circumstances and as an officer of the ship I'm still legally bound to have you delivered to Botany Bay."

"To which I agree," chirped up Mrs Hamlyn.

For a moment he glared at the intolerable woman. "Mrs Hamlyn, I thought we just agreed to be more friendly, let's keep it that way. Alright?"

"Oh, I suppose so, Mister Malone."

"Good. Now as I was about to say, despite my obligations there might be reasons for me not delivering the convicts to the penal colony. Prior to sailing and during a briefing by Captain Stricker, he told us the six convicts aboard had all committed violent acts and should have been hanged. However due to justifying circumstances the judges had not imposed the death penalty. Captain Stricker didn't feel it necessary to go into actual case details, only to say as officers we should always remember you were all to be considered dangerous. I think now before making any decisions about your futures I should be told of those circumstances, in other words why you committed your crimes, and please don't lie. Who will start?"

"I will," Emily volunteered, holding her arm up.

For the next half-hour each woman related the reasons for their crimes, all except Ann Lingos of course who wasn't guilty of any infraction of the law except perhaps naïvety. Wilf had seemed genuinely touched when hearing how representatives of King George had obviously arranged matters to have Ann transported for life so she could cause no further trouble. By the expression on Clare Hamlyn's face it seemed even she too felt some pity.

Wilf sucked on a rabbit leg bone before rendering his decision.

"Hearing your stories eases my conscience considerably. You all did wrong, of that there is no doubt, but in my own humble opinion transportation was a little severe, a prison sentence would have been more appropriate. In view of this I'm prepared to accept the time you have been in transit as your sentences so I along with Fred will try to ensure we all return to England, unless of course any of you wish otherwise. Do you?"

Sophie looked at Fred. "Speaking for myself, I'd like to return home, Wilf."

"So would I," Emily added.

Catherine held her hand up. "I think Ann and I would like to return, if only so Ann can vindicate herself, with my help of course. I'd also like to say, Wilf, on behalf of all of us, we thank you for your support and promise not to let you down."

"Thank you, Catherine, for saying that, it means a great deal to me." He winked in Emily's direction and continued, "Now that our meal is finished and the sun appears to be setting I suggest we should all set about making ourselves comfortable for the night. I know we're above the high tide line so in that respect we're safe although I'm not sure about wild animals which may prowl at night. I suggest we each find a place to settle down and light a fire beside us. That will keep animals away and ourselves warm."

"Good idea," Fred added. "I'm also a light sleeper so if anything comes snooping around I'll wake up."

They all began to stir. Sophie paired off with Fred. Wilf and Emily said they would remain where they were along with Clare who was obviously still in great pain. Catherine and Ann moved about fifty feet, almost to the base of the cliff.

Catherine carried a pile of wood and Ann took a lighted piece to kindle their own fire. Then between them they dragged a section of sail to their area to act as a blanket. As they settled themselves Ann observed Sophie and Fred were snuggling down together. Catherine smiled.

"A convict one day, Ann, the very next a lover with the ship's cook. That is progress."

"Thanks to nature, my love. If that storm hadn't arisen we would be miles from here by now, cooped up in that smelly hold and weighed down with iron chains."

"Although still in love," Catherine added. "Now do you feel like making love?"

"Of course I do. We should cover ourselves up to maintain our dignity; it is better people don't see what we're doing. This is just between ourselves and I for one can't wait to feel your beautiful body pressed against mine. Let us heap the fire a little more."

Wilf Malone looked over to them in the twilight and said, "I think, Emily, two of your fellow convicts are deeply in love."

"I know they are, Wilf. You were wonderful making that decision about our futures. Fate has certainly taken a hand in all our lives."

"A cruel fate in my case," Clare said with tears in her eyes. "I have nobody. Could I at least have another measure of rum, please, Wilf? It may put me to sleep."

"Yes of course."

He poured a generous measure into a shell and handed it to her. She forced a smile despite her body being wracked with pain. Wilf did feel sorry for her but he didn't know what else he could do.

Under the canvas Catherine and Ann became tightly embraced, exchanging tender kisses.

Finally after many blissful minutes Ann said, "Beneath us are the sands of time and far above is the endless universe of stars of which I think we are a part."

Catherine gripped her even tighter. "Oh, Ann, you say such wonderful things. Were you taught them?"

"No, they just enter my head. They have always been there but there was nobody to appreciate them, now there is. Obviously it is you, my love."

"Wasn't your mother interested in your statements?"

"No. All she cared about was who her next gentleman friend would be."

"How did she come to be with King George?"

"He stopped in our village while deer hunting. I believe they met in the one and only tavern and after plying her with gin he induced her to his room. She was very attractive, and was obviously willing."

"But there must have been many people with him. From what I know a king never travelled alone."

"That is true but as you must know, a king also does exactly as he wants. Taking a woman was common and servants were too scared to say anything. If they did instant dismissal was normal, some were even put to death. Look what happened to me, an innocent victim. I was fortunate not to have my head chopped off."

"What about George's wife, wasn't she aware what her husband was doing?"

"I suppose so, but there were her children to look after and educate so she probably ignored her husband's antics plus he may have wanted to indulge in certain sex acts which might have revolted her. There were those who said his madness was caused by frolicking with many women performing unnatural acts. I also know my mother wasn't the only one, she told me that one night after she'd been drinking heavily. Enough of George though, it's you I want and I will never be unfaithful to you. Now let us come together in the present."

Catherine turned on her back and allowed Ann to come over her.

And above a bright, almost full moon shone down as if it too was happy for them. It was ideal, they were alive and semi-free at least. Plus their future prospects looked hopeful, their bellies were full and best of all they had each other.

They continued to make love.

* * *

The following morning while Fred was stacking more wood on the fire Sophie spotted a bloated body being washed about in the surf. All except Wilf and Clare went to see who it was. When Fred turned it over the face was partially eaten away but it was obviously Eduardo Vicosa, the topsail man who had acted as Captain Stricker's interpreter in Lisbon. The body was dragged ashore and Fred suggested they dug a shallow grave for the man above the high-tide line. With pieces of driftwood acting as shovels a hole was quickly gouged out of the soft sand.

Wilf hobbled up and bowed his head. "He was a good and reliable seaman and I know Captain Stricker thought highly of him."

"Do you think Eduardo would mind if I took his shirt as I gave mine to Ann," Fred said.

Wilf smiled. "I wouldn't imagine so, Fred. Take it."

Due to its wetness and the unresponsive body Fred had difficulty removing it but finally he succeeded. It was wrung out and put on. Then Sophie helped her new lover roll Eduardo's heavy body into the shallow grave.

"Shouldn't we at least say something?" Ann said.

Fred nodded and brought his hands together as they all bowed their heads. "May the good Lord Neptune bless his soul. Amen."

They all said amen before starting to fill the hole. Wilf said he would fashion a cross from some of the driftwood but first they would eat.

"It won't be stodgy gruel this morning," Ann whispered to Catherine.

Following a meal of cold rabbit and a small measure of rum they held a meeting to plan their future. Fred wondered if the best idea would be to wait for a ship to pass by and attract it by lighting a large fire. Wilf wasn't keen for two reasons. One, it could be weeks, even months, before another vessel passed within sight of land. The only reason they were in so close when the storm hit was their call at the Swan River. Two, it would take some explaining why four of the women wore ankle shackles which were obviously not ornamental and unfortunately for the moment they had no means of removing them. Finally it was agreed they had no alternative but to move on even if they were hampered with Clare Hamlyn although Wilf did admit he would find it difficult walking any distance on his injured leg.

Fred explained again how he and Sophie thought they had seen a lake a mile or so north of the cliff top. They needed fresh water urgently so Fred suggested that himself, Sophie, Catherine and Ann would explore the area and try to catch more game in the process. Wilf volunteered to remain on the beach with Emily and Mrs Hamlyn. Emily said she'd collect more driftwood and see what else could be salvaged from the shoreline which was now littered with debris after the tide had receded although they had given up hope of finding more survivors. Even Albert's body was nowhere to be seen.

Unfortunately Clare's leg looked even worse this morning and she had obviously developed a fever overnight. The area around the break had gone almost black and there were signs the wound was beginning to fester. Wilf had seen such a condition before and knew it could end in death even if they had a qualified doctor to treat it. All they could do was make her comfortable and hope she didn't pass away.

Emily silently hoped she would, knowing the woman could cause a lot of trouble should they ever reach civilization again. She realised it was a callous attitude but the world had not been kind to her so why should she show any benevolence to someone like Clare who sneered at anybody below her own status in life. Being optimistic, Emily saw a definite chance of living in freedom once again even if it meant changing her name. After last night she knew Wilf would do all he could to protect her and the others and he was a person to be trusted. Clare Hamlyn wasn't.

Wilf hobbled to the base of the cliff with the exploration party and wished them luck. They were told to take as long as they needed as he and Emily could keep a fire going and they still had four skinned rabbits. Emily may also be able to salvage some rope which could be untwined and made into a fishing line.

"Don't catch a shark though," Ann advised him.

They departed upward still laughing. Ann Lingos had become that tonic they all needed.

Once on the cliff top the lake seemed further away than yesterday and appeared to be shrouded in mist. Undaunted they began to walk but found the going rough through the thorny grass with their skirts continually getting snagged and at times it was painful on their bare feet. A good sign though were rabbits scurrying everywhere and Fred killed two quickly. Obviously food was not going to be a problem despite the diet being bland. Yet Fred as a seaman was used to the same food day after day. A ship no matter how large could only carry so much.

After two hours they had to take a rest and tend to cut and blistered feet. Despite earlier advice Fred suggested strips were torn off their skirts and used as bindings. When they had all done so, progress was much faster but now the sun was beating down and they all sweated a great deal. This was the most strenuous effort they had put in since boarding the *Bromley* although all agreed it was well worth it. They were toiling for a future.

Finally the lake was reached and fully clothed they all ran into the crystal-clear water and wallowed in it like children in a pond at home. The bottom was sandy and firm. Although Fred was the only one who could swim they ventured in until the water came well above their waists. They could also see a myriad of fishes swimming around but not seeming to take too much notice of the intruders who were cupping water in their hands and drinking it. To them it tasted like fine wine.

On the far side Ann suddenly spotted smoke rising above the forest trees and pointed. "There must be people in there," she whispered as if not wanting to be overheard.

"If there are people, Ann, they must have seen us by now," Fred replied.

Then out of the trees emerged some very black people carrying what looked like crude spears. Their hair was long, black and fell well below their shoulders. They all wore brief dark brown cloths around their middles, even the females.

"Return to the shore," Fred instructed.

Nobody needed to be told twice.

Once there Fred tried to reassure them. "We shouldn't worry, girls. Those people are probably more scared of us than we are of them. I've heard it said there are many aboriginal tribes who occupy various areas of this land. They are the true Australians, we whites are the intruders although they need us for our technical abilities. If they come to us I think we should try to make friends. We need help anyway. Does anybody disagree?"

Nobody did although by the expressions on their faces they were not fully at ease. Sophie clung to Fred's arm and Catherine held Ann's hand tightly. Their heartbeats increased rapidly when they saw two rafts being launched and poled towards them with four natives on each.

"Stand your ground," Fred told them. "Try to look calm and for heaven's sake smile although we must look a motley lot dressed the way we are. Show your hands to demonstrate we don't carry weapons."

"Will they speak English?" Sophie whispered.

"I very much doubt it," Fred replied. "In fact they may not have much language at all. Anyway we'll soon find out."

The rafts had now been stopped about thirty feet offshore and very deep brown eyes were staring at these white people with great intensity. It was now obvious this party were all males.

Ann smiled and said hello.

There was no reaction.

They all said hello and waved.

One of the men grunted and raised his spear which was no more than a sharpened stick. They could see each man had a painted red line running down both cheeks. Fred imagined it could be an insignia of rank although he had no idea what. He stepped forward with arms outstretched, holding a rabbit. "Hello," he said again.

The tallest one grunted and the rafts began to move forward until they ground to a halt on the sand. The grunter pointed his spear at the rabbit. Fred took another pace and handed it to him. The man smiled, displaying a huge set of yellow teeth. He took the rabbit and held it up by its ears. All the others raised their spears and began chanting.

"I think we've made friends," Fred said.

"I hope so," Sophie replied. "I don't fancy being attacked by them. They look savage."

"We may look savage to them," Catherine replied just as another of them stepped forward and raised the hem of Sophie's skirt with the tip of his spear. Fred advised her not to move suddenly, he didn't think they meant harm.

"It's not you who's being explored, Fred," Sophie mumbled as more of her legs became exposed.

All the natives laughed and pointed to the iron bands around her ankles. One brandished his fists, showing he wore braided leather thongs around both wrists. Then others followed suit.

"They think your shackles are jewellery," Fred told her.

"Well, they can willingly have mine if they can get them off," Ann said as she too lifted her skirt to display similar ankles.

Catherine followed and much jabbering erupted from the thick-lipped mouths. One approached Catherine and rubbed her flaxen hair before muttering something.

"They like your golden hair," Ann told her.

"Well, I hope that's all they like about me, Ann. I have no desire to have male rites forced upon me."

"I don't think they mean any harm," Fred told them. "Just try and remain calm and remember we could be the first white people they've ever seen."

Finally the obvious leader pointed with his spear across the lake and muttered something.

"I think he wants us to go with them," Fred said. "Do we or don't we?"

"It may be safer to do so," Catherine replied. "I don't know anything about natives like these but I do know to refuse an invitation back home can be taken as an insult. My stepfather once beat me with his belt for refusing to go with him to a tavern."

"I agree," Fred said. "We must also try to get it across that there are another three back at the beach."

"Wilf did say for us to take our time," Ann reminded him.

"Then are we all in agreement to take them up on their offer?" Fred asked.

"I don't think we have a choice," Sophie said. "And if they were hostile I think we'd all be dead by now."

"Or something much worse," Catherine added, seeing the leering looks in their eyes and three of them were now showing obvious male reactions.

Fred broke the impasse by moving forward and stepping on the rough timbers of a raft. The others quickly followed. Suddenly the leader grabbed Ann's arm and guided her towards the other raft. Catherine quickly joined her and smiled bravely. The guests sat down cross-legged as the rafts were poled out.

As they approached the far shore many other natives including women had now gathered on the sand. Their sex was evident by bare breasts of various shapes and sizes. Also most women had bits of bone sticking in their wiry-looking hair. Others wore woven flowered garlands around their wrists and ankles. This explained why the natives had been attracted to the ankle shackles. Catherine hoped they might have some method of getting them off but thought it unlikely. They all seemed very primitive but she realised this was a different world to England.

As the new arrivals slowly stepped off the rafts curiosity began to take over, especially from the women. They ran their hands and fingers down the white faces, across the lips and through the hair, especially Catherine's. All the time they smiled and continued to jabber in their own language.

To Ann the women smelled of smoke and she imagined like at home the females spent much of their time preparing food over open fires. Then strange things began to happen. Three of the men lay down, exposed themselves and parted their legs.

"I hope that isn't a hint for us to offer ourselves," Sophie said with obvious concern causing Catherine and Ann to look at each other.

Last night it occurred to them that due to their fortunate circumstances they may never have to suffer the penal colony's impositions, one of which would have been to accept men either willingly or unwillingly. So in their partial freedom they had sworn that no men would ever again be permitted to enter their most private parts. It was accepted they may never bear children or even become married although in all other respects they would consider themselves to be a bonded couple. Their pledge was sealed with more kisses and further expressions of their love for each other.

When it was obvious to the native men these women were not going to offer themselves they jumped up and began walking towards the trees with signs their guests should follow. With some relief they all did.

Deep within the trees they entered a clearing with substantial-looking round straw and mud huts arranged in a large semicircle with one in the centre being twice the size of the others. Many children ran around totally naked and like kids the world over they screamed, laughed and shouted although it couldn't be understood what they were saying. Large black dogs loped about, scratching at the dirt as if looking for food. In the trees there were koalas. There were also large brightly coloured birds which Fred had to explain were parrots.

Central to the compound was an arrangement of four open fires with large cast-iron pots hanging over them. Some steamed, others simmered as the contents were stirred by young girls, one of whom was obviously with child and Catherine was truly amazed how long her nipples were. Slightly to the left there was a glowing pit with some type of animal being turned on a spit. It could have been a pig although Fred suspected it was a wild boar. Whatever, it made all their mouths water. To

Fred the cast-iron pots indicated these people had been in contact with some form of civilization at one time or another. The nearest place he could think of was the Dutch settlement on the Swan River but he had no idea how far away it was. Perhaps there were other settlements nearby? In a way he mentally likened Australia to that other vast continent of Africa with both being largely undeveloped.

Suddenly all chatter ceased when a very tall, dignified-looking man emerged from the largest hut, beaming a wide smile. Surprisingly he wore an English-style maroon top hat, a black gentleman's morning jacket, a plain blue pleated kilt which terminated just below his knees and on his large feet were a pair of brown highly polished buckled brogue shoes. There were no socks. He also carried a feathery object which was obviously a fly swatter. The man could very easily have been an actor ready to walk on the stage of a Shakespearean comedy. As he walked towards the newcomers everybody bowed as he passed. A huge hand was offered to Fred and they shook heartily before the man said in perfect English, "Welcome, friends, whom I assume are from that mighty and wonderful land called England. I was there once to learn your eloquent language and meet the Prime Minister William Pitt the Younger. He wanted me to oversee the development of an area around the Swan River as it was a potentially good port for English shipping. However I declined the offer, knowing it would consume too much of my valuable time. You see, I owed it to my own people the Myalls who needed me far more than the white man. As it is, the Dutch agreed to develop the area and now operate a port with great efficiency despite a sandbar blocking access up river. One day though this will be overcome to allow it to develop into a major trading area and perhaps a city. However I digress. All I will say is that my people know me simply as Mister Cromwell. Why that name? you may ask. I will explain. I use it because I greatly admire your Oliver Cromwell who was Lord Protector of England and I consider myself a protector to my people here. What, sir, is your name?"

"Fred, Fred Pankhurst, sir. I'm very pleased to meet you as are my friends."

"What are their names, Fred?"

As Fred reeled them off each woman bowed to this obviously dynamic person whose English was almost perfect. In fact Catherine knew many at The Grapes tavern who couldn't speak the language half as well.

Cromwell's face beamed laughter as he said, "They are a fine if rather dishevelled-looking lot of women, Fred, but tell me how do you come to be here? This is not white man's land, in fact it is fortunate you came across us rather than others over the mountains who are not quite so civilized. You, Fred, would have been roasted over a fire to be served as supper later while your women were being subjected to certain humiliating aboriginal rites." He roared with laughter before pointing his swatter at Catherine. "She would have been a great favourite with her golden hair. We have gold in the earth, unfortunately no women with hair that colour, which is a pity. Anyway explain your presence, my good friend Fred."

Over the course of the next ten minutes Fred explained they were sailing to Port Jackson when they encountered a very severe storm which totally destroyed their ship. Fortunately he didn't say the three women with him were convicts and heading for the Botany Bay penal colony. He did tell Mister Cromwell there was another man and two women back on the beach. He also explained the man had a gashed thigh and one of the women had suffered a badly broken leg. She was in a critical condition.

Then both Ann and Catherine began to worry when Cromwell stared in silence at their rusted ankle shackles. He licked his very fat lips and Ann had already formed the impression if he kissed anybody it would be like kissing a cow. He looked directly at Fred.

"It seems to me, friend Fred, those anklets the women wear are of the type worn by convicts with a length of chain separating them. I have seen similar in London. Is this not so? Speak the truth, friend Fred, or I will sell you all to a tribe who enjoy tormenting white folks."

Fred looked at the women before replying, knowing full well this flamboyant man was quite capable of carrying out his threats.

"Indeed, Mister Cromwell, the women were convicts. However I don't know whether you are aware of it but by a royal decree dating back goodness knows how long if convicts being transported are involved in a shipwreck then by tradition the king grants an automatic pardon."

Cromwell roared with laughter again, causing his jowls to quiver and his top hat to tilt at an alarming angle. He straightened it before replying.

"My friend Fred, I have never heard such a preposterous untruth in my entire life. In the first place, I'm very much aware your system of transportation only began eight years ago so such a decree could not have been issued, how did you say? goodness knows how long ago. In the second place, no English monarch would be stupid enough to grant pardons because of shipwrecks. If any of my people uttered such an outlandish fib I would have them fastened over an ant hill from sunrise to sunset. I am aware though your King George the Third commuted some death sentences to celebrate his welcome release from madness. However since I'm unable to confirm or deny this royal decree I am willing to accept the ladies are free citizens. Now what can we do for you?"

The three women breathed a collective sigh of relief and Fred wiped his sweaty brow.

"Firstly, Mister Cromwell, we would appreciate your help in bringing our other friends here. Secondly, if at all possible the women would appreciate having the iron anklets removed as we have no means to do so. Finally, we would like something to eat and drink."

"Your commands will be met, friend Fred. I think you said the others were on the beach."

"Yes, almost in direct line with the lake. The woman with the broken leg must be moved with great care."

"She will be. I will dispatch strong men immediately." He pointed his fly swatter at one of the men who had come over the lake on a raft. Instructions were given in what they assumed to be the Myall language. When Cromwell finished six men bowed and departed.

Cromwell turned back to face his guests. "You will start your meal by having a tasty fish. In the lake it is a predator, in your stomach it greatly satisfies. To follow will be turtles' eggs and kangaroo meat, very tasty. Then we will see about removing the leg irons and having my women make some repairs to the ladies' tattered clothing. We cannot offer new for as you see my females wear very little. However they are happy as of course are the men. We are a free and open society. In this glade there is no such thing as man and wife, simply relationships. It is a system which I find functions very well and we rarely have disputes. As you can see all our children are happy and they know who their parents are. It is a system which could only exist in a close-knit society such as we have here. In a way England and Europe generally have much to learn. Still as they say, to each his own." He paused and pointed his fly swatter at Ann and Catherine. "Tell me, friend Fred, are those two related? I observe they hold hands."

"To be honest, Cromwell, while on the ship they became lovers and still are. I know this is very unusual although we have accepted the fact and I hope you will too."

"In matters of the heart, friend Fred, who am I to say what is right or what is wrong? Perhaps your fictitious king of goodness knows how long ago should also decree that those of any sex be permitted to cohabit freely with each other. Love when all said and done is a matter of the heart so whether it is passed between man and woman, man and man or woman and woman it should be accepted. I allow it among my own people while we are here in our secluded glade. However if it is necessary for any of my people to mix with other tribes or Dutch people in the settlements I tell them to be very careful. There are those who would bring harm upon such people. I have witnessed many being subjected to great cruelties when they have been caught together."

"Do you refer to the Swan River settlement?" Fred asked.

"Yes, and a developing one further up river which is occupied mainly by the Noongar Tribe. Presently the area is lightly populated but will expand as the sandbar is gradually dug away so the river becomes navigable to larger ships. It is but a week's cart ride from here. There we buy supplies off visiting ships and if possible clothing for myself such as a new top hat. We use gold to purchase these supplies."

Fred's eyes lit up. "Do you mine for gold?"

"Not really. It lies in many areas just below the surface and my people know where to look. European prospectors don't so they have to search for months for very small amounts. My people possess lots of gold, Fred, and are therefore very rich although we still prefer to live the way we do. We Myalls are an original Australian aboriginal race who are proud to be disease free, a simple peace-loving tribe who wish nothing more than to live our lives in harmony within this peaceful glade. Large congregations of people are not for us, too many criminals," he paused and winked, "criminals who have not received a king's pardon, I may add. You should all feel honoured to mingle within us, my friends."

"Oh, we do, Cromwell, we certainly do," Fred replied.

"That is good, friend Fred. Now come, let us eat."

They assembled themselves around the fires and sat cross-legged. The young men stared at the women's legs which had become exposed to the knees and once again natural reactions were taking place.

"Try not to look," Catherine whispered to Ann.

"Between their legs men are ugly, women are beautiful," Ann replied.

Women served them the fish course on large leaves. It looked like all the bones had been removed so it was ready to eat with their fingers. They all agreed the fish was very palatable and tasted somewhat like salmon. This was followed by turtles' eggs still in their shells. Cromwell demonstrated how to eat them. He simply bit off the top, spat the shell out and sucked. They all followed and discovered the taste was not unlike hen's or duck's eggs. Next came the kangaroo meat which had been cooking on the spit. Ann asked Cromwell what a kangaroo was.

"A unique animal, my dear. One which hops on its hind legs and delivers its offspring in a sack which is part of its stomach. The animal is unique to Australia."

Ann thanked him and made comment that the meat tasted very much like venison but perhaps a little greasier. Nevertheless it was most welcome and certainly better than anything they had been served on the *Bromley*.

Cromwell asked if they enjoyed the meal. They all had. He patted his ample belly and said it was time for a toast, drinking a concoction brewed from coconut milk and a selection of ground-up berries. A huge pot of the liquid was produced and they were each given a coconut shell half. They helped themselves and after the first sip it caused them all to cough and splutter. This was far stronger than the rum they'd found washed up on the shore.

Cromwell put the drink into eloquent perspective. "Drinking four coconut measures of this enables all our young men to retain the hardness of their manhood for a considerable time. This helps them deliver our maidens into sexual heavens." He looked at Fred as if to say Sophie would be well satisfied the next time they came together.

Then he stood up and announced they should all join him for a swim. He quickly removed everything he wore except the top hat and ran towards the lake in all his blubbery nakedness. In unabashed nudity all his citizens followed.

Fred looked at the girls, stood up and said, "There's a saying among sailors, when in Rome do as the Romans do."

Mildly surprised they watched him strip off and run to the water. Sophie followed and not to be outdone Catherine and Ann disrobed. As they entered the cool water nobody took any notice of their nakedness as they waded in up to their waists. Catherine had never felt so free in her entire life. It was as if they had landed on a different world to the one they had sailed from. A world not of London, not even Australia, a place where everything was peaceful and pure. She wondered what the patrons of The Grapes would think about these displays of total nakedness. She could also easily imagine all the filthy bodies which would have been revealed as many only washed two or three times a year. It was then she realised their own bodies were perhaps the cleanest they'd ever been due to the amount of time spent floundering in the sea following the shipwreck. Now holding hands she and Ann were not at all surprised to see Cromwell kissing one of the maidens while others simply watched.

"These people have quite a different outlook on life than English people, don't they?" Ann whispered while running a hand across Catherine's stomach just below the waterline.

"They have a freedom most English citizens don't enjoy, my love. They may be very primitive but obviously cherish their style of life."

"Would you like to stay here forever?" Ann asked while stroking Catherine's cheek.

Catherine thought for a moment before answering. "No, quite honestly I don't think so. England has so much more to offer."

"Provided you have money," Ann interjected. "The rich seem to have everything while the poor have nothing except aching backs and arms from working long hours for very little pay. And don't forget we women are not even permitted to vote so we have no control over who administers our own country. Take yourself as an example, you had to partially maim your stepfather in order to hope for a better life. And look where it got you, a sickening journey in the steaming-hot hold of a ship bound for prison in a land which is virtually untamed. Yet here in this same land we have seen at least one tribe which exists in harmony and with total equality. However to answer your question, I too would like to return home provided you were at my side. We'll just have to see how things transpire. For the moment though I'm very happy."

"So am I. We have our lives and our love, so what more could we ask for?"

She stopped talking because someone had gasped loudly behind them. They both turned to see who it was and were confronted by a wizened old woman wearing a long knitted shawl, the ends of which hung in the water. She was waving Cromwell over. When he arrived some conversation took place before Ann was asked if she'd been flogged while aboard the ship.

Ann looked at Catherine before explaining what she'd done to the first mate when he tried to attack her. Then of the punishment she was forced to endure.

"Is this man now dead?" Cromwell asked, holding a fatherly hand on top of Ann's head.

Catherine explained he had survived and was on his way back to England for treatment, perhaps he had arrived by now. They just didn't know.

Cromwell continued stroking Ann's hair. "He should have been sent to hell for attacking a beautiful young lady who is in love with another beautiful young lady. This lady is my medicine woman, her name is simply Tarfa. She will rub some special leaves soaked in a soothing oil on your back, Ann. It will heal the scars quicker, also make them fainter. A graceful female back should not be sullied with scars created by strips of wicked leather. Go with Tarfa, my dear, Catherine may accompany you. Tarfa is a great healer and we think she is over a hundred years old."

Tarfa took Ann's hand and led her out of the water with Catherine following. Chief Cromwell returned to another maiden who embraced and kissed him before working her body against his.

In one of the huts Tarfa helped Ann lie face down on some soft matting. From a woven basket she produced a quantity of large green leaves which she first crumpled up in her gnarled hands before dropping them in a thick oily substance with a white mist rising from it. As she stirred the mixture Catherine noted it emitted a very strange odour. Once well soaked Tarfa scooped some out with her hands and began rubbing the concoction quite firmly over Ann's back, causing her to wince at first but gradually Catherine saw her entering into a totally relaxed state.

"It feels so soothing," Ann finally said, smiling up at her lover.

Three more rubbings were applied before Ann got up and admitted her back felt much easier already. Then she made one of her coy comments which so captivated Catherine.

"Perhaps we should take Tarfa back to England with us so she could cure all those with diseases which our doctors cannot."

"I don't think Cromwell would allow Tarfa to go anywhere, my dear. Obviously she is the reason why everybody is so fit and disease free here. I wonder if she'll be able to do anything with Clare Hamlyn's leg?"

"Or even Wilf's cut. It was a miracle us finding this place, Catherine. Now I'm filled with an urge to make love. Do you think Cromwell would give permission?"

"I don't see why not. He appears to make enough of it himself. Let's go ask."

They didn't need to go far, he was just about to enter the hut. He studied Ann's back and proclaimed there was a definite improvement already.

Ann thanked him and asked if it was permissible to find somewhere private where she and Catherine could be alone for a few minutes.

"By all means, my children. Be happy in your own way. In the forest you will find many areas covered in soft moss. Then by the time you return your other friends from the beach will have arrived. I shall instruct that a special feast is prepared. Go make love now."

After they had gathered their clothes he watched them walk off hand in hand and smiled. It was nice for him to have visitors from England, very unexpected visitors. He must also ensure those horrible metal bands around their ankles were removed. He would send for the horse breeder Garrogerald who lived in the place they were calling Bridgetown. He had tools to cut the bands off. In fact he beckoned a sprightly youth over and told him to go and get the breeder. He was to tell the man gold would be part of his reward, a very willing maiden the other.

* * *

Catherine and Ann quickly found a very secluded area where the ground was covered in downy moss just as Cromwell had described. As they lay down they saw numerous strange birds flitting about in the branches of lush trees, completing this idyllic setting. Catherine was aware the Bible mentioned a 'Garden of Eden', to her mind this could well be it. However the trees and birds were quickly forgotten when their lips made soft contact.

Ann slowly turned Catherine on her back and snuggled her face in the valley of her lover's breasts. Catherine lay perfectly still, looking up at the green foliage of trees she didn't even know the name of as Ann continued to kiss her delicate flesh which had never experienced such total rapture.

They were so alone and at peace yet in the wide world both were aware new children were coming into it while others were dying, many from hunger, or violent crimes and some naturally from old age. A perpetual motion of life and death. But for Catherine and Ann these were moments where nobody or anything else existed. They were alone and in love.

* * *

When they returned to the village most people were standing at the lake edge, watching the two rafts returning. Wilf Malone and Emily Kilpatrick were easily seen on one while Clare Hamlyn lay flat out on the other on some kind of frame. It was comforting to see Cromwell and Tarfa standing and waiting.

Once he had limped ashore Wilf shook Fred's hand while the females kissed and started to explain this unique village whose head was an educated man simply named Cromwell. A man who at the moment was knee-deep in the water with Tarfa looking at Clare's leg. The expressions on their faces were grave.

Wilf explained, "Her condition has deteriorated drastically since you all left. Clare realises death is near and has made her peace with God. She has repented all the hate expressed against you convicts and wishes to atone in some way, unfortunately I couldn't think of any. She has asked me if it's at all possible to get a message to her husband in Port Jackson that she has departed this life but hopes they may meet again in the next. I know nothing about life after death so I simply said I would do all I could."

"What can you do?" Fred asked.

"I've thought about that a great deal and the only thing I can think of is writing a letter, going to the Swan River settlement and asking that Hoorn Helderden to give it to the captain of a ship bound for Port Jackson. I think before she passes on

I should tell her this, it may ease her troubled mind somewhat. Perhaps the village chief can help... What's his name?"

"Cromwell," Catherine told him. "He's a remarkable man, Wilf. He's sent a runner off to bring someone here who can remove these shackles around our ankles. Also the old woman, whose name is Tarfa, has applied a mystical potion to Ann's back so it is much improved since you last saw it."

Cromwell walked ashore and introductions were made. He even doffed his top hat as Wilf asked him what he thought of Clare's condition.

"It is not good, she is in an advanced state of shock and has a severe fever. Tarfa says her leg is broken beyond repair. She has seen similar breaks and says a rotting disease of the skin has already begun, therefore the leg must be removed without delay or the woman will die." Cromwell's eyes met Wilf's. "Are you the senior man of this group?"

"Yes, I suppose I am. Why?"

"The woman is incapable of making any rational decisions so you must decide if we take the leg off."

"How much of the leg?"

"Just above the knee. Tarfa says if this is done the woman may perhaps live but nothing is certain. Even your doctors in London wouldn't be able to guarantee success. Make your decision quickly, Mister Malone, the woman hasn't much time."

"Will she understand if I tell her what we propose to do?"

"No. I have already tried, you see her mind rambles. I think you say delirious."

Wilf looked around the survivors and they could easily see the pressure he was under. Cromwell was asked if Clare would suffer much pain.

"Not while the leg is being severed. Tarfa has powerful potions which numb the senses. Afterward there will be some pain and discomfort. However that is better than death, don't you think?"

"I suppose so."

"You must agree, Wilf," Ann told him. "I openly admit not liking Clare although I would hate for her to die if it can be avoided."

Wilf nodded. "Alright, Cromwell, go ahead."

Cromwell laid a hand on his shoulder. "Your decision is a wise one, Mister Malone. Tarfa will proceed immediately."

He left the group to tell the old woman. She smiled and beckoned two stout men over to take the stretcher into her hut.

The survivors sat down in a circle to wait. Food and drink was brought to them. As they started to eat they noticed a strange silence had fallen over the entire village. Even the dogs had stopped barking and they themselves didn't feel like talking. A white woman of some breeding was at the mercy of an untrained native who it was claimed had lived for over a hundred years. The outcome remained to be seen.

* * *

Being a man of the sea, time had always been an important factor in Wilf Malone's life and yet to Cromwell's people it appeared to mean nothing. Even Cromwell didn't carry any sort of timepiece, leaving the rising and setting sun to decide the patterns of their days. Apart from cooking, tending a multitude of crops, sheep, cattle and poultry, fishing, hunting and maintaining the thatched cottages there didn't appear to be too many schedules and nobody seemed hurried or rushed. Their lives were basic in almost every respect and perhaps more importantly they all seemed very happy. Ann had not seen a tear being shed and certainly she had not heard anybody squabbling. These simple folk had attained a peace and certain quality of life which would be impossible to attain in places like London. Here a clean, pure atmosphere, there the soot and grime of countless chimneys, the stench of decomposing food and human waste, mangy half-wild dogs running rampant, to say nothing of rats. Then there were the pickpockets and beggars or the aristocrats who exploited almost everybody below their own station. Even to the king himself who eighteen years ago had taken a woman and implanted his seeds of life without a thought that a child might arise from the forced encounter. When it did he simply provided the very basics to the mother although he never came to see his child. Yet when that child tried to obtain some recognition after her mother died, what did the king do? He or some of his trusted aides arranged to have the girl transported to Australia where she stood little chance of survival, or so he thought. Now a twist of fate may give Ann Lingos her chance of retribution. And that same fate may also give new lives to three of the remaining convicts. Two of their number had perished in the shipwreck but so had other good seamen including Captain Algernon Stricker. Yet nobody knew who dictated which persons should live and who should die. There lies the eternal mystery which may never be resolved. Perhaps there was an order somewhere within the ethos but it is one never to be seen yet will have an impact on life in all its facets into what some would call eternity.

* * *

It was dark when the survivors saw their benefactor Cromwell approaching with his face being illuminated by the bright moon which glimmered through the tree branches. He sat down among them.

"It is over, my friends, Clare Hamlyn is minus a leg but happily her fever is already subsiding. Tarfa expects she will make a good recovery although it will take much time and patience."

"Can we see her?" Wilf asked.

"She still sleeps, Wilf, it will be tomorrow morning before she recovers consciousness. Tarfa gave her a very strong sleeping potion because her nervous system needs time to readjust itself, you see; it has been subjected to a great shock. However I think after Tarfa has treated your leg we should rejoice, eat a hearty meal and drink. Then it will be time for romance and enjoyment." He glanced at Ann and Catherine and added, "Each in our own way."

He looked at the faces of his unexpected guests and saw happiness and contentment. Also relief that Clare would live despite her attitude.

* * *

The new day arrived with Tarfa treating Ann's back again and looking at Wilf's leg. Since last night the gash had closed nicely although she had advised him not to do much walking for the rest of the day. He should also be careful if he went swimming. After this advice she went to see how her patient was doing.

During the morning while they were bathing, the women's torn clothing had been washed and stitched by very skilful hands so at least they all looked a little more presentable. Each woman had also been given a pair of bootees made from rabbit fur. Now as the four of them sat drinking coconut milk young maidens were combing their ever growing hair. Thanks to Cromwell and his people they were beginning to feel like human beings again although they were still slightly perplexed at their astonishing good fortune which they all hoped would continue.

Cromwell had been asked if any other ships in this area had suffered a similar fate as the *Bromley*. Not surprisingly he said no. It seemed storms such as they had encountered were very rare indeed, in fact he couldn't remember one so fierce as that which struck them. He did say the storm must have been very localized because it had completely bypassed the glade. They had seen the dark clouds, heard the whistling wind, the flashes of lightning and rolls of distant thunder but that was all. Even the lake had barely rippled.

"We consider the storm a miracle, Cromwell, because it gave us our freedom," Sophie interjected.

Cromwell leaned back and laughed loudly. "I'm sorry, Sophie, I thought, according to Fred, your freedom came by a royal decree issued goodness knows how long ago."

Wilf looked puzzled so Fred quickly related how he had explained their freedom when they first met Cromwell and his tribe.

Now Wilf laughed. "I don't think any monarch would dare issue such an edict. Neither the government nor the people would ever accept criminals being granted freedom before their time had been served."

Ann perhaps put it in a true perspective. "I think by some divine intervention our lives have been spared and freedom is just a part of it. Unfortunately it is a liberty we will never be able to talk about otherwise we may all be arrested again and face yet another long voyage."

They all smiled and agreed just as one of Cromwell's women whispered something in his ear. It seemed it was time to eat again.

The meal consisted of fried gull's eggs along with grilled kangaroo strips which were very similar to fatty bacon. There was also a mixture which Cromwell claimed to be like tea although they all found it too bitter and there was no sugar. Nevertheless they didn't complain, Cromwell's peaceful domain was almost beyond their wildest imaginations. In fact last night Wilf had made a general comment before they all went their separate ways, either to sleep or make love.

"You don't think we're all dead, do you and this is what the hereafter is like?"

"I don't care what it is, Wilf," Emily replied, "with you I'm in heaven anyway."

They all agreed and thought Emily had put it rather well.

It seemed after the morning meal every villager went down to the lake to wash and bathe. They were joined by the survivors who despite language barriers wallowed beside them as if they'd known each other for years. Wilf silently wondered how many other white people knew about this place where the population didn't appear to have a care or worry in the world. He hoped not many, realising foreign intruders would spoil everything within a short space of time. The English were like that, things had to be run their way or not at all. Wilf was aware Englishmen had founded empires mainly in the East although to do so they had trampled on and subjugated the locals. Those in power realised these impositions would eventually lead to the oppressed wanting to govern themselves again but such events could take years, if not centuries, they therefore became other government's problems.

As they splashed in the warm water Catherine saw Emily and Sophie wading over to join them. When they arrived their futures were discussed. It quickly became obvious none of them wanted to stay here forever no matter how peaceful and idyllic the lifestyle was. They agreed that a basic difference existed between themselves and Cromwell's people. Here there was no motivation to make progress, time for them virtually stood still. It didn't even appear as if there were days, weeks, months or years in their lives, simply sunrises and sunsets. In London and cities like it progress could be seen in the buildings or in the clothes people wore. Here these grass huts and fire pits could be a year old or a thousand, nobody would know the difference. It was a pity trees couldn't speak. And apart from Cromwell himself both men and women wore identical cloths about their middles to conceal that difference between male and female although they all revelled in nakedness and made love freely. In Britain there were those inherent ambitions of its peoples to better themselves and advance so the next generation could enjoy higher standards of living. It wasn't the point that life in Britain was repressive for at least three quarters of the population, however that in time would change for the eventual betterment of all. Now though the question uppermost in their minds was not that of economics or life generally, rather would it be safe to return home? To be taken into custody again didn't bear thinking about. For now they had been spared a life in the penal colony although technically under English law they were still guilty. Plus there was another factor which had developed since the shipwreck. Two more of their number had fallen in love. Emily Kilpatrick with Wilf Malone and Sophie Hart with Fred Pankhurst. Obviously if these loves resulted in marriage both Emily's and Sophie's surnames would change, giving them a fair chance of not being detected. Or they could enter England on some remote area of the coast and simply live as man and wife. For the moment however, they were all happy to leave these decisions for another day. England was still a long way away.

While they were still talking Cromwell came to them and announced that the horse breeder Garrogerald should arrive shortly to rid them of their ankle shackles. This of course was another important step to freedom. The final vestiges of their criminal past were to be removed, only the scars would remain. Further, when they had finished bathing they could visit Clare who had just awoken. It seemed Cromwell had already explained to her what had been done and although she was greatly shocked at losing a limb she accepted it because the alternative was almost certain death. Cromwell had a man making her a pair of crutches so she wouldn't be totally immobile once fit enough to attempt walking. She had been advised though this could be weeks ahead. Plus the stump of her leg would require many more treatments by Tarfa. Nevertheless they all considered it a remarkable achievement that Clare still lived.

* * *

It was heartening to see Clare smiling as she greeted them. Her ashen face looked more relaxed than it had been since they found her on the beach. A brightly coloured blanket covered her legs although it was obvious one was absent as only a single foot raised the cover. It also seemed the operation had changed her entire demeanour. Gracefully she said, "I'd like to thank each and every one of you for treating me with civility when I didn't truly deserve it. I was a bitch and realise it now. I'm sorry. I consider it a miracle I'm still alive, having gone through that terrible storm and the shipwreck in which so few of us survived. I shall miss my dear friend Alice Edwards and of course Captain Stricker and his crew who were all so kind. So what are your intentions now, Mister Malone?"

"To be perfectly honest, Clare, we don't actually know. I think most of us would like to return to England but there are the obvious complications."

"You mean Catherine, Ann, Emily and Sophie?"

"Yes of course."

She glanced at each of the convicts' faces in turn before saying, "By way of my own atonement you can be assured if questioned I shall not say who else survived the shipwreck, I owe you that much. And from what each of you told Mister Malone on the beach it seems there were justifiable reasons for committing your crimes. In that respect I agree the law may have been a little too harsh. However it seems God has intervened and given you all a second chance so I say make the most of it."

She turned her head to one side because tears had suddenly filled her eyes. They each thanked her, pleased in the knowledge she didn't intend to tell anybody they had survived. This improved their chances enormously, in fact Catherine felt like kissing her but didn't. Instead she kissed Ann.

Tarfa entered the hut along with Cromwell. He told them it was time for Clare to sleep again while Tarfa attended to the stump which was vital for her future survival. Fred was truly amazed, having known a shipmate on a previous voyage who'd had a leg amputated and he survived less than twenty-four hours.

Once outside the hut Cromwell asked Wilf what his intentions were now.

"After the girls' ankle shackles are removed, I think we'd all like to head for the coast and hopefully pick up a ship bound for England or somewhere close. However we may have to earn some money first to pay for our passages."

Cromwell laughed in his usual hearty manner and tapped his top hat which never seemed to leave his head. "Don't worry about money, my friends, as I said, we have lots of gold. Over the years our people have amassed vast amounts but as you will have observed our lifestyles are very simple so we spend little. It has been this way since I returned to my people from England where I saw the evils which money can bring. Above all it breeds greed and animosity between those who have it and those who don't and sadly I fear it will always be so. Here we are one united people, nobody is better than anybody else and that includes myself. I'm proud to say we have achieved a certain perfection and that is why we live in virtual seclusion. As for money however, I could give you enough gold to buy your own ship, my friend Wilf."

Now Wilf laughed. "I'm not qualified, Cromwell, just a simple bosun who takes orders. Nevertheless your offer of gold is more than generous and we would be fools not to accept. Thank you."

"It is my pleasure, Wilf. I have never known any white man to refuse gold, not that I blame any of you, it is your way of life. I must go now as there is much for me to do. I have a tribe to run, you know, and must supervise our crops and livestock. We will meet again later when Garrogerald arrives."

"What a man, what a bloody man," Fred Pankhurst said when Cromwell was out of earshot.

Wilf nodded his head in agreement as he looked at the others. "I assume we accept the offer?"

They all agreed and started babbling excitedly at the prospects Cromwell had opened up for them.

"You could start your own shipping line," Emily told Wilf while hugging his arm.

"Aye, lass, that I could. I'd need a good wife behind me though."

"I'm yours, Wilf. Just say when."

"Perhaps when we're aboard a ship bound for home. Captains have the authority to marry couples, you know."

"I didn't but it's nice to know."

Fred asked Sophie how she'd like to become Mrs Pankhurst.

"There's nothing in the wide world I'd rather be named, Fred. We could wed alongside Wilf and Emily. And changing our names would make it a lot safer for us in England." Then she looked at Catherine and Ann and asked what they could do. Ann answered, "I don't imagine there's a ship's captain in the world who would marry two women, Sophie, but we could certainly change our names. Catherine Farrow could be altered to Harrow and I could become Annie Ingol or something like that."

"It sounds wonderful," Catherine told her as they embraced.

"That's all settled then," Wilf said rubbing his hands in glee, knowing in the space of a few days all their lives had changed significantly, thankfully for the better.

They started walking towards the lake when they saw Cromwell approaching with a huge heavily bearded man who could only be Garrogerald, the horse breeder. He walked with the aid of a thick cane as his right foot didn't seem quite in alignment with the left.

While being introduced they could actually smell animals on him and he shook hands as if holding a horse's hoof. Cromwell explained that the man couldn't speak because his tongue had been cut out by Spanish pirates who had attacked the galleon he used to sail, marauding in the Caribbean Sea. While trying to get treatment in Kingston, Jamaica the authorities arrested him for plundering on the high seas. He was eventually tried, found guilty and deported back to England where he eventually became a crewman on a ship bound for Port Jackson but skipped ship when they called into the settlement on the Swan River. From there he moved inland to breed horses which he sold mainly to sheep farmers and prospectors. He was very successful as everybody needed transport. Other than that the man was a total mystery who lived alone on his ranch. Cromwell called Garrogerald an enigma, before asking the women to hoist their skirts so the man could inspect their shackles.

Garrogerald smiled to reveal a mouth which was not only devoid of a tongue but teeth also. There were a few stumps although nothing much and Catherine wondered how he chewed meat. Still his diet was no concern of theirs.

After assessing every ankle carefully he stood up and scribed the word 'easy' with his cane in the dirt. Then he pulled a pained expression which Cromwell interpreted as meaning the procedure might hurt a little. This didn't bother the girls, they would tolerate anything to be rid of the remaining evidence of their past misfortunes.

Cromwell instructed two of his lads to find a large flat pebble to serve as Garrogerald's anvil. This proved easy as the lake edge was littered with them. In the meantime Garrogerald had fetched a huge hammer and chisel from a satchel slung behind the saddle of his horse.

It was decided Ann would be first. She lay on the sand, hoisted her skirt to the knees and placed her right ankle on the pebble as Catherine knelt to hold her hand. One of Cromwell's lads held the chisel over the flange where the chain had been attached and Garrogerald brought the hammer down rapidly. Ann's face grimaced in pain and she screamed as the second blow landed. The third severed the anklet and it fell off. The other girls cheered.

Cromwell suggested that to save Ann further pain for the moment one of the others had a turn. This was agreed and within the hour they all danced a little jig saying how light their feet felt. Tarfa had applied some of her magic lotions around their bleeding ankles and through Cromwell she said the scars would gradually fade.

Some of Cromwell's potent coconut milk concoctions were produced and they all sat around drinking the liquid which made their heads spin. Two maidens fawned upon Garrogerald and began removing his shirt. He stood up and they walked arm in arm into the trees.

"That's part of his reward," Cromwell told them. "He will be a well-satisfied man today, as of course will the women."

"Can he be trusted?" Fred asked, his speech slurring slightly.

"Of course, my friend. Remember he cannot speak and I know he hates authority as most of his life has been spent breaking the law in one way or another. You may have noticed he walks with a slight limp. While in custody in Kingston, Jamaica, awaiting a trial, he was questioned about the whereabouts of other pirates roaming the seas but he refused to write down where they were. They tried to induce him by cutting his toes off one by one. When none remained on his right foot they gave up but still tried him for piracy. You've heard the rest so why don't you enjoy yourselves tonight by drinking and making love. Tomorrow you can all start out for the coast and get a ship home."

"What about Clare?" Sophie asked.

"For her own sake she must remain here. When she's fit enough to travel I will arrange for someone to accompany her to Port Jackson where with luck she'll be reunited with her husband. She has expressed that desire to me already. It will also be better for you people as she would only impede your progress. Now as I have just said, enjoy yourselves tonight and wake up fresh for your journey tomorrow."

Catherine turned to face Ann. "Let's go to our glade."

They got up and left. Gradually they had all dispersed and Cromwell went about running his tiny empire.

* * *

In the morning following a breakfast of freshly caught fish Cromwell had three surprises for them. One was a horse-drawn four-wheeled cart fitted with crude benches but large enough to hold the six of them. In it were numerous woven blankets for them to sit on while travelling and to use as covers when they camped for the night. Two of Cromwell's strong lads had been detailed as guides until they reached the developing settlement occupied mainly by the aboriginal tribe of Noongar. From there they would have no trouble finding a boat to take them down the Swan River to the Dutch settlement where trading ships called in. Cromwell's second surprise was almost beyond belief. For each he had a large kangaroo leather purse filled with small gold nuggets. Neither Fred nor Wilf could estimate their value, only that it had to be considerable. Their host advised them to conceal the purses about their persons before they arrived in any populated area as thieves of almost every description abounded. The third surprise was more down to earth. A cut-throat razor so the men could shave. And they needed to, they hadn't shaved since the shipwreck and their stubble was starting to look like beards.

Before leaving they all went to say goodbye to Clare Hamlyn who looked better than she ever had, even when aboard the *Bromley*. Tarfa had worked a miracle. Tears flowed as goodbyes were said because in one way or another they had been together for over half a year although nobody could have anticipated it would end this way. Many had perished in the shipwreck and of the six original convicts only four remained but all being well they now faced a prosperous future with the money Cromwell had given them. And perhaps the most ironic thing of all, nobody except themselves and their host were yet aware the *Bromley* had been shipwrecked. Naturally questions would be raised when it didn't arrive in Botany Bay and Wilf assumed word would eventually get back to the ship's owners in London. However his seafaring life was over as he intended settling down with Emily in a yet to be determined location.

It was a wrench for them all saying goodbye to the flamboyant one they only knew as Cromwell. If the horse dealer Garrogerald was an enigma Cromwell was a bigger one. Probably one of the most educated men in Australia and yet his lifestyle couldn't be simpler. A man also of inestimable wealth although rarely spending any of it. He could even buy a nation if he so wished although the urge wasn't present.

He enjoyed the uncomplicated life which gave him good health, food and drink and all the female company he could ever want.

As they all shook hands he said, "Today, my English friends, you depart, I remain but please think of me from time to time. You will be very safe with my two trusty guards whom I have named Hamlet and Macbeth because of their desire to learn the English language. They will provide escort to the head of the Swan River where you will meet Europeans. Along the way you may like to teach them some English, I know they will appreciate it."

"We'll all try," Fred told their benefactor.

Cromwell smiled. "That is good and I thank you. Now finally I'd like to say you are all ready to go back into your own world but please don't tell anybody about mine. Can I rely on that?"

"You certainly can, my friend," Wilf answered as they all began to get in the cart.

As it started to move off with their two escorts sitting up front Cromwell doffed his top hat which brought tears to the women's eyes while Wilf and Fred tried not to show any emotion. Slowly they emerged out of the forest to pass through sweeping fields of wheat and many other basic crops. Ann took Catherine's hand when happy, contented workers smiled and waved at them.

"We must remember these sights, my love, for they represent a tranquillity of life we may never see again."

Catherine licked her lips. "I agree. During our nights at home we must take a few moments to think of this place and its people before making love. In that we will always have peace of mind."

Wilf had overheard them and smiled to himself. In themselves they were a unique couple and he inwardly vowed to do all he could to ensure their safety.

Then the cart started to descend down a steadily sloping trail towards a flat, bleak-looking plain which hopefully in a week to ten days would see them arrive at the coast where their new lives should really begin.

* * * * *

PART FOUR

HOMEWARD BOUND

CHAPTER 19

WILF DECIDED TO MAKE CAMP FOR ONE final night as they were less than a day's ride to the Noongar settlement and the Swan River, this according to their escorts Hamlet and Macbeth. In their limited English they had made it clear on their first night out that it wasn't safe to travel during darkness. For one thing bandits and wild animals roamed the plains.

Their journey from Cromwell's haven in the forest had been accomplished with only one major delay when a cartwheel came off after hitting a large rock. This caused the cart to tilt at a severe angle but luckily none of the passengers were thrown out although it did put a strain on Wilf's leg. Two spokes had been broken which their faithful and resourceful guides lashed together with splints and lengths of rein before replacing the wheel with Fred's able assistance. Wilf volunteered his services but Fred insisted he didn't put any more strain on his leg which was healing nicely although it had a tendency to stiffen when he sat for long periods of time.

To exercise the leg he and Emily walked alongside the cart for half an hour or so every couple of hours accompanied by either Hamlet or Macbeth so they could learn as much English as possible. Not unexpectedly Ann had proved to be an excellent and patient teacher despite the fact she couldn't speak their language. Her approach was to pick out objects such as trees, rocks, ponds and animals then say the words in English and make the two men repeat them over and over again. Four days ago Hamlet had become very brave and pointed to her right breast. Ann realised this question had arisen from the previous evening when all the women had removed their blouses to wash in a pond. Both guides had stared at them and one could only imagine what was going through their minds although neither youth had tried to make advances. Obviously Cromwell had alerted them to the fact the girls had their own lovers. Both men were told the correct word for these female glands.

Throughout the journey they had encountered some fairly hilly terrain and were forced to make detours around steeper slopes. Of course had they been on foot it would have been easy to traverse over them. The going was rugged at times and they all had to help push the cart through boulder-strewn regions and across streams and swiftly flowing rivers. These hazards were obviously why Cromwell limited his visits to the river settlements. And one of Wilf's comments added a lighter note.

"At least in a sailing ship you don't have to get out and push."

One thing in their favour as they progressed onward was the abundance of food. The area teemed with rabbits which were almost too easy to catch. Larger ponds and lakes were sources of fish and Fred was able to confirm if they were edible or not. Game birds were plentiful although difficult to catch as they had no guns. A blanket was used to trap some while they were in the trees but this made for frustrating hunting and consumed too much time so by and large their staple diet was rabbit and fish. However thanks to Fred's culinary skills he managed to vary what they ate by adding various herbs, spices and berries which grew wild. What rum remained in the keg had been brought with them and Wilf had taken it upon himself to ration the measures to ensure there was enough for a tot each until they reached the coast.

For the first time in their lives they saw numerous kangaroos which according to Emily looked like enormous rats. Quite a few carried offspring in their belly pouches. One which didn't was killed by their guides for its meat. They also saw many large strutting birds which Fred knew to be emus but only because of their plumage which English women of quality had made into stoles. Snakes though were a constant problem as they appeared suddenly out of the rocks or scrub grass, hissing at the two horses. Hamlet and Macbeth fearlessly clubbed them to death.

After skinning the rabbits their pelts had been put to good use. It was the ever resourceful Sophie who suggested they made spare bootees in case their original ones wore out due to the rugged terrain. Threads were created from the hems of the girls' skirts and gorse spines made perfect needles. Making the footwear also passed the hours away as they progressed in a north-westerly direction under a hot sun. It was as Sophie had said, "In preference to just sitting, I'd rather sit and work." The others could only agree.

Each night they stopped and slept under the stars, near fires lit by Fred's supply of flints. They also tried where possible to camp by a small lake or simply a pond so they could wash and the men shave.

As their progress brought them nearer to the Swan River the ladies became concerned they may bump into the farmers they had dropped off. As a result of this any time they saw another group, either on horseback or driving carts, they took whatever cover was available and waited while the party passed. At night they ensured their campfire couldn't be seen. It was obvious Cromwell's lads didn't understand all this secrecy as they were unaware of the ladies' backgrounds. Tactfully Cromwell had not told them but Wilf doubted there was a word for transportation or convict in their limited vocabulary.

And of course before sleep came each night love was exchanged and memories stored. What had started out for the convicts as a nightmare had now become an adventure although it still lingered at the back of their minds they were somewhat vulnerable and this would only increase once they reached the coast where they may have to wait a long time for a ship. Wilf tried his best to ease their concerns by telling them it wasn't necessary to take a ship bound for England. Anything heading west would do and of course they had gold to pay their passages.

It was a source of amazement to them that since leaving Cromwell's glade they had not seen a single residence of any shape or size. They had come across one hut by a narrow river although it appeared to have been abandoned years ago. They assumed its occupant had been a prospector for gold who had either found a fortune or died in the attempt.

From his nautical experience Wilf had taken it upon himself to count the days they had been travelling. When he estimated they were within two days of the Noongar settlement he called a halt to discuss their future strategy around a crackling campfire.

"During my many walks by the cart I've given the matter of our security a great deal of thought and I suggest we all agree on a cover story. Six total strangers travelling together are bound to draw attention and the last thing we want is to be questioned by anybody, especially somebody connected with the law, that is if there are such people in these parts. Fortunately neither Fred nor myself went ashore when we dropped the farmers off so we won't be recognized. As you know, only Captain Stricker and Felix Bloom actually landed to organize the provisioning, plus locals manning supply boats didn't come aboard. All provisions were simply hoisted up on deck." He paused to take a sip of water so they all did.

After five minutes he continued, "I think it's wise to keep our story simple and stick to what actually happened wherever possible, that is except with a slight modification. I suggest that rather than sailing east to Port Jackson we would have departed from there heading for London, carrying a cargo of fleeces, when we were shipwrecked in the area off Brookes Inlet with all hands except ourselves being lost. It also helps that myself and Emily have genuine wounds to show. Luckily after spending two days on the beach we met up with this tribe who fed us and provided transport and escorts to the Noongar settlement. In view of our promise to Cromwell we won't mention his name. How does all that sound?"

Nods of agreement were made before Fred asked what their bogus ship was called.

"The *Whitby*," Wilf replied after a moment's thought, being aware of a genuine vessel named the *Scarborough* which carried convicts to Botany Bay. Before continuing he poured each a measure of rum. Hamlet and Macbeth were also given a tot and they responded by saying one of their new English words, "Cheers."

"Now as for our own situations," Wilf continued. "It would be less complicated if Fred and I simply say we are married to Sophie and Emily, this on the very logical reasoning that nobody can refute it. As for Ann and Catherine, you will simply assume your aliases as previously agreed and be travelling companions who were returning to families in England when disaster struck. How do we all feel about this?"

"Everything sounds excellent," Catherine and Sophie replied in unison.

In fact they all agreed which left them with much easier frames of mind. They went over the story two or three times until everybody was sure of the facts. Questions were asked and answers came very convincingly. As Ann said, "We are becoming accomplished liars but for my freedom I'm quite willing to distort the truth."

"Aren't we all," Emily added with a smile before kissing Wilf on his cheek.

Then as usual Fred and Sophie started to prepare a meal as the others gathered firewood and arranged blankets to sleep on with a canopy of stars as their roof. And once again they were all amazed at the utter stillness and silence which prevailed all around. It would be a pity to leave it, yet on the other hand they were all longing to hear the clip-clop of horses' hoofs and the sound of cartwheels again as they clattered over the cobblestone streets of England.

* * *

Next morning Wilf claimed he could smell the sea as they headed west towards the Noongar Settlement beyond which lay the Swan River estuary and hopefully a ship to take them home. The women were obviously edgy as today they would be entering into unfamiliar populated areas which didn't offer the security of

Cromwell's glade. For comfort Catherine and Ann held hands and the men had their arms around the ladies' shoulders. Up front Hamlet and Macbeth stared straight ahead, knowing this would be the last day with their charges.

All was quiet until Emily suddenly said, "I don't believe it, look."

Appearing out of a shimmering heat haze there was a medium-sized log cabin complete with a neat garden in which a white woman was hanging out washing, surrounded by free-roaming chickens, sheep and geese. What looked like a young native girl was helping her. The woman saw them and hailed, "Good morning. Who are you? It's nice to see strangers. We don't get many travellers passing as we're a little off the beaten track, as they say." Her accent was very English, more suitable to certain areas of London rather than this rather desolate area of western Australia.

Hamlet who had the cart reins stopped it at Wilf's request. He got out realising this would be their first test of themselves and their story. As he approached the lady he just hoped she wasn't too inquisitive.

"Good morning to you, madam. Another pleasant day."

"All days are pleasant here, sir, so much fresher than England, none of that dreadful fog ever. I assume you are heading for the coast because few people pass here going inland into the most inhospitable wilderness."

"Yes, we're aiming for the coast where we intend getting a ship to England."

"Well, I don't think there are any ships in at present so why don't you and your friends tarry awhile and take morning tea with me? You will be most welcome."

Wilf looked at the women.

Emily hunched her shoulders. "Why not? I fancy a nice cup of tea."

The others agreed and started to get out of the cart. All the women felt slightly embarrassed at their dishevelled appearances although they would serve to support their story which was bound to be raised. In fact Emily's blouse continually slipped off her slightly sloping shoulders but up to now it hadn't seemed to matter and she knew Hamlet and Macbeth had no objections to displays of suntanned English flesh. Emily hitched her blouse up again as they all walked towards the tall woman who looked quite robust. Wilf made the introductions and for the first time Emily heard herself being called Mrs Malone. Catherine became a Harrow and Ann was now Annie Ingol. They both curtsied but were told it wasn't necessary, this was not England, everything in Australia was far less formal. Then she introduced herself.

"My name is McFarlane, Martha McFarlane. My husband Brendon is presently out on the range tending sheep. Please, all of you, come in. Kiri, my maid, will prepare tea." She said something to the attractive young Kiri which they all recognized as the language used by Cromwell to his people the Myalls. Kiri nodded, smiled and bowed.

After speaking with Martha for a few moments Wilf knew they were within a mile and a half of the Noongar settlement which meant Hamlet and Macbeth could return home. He went to them and explained the situation as best he could and by their smiles it seemed they understood. Despite all they had learned and seen on the journey they obviously wanted to be back among their own people.

Before they departed all the women gave them a hug and platonic kisses on their cheeks. Fred shook their hands as did Wilf while thanking them in English, hoping they understood. They geed the horses and drove off, heading back to the glade and their leader Cromwell. Their faces reflected contentment and they were returning with a better understanding of English, thanks mainly to Ann.

It soon became obvious the McFarlane residence wasn't palatial which caused them all to wonder why such people were here at all. From what Hamlet had managed to tell Wilf there were very few Europeans in this area of Australia. It seemed Port Jackson was the place of preference despite the fact it added thousands of miles to a voyage. However the McFarlanes really didn't concern Wilf, all he wanted to see was the western coast of Australia disappearing into the haze from the aft deck of a ship bound for England. This country held nothing for him or the others.

They were all shown into a medium-sized room whose main asset seemed to be a sweeping fireplace with a mantle bedecked with porcelain figures and miniature watercolours of presumably family members. It was also obvious the room was used for both dining and as a sitting area. The furniture was all handmade and didn't look too comfortable. Despite this they were asked to sit down. There were only four chairs plus a rocker so Catherine and Ann sat on the floor.

In a fleeting moment of reflection Catherine realised that had she not been sentenced in the first place and shipwrecked in the second the McFarlane residence would still have existed although she would never have seen it. Then her gaze fell on Ann causing her heart to miss a beat, realising she would not have met her either. Her crimes had opened up vistas which a year ago would have been unattainable.

As Martha fussed around rearranging some limp flowers Fred asked how many sheep Mister McFarlane owned.

"Oh, he doesn't own any, Mister Pankhurst, he simply manages for a mixed group of Europeans who run their stocks in the outback. It's hard work but it keeps Brendon out of trouble and it is he who does much of the bargaining with traders for the sheep's wool. Financially he does quite well and without the worry of running his own business. Now I know you'll think it odd a Scotsman and an English woman are out here seemingly alone but to be perfectly honest we were not welcome at home. All I'm willing to say is Brendon wasn't what you may call an honest trader and certain factions were after him in Scotland and England so we bought passage on a ship and came here. It isn't an ideal life but it's better than being constantly on the run. I say all this in confidence, you realise, and if the truth be known, hasn't everybody got something to hide?"

Wilf coughed, hoped he hadn't blushed and said, "I'd say that's quite true, Martha. To coin a phrase, where I come from there are more black sheep than white." He winked and Martha smiled.

"Ah, here's Kiri with the tea. Remain seated, she will serve you. We also have biscuits and fruit cake, I do all my own cooking and like to preserve the English traditions despite being so far from home. Now please tell me how it is you have arrived here out of the blue, as it were."

As they all sipped their china cups of tea Wilf with occasional prompts from Fred related their story exactly as planned. Ann thought they were very convincing and Martha seemed to be taking it all in.

"Quite an adventure," she said once the men had obviously finished. "You were all very lucky. Naturally I've heard of such storms at sea but fortunately have never had to experience one." She cast her eyes at the four women before posing a question. "This may be very rude of me but did you all have your hair cut short specially for the voyage home?"

Sophie answered, "Actually, yes. We were advised by the ship's doctor that shorter hair prevented head lice and as I detest the little mites I decided to get a haircut. Emily, Catherine and Annie also thought it a good idea."

"And under normal circumstances our hair would have grown again by the time we arrived in England," Catherine said, adding impact to the lie.

Martha nodded her head. "It sounds like a wise idea to me and I shall certainly consider it if Brendon and I decide to take a trip home although I fear it won't be for quite some time yet."

She stopped talking to take a sip of tea before looking across to Wilf.

"So, Mister Malone, it is obviously your intention of returning to England with the least possible delay. I take it you have money."

"Gold actually. I managed to salvage some from the captain's secure locker before the ship went down."

"Very fortunate for you all, Wilf. Be warned though, guard your treasure carefully because all settlements around here are rampant with criminals and hooligans looking for easy pickings. Much drinking and gambling takes place which eventually leads to fighting and robbery. I believe such events are similar in every port town. Do you know anybody at the Swan River settlement?"

Wilf answered. "We have a name. One Hoorn Helderden who we understand attends to all shipping, both incoming and outgoing. Do you know him, Martha?"

"I've heard of him although we've never met. Brendon tries to keep me away from dockland types."

"Have you any friends?" Ann asked. "This place seems very remote."

"There are a few European women about, Annie, and we meet occasionally. Usually around shearing time when wool is brought in for shipment. Rates have usually been negotiated earlier in the season so payments are swift. Once all business is settled the men get drunk, leaving us women to look after ourselves. Our time comes when they sober up. Usually a ship has brought in clothes and cheap jewellery which the men buy for us. Then we too will have a party. After a week or so everything reverts back to normal, that is if you can call anything normal out here. Many a time Brendon and I wish we could return home although if we did it could mean prison and nobody wants that after experiencing freedom here. An isolated life is far better than a cell in Newgate or some other dreadful rat-ridden establishment. I hope you all see my point."

"Oh, we do, Martha," Wilf replied. "Nobody likes confinement in any form."

Ann looked at Catherine as if to say, 'Be careful what you say, Wilf.'

Catherine by way of a reply simply raised her eyebrows.

Wilf finished his tea, stood up and placed his cup and saucer on the tray Kiri had brought in. He looked at his hostess.

"Well, Martha, you've been very kind but we must be on our way. We'd hate to miss a boat and we've a way to go yet."

"Oh dear. I was rather hoping you may all stay the night. It isn't often I have such agreeable company. I can't offer luxury but I guarantee a hearty breakfast before you all depart in the morning. As I said, I'm pretty sure there are no ships in at present, if there were I'd have heard. So please reconsider, even just to give me your companionship."

Wilf glanced at the others and saw 'Why not?' in their faces. He asked where they would all sleep.

"You, Wilf and Fred, could sleep in my bedroom with your wives. You'll have to decide among yourselves who gets the bed. Catherine and Annie can take the small spare room so long as they don't mind sleeping on the floor as there is no bed although we have plenty of blankets."

"I'm sure they won't mind that, Martha," Wilf replied. "Since the shipwreck we've all been roughing it anyway. Where will you sleep?"

"In the kitchen with Kiri. It won't be the first time. If Brendon brings any guests home to drink themselves silly that's usually where I sleep. As you can see it's still fairly primitive in this part of the world but I'm sure things will get better eventually and at least being so far from home we know the sheriff won't be knocking on the door holding a pair of handcuffs. Shall I tell Kiri to put a lamb over the kitchen fire?"

"That would be nice, Martha, thank you."

Wilf smiled at the others as Martha got up to continue being a hostess and it seemed she was enjoying every minute of it. In a way Wilf felt sorry for her having to suffer the privations she was forced to live under, she was a true pioneer in almost every respect. He used to think his life aboard ship was rigorous enough but for a woman to be usually left alone was the ultimate in hardship. Yet she was doing it for the love of a man and it proved to him yet again what fortitude women possessed. He looked at Catherine and Ann, realising they were in a similar vein, especially Ann who had taken her punishment at the mast almost like a hardened seaman. Of course she screamed but he knew that was a natural reaction for anybody being subjected to intense pain. He knew hardy sailors tried to suppress displays of emotion and preferred to faint rather than cry out in their anguish. He smiled when seeing Catherine winking at Ann. He knew their youthful minds were already in the spare room, making love. And tonight at least there would be a wooden floor beneath them, not hard-baked Australian soil.

Before Martha left she had an afterthought and suggested it may be a good idea to show them their rooms where they could wash their faces. They all agreed and followed her out.

It was a short, rather narrow corridor which by its position could have been an addition to the original property. The drabness was broken with not-too-well-painted pastoral scenes which depicted the English countryside. Rolling hills formed the backdrops with bluebell-strewn slopes and cascading streams in the foreground. Birds of prey hovered in the cloudless sky, ready to dive on an unsuspecting vole or other earthly creature. Obviously memories for Martha and by their questionable quality she must have painted them herself.

Martha opened one door to the left and one to the right. The one on the right was the spare room for Annie and Catherine. The other was the master bedroom, Martha proudly proclaimed. In a few moments Kiri would deliver water, soap, cloths, towels and a bottle of scent to each room.

Once inside their sparse room Catherine and Ann kissed and yearned to go further but didn't dare until Kiri had delivered the water. It was similar for Wilf and Fred in their room.

"Well, Mrs Pankhurst, does your husband get a kiss?" Fred asked, knowing he would not be refused.

Their lips came together and Fred's hands pushed against Sophie's bottom, intimating what she could expect after Kiri had made her deliveries.

"Mrs Malone desires to be kissed," Emily said to her bogus husband as they became embraced. It was obvious from the way Emily gyrated her body against his she desired much more than a kiss but Wilf broke away.

"In deference to our hostess, Emily, I think we'd better delay going further than a kiss, for the moment anyway."

"Reluctantly, my husband, I agree."

* * *

Within an hour they all looked much fresher than upon arrival. All of them had applied sweet-smelling scent and powder to various parts of their bodies, unfortunately there wasn't any lip make-up for the women. However that was of little concern as they all felt like somebody again. Of course there was still much uncertainty to face and it may well be their idylls would terminate abruptly if the authorities got so much as a whisper that the four women were to all intents and purposes convicts on the run. For the moment however, they were all pleased to accept Martha McFarlane's hospitality.

After washing and before replacing their blouses Ann and Catherine had exchanged soft kisses for a number of beautiful minutes before they finished dressing. They had also assumed the two would-be married couples had been indulging in acts genuine husbands and wives performed on a regular basis.

In deference to their hostess though they all returned to the living/dining room where they were offered goblets of home-made red wine and from somewhere two extra wickerwork stiff-backed chairs had appeared. Catherine and Annie were offered these and silently they relished the comfort, their first in at least seven months, having lost track of actual times although they assumed it must still be January.

Martha finally announced their meal was ready.

As guests they had to act their parts as if suppers such as the one they faced were normal occurrences. For the women it seemed strange after so long to be sitting at a table eating off china plates and using knives and forks. Fred had volunteered to carve the lamb but Martha said Kiri would do it. More home-made wines were available and after the meal the men were promised Scotch whisky or a brandy and a cigar if they wished.

Wilf proposed a toast by thanking Martha and Kiri for their hospitality. He did note however, that Kiri seemed very reserved and shy. Even after Fred complimented her on the food she simply replied with a bow and a thank you.

Martha explained the girl's reticence in the presence of men. It seemed she had been forcefully removed from her tribe by four drunken Belgian prospectors who raped and generally tormented her in their cabin for almost a week before Brendon and some aborigines came across them. Naturally Kiri was in a state of near insanity and had almost lost her ability to speak. For their crime the tribesmen slit the men's stomachs open and staked them outdoors to die. Brendon brought Kiri here and she had been a faithful servant ever since. Martha was hoping that with some loving care she would return to her normal self one day. At the moment she was still terrified of most male strangers although it was obvious by her manner she wasn't scared of either Wilf or Fred.

Catherine well knew what it must have been like for the poor girl and hearing about her experience put a damper on the otherwise cheerful meal. Catherine was careful though not to say she had suffered similar indignities. In fact all four of them had to be constantly on their guard not to let it slip they had been convicts in transportation to Botany Bay. Martha seemed the type who would say nothing but they couldn't take that chance. They had come this far, it would be a disaster to be recaptured at this stage.

Dusk was setting in as they completed the meal so Martha went about her usual evening ritual of lighting oil lamps. After the two men had settled down to drink a generous measure of whisky and smoke a cigar Emily and Sophie volunteered to help washing the dishes but Martha wouldn't hear of it. They were her guests. It was just a pity Brendon hadn't been at home. He too would have enjoyed their company.

It was about nine o'clock when the guests retired to their rooms. Once in theirs Catherine and Ann went to the small window and looked out on the bright moonlit expanse of wilderness. In the far distance smoke could be seen rising and the silhouettes of two people were visible riding across the horizon, it was impossible to distinguish if they were male or female, probably male though as this was a country for men. Martha had emphasized this at supper but in the usual pioneering tradition hard-working men were pleased to have a woman waiting at home.

"I think Martha misses England more than she admits," Catherine said as she moved behind Ann to kiss her swanlike neck as a prelude to more amorous activity. "I love you so much, Ann."

"And I you. Let us undress."

In silence they embraced.

Moments later they began the arousals they knew would terminate in raptures which always seemed to exceed anything they had attained previously.

"Oh, Ann my love, it has never been so wonderful."

"Nor for me, my love. Now lie still so I may give you even more pleasure."

Catherine's body began to tremble when sensing Ann's silky tongue probing into the very depths of her being until that wonderful moment arrived where she was transported into an alternate universe.

Ann returned up to her and whispered softly, "I have just visited the gates of paradise." She kissed Catherine's eyes which had become glassy with tears. "You weep, my love. Why?"

"Because you say such wonderful poetic things. It's strangely ironic that through my crimes I've met the most wonderful woman in the entire world. Kiss me again before I return that pleasure which you have just given to me."

And tonight there was no hurry. It would be a while yet before sleep overcame them despite their tiredness.

* * *

In the hostess's bedroom both Wilf and Fred were doing what was expected of them. For the moment Fred and Sophie had the bed but Wilf and Emily would get their turn. This was an interlude they had not expected yet they realised tomorrow they must start their quest for a ship. Any ship which was leaving Australia. For the present though all their trials, tribulations and futures were forgotten. Tonight was for love.

* * *

Following a hearty ham and egg breakfast the six of them bid Martha goodbye and expressed their regrets that they had not met her husband. Both Wilf and Fred had wanted to kiss Kiri but she had shied away the moment they approached. She did however accept the women's kisses. Martha as a final gesture of hospitality offered Fred one of Brendon's jackets as his own was falling apart at the seams. It wasn't a perfect fit although much better than the one destined to be thrown on the kitchen fire. She had also given the four women some coarse stockings as it was unseemly walking about bare legged. She also gave them two corked jugs of water to slake their thirsts along the way.

At the garden gate Martha bid them all goodbye, saying it was less than two miles to the Noongar settlement. She also warned them again to guard their gold carefully as nobody could be fully trusted.

It was a hot day so their pace was slow and they were glad of the water. Emily was worried about Wilf's leg although it didn't seem to be bothering him. After a week of idleness his main aim now was securing them a ship so they could depart this land once and for all. It may be ideal for Cromwell, even the McFarlanes, but it wasn't for him or his charges.

Undaunted they trudged on.

* * * * *

Chapter 20

INALLY THEY MOUNTED YET ANOTHER RISE AND there set before them was a sweeping bay where to the west Wilf could just about make out the head of the Swan River. He knew from memory that beyond the river estuary lay the immense area of seawater known as the Indian Ocean. He felt elated at the thought and imagined the others did also. He was aware they were still a very long way from home but further downriver lay the stepping-off point to sail west.

They each surveyed the settlement of Noongar spread out randomly before them. A mish-mash collection of thatched shelters, tents and wooden buildings, the largest of which appeared to be a general store with a tavern attached if the number of horses tethered outside was any indication. A badly tuned piano could be heard playing a tinny tune of unknown origin. Dogs and children hovered around outside, possibly waiting for owners and parents. In front of many structures open fires burned, some of which had large cast-iron pots hanging over the flames with squatting women constantly fanning them. Others had meat being turned on spits. Nothing looked too permanent, as if the settlement was in transition.

At first glance the population seemed mainly aborigine although there were a smattering of whites who were most probably Dutch. A good sign to Wilf though was the many longboats and fishing smacks tied up at a lengthy pier and along the sandy shore men were sitting on barrels, repairing trolling nets. Numerous wicker baskets contained the morning's catch with pipe-smoking buyers making their selections. Also in evidence were numerous wicker pens containing sheep ready to be sheared or slaughtered. To Wilf's experienced eyes the Noongar settlement seemed larger although more primitive than the one at the mouth of the Swan River where they had dropped the four farmers off. This thought caused Wilf and Fred to wonder what had become of the four men. Both hoped they had already moved inland for the last thing they wanted to was to bump into them, realising complications could arise if they saw the women.

Wilf took a deep breath and said, "Well, it's no use standing here looking. Let's get down there and try to get a boat to the Swan settlement."

The women hitched up their skirts with frayed hems and followed their men down the dusty cart track which could easily become a quagmire if it rained. This was unlikely at the moment as Martha had told them months could go by without a drop of moisture falling.

Each tried not to show their anxiety as they entered what had to be the settlement's main street. It was natural for people to stare for they were strangers in town. Wilf advised his charges to smile but not speak unless spoken to. They didn't need to be told this would be their first contact with total strangers since boarding the *Bromley* except of course for Cromwell although he was the exception to almost every rule written. What encouraged Fred and Wilf as they walked slowly towards the pier was the obvious lack of anybody who looked to have connections with maintaining law and order. A wild frontier town if ever there was one. Wilf had heard of such places in mid-western America where there was always a law officer, a courthouse and a gallows waiting for any bandits stupid enough to get caught by bounty hunters or the numerous posses which roamed at large, hoping for an arrest and a reward. Here it seemed similar to the stories he had heard. Thugs, both male and female, black and white, who seemed to lurk aimlessly everywhere looking for an easy mark. Many pairs of wild-looking eyes stared at this strange party of six who lacked any form of transport. Offers were made to both the men and women that good times could be had in the tavern where whisky and rooms were available at reasonable rates. And the white women could earn themselves a fortune from sex-starved prospectors who had found a few ounces of the golden rocks or simply dust. There were also card games where much money could be made if they had a bankroll. Strangely these touters never seemed to mention more money could be lost than won when newcomers were playing against stacked odds and marked cards.

"Don't reply to anybody," Wilf advised. "If any come near enough I've got the cut-throat razor which they'll feel across their throats if they start anything. It wouldn't be the first fight I've been involved in."

"Nor me," Fred added. "My feet can be lethal if called upon."

"And I know exactly where to kick a man so it bloody hurts," Emily said and Catherine knew exactly what she meant.

What did catch their eyes though was the water's edge where many boats were tied up to stout posts sitting a few feet offshore. Some were obviously water carriages with native men standing idly around either looking for work or a fare. As a precaution before leaving Martha's house they had tied the sacks of gold between their thighs as it seemed the safest place should any form of attack occur. Now they realised what a good idea it had been because many of the idle men looked like they would slit a throat for a few pence. Undaunted and with his right hand on the razor Wilf sauntered into their midst and asked if anybody spoke English.

"Who's asking?" a deep resonating voice replied in passable English with a foreign accent. The man was huge, well over six feet with broad shoulders and very muscular arms, similar to those on Felix Bloom who was now sadly with his maker.

Wilf took a deep breath, realising this was probably a man who could help them.

"My name's Wilf Malone, former bosun of an English vessel shipwrecked off Brookes Inlet almost two weeks ago. Myself and these five people were the only survivors and we're hoping to get a ship back to England, or some part of Europe. I was hoping to find a man called Hoorn Helderden, head of the Swan River shipping depot. Do you know the man, sir?"

The man grunted and pointed. "See him just coming out of the tavern, that's him but I caution don't upset the man or else he turns nasty. He's God around these parts and runs just about everything, legal that is. Get on the wrong side of him and you can count the remainder of your life in seconds. Plus if it weren't for him there'd be no work for the natives. I'm one of his right-hand men as they say so just call me Sam, simply Sam. A man with a past but it ain't healthy to ask what he's been up to in these parts. Almost every European round here has something to hide, believe me, godforsaken, festering hole that it is."

"I fully understand, Sam," Wilf replied, wanting to be on the right side of the man. Getting a ship may rest on these two men. Sam introduced Hoorn after asking Wilf what his name was again.

Wilf took the offered hand which was as hard as nails with a grip equal to that of a vice. They shook vigorously.

Hoorn smiled. "Well, it's nice to meet a civilized person for a change. All this country seems to breed are greedy cheating bastards who'll slit your throat and have your bankroll in a jiffy. Do you have money?"

"Some. Do you have a ship?"

Hoorn smiled, revealing a mouth full of bad teeth. "I may have, I may not. We have to discuss first, not here though. Downriver in my office." He pointed at Fred and the women. "Them lot with you, I have to assume."

"Yes. The black-haired one's my wife. The tall one is married to the other man, Fred, he used to be the ship's chef before we got shipwrecked. The two younger females are travelling companions who were returning home after visiting relatives in Port Jackson."

"With those haircuts they could well be convicts, Wilf. They're not on the run, I hope. We do get a few who got fed up existing in that shit hole they call Botany Bay. Easy to spot 'em as they usually carry a few lash marks across their backs. Never had women runners though. The outback is too tough for 'em. Plus most pick up lodgings with sheep farmers or prospectors who are looking for something comfortable to lie on at night."

"No, we're not on the run from anywhere except a sunken ship," Wilf confirmed.

"That's good then. What did you say the name of your ship was?"

"I didn't, but it was the *Whitby*, out of Hull. Heard of her?"

"Can't say I have. Has she ever sailed into the Swan estuary?"

"Not since I've served on her. So what happens now, Hoorn?"

"We'll go to my office where we can talk in private. I don't want all these lazy buggers to know if there's a ship due or not. If they find out they'll be on me like swarms of hornets, wanting to help offload. That's my longboat over there. Get your lot in it. No luggage, I assume."

"No, we lost everything in the wreck. Only the six of us survived."

"I've known wrecks off this rough coast where everybody perished."

Wilf was most pleased to tell Fred and the others they were going to be sailed downriver to the inlet. Last night he had raised the possibility they might have to walk and Martha had estimated it was almost twenty miles to the inlet. For Wilf not a happy prospect on a bad leg.

Willing hands helped the ladies aboard after introductions had been made. The longboat had a canopied padded seating area at the stern with room enough for nine passengers. Hoorn and his man Sam sat with them and straight away each was offered a tot of rum. Two muscular aboriginal men manned the oars and other willing hands pushed them out. They were on their way and Wilf welcomed the aroma of salt water again. It was only now he realised he'd missed it during their inland travels. He took a deep breath.

"Ah, smell that, ladies. Now I really sense we're about to resume our voyage."

Catherine and Ann exchanged smiles but didn't hold hands, not knowing what Wilf had told Hoorn about them. He didn't look the type to tolerate convicts on the run under any circumstances although their situation was not quite normal. Strictly they hadn't escaped, the shipwreck had simply provided the means of freedom. Nevertheless until they were safely afloat heading west they would not be fully at ease.

The longboat made swift progress across the bay, heading towards the narrower Swan River. Overhead, literally hundreds of seagulls and other birds flew, obviously hoping for morsels cast off by the fishermen. Various plumes of smoke rose from the trees, giving evidence that people lived within the forest because not many residences of any kind could be seen. In fact Fred asked Hoorn how many people populated the area.

"Probably a thousand or so around this area where we can see but there are many more up and down the coast. Most live by their ancient traditions of hunting and fishing. A few work for me on a permanent basis by helping to unload or load ships but they have to be watched like hawks as they'll steal anything they can carry. Plus they make their own alcoholic concoctions and get into day-long binges. Many die but in passing they believe they fly to a better world. Bullshit of course, yet this country thrives on aboriginal folklore. They believe in heaven, I don't. You see I'm just a simple working man trying to make the most out of life. I'm boss around these parts and everybody knows it. Another few years and I'll retire and build a house somewhere, not round these parts though. I've heard Tahiti is a nice place to settle. Now, who wants another rum? We've a way to go yet."

Nobody refused as Wilf asked how many ships they handled, knowing there was no actual port yet because of the sandbar.

"Oh, we get quite a few traders, mainly English and Dutch, some American but I hate those bastards, always think they're better than everybody else. Well, to my mind they're not and I wouldn't trust one for a minute. Pirates mostly dealing in slaves. Many ships bypass us though on their way to Port Jackson where all the action and money is. It's a bustling place as I suppose you know having sailed from there."

Wilf nodded. "Yes, the place is expanding by leaps and bounds with much of the work being done by convicts as I suppose you know."

"Oh yes, I know. Smart of you English to send criminals out there. Dirt-cheap labour and for those that want 'em, willing women." He looked at each of his female passengers. "No offence to you, ladies. I suppose you know they send the dregs of society to Botany Bay."

"Yes, we're well aware of what types are sent there, Hoorn," Emily told him.

"Aye, the scum of the earth. That aside, I suppose you saw a bit of the land coming here from Brookes Inlet."

"Yes, we did and as you say it's a wild country," Fred told him. "We had good escorts though."

"Who supplied them, Cromwell?"

They all looked shocked at the mention of their benefactor.

Hoorn noticed and said, "Oh yes, I know Cromwell. Without doubt one of the cleverest men in Australia and yet he chooses the simple life, but who's to say which one is best. I work my guts out when we get a ship, Cromwell has a life of ease and plenty where everybody works willingly for him and he doesn't do too bad for women either. He's also rich beyond measure. There's many a prospector tried to bribe the man for information where the gold lies buried but he'll never say. I suppose he gave you lot some gold, did he?"

"As a matter of fact, yes," Wilf answered. "Just so we could pay our passage back to England, or somewhere near. Honestly, what are our prospects, Hoorn?"

"Pretty good, I'd say. Luck seems to be with you. First surviving the shipwreck, then meeting up with Cromwell and now bumping into me. I have a ship expected in a day or so actually. A Dutch merchantman coming from Canton and Jakarta, carrying tea and spices. It's calling in here to pick up a hundred bales of raw wool which you'll see are piled up on our dock ready for loading. I'm sure it'll carry a few passengers, most do. It's the *Rotterdam*, I'll introduce you to the captain," he winked, "for a small fee of course."

Wilf smiled. "Of course, Hoorn, we expected to pay. You'll accept gold, I hope, as it's all we've got."

"Oh yes, I'll take that. In fact I'm hording the stuff for my retirement. Gold is good anywhere in the world as I expect you all know. It's the front-door key to almost anything a man can want." He turned, shielded his eyes and looked forward. "We're nearly there, just round this next bend and you'll see our settlement which I imagine one day will become an important port town, that is once we manage to dredge the sandbar deep enough for vessels to sail over. Presently we have to offload and load with longboats. Bloody nuisance but that's life. It's a big job shifting countless tons of sand and much of it washes back in with the tides. What we really need are massive dredgers." He shrugged his broad shoulders. "Ah well, I suppose one day."

Of course Wilf was well aware of the sandbar but was careful not to say so. In fact he considered it very fortunate Hoorn was away when the *Bromley* dropped the farmers off. If he had been present and seen either him or Fred some very awkward questions would have been asked and things may have not been so rosy as they seemed now.

As they rounded the bend they saw numerous wooden buildings, including the large warehouse. Otherwise the buildings were very similar to those in the Noongar settlement. Scattered here and there were conical-shaped grass dwellings obviously occupied by aborigine families if the number of children running around was any indication. They seemed happy though and waved to the longboat. Men at the river edge were fishing and they too waved. Both Hoorn and Sam waved back.

"Still a bit primitive by European standards," Hoorn said. "They may be simple folk but when pushed they're good workers and I try to pay them a fair rate."

"You don't realise how advanced places like London are until you see how these people live," Wilf added, "yet at times I wonder who's best off, us or them. I know we all enjoyed our time in Cromwell's glade although we agreed our preference was England … didn't we, girls?."

They all nodded and smiled.

"They don't say much, do they?" Hoorn observed.

Wilf hunched his shoulders. "Still suffering the effects of the shipwreck. They were in the water a long time, seeing numerous drown and one deck lad being bitten almost in half by a shark. That's enough to give anybody the willies."

"Aye, I suppose so," Hoorn agreed. "Anyway we're nearly there now, then we can eat and have a drink or two. I've got some home-brewed wine, that should steady the lasses' nerves."

Now they could all see a sturdy landing stage which still seemed to be under construction if the number of men lashing tree trunks together was any indication. Hoorn told them he was having it built so it could accommodate the largest ships. When finished it would be well over a hundred and fifty feet long and sturdy enough to withstand the pounding seas which rolled in almost constantly. A few scows were tied up alongside and another four were in mid-stream with men dragging thick lines, obviously to deepen the channel. Even Ann realised it would be a very long job to dredge a channel deep enough for ships like the *Bromley* to sail over. However she did realise they had plenty of time and didn't imagine there was a deadline.

Wilf asked Hoorn who was paying for all the dredging work.

"We charge a levy for every boat which calls in. Most pay willingly but a few captains grumble saying even when the sandbar has been cleared they would never want to travel further up river. I tell them it's for the benefit of all and if they don't pay up we won't unload them, supply provisions or any other facilities, most then divvy up without further argument. After crossing the Indian Ocean most ships are low on just about everything, especially fresh water and many crewmen are almost ready to mutiny. Well, you must know how it is."

"I certainly do," Wilf agreed.

As they pulled alongside a finished portion of the wharf they looked at the large warehouse inside which, it had to be assumed, were the bales of wool destined for

Holland and possibly other supplies for a ship with thousands of miles to cover
before land was made again. One or two aboriginal men were fishing off the end
of the pier, probably catching their next meal. Other quite wild-looking men ran to
tie their boat off. It was only then they all saw a large log cabin set back fifty yards
or so in the trees. Two brawny white men were emerging from it. They waved and
Hoorn waved back.

"My senior staff," Hoorn said with obvious pride.

Sam helped the passengers disembark before announcing he was going to look
at what progress had been made on the quay since he and Hoorn had been away.
Then out of the corner of his eye Fred saw a very attractive native woman appearing
from the office. Hoorn introduced her as his companion and lover.

"When I found her she didn't have a name so I christened her My Sunrise
which she seemed to like so the name stuck. Now though she's simply Sunrise and
good company before going to sleep and she's always waiting when I wake up.
Course she does know when she's well off."

She waved and bowed to them all before giving her lover a kiss, one which
conveyed she hadn't seen her man in a year but Wilf assumed it was probably no
more than a couple of weeks. Wilf and Fred shook her hand before the girls gave
her a light hug while kissing her cheek.

They were invited inside the residential side of the building which they quickly
discovered was lavishly furnished by any standards and certainly far better than
anything the McFarlanes possessed. All the furniture was quality teak with brocade
upholstery in an oriental flavour. The dining table was large enough to seat four
down each side and two at the ends. Two triple-stemmed candelabras were set on
the tables and highly polished oil lamps hung from the rafters. Hoorn obviously
lived very well but he seemed genuinely concerned when having to tell Wilf and
Fred they would have to share a bedroom with their wives and that Catherine and
Annie had to share the same bed.

Of course this didn't bother them in the least and Catherine told him they were
used to sharing. Of course their host was not to know both women were thrilled at
the prospect. It had been the floor at Martha McFarlane's, a proper bed here. Things
were steadily improving and soon they would be sailing west towards home.

The sitting room overlooked the bay entrance with the surf pounding on the
sharp rocks beyond the sandbar. Wilf knew that those jagged rocks and those like
them the world over had been the doom of many mariners. He silently counted his
blessings now that there had been no reef or rocks where they had come ashore
following the shipwreck. Had there been they would not be here now accepting

Hoorn's hospitality. They all became seated as Sunrise poured each man a dark beer out of a giant enamel jug. The women were offered the home-made wine. Toasts were said after Sunrise had left to prepare a meal.

Hoorn downed his beer in two gulps and shouted to Sunrise for a refill. She entered with a full jug and left it on a casual table after filling Hoorn's goblet. He rubbed his belly and said he was looking forward to a lamb supper.

"I suppose you eat lamb fairly regularly," Fred said to make conversation.

"That plus beef, Fred. That's one thing about this country, there's no shortage of meat and poultry. In fact I'd go so far as to say me and my men consume more lamb and beef in a month than the average English person eats in a year. We need it to build up the muscles, it's a hard life servicing the ships which come in after a turbulent crossing, especially in the winter months. Many arrive in bad shape so I make a pretty fair income carrying out repairs and labour is cheap as you've no doubt guessed. Within the forest we have a timber mill so we can replace almost any part of a ship. My second in command Karl DeGrutt looks after most repairs, he also handles provisioning and oversees the workers."

"Are they reliable?" Wilf asked.

"Some are, some aren't, a slacker doesn't last too long with us though as there's always others willing to work. We've also to be careful of theft. Sly buggers these aborigines, they'll steal anything given the chance. Any we catch usually don't do it again."

"How do you treat thieves?" Sophie asked.

"Depends on the crime. For theft it's lashes, I determine the number. If the criminal is a kid, and many are, he or she gets caned across the backside. For more serious crimes we usually chop a hand off. In very severe cases and murder, hanging is the only answer. You must remember, Sophie, this is a new emerging country so we have to administer the law ourselves. Some day, I suppose, a police force will emerge, although not yet. I know they're working on such a force in Port Jackson but it'll take time. This is a big country. You could drop Holland in the middle of Australia and nobody would ever find it. Why, I've only been to Port Jackson once and that's where I landed this job."

"Have you ever been back to Holland?" Catherine asked.

"Just once but soon realised at home I was just one of the masses while out here I'm a somebody. Plus I'm making much more money …" He paused and looked around to see Sunrise in the doorway. She announced in broken English the meal was ready.

They all got up and took their places at the dining table. Much to their surprise after Sunrise had set the huge roast of lamb in front of Hoorn for carving she left but reappeared moments later with four bottles of French champagne and tulip-style glasses. She poured and Hoorn proposed the toast.

"To my new-found friends. May you all have a pleasant voyage home without suffering further hardships."

He raised his glass and they all drank, including Sunrise.

Wilf replied, "We thank you, Hoorn, for your hospitality and indeed we all look forward to our return and feel fortunate we are able to do so."

"Aye, there's many mariners who never make it from a shipwreck."

They all proceeded to eat and drink. When they were finished only Hoorn and Sunrise were sober. Wilf and Fred had to assist their bogus wives to the bedrooms and Sunrise helped Annie. Catherine could just about manage herself although she realised any form of passionate exchanges were out of the question. In fact once in their room Ann fell on the bed face down and was asleep in seconds.

Catherine went to the window to take a few breaths of fresh air and saw Sam walking with a dark-skinned young woman towards what must have been his living quarters. She smiled, knowing the man would be well satisfied tonight. Then she removed her blouse but decided to leave the skirt on. After getting in the large bed she turned Ann over. Moonlight shone on her ever growing russet hair and in slumber she looked perhaps even more divine, an angel.

She lay beside Ann and following a couple of rotations of the bed sleep overcame her.

* * *

In the morning Catherine awoke to see Ann's sweet face looming over hers.

"I don't remember last night, Catherine. Was I bad?"

"No, not really. We all got drunk. Sunrise helped you to the room as I wasn't capable."

"We must never get into such a state again, Catherine, otherwise we might say something which will give us away. Now we've got this far and experienced freedom again I couldn't tolerate being rearrested."

"Yes, I agree. In future we shall ration our intake of drink, drink which neither of us are used to. Now bring your delightful lips down to mine so our heads may swim in rapture, not drink."

They kissed each other for over fifteen minutes, making up for what they'd missed last night. During one short break Catherine told Ann about seeing Hoorn's man Sam going to his quarters with an attractive aborigine woman.

Ann smiled and ran the tip of her right index finger across Catherine's moist lips. "I say good luck to him. I imagine having a woman is one of the few enjoyments around here."

"Yes, I agree, but I have the only woman I'll ever want, my love. Now let's wash our faces, get dressed and see what the others are doing."

They kissed again before doing so.

* * *

While Hoorn was out attending to business on the dock Sunrise prepared them all a ham and fresh-laid eggs breakfast. Sophie wasn't too keen to eat anything but Fred insisted she did, claiming the best cure for a hangover and upset stomach was to get something in it and Wilf endorsed the advice.

Sunrise simply smiled, knowing how they all must feel. She explained with her limited English that she and Hoorn frequently felt like that in the morning. Following the meal she suggested they all took a walk along the jetty where the fresh ocean breezes would do them good. Wilf agreed, saying he used to walk around the ship's deck if he felt queasy some mornings when the captain had been generous with the rum ration.

After numerous cups of strong coffee they set out for their walk. The sea was even rougher today and at the inlet huge waves were pounding the rocks, sending spumes of spray high in the air. A few fishing scows tied up at the jetty were being tossed about like corks and Hoorn could be heard shouting orders to the men passing up baskets full of today's catch. There were no boats out dredging the sandbar as the tide was too strong. The walk was refreshing though and helped to blow their cobwebs away.

"We could have had a swim if it wasn't so rough!" Ann shouted to Catherine.

"I think I had enough of swimming after the shipwreck," Catherine replied with a fond smile.

"Didn't we all," Fred replied before kissing Sophie on her cheek.

At the far end of the jetty they all peered north, hoping perhaps to see the large three-master which would be their transport back to Europe. Unfortunately there was nothing in sight. Hoorn appeared and told them it would be another day at least. He suggested they just try to relax as there wasn't anything to do. He explained that even for him this was the way of life here. Unloading the fishing smacks, salting the catch and waiting for the merchants to pick up their choices. After that he would check on his farm stock and tell those who worked for him what animals they could kill for their weekly ration.

He was asked if they ever ran out of basic needs like yeast and flour. It seemed this happened frequently when a ship was late, then they just had to make do. This was not Amsterdam or London where you could go to the local market and take your pick. Sophie asked him how they got clothing.

"We have a tailor who travels around the scattered settlements, selling his wares and taking orders for new clothing which comes in by ship two or three times a year." He looked at the women's tattered skirts and said Sunrise would have spare ones which they were welcome to. He may also have fresh shirts for the men but not jackets.

Happy with the prospect of new clothing, the women left with Sunrise.

Once the women had moved indoors Wilf asked how long the *Rotterdam* would remain in port.

"No longer than the captain needs to, Wilf. He and his crew are on their way home so no man will want to linger, especially those with wives and kids. Some of the crew no doubt will be carrying disease because they've been associating with loose Eastern women who had been hoping to net a husband." He winked. "Well, you know."

"Oh yes, I know, Hoorn. I also know many English captains lay the lash if a crewman is caught carrying the pox."

"So do Dutch masters, Wilf, or they have the man thrown overboard. It's the only way to stop spreading the disease which can take over a ship like wildfire. I suppose you know there are few cures. In fact I predict any doctor who invents a cure for pox would make himself a fortune in no time."

Wilf nodded as Hoorn paused to bellow at a native who had just dropped a basket of fish back into the sea. Knowing the catch would be lost Sam was told to have the offender thrown in to retrieve the basket..

"He may drown," Fred suggested.

Hoorn smiled. "If he does he won't do it again, will he! Like I've said, it's a harsh life out here, this isn't London. Anyway the unloading is almost finished then we can all have a quiet drink. How does that sound?"

Although both men thought it a little early they didn't refuse. In many ways this lull was like shore leave at home.

* * *

While they were all in the cool lounge sipping beer and wine and admiring the women in their fresh skirts they could hear Sam shouting orders to start dredging as the seas had calmed enough.

It seemed Hoorn had an infinite capacity for beer as he drank two pewter goblets to every one Wilf and Fred consumed. The women simply sipped their wine, wishing they could be on their way again. Wilf perhaps more than anybody was hoping the *Rotterdam* would arrive when expected. His mind couldn't help make him wonder what would happen to them if something had befallen the ship. They would be well and truly stranded because Hoorn had told them at supper last night it was sometimes a month or more between ships. The Swan River wasn't the busiest port in Australia as most shipping headed directly for Port Jackson which was becoming the main centre for commerce, trade and of course the penal colony. This would have been the case for the *Bromley* had it not been for the farmers. What made it worse for Wilf was the nagging thought he still had four convicts on his hands and if the authorities were to find out it could mean serious repercussions for himself and perhaps even Fred. The shipwreck had changed all their circumstances in that for the first time in their lives they had found genuine love. If the *Rotterdam* didn't arrive everything could change, and for the worst unfortunately as it would be difficult to maintain a façade for any number of weeks. Added to which if Hoorn, Sunrise, Karl DeGrutt or Sam saw the lash scars on Ann's back awkward questions were bound to arise. Plus both men knew Emily was apt to talk in her sleep especially in reference to her experiences on the *Bromley* before the shipwreck. Wilf knew outwardly Hoorn was a friendly person but he had a reputation to uphold and if he suspected anything was amiss he would turn them in to somebody. That would mean the girls continuing on to Botany Bay while he and Fred were returned to England to face charges of aiding known convicts.

Hoorn must have sensed something was on Wilf's mind when he asked what was the matter.

"Nothing really, Hoorn, it's just frustrating having to wait like this."

"Better to wait than have drowned, my friend, so count your blessings. Don't worry, the *Rotterdam* will arrive tomorrow. It is a sturdy ship with an excellent master who has completed numerous voyages and weathered many a storm. Now relax and have another drink, I'm going to."

"Yes, very well then."

In fact they all agreed another drink was in order and if nothing else it would pass the time.

* * *

It was only natural for them all to be up early the following morning. Immediately they emerged outdoors they saw Hoorn with a telescope peering north. He saw them and beckoned.

"There, my friends, what did I say? That's the *Rotterdam* approaching and already they've started to reef in the main sails. I estimate it will be another hour or so before they drop anchor so I suggest you at least get a coffee from Sunrise. I have to organize a longboat to bring the captain ashore then we can start provisioning and loading the wool."

Wilf thanked Hoorn for them all. The *Rotterdam* was indeed an impressive sight and from a distance it looked slightly larger than the *Bromley*. Catherine hugged Ann.

"We're almost on our way home at last, my love."

"I'll feel happier when we're aboard and under sail. Now I like Hoorn's suggestion of a coffee. What do you think?"

"Yes, let's get one and then watch the loading."

They both gathered up their newer skirts and headed for Hoorn's cabin.

* * *

They all watched the heavy cast-iron anchor splash into the water. This was followed by three of Hoorn's longboats tying up alongside. With their keen eyesight they could see crewmen still furling sails under the watchful eye of a stately looking bearded man on the quarter deck. He was obviously the captain as a bosun's chair was being prepared to lower him down to a longboat under Karl DeGrutt's command. Once aboard the rowers started to pull towards the deeper water over the sandbar before heading for the wharf where Hoorn waited with his expectant passengers.

Willing aboriginal hands finally tied the boat off and others assisted the captain ashore. Moments later Wilf was being introduced to Captain Gustav Van Der Sanden, he then introduced the others. Gustav clicked his heels with each handshake saying he was delighted to meet them. Wilf was pleased the man spoke good English as he couldn't speak a word of Dutch himself.

Hoorn quickly explained their situation and asked if the *Rotterdam* had space for them.

Captain Sanden stroked his elegant beard and the four women held their breath, waiting for his reply.

"Unfortunately my space is very limited, ladies and gentlemen, as the *Rotterdam* is mainly a cargo vessel. However I do have two spare cabins. The single females are welcome to one, you gentlemen and your wives would have to share the other. As your ultimate destination is England we could disembark you at Calais where there should be no problems getting a vessel to cross the channel. Your passages will cost twenty guineas each, including meals. Charges for alcohol will be at my discretion. Company policy dictates I must ask you to pay your fares in advance. If these terms are agreeable we can shake hands, or perhaps you would prefer to view our facilities first?"

Wilf declined the offer, knowing they would have accepted space on the deck if that was all Captain Van Der Sanden had to offer. As it was, he knew almost exactly what cabin space to expect aboard the *Rotterdam*. Although it was slightly longer and wider than the *Bromley*, this class of ship was basically identical. Inwardly he breathed a sigh of relief, his fears of yesterday had evaporated to nothing today. He did however consider the fares rather excessive considering he, Fred, Emily and Sophie would be sharing a cabin but he was not about to haggle. They had Cromwell's gold, now they had a ship and he knew the women were delighted just by the expressions on their faces. He looked at Fred who nodded his head. Captain Van Der Sanden was told they could accept his terms if he would accept gold.

The captain readily agreed, clicked his heels again as they each shook his hand. "I look forward to a pleasant voyage, gentlemen. We sail immediately our cargo is stowed and provisions loaded; as you may know it's a long haul to Cape Town which will be our first stop. You may board whenever you wish. I shall be pleased to show you your cabins."

"And I'd better get my men organized loading the wool," Hoorn said, already gesturing to Karl who immediately started barking orders. Whether they were understood was another question but the men seemed to know what to do.

Wilf suggested they returned to Hoorn's house to collect their few bits and pieces.

*   *   *   *   *

Chapter 21

Captain Van Der Sanden showed his new passengers to their cabins located on the port and starboard sides one deck below his own quarters and those of the ship's officers. The galley was located at their level and when Fred smelled bread baking he knew at some point he would have to poke his nose in. He also knew chefs were a unique breed who enjoyed swapping recipes.

It pleased Wilf that Captain Van Der Sanden had not probed too deeply into their reasons for being in this area other than it had saddened him to hear they had been shipwrecked. Wilf however expected the subject to be raised again at some point on the homeward voyage, knowing mariners always liked to hear of shipwrecks and the possible causes. He also knew their story was well rehearsed by now and the four women had assumed an air of quality in their new skirts which were a mosaic of colours. The men sported serviceable shirts, thanks to Hoorn's wardrobe.

Captain Van Der Sanden explained there were four other passengers aboard, two were experts in selecting Chinese tea leaves which would be blended in Amsterdam. The other two had been purchasing Eastern spices to flavour food suitable for Dutch palates. Presently they were having drinks with Hoorn, Sam and Sunrise as the loading and provisioning progressed.

It was with a decided sigh of relief when Catherine and Ann entered their cabin. They kissed before sitting down on the lower bunk. They could decide later who took the narrow upper one. The cabin wasn't large although it did have a small porthole which was open at present. To the porthole's left was a narrow dresser with three drawers, more than enough space for their meagre belongings. On top of the dresser stood a large-diameter ceramic bowl with a jug of water standing in it. On either side were medium-sized towels draped over cast-iron rails. The furniture comprised two wooden high-backed chairs with wicker seats. Not much for their money although certainly far superior to their accommodation on the *Bromley*. In fact to them it was a palace. They also felt more at ease now than at any time since leaving Cromwell's forest glade.

Although they had enjoyed their overnight stay with Martha McFarlane it had been worrying that she may have suspected they were not exactly who they claimed to be. Because of this they were constantly on edge that somebody might arrive and clamp them in irons again before starting out for the penal colony be it by ship or overland, knowing this time they couldn't expect another miracle. However their fears had not materialized and very shortly they would be at sea and safe, at least until reaching England.

Catherine and Ann took advantage of their privacy by lying together and hugging on the lower bunk despite its somewhat narrow width. They decided there and then that when full love was to be made they would lie on the floor. Now however was not the time although like all lovers they couldn't resist exchanging a few kisses. For them every day was a honeymoon as they rediscovered each other both physically and mentally.

"They must be preparing to sail," Ann whispered in Catherine's ear as they embraced tightly.

Aloft they could hear orders being shouted in a foreign language which they assumed to be Dutch. There were also those commonplace sounds of ropes running through pulley blocks and sails being hoisted. Sounds they were familiar with from their previous voyage. Now though these sounds offered hope, not despair. And the aroma was not that which permeated up from the bilge or the sweat of themselves but coffee beans and baking bread which made them feel hungry. Then outside in the passageway they heard more foreign voices and assumed they were those of the other passengers. They sounded merry so it was assumed much beer had been imbibed.

Catherine heard one word she was very familiar with. "Fuck." One which her stepfather Patrick O'Grady used frequently and in various contexts. When he hit his head on the street-door lintel as he came in drunk. Or when he stubbed his toe going for a pee in the backyard privy while it was still dark. And of course he used it when requiring the sexual services of her mother.

"Come on, Vera, let's fuck."

"I'm sore. Have Catherine instead."

Ann smiled at Catherine. "Soon, my love, we shall be safe."

They kissed again.

* * *

Hoorn had been thanked and paid off with a small gold nugget which he considered more than generous. Now Wilf and his party were standing on the quarter deck, watching as a pair of longboats slowly pulled the *Rotterdam* around so it faced the open sea. Mainsails were being hoisted by sailors happy to be heading home again. There was that familiar flapping as square yards of canvas filled with wind, making the three masts creak as they took the strain and gradually the large ship began to develop a wake. The stately Captain Van Der Sanden stood by the helmsman, issuing orders as they cleared the headland. Quite a large swell was running and the ship heeled slightly as it picked up speed, ploughing through the oncoming waves. Behind them the Swan River inlet and the wharf were receding rapidly with Hoorn, Sam, Karl and Sunrise waving. Hoorn had his beefy arm around his lover's waist and no doubt once the *Rotterdam* was well away they would retire to his comfortable residence and make love. On the ship itself neither Wilf nor Fred cared if they never saw Hoorn or Australia again. Their voyage had started out as a job to do, now by unforeseen circumstances their outlooks on life had changed radically. For one they had both found love.

"Come on, ladies, let's go to our cabin and drink a toast to our futures," Wilf said as he waved to the captain.

Sunrise had given them six bottles of rum to ease the chill on cold nights, or simply to drink. As they each said their goodbyes there was that look in her eyes saying she'd like to be going with them despite her closeness to Hoorn. For the moment she was happy and this was after all her home but she imagined Hoorn's country had so much more to offer. Australia was a land of hardship and hot dry weather, a country for men, not women. Men who strived for months raising thousands of sheep or mining for gold in the unrelenting hard ground, then what did they do? Go into town, gambled, got drunk, took a woman, drank again until they collapsed in a drunken stupor and got robbed. When they recovered their only course of action was to go into the outback again and resume working for another year or so. An endless cycle of futility and stupidity where very few made their fortunes. Those who did were the bankers, money lenders, purveyors of tobacco, liquor, opium and sex. And of course that singular and most remarkable man Cromwell who lived a life which would be the envy of many.

Wilf and Fred's cabin was much larger than Catherine and Ann's. It was fitted with one three-quarter-size bed and two bunks, one above the other. There were two windows, a small table and two chairs plus a large dresser. On the table was one of the rum bottles and Fred had managed to acquire six pewter goblets from a steward. Fred poured.

Toasts were said to a pleasant voyage home and a sunny future for them all.

Actually none of them had any idea what lay in their futures. Both Wilf and Fred realised they could be charged with harbouring and abetting criminals if caught. In another few weeks when the *Bromley* didn't arrive in Port Jackson questions would be asked and perhaps an enquiry launched. The logical assumption would be exactly what happened, a shipwreck. There was even a chance some other ship had picked up floating debris and reported it at their next port of call. Eventually word would get back to London of the *Bromley*'s demise although this could take well over a year, during which time Wilf and the others would have dissolved into the countryside to be known only as law-abiding citizens. As for the ship's owners they would make an insurance claim and hope for an amicable settlement. Unfortunately the relatives of the lost seamen would in all probability never know how their loved ones had perished. Those were the risks a seaman took. Like dockyard workers, they were expendable. Wilf wondered if Albert Brooks's father would ever hear how his son met his end, or Alice Edwards's husband.

Wilf also wondered what had become of Hector Pimm since his assumed arrival in England. Would his condition have improved or worsened during the long overland journey? They discussed the situation for a few moments but it soon became obvious nobody cared just so long as they didn't meet up with him. Ann visibly shuddered at the thought, knowing he would still hold a grudge against her. It had taken mere seconds to stab him with that pencil yet it could affect his entire future life, if in fact he lived. She carried the lash scars as a reminder of the incident but nobody was ever likely to see them except Catherine.

"You're not really worried about Pimm, are you, my dear?" Catherine asked as she reached out to take one of Ann's dainty hands.

"I'll not deny he's on my mind at times. If we ever came face to face I'm sure he would kill me."

"Well, none of us would let him do that," Fred told her in a most reassuring manner. Then he summed the situation up nicely as he poured another round of drinks. "Whatever happens is at least six months in the future so for now let's enjoy the voyage and what it may entail."

They all drank to that. Another bottle was broached as the massive island of Australia disappeared into a shimmering heat haze.

Finally Catherine announced she and Ann were returning to their cabin for a short rest although the others realised an actual rest was the farthest thing from their minds, but they themselves had similar thoughts. Wilf and Fred tossed a coin to see who got the bed first. Fred won so Wilf and Emily had to make do with a bunk for the time being.

With the bed linen provided Catherine and Ann laid it all out on the cabin floor before undressing completely. Then with waves crashing against the hull and the rigging creaking they lay down on the slightly angled deck to become enveloped in each other's arms. Before closing their eyes they saw two seagulls flying past the porthole.

"We're as free as they are now, my love," Ann said before nestling her face between Catherine's breasts.

"Just the two of us, Ann. This cabin will be our world and love nest for the next six months."

Slowly their hands began the arousals.

* * * * *

The orgasm does not differentiate between male and female nor does it know whether the arousal had been brought about by a man or a woman. The clitoris has no idea if the finger stimulating it belongs to a male or female although the final outcome is identical. Sheer pleasure for the individual. And the same may be said for a hand performing masturbation. In these matters all things and all people are equal. It is simply a question of communication, one with the other.

* * * * *

CHAPTER 22

URING THE EVENING OF THEIR SECOND DAY out Captain Van Der Sanden had introduced their fellow travellers, the four Dutchmen who were skilled in the art of selecting tea blends and spices which their countrymen would enjoy provided they could afford the price. However it was difficult making conversation as they didn't speak English and Wilf and his friends had no Dutch. Captain Van Der Sanden came to their rescue by acting as an interpreter. This he promised to do whenever possible.

So as the weeks progressed and by using sign language they had all managed to pick up a few words, especially Ann who seemed to have a natural knack. Wilf of course warned her to be very careful what she said as he didn't want to raise any alarm bells. Plus it would have been very unwise to reveal the fact she and Catherine were physical lovers as men tended to be very disdainful of such relationships. Despite this Catherine and Ann were almost certain two of the men were having a sexual affair because they had seen them one night embracing in the passageway to the cabins after they returned from a stroll around the deck before bedtime.

Once in their own cabin they giggled while getting undressed and Ann put what they had seen in perfect context.

"We are not alone in a fondness for our own sex, Catherine my love."

"And I wouldn't have it any other way. I have experienced what it feels like to have a man inserted into myself and have no desire to undergo such an indignity ever again. You give me everything I could ever wish for. Now for heaven's sake kiss me."

And she did.

Lovemaking had consumed many pleasant hours for the six of them, each in their own individual way. With Catherine and Ann their acts of love from one session to another seemed slightly different each time. The simple touch of a finger today was not quite the same as yesterday. The induced conclusion in whatever form it took was unique to that very moment. They knew these things and that was why they were so compatible. Emily tended to be slightly noisy as her conclusions were attained, whereas Sophie simply trembled and gripped Fred with her strong legs. Either way total satisfaction was accomplished and usually after lovemaking their futures were discussed.

Emily and Wilf had become convinced an actual marriage ceremony wasn't necessary. They could return to Ireland and live quietly as man and wife and perhaps undertake a small business venture. Thanks to Cromwell they had money and Wilf had no intentions of returning to the sea for a living. One shipwreck was enough for him.

Fred, on the other hand, insisted Sophie officially became Mrs Pankhurst so any children which resulted could be properly christened. She agreed provided the ceremony was very discreet and conducted in a community far away from where she was known. As Fred had been born in the north of England in the town of Hull it seemed logical to make their new start there. A seaman returning home with his future bride.

As for Catherine and Ann they would be happy just to remain together in as much anonymity as possible. At a meeting in Fred and Wilf's cabin it had been agreed their final destinations would only be decided once they set foot on English soil again. And of course to assist them in their individual pursuits they each had Cromwell's gold which in itself would be a major asset. All of them in one way or another realised money couldn't buy good health or even happiness although it could open many doors and even buy security. The affluent of British society had been proving that for centuries.

* * *

Wilf had not been in the least surprised when he saw how Captain Van Der Sanden treated his crew. This with the utmost civility and respect from the traditional deck lad all the way up to the first mate. And the crew in turn rewarded his treatment by being efficient in everything they did. Wilf knew one or two English skippers who would have been well advised to take a lesson from the captain's book.

Fred of course had done numerous shifts in the galley and had actually been able to make some meat pies so his New Year's Eve promise to Sophie was finally fulfilled. Actually he made enough for themselves and all the ship's officers except he had fashioned Sophie's name in pastry on her pie top. She cried when it was shown to her.

Another feature of the ship was the trolling of a fishing net off the stern. It may have slowed their progress marginally but their rewards were numerous edible fish. One day they even netted a tuna which not only provided a tasty supper but it gave them a source of cooking oil. Generally the food had been very good with the staple diet being lamb and chicken. With the extra six passengers they ran out of eggs when about a thousand miles east of Cape Town where the ship would be completely reprovisioned. Nobody was about to quibble but as Wilf had said, "If Clare Hamlyn were aboard Captain Van Der Sanden would have been subjected to one of her endless tirades."

Mention of Clare brought speculation of whether or not she was on her way to Port Jackson yet. In all truth though, nobody really cared. All she represented was an ugly chapter in their lives despite her making an effort in Cromwell's forest glade to be amicable. Of course without the survivors of that shipwreck she wouldn't have lived. And Ann felt pity for her husband. Fred suspected he had married for Clare's money and for that was prepared to tolerate her many mood swings.

* * *

They had passed numerous ships heading east during their passage across the vast Indian Ocean with greetings being hailed across the water. One ship was the *Romney* which Fred knew carried about thirty passengers. It was a ship he had tried to get a position on as chef but had been beaten by an older seaman with slightly more experience. He did however secure his station on the *Bromley* which transpired to be good luck for both him and Sophie. Another ship they passed was the *Minerva* which Wilf thought was one of the fleet taking transportees to Botany Bay. They all said a silent prayer for those incarcerated in the holds, more than likely clad in leg irons.

"If there is a God," Ann had whispered, "I think he has helped us more than he'll help them. We must be thankful."

"I am thankful," Catherine replied in an equal whisper for there were crew members fairly near.

When the *Minerva* was out of sight they retired to their cabin until it was time for lunch which was served promptly at twelve. Timekeeping was a vital element of Captain Van Der Sanden's daily meal routines. Breakfast at eight, lunch at noon and supper at seven. Between times he would write up his log, inspect his crew and the ship in general. Sail repairs, painting, varnishing and the greasing of tackle was carried out continually during daylight hours when the ocean was calm enough.

Crewmen sang as they worked and one member had told Wilf that Captain Van Der Sanden never applied the lash. If any of his men committed a serious offence the offender was clad in irons to be handed over to the owners when they docked at their home port. Let them decide what to do with the man.

* * *

By and large it had been a peaceful passage marred only by one incident, that when they encountered a violent storm rounding the Cape of Good Hope, heading for Cape Town. Many sails had been torn and two crew members were washed overboard while another fell from the high rigging and smashed his head on the starboard rail. A tearful burial service had been held by Captain Van Der Sanden before they sailed into Cape Town for emergency repairs and to replace canvas. They were in port for five days which gave the passengers time to look around the town. It seemed slightly strange and certainly ironic that the four women had seen Cape Town less than a year ago but only from the aspect of the *Bromley*'s deck rail. Now they had been rowed ashore as if they were very important people.

Sophie was surprised just how many white people resided in the colony, many of whom it transpired were Dutch. In fact Captain Van Der Sanden had stated at supper one evening he almost felt as much at home in Cape Town as he did in Amsterdam where he lived when not at sea. To Ann it seemed the more affluent areas of London had been transferred here. The homes of the whites were luxurious and it appeared all the families had servants galore. Of course one thing London didn't have was Cape Town's almost perfect climate. The only fogs they got were occasional sea mists and with burning logs on domestic and industrial fires there was little of the soot that coal created.

Sophie quickly discovered through Fred the main industry was diamonds which were mined by the natives either underground or in open casts, as they were called. The deeper mines naturally paid rather better wages although there was more danger from flooding and cave-ins. Yet Sophie heard tales of sadness from native miners' wives who were not happy. Their Dutch masters exploited them to the point where they were not much better than slaves and to be caught with a rough diamond at the end of a shift almost amounted to a death penalty. The overseers were hard, cruel white men who to set an example tied the thief to a frame and thrashed him with flexible canes until he stood in a pool of his own blood while his relations including children were forced to look on. Then he was sent packing with no prospects at all. Nobody wanted to hire a thief.

Farming and the manufacture of wines were other profitable ventures for the whites and again they benefited from the abundance of cheap labour. Sophie was fully aware people were exploited in England although not to the extent which appeared to exist in Cape Town at least and she assumed South Africa generally. Even house servants were required to work at least fifteen-hour shifts seven days a week all year round. And if they should choose to leave for whatever reason there was a long line waiting to take their place. Even a pregnant house servant was only permitted one day off to deliver her child.

The gross inequality opened Sophie Hart's eyes and she wished it was possible to do something about it. Sadly she knew working females generally wielded little or no power. The owners and managers were the masters in South Africa just as they were in England. And before her sentencing it had always annoyed Sophie that women were not allowed to vote although in the northern woollen mills of England females represented over seventy percent of the work force. They toiled yet had no say in who represented them in parliament and to launch any sort of protest would result in instant dismissal, or worse, prison. Every week women were being incarcerated for raising their voices against inequality. And once released they stood no chance of gaining other employment because the word had been spread. This forced many to a life of crime or prostitution as their only form of income. And in Sophie Hart's case her crime had resulted in transportation.

During their stay all four women had gradually formed the opinion it was a very unbalanced world they lived in and ironically being transported had opened their eyes to much of it. On the one hand there was Kiri being exploited by the McFarlanes in their remote Australian residence and yet she was grateful, having been rescued from countless days of pain, anguish and of course sexual abuse. Here in Cape Town there were native Africans being used and abused yet without the white men there would be virtually no work at all. And of course there was Catherine Farrow who had been subjected to virtual slavery from a very early age. A world of exploitation where only the locations were different. However there were exceptions to every rule and Cromwell was a very good example of treating people with dignity and equality. Unfortunately he was in the minority.

Once the *Rotterdam* had been provisioned and set sail again it gave all the passengers time to reflect on worldly conditions they may not otherwise have seen. They were all sympathetic for the native Africans but sadly knew little could or would be done. The white man was master and in almost all cases he was blind to the needs of others. Yet as Fred had said to Sophie in bed while Wilf and Emily were taking a stroll around the deck, "I agree these inequalities should not exist, my dear, but please don't try doing anything about them yourself. I love you to the very depth of my being and I don't want to see you being carted off again to face the governor of Botany Bay who thinks a bull whip solves all problems. Promise me that."

"You speak words of wisdom, Fred, and I will obey. Now interpret that wisdom into satisfying me greatly. In this bed, in any bed there will always be equality between us."

They became enveloped within themselves.

Now they were heading north towards England it was natural for the women to begin feeling a little uneasy again although they had many miles to sail yet. After a scheduled stop in Tenerife their next would be Calais but first they would have to face the Bay of Biscay although this time their circumstances were far more comfortable and the *Rotterdam* had proved it rode ocean swells slightly better than the *Bromley*.

* * * * *

Chapter 23

As Calais wasn't a scheduled stop for the *Rotterdam* it simply anchored outside the small harbour so the six passengers could be taken ashore in a dinghy. In the harbour there were many ships lying at anchor, an assortment of fishing smacks, two brigantines and three sloops, one of which was armed and flew the Spanish flag. Wilf wondered if a war had broken out since they had been away, after all it was well over a year and a half. But unless the war was against England it didn't concern him.

For the women it had been nostalgic sailing up the English Channel again, setting eyes on their home country, this time under much happier circumstances. Of course they regretted not being able to actually land in England but Wilf considered Calais would be safer in the long run. From there they had a choice of which English port to make their entry. It had to be remembered the women were still fugitives so extreme caution was their number one priority. One city to be given a wide berth was obviously London, that being where they had been convicted and lawful elements may still remember their faces. Catherine could easily recall the stern faces of Chief Constable Henry Random and Judge Harcourt Longman. In fact they all had vivid memories of those dark days standing in the prisoner's box as their sentences were delivered. A single word by Crown-appointed judges had shattered their lives. *Transportation.* Yet the one who bore no guilt at all had suffered the most. Ann Lingos was returning with bitter memories and a scarred back. Yet even her animosity towards royalty had moderated to some extent because she had fallen in love with Catherine Farrow. The equation of life had achieved a kind of balance.

Before leaving the *Rotterdam* Captain Van Der Sanden was warmly thanked and complimented on his efficiency. For his part he had enjoyed having them aboard and was glad to have been of service. He was lightly kissed by the women before Fred and Wilf shook his hand. Remembering their passage fee didn't cover the cost of drinks they had consumed aboard, Wilf asked the captain what it was.

The answer was somewhat surprising. "Your company has been payment enough, ladies and gentlemen. I wish all my passengers were as agreeable as you have been."

Hands were shaken again which caused Wilf to recall how bitchy Clare Hamlyn had been with Captain Stricker.

Once ashore in the French port the women and Fred went to a small dockside bar while Wilf searched for the harbour master to enquire what was available for the crossing to England. He didn't speak French although he was fairly sure somebody would be able to converse in English.

Fred wasn't in the least surprised that the bar was almost full of unsavoury characters, both male and female, and Catherine mentally compared it to The Grapes in Limehouse except the loud chatter was in a language she didn't understand. It would have been easy to choke on the thick smoky atmosphere which wasn't all cigar or pipe smoke. Numerous gaudily dressed women sat at small tables drinking smaller drinks while obviously looking for customers. One or two had their eyes on Fred because he was a stranger, new business perhaps? Unfortunately Fred didn't have eyes for them. It seemed knee-high, tight-fitting leather boots were the fashion, complemented with tight skirts and loose blouses which displayed ample amounts of bosom. Most of the men carried knives or pistols in their wide belts as if expecting trouble to erupt at any moment. From her limited experiences Catherine realised places such as this bar existed in every town and in every country around the world with the common element being poverty and where any one of the customers could be candidates for transportation. And what a contrast it was to Cromwell's sedate glade where the only sounds were those of happy children at play and perhaps dogs barking.

Most disquieting to the newly arrived group was the way customers and staff stared at them with suspicion. What really raised eyebrows were the women's sensible everyday clothes they had purchased in Cape Town. They had all expressed a desire to retain their original clothes as mementoes of harsher times so they had each bought lace-up brocade travelling bags to put their rags in. These bags were eyed with suspicion. Had they committed a robbery or were about to? Emily was pleased they had decided to wear bonnets as they denoted an element of purity but if called upon she was ready defend herself. It was Emily who had suggested before they disembarked from the *Rotterdam* that they once again hang the purses filled with gold between their legs as that was probably the most difficult place to get at. Although for most of the men present this was the only area they were interested in.

Wilf had given Fred some gold coins to pay for the drinks so they wouldn't have to show they all carried small fortunes. They had no idea exactly how much their gold was worth but at some point in the not too distant future it would have to be converted into real money. Gold was the world's most valuable metal although many merchants were reluctant to take it for goods or labour as its actual value was difficult to assess. They wanted coins or paper money on which denominations were clear.

Ann desperately yearned to hold Catherine's hand but didn't dare as a surly waiter with only one good eye came to them and in a language they didn't understand asked what they wanted to drink. Fred tactfully pointed to a rum bottle on another customer's table and held five fingers up. The waiter seemed to understand, nodded and went off.

Moments later he returned with five bottles and one pewter tankard with a glass bottom. In sign language Fred was finally able to convey he wanted one bottle and five tankards. The error was rectified and a gold coin offered. It was taken and bitten. Fred had no idea if any change would be returned although he really didn't care, the sooner they were out of this dump the better and the smoke was getting thicker by the minute. It seemed they were the only customers who were not smoking and they all hoped Wilf was making swift progress.

As Fred started to pour them each a rum, a rake wearing an unusually tall top hat and a bright green suit sidled up to Sophie and ran a finger through her hair which hung below the bonnet.

"Please don't," she said, brushing it away.

Fred stood up and in plain English said, "Stop that, mate, she's my wife. There's plenty of other tarts around, go mess with one of 'em."

"Sorry," the man replied in English while tipping his hat. "I just thought you ran these four attractive women for a customer's pleasure and I needed a change from the regular tarts as you so aptly put it. Sorry again."

"Accepted, mate. You sound English, where you from?"

"Plymouth originally. Sailed from there for a few years then got involved in smuggling hemp and opium from the Near East. The law were after me so I came to Calais; I've lived here ever since. Here people tend to keep to themselves and ask no questions. I'd say sixty percent of the population are into one form of crime or another. You want it, you can get it in Calais. Charles Hastings's the name. Are you seeking something?"

"Rather not say, matey," Fred replied tactfully, adopting the Australian expression for friend.

Charles winked. "A wise answer. Everything around here has ears, you know, so I'll say no more."

"There's one thing you can help me with," Fred said while sitting down again. "I gave the one-eyed barman a gold crown for this bottle of rum. He ain't brought change yet. Am I due any?"

"Of course. He saw you were new and took advantage. The French are like that." He beckoned the barman over and they conversed in French for a moment.

Finally the barman produced some coins from a purse and slapped them on the table. Fred thanked him and handed what looked like a low-denomination coin back. The barman used his good eye to wink and left.

"You've just made an enemy," Charles whispered. "If I were you lot I wouldn't linger too long in here, even with a man present the women are not safe. Abducting females for prostitution is a very common crime, so is murder but nobody seems to care. France is in a state of flux. Anyway enough of that, if you need anything you'll always find me here. For now though I wish you the best of luck with whatever you may be up to."

He tipped his hat again and walked over to one of the other ladies who seemed pleased to see him. He dropped a coin down her cleavage before his hand followed it.

It was with relief the group saw Wilf coming in. He drew up a rickety chair and sat down. Emily pushed her tankard of rum over to him and they all watched as he took a long draw. He was just about to say something when Fred put a finger vertically over his lips. Wilf took the hint and winked. They all drank up and left, taking the bottle with them.

Once outside Fred explained the general situation and of meeting Charles Hastings.

"Then I agree with Charles, Calais is a nest bed of criminals," Wilf replied. "I was told anything can be arranged for a price. I did however manage to secure us a passage on a mail boat sailing for Dover at two this afternoon. From there I suggest we take rooms in a tavern to discuss our future plans. One thing I consider most important is that we all go our separate ways. We do attract attention as a group. Does anybody object?"

Nobody did and it was a relief they would be sailing again so soon. Ann in her usual practical manner asked if it wouldn't be wiser now they had come this far to convert their gold to cash, then at least they would have some concept of value. Everybody agreed. Fred suggested they contact Charles Hastings, despite him

being a little on the shady side he was at least English and they could understand
what he said.

Charles was brought outside to discuss their business. He was surprised they
even carried gold and suggested going to a bank he knew which had a slightly better
reputation than most in Calais. He of course would expect a small commission for
his services. This was agreed although he advised taking a chaise as it wasn't too
safe walking the streets with attractive young ladies.

* * *

Once in the stuffy bank and knowing where the women carried their gold Wilf
suggested it may be a good idea to get a private room while they conducted their
business.

Charles was very much surprised when he saw the amounts they each carried,
as was the bank manager, a short, bloated man named Rollo le Dreux who limped
and wore a monocle through which he eyed them with suspicion.

To allay distrust Wilf related an abridged version of their sad story. He also
insisted through Charles they were paid in English currency.

Monsieur le Dreux objected at first but when Charles tactfully told him they
would take their business elsewhere he relented and began to weigh the metal out.
Charles haggled on their behalf for at least fifteen minutes before an exchange
agreement was reached. The banker made a quick mental calculation and said there
would be slightly over three thousand pounds each. This stupefied them, realising
they were rich by any stretch of the imagination. Fred wondered if Cromwell was
aware just how much he'd given them. Of course they would never know, but
knowing him, he wouldn't have cared anyway. To complete their transactions
Charles was given twenty crowns and they were all sure he would get a cut from the
manager. Once again the money was secreted within their clothing before leaving
the bank.

Now came perhaps the most nerve-wracking part of their adventure. Their
return to England. Two more bottles of rum were purchased for the crossing which
they hoped would be calm because Wilf had alerted them to the fact the Channel
could become very rough. For safety against robbers they decided to take a chaise
to the dockside.

* * * * *

CHAPTER 24

I T HAD BEEN AN UNCOMFORTABLE CHANNEL CROSSING, the sea was choppy plus a gusting cross wind pitched the vessel at a fifteen-degree angle for most of the time. This meant they had to hold their goblets of rum rather than set them on the cabin table and Wilf kept the bottle in his pocket. Despite this it was the final leg of a twenty-four-thousand-mile saga, one unfortunately which they could never speak about, nevertheless they had no complaints. If it hadn't been for the shipwreck five months of their sentences would have been served by now. For Sophie that would have meant being confined and shackled in a solitary cell until morning and she didn't even dare to contemplate what else may have befallen her during the night. As for Catherine and Ann they realised their nightly romantic sessions would have been nothing more than memories, even if they were still together. Emily who had no thoughts at all did suggest they held a moment of silence for Lydie Denner, Barbara Henshaw, Captain Stricker and the rest of the *Bromley*'s crew. Sadly they were gone but hopefully at peace somewhere.

Once their ship docked in Dover they were all questioned by a pair of very obnoxious and suspicious port officials who wanted to know where they'd been and what was their reason for being in Calais. Fred suspected they may have thought the women were being brought in for the purposes of prostitution. Fortunately Wilf allayed those suspicions by relating their story once again, placing emphasis on the fact that all their documents had been lost in the shipwreck. By the time he was finished the two officials were full of sympathy, especially as he'd concluded by asking if the beer had improved since they'd been away.

"Nay, sir, it's still piss but it does dull the senses when you have a miserable wife at home who'll only grant marital rights on New Year's Eve. She says if we start five minutes before midnight and finish five minutes after I can brag we were at it for a full year. And I know she fakes her conclusion. I don't complain though, there's many a willing lass hanging around the docks which the wife don't know about."

Both officials then broke into raucous laughter before telling the group to move on.

They all felt relief and the women removed their bonnets to free up heads of thick hair which had grown during the voyage home. It was also good to be back among familiar accents despite the hurdles yet to cross. Of course Catherine now went under the name Harrow and Ann was Annie Ingol. And as before Emily was Mrs Malone and Sophie Mrs Pankhurst.

It soon became obvious Dover was very similar to any port town throughout the world with its fishy smells and seagulls cawing overhead, hoping to swoop and pick up morsels from the decks of vessels which brought the catch in. Carts loaded with all manner of goods were on the streets, being drawn by massive Clydesdale horses. Lower life also abounded with many drunks sleeping last night's gin intake off in the gutter while being robbed by urchins, both male and female. In fact the lasses seemed the more aggressive. They saw a constable walk past one incident, totally ignoring the bodies as if they were nothing but mirages. Plus there was the usual complement of seedy-looking characters hanging around the docks, looking for some form of work. Men who promised the earth before employment was given and then did virtually nothing after they were hired. Buildings generally were ramshackle, having suffered the ravages of wind and rain and almost all needed a coat of paint. Rats abounded as did mangy flea-ridden dogs which roamed the cobbled streets, peeing and messing as they went. Cats seemed more discreet. Scruffy young children roamed everywhere, begging for a copper or two or offering their sister for a few coppers more on the promise she would give you a real good time. She may but another would be picking your pocket while the good time was had. Despite it being August thick black smoke belched from hundreds of chimney pots, depositing its grime everywhere. Washing hanging on lines across the streets was getting dirtier by the minute due to falling soot. Merchants bellowed out, trying to sell freshly caught fish directly off the boats. Of course there were the usual smattering of toffs who operated on the fringes of the law, such as it was. These were the money lenders who extracted exorbitant interest rates and if you couldn't pay on time whatever you possessed was taken and of course the debt was still owed.

"And don't report me to the constable 'cause your wife or daughter will suffer," was the usual threat. These were men without morals but every city, town, village and hamlet in England had them. There was little control of law and order, giving the unlawful carte blanche. Wilf thought it was about time somebody in government put a legitimate law force together.

And of course like everywhere there were the taverns on almost every street corner plying their cheap ale, watered-down whisky, gin, rum and meat pies of questionable quality, plus the cauldron of soup could have been mixed weeks ago. Barrel organs played tinny music outside many of these drinking establishments, hoping to attract customers. Some even had a monkey that entertained by dancing a jig first then performing an act upon itself. This to the great amusement of little boys who, when the act was finished, went to a corner to try it themselves or better still have a lass to do it for them.

"Welcome back to England," Fred said somewhat sarcastically. "Cromwell's forest glade was a paradise by comparison."

And for an instant they all wondered if it wouldn't have been better staying with the man. It also prompted them to think about what he was doing at this particular moment in time. They had travelled halfway across the world while he simply managed his small but very happy tribe. Ann wondered if perhaps one day he would return here, if only to purchase a new top hat?

"So where do we go from here?" Catherine finally asked, realising the time to part company had almost arrived. For over a year she and Ann had enjoyed the security of others, now very shortly they would be on their own, two vulnerable young women although due to their travels they were more worldly now than when the *Bromley* first set sail. It also went without saying that they were far happier.

Wilf glanced at two seedy-looking taverns before suggesting they tried to find a better quality establishment which offered more privacy and where it would be safe to talk. They all agreed so he hailed a passing chaise. The driver was asked if he knew a quiet inn where some weary travellers may rest a while.

"I do know such a place, sir, about a mile up the coast road, high on the white cliffs. The Strait of Dover Inn, it's a reputable establishment where they serve good food and drink and have rooms for rent by the day or week. You'll find it frequented by wealthy gentlemen who desire a little privacy to discuss business deals, usually concerning cartage by sea. Of course there are other amenities on offer as well, sir, although it seems to me you already have attractive company. I envy you. My own wife is bloated but comfortable, if you know what I mean."

Wilf nodded and asked if six could be squeezed into his carriage.

"Aye, sir, but four is normal. I charge extra for six. Two pennies more per passenger."

Wilf agreed and they were on their way. It was a tight squeeze with Emily and Sophie having to sit on their husbands' laps; however they had no objections.

* * *

The private bar of the Strait of Dover Inn was occupied by well-dressed portly men of obvious wealth and station. They were sitting in groups of threes and fours with parchments in front of them, discussing business in one form or another. Wilf knew Dover was one of England's principal ports, giving access to the continent of Europe and thence the world. Every man was either smoking a cheroot, a thick cigar or puffing a pipe, filling the room with a variety of scented odours. Some had tankards of beer in front of them, others silver goblets probably containing gin or whisky. At one large round table another group were playing cards for money and passing an ornate snuff box around as they either added to the kitty or threw their hand in. In a dark corner sat four fairly young women flaunting their natural endowments, hoping to attract a customer for an hour or so. Each sipped some form of beverage from thimble-sized glasses but their bright red lips suggested they were willing to accept more than food and drink into their mouths. One word would describe them all: loose, and the only thing which differentiated these women from those in Calais was the fact they spoke English not French. Candles burned in profusion as if the inn had an aversion to smelly oil lamps or that they cast too much light. From another room came the distinct clink of snooker balls.

A burly bartender eyed the newcomers suspiciously for their clothing was badly creased and crumpled after all their travels although the women's skirts and blouses had been washed prior to arriving in Calais. More clothes had to be a priority once their plans of campaign had been settled.

Wilf was just about to approach the barman when another person appeared through a side door. He wore a maroon suit complete with a matching tight waistcoat. His face was florid, the gut copious, his hands large with diamond-encrusted gold rings on every finger, jewellery now, knuckle dusters later if the situation demanded it. He half bowed to this new group who were strangers to him, which wasn't surprising.

"Welcome, ladies and gentlemen, what can I do for you? I'm Peter Morgan, by the way, owner of this fine establishment." His accent was lilting which Fred suspected could be Welsh for he had once sailed out of Cardiff.

Wilf introduced himself and said they were looking to rent a private room for an hour or so.

Idris smiled and glanced at each woman. "A room with or without beds, sir?"

"We have serious business to discuss, sir," Wilf replied firmly. "This very day we have arrived from Australia after many months at sea and have business to settle. If you're in the least interested this lady is my wife, this one is married to my friend Fred Pankhurst and the other two are travelling companions returning home to families eager to be reunited. Our intentions are perfectly legal and we have money to pay. Now will you accommodate us or shall we take ourselves elsewhere?"

The Welshman bowed deeply. "My apologies to you all. You must understand we have many requests for rooms on a short-term basis and I must be careful. Not all people are what they seem. Why, just last week we found a young lady in one of our better quality rooms, totally unclothed with her throat slit. The sheriff is still looking for the culprit although I fear he or she will be long gone, they always are. Anyway that's none of your concern and I can see you are people of means. Of course I have a room available and for a crown it's yours for two hours. I shall also include a jug of quality red wine or is your choice gin?"

"Wine will be fine," Wilf answered, producing the coins.

Peter slipped them in a waistcoat pocket and gestured they should follow him.

It was an ornate, lavishly furnished room with a window overlooking a large well-manicured lawn surrounded by clipped hedges over which the sea could be seen. It looked a lot calmer now than when they'd sailed across. Wilf told them it appeared that way because they were much higher up.

Then Ann had a question for Peter which stunned them all. "What is the present status of King George, sir?"

Peter's rather high brow furrowed for a moment before he answered.

"As I believe it, young lady, he hasn't suffered a relapse as some of his enemies hoped. It is being said by doctors he suffered from a disease which affected his central nervous system and we must take their word for it. Presently his popularity and energy is high so he attends many public and private functions. He was actually here in Dover six months ago to open a hospice for the needy, of which there are many. The dreaded opium, heroin and gin reduce many people to the state of vegetables. However these are no concern of mine and I must say you all look remarkably fit." He glanced back at Ann. "As for our king, that's all I know."

Ann smiled. "It is far more than I knew, sir. Thank you."

Of course the others were aware why Ann asked the question.

As they became seated a huge decanter of red wine and six glass goblets were brought in by a buxom young woman with her blonde hair done up tightly in a bun.

Peter told them if they required anything else all they had to do was pull the silk cord to the right of the fireplace.

Fred poured the wine and a toast was said to their continued good fortunes before Wilf got down to business and asked what their future intentions were. Fred answered first.

"Sophie and I have agreed it would be wise to travel north up to Hull where she is not known. We shall also marry there as I know a vicar, if he hasn't died in my absence of course. From Hull we may head for York where I intend to open a dining room. I do know it's a very affluent city."

Wilf nodded his head in approval then looked to Catherine and Ann who were holding hands. Catherine answered, "I shall leave Ann to outline our plans for her getting some form of compensation. All I will say is we have pledged to remain together for the remainder of our lives. Of course we realise at times this association may not be easy. However we intend to overcome any and all adversity. Neither of us know how we fell in love, we just did and whatever the circumstances it is our belief we would have met somehow or other. We all know our coming together was not in the happiest of circumstances but all that changed by what we are calling a supreme act of fate. If you weigh all the factors there really can't be any other explanation. We have been given a second chance in life and, thanks to Cromwell's money, we intend to make the most of it. It is also our intent to help others who have not been so fortunate. That's all I have to say, now Ann will continue."

There was a polite round of applause which gave Ann time to take a sip of her wine.

"We intend to make our way gradually to a place somewhere near where I used to live with my mother. There we hope to locate my friend the cobbler to King George, Henry Lastman, who did have the king's full confidence and we're hoping he still does. If this is the case, through him we shall try to arrange some form of a financial settlement. Of course we'll be discreet and with our changes of name we should be able to remain anonymous. It's my belief the king may never have been informed of what became of me following my mother's death. Such things are not unusual, the monarch has enough to worry about without having to bother over trivial matters, of which I was one unfortunately." She stopped talking because Wilf had held a finger up.

"On the other hand what if the king does know of your sentence, surely that will raise suspicions if this cobbler friend tries to negotiate as you have said? Remember, Ann, there are Emily and Sophie to think about, plus Catherine of course. Well, all I'm trying to say is be very careful."

Ann looked at Catherine before answering. "Oh, we'll be very careful. Don't forget we've tasted captivity and have no wish of a return to it. You can be assured I have no intentions of making my name known or that of Catherine. We shall instruct Mister Lastman to make his plea in the name of a person who would prefer to remain anonymous. If George is fully recovered as the landlord said then I think he would be happy to make a discreet settlement simply to avoid a scandal. No monarch wants it known he has illegitimate children running around the countryside." She hunched her shoulders. "It's fairly certain I'm not the only one. And if we don't succeed, well it really doesn't matter, it's not as if we'll need the money. In retrospect the sensible thing for me to have done was use Henry Lastman in the first place instead of trying to go it alone." She paused and looked at Catherine. "Then of course Catherine and I would never have met so I have no regrets. Now we have each other and in that is our strength."

She leaned over and kissed Catherine's cheek.

"It all sounds very complicated to me, Ann," Sophie said. "Don't you think it would be wiser simply to leave well alone? After all, as you said, you don't need the money."

"That's correct, Sophie, but during our private hours aboard the *Rotterdam* Catherine and I discussed everything in great detail. We agreed it wasn't the money, rather a matter of principle. I think you will all agree I have suffered grievously and unnecessarily so I deserve some retribution. I also believe a person must stand up for their rights. England didn't become what it is in the world today by sitting back and letting others push it around. These are chances we are prepared to take. In each other we have the fortitude. Let it remain at that."

As the others clapped she and Catherine kissed passionately.

After a short break Wilf took his turn.

"It's Emily's wish to return to her native country of Ireland. As my roots are also Irish I agreed with her. With our money I may venture into some form of shipbuilding while Emily gives me many children, of course I shall assist in that respect."

There was a pause for laughter and to pour more wine.

Wilf then continued, "It seems our plans are all pretty well settled so I would like to propose that two years from today's date we meet here again to see what headway has been made. By an act of God four women and two men have been given a chance in life very few are granted. I know the shipwreck was a disaster for many of my shipmates but ironically we have benefited from it. In their name and that of our friend Cromwell we must ensure our success. Now it is my intention to seek out our landlord and take a room here for the night. I suggest you others do similar. Then tomorrow we shall take breakfast before going our separate ways. What do we all say?"

They all agreed and the cord was pulled to summon their landlord Peter Morgan.

* * *

In their room Wilf and Emily stood at the window holding hands while overlooking the sparkling English Channel.

"Won't you miss the sea, Wilf?"

"It will always be in my veins, Emily, although I think from now on it will be safer to build ships rather than sail in them. That I shall do. Together and with our children we shall forge a shipbuilding empire such as England or the world has never seen before. My first vessel will be named *Kilpatrick*. Your first voyage commenced in a cramped and smelly hold, fettered about the ankles. In time we'll take a voyage again, this time on the finest vessel afloat. It's strange, Emily, but before meeting you there was nothing I wanted more than to ply the seven seas, now that's the farthest thing from my mind. A ship was wrecked off the coast of Australia yet within two hours a relationship was founded. One which will endure, my love, because a bond has been created out of necessity at first until it has developed into a love deeper than the deepest ocean. Now I've said enough, why don't we act like a man and wife."

"I'm all yours, Mister Malone."

* * *

In their room Sophie sat on the huge comfortable bed, looked up into Fred's eyes and said, "Let us start our family here and now in this room as I feel it will bring us luck and prosperity. Together we have forged a passage from the gates of hell for me and to paradise for both of us. Come to me."

"I do so willingly, Sophie my love. As we set sail on the *Bromley* I never imagined it would end like this. I saw you then as a waif who had committed a crime and was destined to spend the remainder of her years as a captive in a wild, untamed country. I see that same person now as the mother of our children."

He came over her and they kissed passionately for many minutes before undressing to become blissfully interlocked. It was not necessary for Fred to take precautions this time.

* * *

In their room overlooking the garden with the verdant rolling hills of Southern England in the background Catherine and Ann came together and embraced tightly. They both cried. It seemed an eternity since they first set eyes on each other in the stuffy hold of a ship bound for Australia with no future to look forward to except one of hardship, cruelty, despair and possible death.

Ann ran a finger down the side of Catherine's face. "We are home, my love. Let us once again experience the harmony which exists between us."

"Yes, my love, we will. Let us wash our bodies first to rid them of accumulated grime."

"I agree. We have travelled a very long way but as the miles increased so did our love for each other. Every second which passes establishes another beautiful memory. Nothing can stop us now. We have money and ambition and perhaps I shall have a royal father who has recognized me even though he may not know who I am."

"He will, Ann, he will."

Twenty minutes later they were washed from head to toe, lying side by side to begin the process which would convey them into a world unto themselves alone.

And in the western sky the setting sun was casting a golden glow over the sea and land.

* * * * *

PART FIVE

HECTOR PIMM
SEEKS REVENGE

CHAPTER 25

W ITH ROUTINE STOPS TO EAT AND CHANGE horses it took Hector Pimm and his party over five weeks to arrive in London from Lisbon. The day was also his thirty-fifth birthday. While in Calais he had wanted to discharge the Portuguese nurse, coachman and guard but they insisted their instructions had been to see him settled wherever he lived. As he was single and usually at sea he had no permanent residence but when ashore he lodged in a quality boarding house in Deptford so his escorts were asked to take him there. A private chaise was hired for the journey.

On the way he was intrigued to see a newspaper placard on which was written in very bold letters:

PROMINENT JUDGE FOUND DEAD IN HIS APARTMENT

Pimm asked for the coach to be stopped so a sheet of the *Daily Gazetteer* could be purchased. Although the print was slightly blurred the report was legible.

> *The prominent London circuit judge Harcourt Longman was found dead in his Belgravia apartment by his manservant yesterday morning. The judge had been stabbed numerous times. According to the Sheriff of London who is investigating the case there appears to be no motive as there is no evidence of robbery. Judge Longman had an impeccable record on the bench. He will be missed.*

Pimm mused on the report as the coach continued on its way. He had heard of the judge who had frequently sentenced criminals to transportation. Naturally it caused him to wonder if those on the *Bromley* had been sentenced by him. Of course it was of no moment to him now. He had other business on hand.

* * *

Finally the coach came to a halt in front of his lodgings.

His old landlady Bella was pleased to see him despite being unexpectedly early. He explained the circumstances of his injury although omitting how it was attained. Nevertheless she was happy to have him back and of course she had a room. Not the one he had used last time but of the same quality, however the bed was new. Bella was a gargantuan woman with many chins, a raucous laugh and a heart of gold. A true motherly sort. While embracing him she promised to help him through his difficulties. He didn't think that would be necessary but thanked her anyway.

Abutting Bella's residence was a tavern which Bella claimed to be for gentlemen of quality only. This meant they washed at least once a month and paid their bills. By mutual agreement the tavern served her tenants meals and drinks at slightly reduced rates. In appreciation of their excellent services en route Hector felt obliged to wine and dine his team so after depositing his bags the offer was made in Bella's lounge. The guard and driver Enrico Douro declined as they wished to enquire about English coaching services with a view to company expansion. Enrico asked Hector for an endorsement which was gladly given, the man had served him well. The nurse Catriona Vigo however accepted Hector's offer gratefully and Bella winked, suspecting a seduction was possible.

If asked Hector would have described Catriona as attractive in her own way although not a ravishing beauty. However she had catered to his every whim en route which made the long journey bearable despite suffering bouts of dizziness and headaches in varying degrees of intensity. Some were mild, others excruciating. Catriona was able to allay most with a special medicine she claimed was developed by her Spanish ancestors. She wasn't able to reveal the contents; however in most cases the thick mixture worked so he didn't press the issue. His ear still had a tendency to dribble blood so when it did Catriona stuffed it with wadding. It didn't affect his hearing because he was deaf in that ear anyway.

Throughout the sometimes bumpy and windy journey Hector had thoughts of making amorous advances towards Catriona. The problem was with the other two present it made things difficult. Now though it was just the pair of them for supper and Hector did wonder if the men were being diplomatic. No expense was spared over the meal and following it Catriona was asked if she'd like to join him for a slightly more private drink. She accepted. A flagon of red wine was purchased and they returned to his room. Bella had winked again before they mounted the stairs.

Once in the spacious room and the wine poured Catriona startled Hector with a statement he had not expected.

"Now my obligations are complete I should be most happy for you to avail yourself of my body, Mister Pimm."

"I accept willingly, Catriona."

She undressed herself first, then him. He was rapidly aroused by the sight of her slightly plump body and in mere seconds after she lay next to him he came over her and they became fused. Unfortunately for Catriona the urgent body below him was not his nurse but Ann Lingos.

For most of his time on the road when he wasn't being tormented by throbbing headaches he began to develop an extreme hatred for the girl who had infatuated him to the point where he was driven to make that assault upon her. Almost every moment when he was off watch his mind had created mental images of her lean, firm body under him with those pert breasts pressing into his chest as he kissed her delectable lips. That was why he was shaving when she arrived for her cleaning duties, he didn't want his stubble to mar the almost flawless skin. In retrospect he realised it had been a mistake to request she showed him her upper legs and go at her suddenly. It scared her and she retaliated with the only weapon near at hand, one of his well-sharpened pencils. He realised that failed attempt had to all intents and purposes ruined his chances of ever becoming the master of his own vessel. A promising career thwarted by a mere convict. As the carriage bumped northward he kept repeating to himself over and over in his head she must be made to suffer far more pain than those lashes had inflicted. There was a way because he was on friendly terms with the Botany Bay penal colony governor, having signed over both male and female convicts into his hands on two previous occasions. He also knew Edgar Boag was open to bribes and had in fact made himself a considerable amount of money selling young female convicts to prospectors and farmers who desired agreeable company at their isolated stations. His colony records simply showed the convict had died due to disease and there was nobody to question him. A few guards and the doctor would have to be paid off but they were more than willing. Transported convicts were the dregs of society anyway and most had no family connections. Even if they had they were too far away from home for it to matter.

By the time he arrived in London Hector had formulated a plan of returning to Port Jackson and buying Ann Lingos. He would then take her to some remote area and firstly claim by force that which she had denied him on the *Bromley*. After fully satisfying his lust he would slowly begin to work on her until she was reduced to a state of insanity. With that accomplished he would cast her out into the wilderness to become prey to the wild animals. His evil mind saw it all, first though there were two items of business in London which required his attention.

* * *

Number one priority was to see a doctor about his ear. His deafness had been accepted but if possible he wanted to clear his headaches and the bleeding. Doctor Mountjoy aboard the *Bromley* had told him about a street in London where reputed doctors practiced; however he must proceed with caution because many were more interested in taking money off rich patients than actually curing them. He was sure those who attended King George III during his madness actually knew little about what ailed him, nevertheless their reputations counted for a great deal to the monarch. Yet numerous physicians had failed to cure George so those loyal to the Crown brought in a doctor named Willis who with unusual methods finally cured the king.

Without much difficulty Hector managed to locate a fairly young doctor named Lawrence Heath who agreed to conduct a cursory examination for a fee Hector considered reasonable. Numerous general questions about his life were asked prior to the main one. How did the accident occur? Pimm didn't like to admit a young convict girl had stabbed him with a pencil so claimed a spar had splintered during a storm and a sliver penetrated his ear. One of those unfortunate accidents which can happen aboard ship.

Following the questions Doctor Heath had his patient seated in a reclining chair and the examination began with the assistance of a middle-aged nurse. For Pimm it was a very painful experience as his ear was prodded and poked a great deal, causing it to bleed quite badly. The nurse cleaned him up and applied a bandage while the doctor contemplated his conclusions. Over a brandy each, Doctor Heath rendered his report.

"The eardrum, Mister Pimm, is damaged beyond repair so you will be deaf on that side forever. I'm sorry. Also from what I have been able to see the passage from the middle ear to the pharynx has received some damage which may or may not cause future complications, sadly I cannot be sure. One possibility is a tumour could develop. I know you expected more but you must realise these areas within the head are at the very fringes of our knowledge. Perhaps in fifty years we may know more."

"That doesn't do me a lot of good, does it, Doctor?"

"No, I'm afraid not. However I have at least alerted you to the fact that further problems may arise so you must be vigilant to physical changes."

"Such as?"

"Increasing dizzy spells. Loss of balance. Feelings of nausea. Headaches more severe than you seem to experience now."

"Is there nothing you can do to at least stop the headaches?"

"I could prescribe all manner of potions, Mister Pimm, although they wouldn't do much good. I'm not a quack as some people call others in my profession. Avoiding bright sunlight will help and if the headaches are really severe you may like to wear eye shades."

"Yes, Doctor, I understand. Just one more thing. These future complications you mentioned, how far ahead do you think they are?"

"Frankly I have no idea. Perhaps months, even years, or they might never arise. As I said, you must be alert for signs. Do you intend going back into seafaring?"

"I haven't decided yet."

"Well, whatever, I wish you luck and I'm sorry there isn't more I can do. A great deal goes on within the head which we may never know about. I would appreciate it though if you could drop by and see me again in a year or so, we could at least discuss what has transpired. It perhaps won't help you a great deal but it may be of use to me, and others. We doctors are always striving to gain more knowledge."

"Yes of course, Doctor, and I thank you for being so honest."

Doctor Heath was given a cheque and Hector left being just a little wiser than when he went in although certainly not cured. He decided while hailing a cab to live as normal a life as possible and still extract his revenge on Ann Lingos. Now though there was something else to do before even thinking of returning to Australia.

* * *

The following day and without making an appointment Hector arrived at the *Bromley*'s company offices in North Woolwich and asked to see Clifford Prosser, the managing director. Being well known within the company he was immediately shown into the lavishly appointed office and asked to sit down. Following a brief account of why he was here and not en route to Port Jackson the manager was handed Captain Stricker's sealed report.

Once read Hector was permitted to read it himself in case there was a disagreement of the facts. Hector, in all fairness to Captain Stricker, agreed it outlined events exactly as they had unfolded. It also stated his reasons why the convict Ann Lingos was only given twenty-five lashes as opposed to the required one hundred. The report concluded by saying First Mate Pimm had exceeded his bounds as a senior officer by trying to induce a female convict into illicit acts. It also added there was a suspicion he was at least partially drunk when the incident occurred although this could not be proven. Even Doctor Mountjoy wouldn't swear to Pimm being intoxicated.

The portly Clifford Prosser scanned the report again before sitting back to deliver his own opinion.

"I'd say you were a fool, Pimm, a bloody fool. As you well know, this company had high hopes for you, in fact you would have had your own vessel within two years. However this incident has changed everything. We cannot have senior officers on our staff who are overcome with lust even if the ones they are entrusted with are common criminals. Is there anything you wish to add to Captain Stricker's report before I render my judgement?"

"The lass enticed me, sir, during the execution of her assigned duties by continually bending down and at least partially exposing her breasts. I should add she did wear a very slack blouse. From this I naturally assumed she desired me, something which is not uncommon among female convicts while in transit. Believe me, sir, they will go to almost any lengths to receive little favours. I know on other vessels even the captains have taken convict mistresses during the voyage."

"That may be so, Pimm, although not on our ships. I'm sure Captain Stricker made that perfectly clear to all hands including yourself. It was your duty, Pimm, as first mate to resist any unbecoming actions and set an example to the rest of the crew. However in this case I don't think it was one of temptation, rather your lust for a vulnerable young woman. I realise convicts generally are not ethical or trustworthy citizens but we are performing a service for which a fee is paid. It is our duty to deliver them in a fair condition to the authorities in the penal colony and I think by and large we do so. By your actions you have not only sullied yourself but our company as well. I can only hope our charter is renewed and that this company will be commissioned for future voyages. I'm sorry for your deafness, sadly however there is nothing I can do about that." He paused, seeing Hector had held a hand up. "Yes, what is it now?"

"What was the nature of the Lingos woman's crime? It wasn't listed in the convicts' log and for some reason Captain Stricker wouldn't confide in me."

"No, I'm aware of that, Pimm, and for good reason. Unfortunately I cannot reveal the reason either as the captain and I were forced to swear an oath. I'm sorry but there it is. Anything else?"

"No, sir, only I would deem it a great honour to still serve you in some capacity."

"Out of the question, Pimm, out of the question. Firstly your deafness in the ear will be a detriment to efficient performance and secondly Captain Stricker discharged you in Lisbon and I do so again now. Naturally you will be paid what is owing. We will also reimburse the consul in Lisbon who covered your overland travel costs. That is all, Pimm, you may leave. Report here again tomorrow and what money is owing will be waiting."

* * *

Still in a huff, Pimm reported the following day and picked up his cheque. Now came the task of finding a ship heading for Port Jackson. He had hoped to work his passage but without references any position of merit was out of the question and he certainly had no intentions of signing on as a deckhand. As he was a single man his bank account was fairly substantial so he could afford to pay.

He made numerous enquiries around various London dockyards only to discover there was nothing in the immediate future heading for any part of Australia. He was advised to try Southampton or even Plymouth.

Plymouth was a long way from London so he decided to try Southampton first. He packed his bags, paid Bella for a month, kissed her and took an express stage.

Luck was with him. There was a ship named the *Romney* due to sail on the fifth of October heading for Port Jackson before continuing on to Wellington on the north island of New Zealand. Its estimated time of arrival in Australia was the third or fourth week of April next year. Hector met with Captain Gerald Mayfield and reserved a shared cabin. His quest to extract revenge on Ann Lingos had begun. Of course he was not to know the *Bromley* would be shipwrecked off the south-west Australian coast next January. Nor that there would be survivors.

* * * * *

CHAPTER 26

HEN HECTOR FINALLY ARRIVED IN PORT JACKSON and had re-established his friendship with the penal colony governor Edgar Boag it came as an enormous shock to discover the *Bromley* had never arrived. It therefore followed Ann Lingos wasn't confined, or any of the other convicts. Edgar explained they assumed the *Bromley* had been sunk, taking all hands and the convicts with her. They were still waiting for confirmation; however in the interim the convicts' names had been struck off the register. It was no great loss except the six young women had been earmarked for breeding purposes.

Hector was livid which didn't help his headaches at all. Twice now Ann Lingos had thwarted him, to say nothing of a twelve-thousand-mile journey and over six months of his life wasted. However Hector was due to have an extraordinary piece of luck.

Two days later at the inn where he was staying and while mulling over his return to England he saw a woman using crutches being assisted by two coloured men up to the reception counter. Her face seemed vaguely familiar. Upon closer inspection he saw she was none other than Clare Hamlyn, one of the *Bromley*'s two female passengers. There was no mistake, but how could this be? According to Edgar Boag it had been assumed the *Bromley* had sunk, taking everybody aboard with it. Hector knew he had to play his cards correctly, something was not quite right here. And why did Clare need crutches? She certainly didn't on board the *Bromley*. He didn't approach her there and then but watched as the coloured men escorted her to one of the rooms. He noted the number.

Fifteen minutes later Hector saw the men leave with smiles covering their handsome faces. Very discreetly and just to be sure himself Hector asked the brawny-looking man on the reception counter the name of the woman who had just registered.

"You ain't a bounty hunter, are you?"

"Do I look like one?"

"No tellin', matey. We get many here lookin' for runners from the penal colony. They stalk their prey like wild animals then when caught they take 'em back and get paid. The poor sod of a runner gets a length of rawhide laid across his back a few times after which he gets a God-awful cell all to himself for months plus steel neck- and ankle-wear."

"Well, I'm certainly nothing to do with bounty hunting."

"Aye, per'aps you're right. Information will cost you though, nothing's free in this town."

"Would a florin make you feel more disposed to answer my question?" He displayed a coin.

The man took it before running a bitten fingernail down a badly smudged list. "The name's Hamlyn, Mrs Clare Hamlyn. Now bugger off and don't try to rape or rob her, just remember I've seen your face."

As he walked away Hector realised once again what a lawless inhospitable town Port Jackson really was. Everybody was on the take and everything had a price. Of course he himself was part of it because if Ann Lingos had been in the penal colony he would have paid Edgar Boag to have her turned over to him. With this accomplished his revenge would begin and only he would hear Ann's screams and pleas for mercy, mercy she wouldn't have got. Plus the beauty of it all was with England being so far away it was very unlikely anybody would discover what he had done. The Lingos girl had been sentenced to life anyway, he knew that despite her actual crime being a mystery to him.

After taking a deep breath he decided to take the bull by the horns and knock on Clare Hamlyn's room door. He imagined she'd be just as surprised to see him as he was her.

After four knocks the door opened a few inches and Clare's eyes peered out. She gasped and uttered two words, "Mister Pimm."

"Please allow me in, Mrs Hamlyn, it's very important."

The door opened and she stood aside, balanced on her crutches. They shook hands somewhat awkwardly.

"I never thought I'd see you again, Mister Pimm."

"Nor I you, Mrs Hamlyn. Please call me Hector, far more informal, don't you think?"

"Agreed. Now assist me to a chair, as you can see I'm incapacitated."

After helping her to a chair he sat at an angle to her so his good ear could take in all she said. Before opening any conversation he eased his cravat and unbuttoned his jacket as the room was hot and stuffy. They stared at each other for a long moment before Hector spoke.

"I'll be perfectly honest with you, Clare, I may call you that I assume?" She nodded. "I came to Port Jackson on my own initiative to extract revenge on Ann Lingos for what she did to me. I saw the penal colony governor who told me she and the other five convicts never arrived. It was assumed there had been a shipwreck somewhere along the way with everybody aboard being lost. Naturally when I was told this I counted myself fortunate that Captain Stricker had dropped me off in Lisbon. Now I meet you here in Port Jackson. I would deem it a great honour if you could explain what happened. Will you?"

Clare sat there feeling rather uncomfortable, knowing the pledge she had given to the survivors when they were with that wonderful man Mister Cromwell. After much soul-searching she decided to modify the story somewhat.

"There was a shipwreck, Mister Pimm, sorry, Hector, off a place called Brookes Inlet as I recall. Three of us survived, the Bosun Wilf Malone, the chef Fred Pankhurst and myself. I suffered a badly broken leg and were it not for what I can only term a miracle we were picked up by a group of aborigines, one of whom was a magnificent man named Cromwell who spoke excellent English." She paused to ease her good leg. "Well, to cut a long story short there was a medicine woman named Tarfa with this tribe and she amputated my leg just above the knee. That saved my life, of that I'm sure. As you are aware I was aboard the *Bromley* to be reunited with my husband here in Port Jackson so despite my incapacity I still felt it my duty to rejoin him. When Tarfa finally pronounced me fit to travel Cromwell detailed two of his young men to escort me here by overland routes as I had no wish to sail again. They carry the rather strange names of Hamlet and Macbeth, then again Mister Cromwell was rather strange himself although totally dedicated to his tribe. As our journey was in excess of two thousand miles I agreed to teach Hamlet and Macbeth English on the way. I'm pleased to say they were quick learners and now speak the language fluently. You may have seen the pair bring me in here."

"Yes, I did. Tell me, what became of Malone and Pankhurst?"

"While I was still recovering they intended returning to the Swan River port to get a ship back to England or at least western Europe. Cromwell told me later they did, on a Dutch vessel named the *Rotterdam*."

"Did they have any money?"

"Yes. Cromwell gave them each some gold. He had piles of it yet such was his way of life he hardly ever used any. As I said, he is a very remarkable man even if slightly eccentric."

"I see. I thank you, Clare, the picture is a little clearer now. May I ask what are your own intentions now?"

"Quite frankly, Hector, now I've seen Port Jackson I'm not at all impressed as it is far more primitive than I ever imagined. Why even this inn is little more than a large shack despite it being considered the best in this part of Australia. Of course I didn't expect London but this town is no better than an average English hamlet with little order and hardly any law. Anyway that is of no moment, such things have to be accepted. During my long journey with Hamlet and Macbeth I came to realise I wouldn't be able to perform my duties as a wife let alone a mother at some future date, therefore I'm going to try and convince my husband it would be better if we returned to England. To this end I have dispatched the two men to bring my husband here. This is no land for a cripple, Hector."

"I agree there. What of Alice Edwards's husband, shouldn't he be informed of her demise?"

"Of course. According to Alice he's developing a mine at a place called Broken Hill somewhere west of here, I believe. Anyway my husband will know where to contact him. Now perhaps if you could be so kind and order us a pot of tea, if they provide such. If not I'll have red wine."

"Yes of course, I'd be pleased to."

He got up and left, not quite believing Clare had been telling the whole truth. The way she had fidgeted while describing the events and the flickering of her eyes indicated she was lying to some extent. He also had a sneaking suspicion Ann Lingos had survived the wreck so there was still hope of extracting his revenge. Then he slapped his head in a realisation. While sailing here they had passed a ship named the *Rotterdam* travelling west. He remembered everybody waving and drinking toasts as they passed. His quarry Ann Lingos could have been one of them. This thought made him tremble and brought on another headache so along with ordering a pot of tea he asked for a very large goblet of whisky.

While awaiting delivery of the tea he and Clare made small talk with Hector trying subliminally to pry more information out of her. Unfortunately she didn't vary her story at all and spoke very highly of her escorts. Hector decided the least he could do was buy Clare a meal in the hopes more wine may loosen her tongue.

He was wrong and by nine o'clock they decided to retire for the night having assumed Clare's husband Gordon wouldn't arrive until tomorrow at the earliest.

* * *

In fact it was two days later before Gordon Hamlyn arrived. Hector was introduced and after taking tea together he excused himself, not wanting to become involved in what he imagined would be a domestic dispute. He wasn't wrong.

Following Clare's explanation of her intentions Gordon was beside himself with rage. In fact he was a man with a disposition similar to his wife's.

"Didn't I tell you to remain in England until I came to get you, Clare? You are an ass, a complete ass. I have made money out here and my future prospects are limitless. In time I would have built us a house, sailed home and we could have returned together on a proper ship, not a rotten hulk transporting pox-ridden convicts. I say again you are an ass. Now you will be nothing but a millstone about my neck. This is a land for fit and able people, not cripples."

Clare broke down and sobbed. "I wasn't expecting such an outburst, Gordon. How do you think I feel having to painfully hobble everywhere on crutches. Do I take it your love for me has waned?"

"Waned puts it very mildly, Clare. I'm founding what I hope will become a construction empire out here and a one-legged wife does not fit into it. I'm sorry to be so blunt but there it is."

"Then I shall return to England alone. Mister Pimm will escort me, I'm sure. And do not think for one moment, Gordon, I shall give you a divorce because it is out of the question. Additionally I shall expect you to support me financially because to me a marriage bond is a contract for life."

"I will not shirk my responsibilities, Clare. I'm willing to settle an annual allowance once I know better what my financial situation will be. In the interim I shall pay your return passage and give you eight hundred guineas. That will have to suffice for the moment."

"I will accept that, Gordon, but shall look forward to hearing from you within two years with a proposal for an annual settlement of at least a thousand guineas, I think that is fair. I also expect you to pay my two escorts who provided excellent service all the way from their village to here. I think twenty-five guineas each will satisfy them."

"Yes, Clare, I'll see they get that. I do however consider an annual payment of a thousand guineas rather excessive."

She smiled. "Separations can be expensive affairs, Gordon, but please remember it is you who have forsaken me. However for the moment I shall make no further demands provided you swear to honour yours. Do you?"

"You know I'm an honourable man, Clare, and will not let you down. My word on it."

"Thank you, Gordon. Now tell me, is Alice Edwards's husband still overseeing that mine in Broken Hill?"

"As far as I know, yes. In fact I believe the mining equipment aboard the *Bromley* was bound for his company. All I could do is send him a letter explaining what befell Alice. He will be heartbroken, I know. He had such plans for them both."

"I thought we had plans, Gordon."

"We did, we did; however they included a complete woman. I'm sorry, Clare, but it would be no use us trying to make a go of it. As you said, this is a rough country and I have to be constantly on my guard against my employees who would fleece me rotten if given half a chance. As it is I have to employ henchmen to ensure my workers give value for money. Anyway enough of that, I shall take my leave now. You will have my money by tomorrow, it's too late today, the banks will be closed."

He got up, kissed the back of her hand and walked out. Clare hobbled to the bed, fell on it face down and sobbed. She would have been even more distressed if she knew Gordon had a young lady waiting for him at a small ranch house three miles north of the town. Things couldn't have worked out better for him. Clare's broken leg had been a blessing in disguise.

Hector Pimm was wondering what had transpired between the couple when Gordon appeared and sat down beside him. He explained it was Clare's wish to return to England and would he be willing to escort her for a fee. Hector agreed because his mood was one of high elation as a result of a discussion he'd had with Clare's escorts when Gordon went to her room.

With nothing better to do he invited both young men for a drink in the men-only bar room where they served beer and liquor. Once they were settled with a large whisky each Hector opened the conversation on the premise Clare Hamlyn hadn't told him the entire truth about the shipwreck and decided to gamble a little. He subliminally asked the men if they knew the names of the other survivors. He wasn't in the least surprised to be told one was called Emily, another Sophie plus two others, Ann and Catherine.

Of course Hector could have leapt out of his chair in elation, Ann Lingos was alive and well, but where was she? That was the important question although finding her could be a daunting task; however he did have one or two clues. If he could be located the captain of the *Rotterdam* may be able to help. Then of course there were Fred Pankhurst and Wilf Malone, they should be easy to locate through Clifford Prosser. He didn't think two career sailors would have any allegiance to convicts, and yet, he thought, they had sailed to England with them and according to Hamlet the men were very friendly with Emily and Sophie. If so locating Ann could be difficult. There was one thing on his side though, he had plenty of time.

He bought Hamlet and Macbeth another drink each before returning to his room with a bottle of Scotch whisky. All the excitement had brought on another pounding headache.

* * *

Gordon Hamlyn kept his word and provided his distressed wife with sufficient funds to purchase a passage to England and give Hector Pimm a generous fee for escorting her. With only one leg she would be in almost constant need of a strong arm, especially aboard ship. Clare and Gordon parted with a formal handshake. Hector sensed a definite chill as he too shook Gordon's hand before they parted.

Now all Hector wanted was a passage back to England on the first available ship. Upon making enquiries he was told the only one expected was the *Romney*, the very vessel he had travelled here on. If all had gone well on its passage to Wellington and assuming there were no delays unloading and loading, it should arrive back in Port Jackson in five to six weeks. He would just have to keep his fingers crossed there were berths available. And so he may live up to his obligations as an escort, he hoped to get adjacent cabins with a connecting door. That way he could give Clare all the help she needed.

* * *

They sailed forty days later. Both Hector and Clare were much relieved as the wait had been frustrating. Hector spent much of his time simply walking around alone as Clare wasn't capable. He realised once again Port Jackson wasn't the sort of town designed for social living and there seemed to be many more convicts than on his previous visits. They had been put to various tasks such as building and assisting in the fields although they were always marched back to the colony compound after sunset. Most looked to be a degenerate, desperate lot who had lost all hope. Many of the younger women appeared pregnant which caused Hector to wonder what became of their children once delivered. It was no fault of their own they were here and he wondered if they would ever get a chance of returning to the land of their mothers. He doubted it and realised many would become criminals themselves when old enough. Hector also spent many hours over goblets of whisky musing about his ill fortune and not being able to extract revenge on Ann Lingos and each night in bed he suffered nightmares about the girl.

She floated above his bed in total nakedness, smiling down at him.

"Gaze fondly now, Hector, at what lies between my thighs although your fingers will never caress it. I have my liberty again and reside in a place where you will never find me. I haunted your thoughts while aboard the *Bromley*, I haunt you now in Port Jackson and once you are at sea again I shall still hover over you yet always outside your grasp. And when I fade away it is to return to Catherine Farrow who enjoys everything about me you are denied for we are deeply in love. Sleep well, Hector Pimm."

Usually at that point he woke up in a cold sweat and with a pulsating headache. His only recourse was in the whisky bottle.

It therefore came as a great relief to himself and Clare when the *Romney* actually departed Port Jackson, a place he never wished to see again and Clare was in complete agreement.

* * *

Luckily Hector had managed to obtain adjoining cabins and by giving the steward a generous tip whatever meals they required could be served in Clare's cabin. This to ease the stress on her leg as she was finding it difficult walking about on an angled and sometimes slippery deck. Captain Gerald Mayfield was very sorry but there wasn't anything he could do about the ship's lie. The winds alone dictated that and at this time of the year they could be very erratic. Perhaps once they entered the Atlantic things may improve although as a seaman he knew there were no guarantees. Of course Hector understood and explained the situation in more detail to Clare. Travelling west they were heading into the westerlies rather than going with them as the *Bromley* had been on the outward journey. Clare made but a single comment.

"Well, I sincerely hope we don't founder this time as I would stand no chance of survival. Now let us enjoy a whisky."

On their second day out while the pair were taking supper in Clare's cabin she decided to fully confide in Hector regarding her marital arrangements with Gordon.

"You may as well know my husband has abandoned me and I suspect he has already taken a mistress. If the rat can do that to me, Hector, I see no logical reason why I shouldn't reciprocate. I may be minus the lower half of my leg but what lies between my thighs is not impaired. In all other respects I have the healthy appetite and normal desires of a woman so I'm willing if you are."

"I always saw you as a captivating woman, Clare, although I didn't dare make any approaches on the *Bromley* as Captain Stricker would have frowned on such an association. That in part was why I tried to have my way with Ann Lingos and we both know the outcome of that."

"Indeed we do, Hector. Further I openly admit to you now I enjoyed watching those lashes landing across her back. Her squeals were delightful, it was just a pity she only had to suffer twenty-five strokes. With more she might have died thus depriving her of Catherine Farrow with whom she exchanged affections."

"So they were lovers. I long suspected it but was never sure."

"Be sure now, Hector."

"How are you so certain? Nobody ever saw them even petting on deck, not at least before I was dropped off at Lisbon. If they had indulged in such activities I would have been informed and instructed to have it stopped. Captain Stricker was a traditionalist."

Clare paused for a moment to consider whether or not to relate the full story of the shipwreck. In her bitterness and despite her word to Wilf Malone and the others she elected to on the grounds they would never find out anyway. She took a deep breath.

"What I told you at the inn when we first met was not quite an accurate account of what transpired following the *Bromley*'s demise. There were more survivors. Emily Kilpatrick, Sophie Hart, Catherine Farrow and Ann Lingos." Hector of course knew this but he let Clare continue. "On the beach it sickened me to see Farrow and Lingos locked together embracing, kissing and doing goodness knows what else with their asp-like tongues and fingers. I must admit though they all tried to make me comfortable so following the amputation I promised them I'd not reveal what I'm telling you now. But when all said and done they were convicts, and still are as far as I'm concerned and should be brought to justice."

"I agree one hundred percent, Clare, and your openness is also greatly appreciated. Do I assume Malone and Pankhurst teamed up with the other women?"

"Yes. Emily became attached to Wilf Malone and Sophie to Fred Pankhurst. I do believe they intended getting married at some future point."

Hector clapped his hands in glee. "Well, if they did their marriages will be short-lived, I guarantee that. After I've dealt with Lingos personally all the women will find themselves back on a ship bound for Botany Bay, manacled hand and foot. As for Pankhurst and Malone, I'll see they're charged with abetting known convicts. It was most fortunate we met again, Clare."

She smiled. "Indeed it was, Hector. Now enough about them, we'll have plenty of time to plan revenge later. For now why don't you lay me on the bunk and remove what clothing is necessary so you may give me what I'd hoped to receive from my husband."

In moments Hector lay over Clare and they became fully coupled. He smiled. Despite his continuing headaches and deafness perhaps it wouldn't be such an unpleasant return voyage after all.

* * *

As it transpired Hector was still to be fated with bad luck.

Less than a day after the *Romney* sailed from their stopover in Tenerife his headaches started to become more severe. In fact they were so intense he couldn't tolerate being in daylight so all his time was spent in the cabin with a thick, dark blanket draped over the window. Even his balance and vision suffered. The ship's doctor was unable to give him much in the way of relief and all Clare could do was bathe his forehead with cloths soaked in salt water and pour him either brandy or whisky whenever he asked for one, which was becoming more frequent as each day elapsed. Sadly even she was restricted in her assistance because if the ship was pitching too much she had no alternative but to lie on her bunk or sit uncomfortably in a chair.

Unfortunately the headaches only got worse, just as Doctor Heath had predicted and now his neck was giving him intense pain. Hector was a strong man but even he was reduced to tears at times. His thoughts now were not of the reprisals he would inflict upon Ann Lingos, rather of his own survival. At all costs he had to hang on until they reached England where he hoped Doctor Heath could do something for him. After all it was over a year now since the consultation so hopefully there may have been some form of medical breakthrough.

Ironically by the time they were passing Lisbon Hector was falling in and out of a coma and couldn't hold any food down, not even watery broth. Two days later when Clare hobbled into his cabin she found him lying face down on the floor with blood streaming from his ear, his mouth and a large gash on the forehead. The captain and ship's doctor were called and they conducted a brief examination. Both men knew well of Hector's condition and reached a similar conclusion. He had fainted and in falling had cracked his forehead on the wooden-framed bunk during last night's rough weather. That in all probability was what killed him. The doctor was prepared to write up a death certificate to that effect in case there were any legal claims arising from the death.

That same afternoon Hector Pimm's body was sewn in canvas and consigned to the deep following a brief service performed by Captain Mayfield. All the crew attended and one had been detailed to support Clare in case the ship was hit by a sudden large wave.

Alone in her cabin Clare cried over Hector's demise as his loss was also a tragedy for herself. Nine weeks ago and in tears Hector had been informed she was carrying his child. In the heights of their passion they had both been careless. Hector had verbally agreed to provide financial support for the child when he was employed again. Presently she knew he was without a situation but after settling his vendetta with Ann Lingos he intended to seek work ashore. An agreement was to have been drawn up when they landed in England. Hector had made it very clear he had no intentions of living with her as she was still a married woman despite her estrangement and reluctantly she had to accept this. Now of course with Hector dead and buried whatever agreements had been reached were null and void. The fact still remained that it would be obvious to all, even her husband, that the child had been conceived at sea and obviously by Hector Pimm, her escort. She knew this would negate any financial promises Gordon had made and despite her own crippled situation this would be a disgrace to her and the family. She realised life was going to be very difficult indeed, or there was another way ...

Next morning when the galley steward knocked on her cabin door to deliver breakfast there was no reply. The ship's first mate was summoned and with a master key he entered the cabin. Clare Hamlyn wasn't in her bunk or sitting in the chair although her crutches were lying on the floor beside it. An alert was issued to find the passenger, who couldn't have moved very far on one leg.

After searching every nook and cranny aboard the vessel by two separate parties Captain Mayfield finally concluded she must have thrown herself out of the cabin window sometime during the night. It must have been awkward for her although there was no other conclusion to be reached. The troubled woman had lost her travelling companion and saw no future for herself. The captain knew it was no use turning the ship around to mount a search. With one leg and heavy clothing she would have drowned almost instantly. Another death had to be recorded in his log. The voyage had turned tragic which was not a good omen for any sailor.

* * *

Of course Catherine, Ann, Sophie and Emily were not to know of their good fortune for had Hector and Clare arrived in England they would most certainly have informed the authorities that the four convicts plus Wilf Malone and Fred Pankhurst still lived. A hue and cry was sure to have been raised and sooner or later they would have been retaken.

Yet it seemed fate was once again on their sides. Knowingly they had survived a shipwreck, unknowingly Ann Lingos at least had escaped the wrath of Hector Pimm and to a lesser extent Clare Hamlyn for it was fairly obvious she would have once again been eager to see the convicts got all they deserved.

* * * * *

PART SIX

REUNIONS

CHAPTER 27

EXACTLY TWO YEARS TO THE DAY FOLLOWING their original meeting a genuine Mister and Mrs Fred Pankhurst arrived at the Strait of Dover Inn only to find it was now simply called the Straits Hotel. A second floor had been added and the courtyard extended. This was now over half filled by a variety of travelling carriages, both open and closed. Footmen stood idly around smoking and chatting among themselves while stable lads wiped the steaming horses down. There was an air of relaxed affluence with the sound of waves breaking on the shore in the background.

As the new arrivals stepped out of their rented coach many pairs of inquisitive eyes watched as the couple made their way to the main entrance where they were met by a liveried doorman who escorted them to a highly polished oak reception counter staffed by a man wearing a morning suit. Fred requested one of their best quality rooms for two days at least. As he signed his name on the register the receptionist told him there was a gentleman and lady waiting for them in the residents' bar through the set of double doors to the left.

"It has to be Wilf and Emily," Sophie said as Fred was being given a second-floor room key. Money had not been asked for as their clothes alone spoke of wealth and prosperity. Their luggage would be taken up.

In the lounge eyes sparkled and faces smiled as Wilf and Emily stood up to shake hands and exchange kisses. It was obvious they too had done well for themselves as their clothes were obviously made to measure and of top quality. Nothing like the ones they wore on their first stay here. Wilf quickly observed Sophie was pregnant and Fred confirmed it wasn't her first. She had delivered a son almost nine and a half months to the day since leaving the hotel before. Peter had been left with his nanny in York.

Then to their surprise Peter Morgan, the original owner, appeared in the bar through an all-glass door which gave access to a mosaic-tiled terrace and a landscaped garden beyond. Peter said he recognized Fred's voice. Hands were shaken and the backs of the women's hands kissed. Their ring-bedecked fingers didn't go unnoticed.

Peter explained his business had increased considerably since they were last here hence the addition and improvements although he quickly added his high-quality services had not suffered. He still catered to those who wished to dine in style, enjoy discreet privacy and have meetings in a relaxed, comfortable atmosphere. This especially so for politicians and businessmen from London which was less than a day's ride by an express stage. He also added the addition was not his only investment, he had acquired two staging posts along the Dover to London road so horses could be changed en route thus providing a speedier service and minimum delays for his valued customers.

"But," he explained, holding an index finger up, "this service only operates during daylight hours as highwaymen frequently hold up and rob coaches during the dark hours." He paused and looked at Emily and Sophie. "Sadly, I regret to say, gentlewomen such as yourselves also find themselves being assaulted."

"Yes, we were warned of the dangers," Wilf replied. "And I say once again it's about time England adopted a fully coordinated police force operating as a single unified body, not the mishmash of so-called law and order we have now."

"I couldn't agree more," Peter replied. "Since transportation was introduced people expected the crime rate to drop, sadly it has increased, in this area at least. It's all the undesirables who filter into the country by one means or another. It also costs me a tidy sum paying security guards to ensure the safety of our valued guests. Still I'm not complaining and I hope you have a pleasant stay this time. Now is there anything I can get you?"

Wilf requested red and white wines and a cheese selection to be sent up to his room while they awaited the arrival of Catherine Harrow and Annie Ingol who must have been delayed. Sophie immediately began to worry that the pair may have been recaptured and were now serving their sentences in Botany Bay despite having seen no announcements in the press. Although living so far away in York news from the south was frequently omitted due to it being out of date when received.

Wilf's room was elegance itself complete with a canopied four-poster bed. The view over the white cliffs was spectacular with the channel shimmering in the background. Happy sights for Sophie and Emily now, not so when they were first permitted on the *Bromley*'s deck, heading for Australia. Two comfortable settees were furnished along with oak casual tables. A full-size table and four chairs were provided by the window. Fred and Sophie said they would check their own room out while the refreshments were being delivered.

The room was almost identical although the decor was pale blue while Wilf and Emily's room was a pastel pink which included the silk bedspread. The pair kissed and washed their faces in a large ceramic bowl before returning to Wilf's room.

Their refreshments and drinks had arrived so Wilf poured. A toast to themselves and the hope that Catherine and Ann would arrive shortly were said before they sat down.

"Did you realise your ambition to open an eating place?" Wilf finally asked Fred.

"Indeed we did, it lies within the walled and historic city of York. With Cromwell's money we purchased a run-down building, had it completely gutted and redecorated. No expense was spared, much of which went into the kitchen. We now boast the most modern cooking facilities in Yorkshire. In no time we had built up a regular and influential clientele who appreciated fine dining and drinking. Many who patronize us are out-and-out aloof, I have to admit, but they are good spenders and the lifeblood of Yorkshire. I purchase most of my meat and poultry from the gentlemen farmers, as they liked to be known. I also attend grouse shoots with them. Quite a change, you must admit, from that small galley I sweated in on the *Bromley*. We also have an excellent wine cellar. Rather than purchasing myself, I've taken on an expert who travels to France three or four times a year buying vintage wines, spirits and of course champagne."

"You wouldn't believe how much profit we can make on a bottle of champagne," Sophie added while giving her successful husband a broad smile.

Emily asked what the establishment was called.

"Cromwell's," Fred replied. "Sophie's idea actually. She said we owed the man that much and we couldn't come up with anything more suitable and agreed Pankhurst didn't sound quite right. Anyway Cromwell is a truly loyalist name and, so it is said, the man himself Oliver Cromwell is buried in Newburgh Priory near the hamlet of Coxwold, some twenty miles north of York. We've seen the crypt there but of course you just have to accept Oliver's bones lie below."

"Do you still cook?" Wilf asked.

"I make up the menus and prepare speciality dishes for some of our fussier, more senior customers who have rather fragile stomachs. I have a permanent cook who has worked in one or two better quality establishments in Paris and London. Actually this feature brings people in by the coach load. Many a time we're fully booked three months ahead. Sometimes we have so many customers their coaches and horses block the street but I pay my taxes so all is usually well. We also provide an out service of food and drink to coachmen and grooms. This feature alone brings more clients in, the ones who treat their servants like human beings that is, not beasts of burden."

"Fred was just what York needed," Sophie told them. "Of course he never tells them he once worked on a transportation ship taking convicts to Australia ..." she paused, lowered her voice and said after a smile, "or that I was one of them."

"Did people suspect anything when you first arrived?" Emily asked Sophie.

"No, not really, and as we had money fashion shops were soon trying to sell me dresses and naughty silk underwear which came mostly from Paris. York was, still is, a very staid city and quite religious. Its cathedral or Minster, as it's called, was built between the twelfth and fifteenth centuries and we do boast an archbishop. Our establishment is within the city walls so Fred and I like to think of ourselves as living inside history."

Fred patted her back. "My Sophie has become very clever as you will have realised. She also delivers excellent children and rides very well. We own one or two hunters as I enjoy the sport plus it gets me out of the kitchen and into the fresh air for a few hours."

Sophie laughed in a friendly fashion. "Actually it's just another excuse for him and his friends to drink before chasing a fox. Following the kill they celebrate with more drink and food. It seems in this day and age everything revolves around drink. Look at us here, we talk and we drink."

"Remember we can afford to, Sophie," Wilf remarked while removing a gold pocket watch from his waistcoat, he opened it and stared at the time. "It's getting late, Catherine and Ann should have been here by now. Surely they couldn't have forgotten."

"I wouldn't have thought so, Ann never forgot anything," Sophie replied while wiping a smut of dirt off her powdered nose.

Wilf snapped his watch closed and suggested they go down for supper and hope the two women arrived while they were eating. As for himself he was starving.

"He's always starving," Emily told them. "You should open an eating place in Belfast, Fred, Wilf alone would keep your accounts in the black."

Wilf kissed her cheek. "Don't forget I work long hard hours, my dear. That develops a hearty appetite."

"Did you get into shipbuilding?" Fred asked.

"I'll tell you over supper. Let's get changed and go down, I noticed suckling pig was on tonight's menu."

* * *

They took a table for six despite there only being four of them. Peter Morgan acted the perfect host and donated a large claret jug of red wine for the table. They drank each other's health under the eyes of many customers and one of the largest chandeliers Fred had ever seen. It was in the style of a cartwheel and was at least twelve feet in diameter with an uncountable number of ornate oil lamps mounted on it. It seemed to be arranged on a system of pulleys so it could be lowered when the lamps needed refuelling.

Most male patrons had cast at least one glance at Emily and Sophie for they both looked ravishing in their new silk and lace dresses, featuring low-cut necklines with almost identical strings of pearls gracing their necks. At the moment it was the fashionable thing for a woman to accent her bosom and suffer a corseted waist but both women were prepared to do this because most of their lives had been spent wearing rags. Now by a great stroke of fortune they had emerged into more prosperous circles. Not to be outdone both men wore finely tailored suits, starched white collars and cravats. One would never have suspected that almost three years ago these same people were sitting on a desolate Australian beach, wondering where their next meal was coming from while planning their future following a shipwreck.

The pig was being roasted over a huge spit being turned slowly by two children whose faces seemed too red for they were in close proximity to the hot coals. Sophie had already expressed the view she didn't like to see such exploitation of children although knowing it was common everywhere. Outside York in the farmers' fields, children toiled alongside men when they should have been in school. Unfortunately a family income was far more important than lessons. And if the children didn't maintain pace with the men they were, more than likely, thrashed. Many a time Sophie had the urge to intervene although Fred usually restrained her by saying: "Remember who and what you once were, Sophie. Don't spoil it all by drawing too much attention to yourself. These things will happen anyway. Cruelty has been around since the beginning of time and will continue long after we're dead and buried."

"I realise that, Fred. Remember I was once forced to witness quite a young girl being tethered before a ship's mast and flogged into unconsciousness because she attacked the man who tried to assault her. That I'll never forget, Fred, however I'll heed what you say."

A liveried waiter took their order while another poured them red wine to accompany their meal.

* * *

Supper was finished but sadly Catherine and Ann still hadn't arrived. Now they were all getting worried that something had befallen the couple. Over their extended meal Wilf had accounted for himself and Emily since they last saw each other.

It took him and Emily almost six weeks to reach Ireland. Wanting to give London a wide berth they first took an express stage from Dover to Southampton where they stayed for two days, buying new clothing. From there it was a series of coaches to Liverpool, unfortunately they encountered numerous delays due to muddy roads and in some areas floods caused by heavy rainfalls in Wales and Northern England. Then upon arrival in Liverpool they found all sailings to Belfast had been cancelled due to unusually rough weather in the Irish Sea. The delay however proved fortunate for Wilf because he met a man by the name of Edward Thompson who had recently embarked on a project to open a shipbuilding yard in Belfast. It seemed Edward intended to become a pioneer and build steel-hulled sailing ships supplemented with steam engines. He also foresaw the time when steam would take over completely, making wooden ships like the *Bromley* obsolete. It was revolutionary thinking and qualified engineers had already been retained to do preliminary design work. Edward said he was also looking for private investors as the banks were reluctant to lend money on the reasoning wooden vessels were proven so why bother to change.

Wilf naturally expressed his interest in this new company. To him it was a way of keeping in touch with sea travel while not having to face the hazards associated with it. Edward Thompson asked if he had experience in ships and sailing.

For the first time since being shipwrecked Wilf explained he had held the rank of bosun on three ships; however due to an unfortunate occurrence during one voyage he had decided to retire. Then he cautiously added he and his wife had funds to invest.

Terms were discussed and when they finally arrived in Belfast Edward Thompson's lawyers drew up the contracts. Sixty percent of the money Cromwell had given them was paid into the new company and Wilf became a major shareholder. The new company was rightly named Thompson and Malone.

Emily took up the story, saying with the money they had to lay out for Wilf's investment it had been somewhat of a struggle at first as she was expecting their first child. She delivered a girl whom they named Caroline who was now almost a year old. They had decided to wait a few years before having another as they didn't want to strain their finances.

"Things only got better," Wilf continued. "Within twelve months the company had a major investor who agreed to buy every ship we produced. This agreement managed to secure us all the credit we wanted and now the banks are almost licking our boots to advance loans. One result of which is we are having a mansion built in the Antrim Hills and we owe it all in part to Cromwell. I certainly intend to name one of our ships after him just as you did your establishment, Fred."

Fred nodded. "However we must remember, Wilf, not to arouse too many questions about Cromwell. We owe him that much."

"I thought about that, Fred, but realised Cromwell is an English name so nobody is going to associate it with a slightly eccentric man living in a secluded forest glade in western Australia."

"Did you ever get married?" Sophie asked Emily.

"No, one day we may though. As agreed in Australia we claim to be married and everybody simply takes our word for it. Even here we signed-in as man and wife and were not questioned." She paused because Fred had laughed.

"I imagine the hotel is well used to renting rooms to bogus married couples. It's similar in York where many of my customers are wining and dining mistresses, but I don't complain. The tips are usually much better. Anyway I interrupted you, Emily. Please continue."

"I was going to say we are also in the process of trying to trace my own heritage although we were so poor I doubt records of my birth will exist. As I told you on the *Rotterdam* I was delivered in a barn because my mother and father were constantly moving around trying to find work. It's very doubtful I was ever registered in church records, in fact I don't even know if I'm a Catholic or a Protestant. However Wilf has been speaking to a priest who thinks he may be able to help. It remains to be seen."

"Aren't you afraid of somebody asking questions which could raise your past in London?" Fred asked.

Wilf put his arm around Emily's shoulder. "Who would ever associate Emily with what she once was to her situation now. She performs a great deal of charity work, especially with children of the very poor. To them she's an angel, as she is to me of course. It came as a wrench when I had to leave her for a few weeks on a mission to ease my conscience."

Wilf saw puzzled frowns on Fred and Sophie's foreheads so he explained what he meant by easing his conscience. After Emily had settled into their lodgings and with the first ship barely started ,he decided to visit the *Bromley*'s owners in North Woolwich to inform them of the ship's demise off Brookes Inlet. They were surprised and sad to learn all hands had perished except himself, Fred Pankhurst, Clare Hamlyn and of course the four farmers who had been dropped off prior to the shipwreck. He explained Fred had returned to his place of birth in Yorkshire with a woman he met on the homeward journey. As for Clare Hamlyn he simply said she had continued on to Port Jackson to be reunited with her husband, which actually wasn't a lie if Cromwell had kept his word. He concluded by asking if First Mate Hector Pimm had arrived back.

According to the Managing Director Clifford Prosser, Hector had arrived and presented Captain Stricker's report. It seemed Mister Prosser wasn't at all impressed with Pimm's actions and had dismissed the bitter man after paying him off. He had no idea where he was now and really didn't care. He did confirm Hector still suffered severe headaches.

Over lunch Wilf was shown Captain Stricker's report and asked if it was accurate.

"To the best of my knowledge it is, sir, although I wasn't present when the assault occurred. I do know the girl claimed that Pimm had been drinking when she entered his cabin. I also know it distressed Captain Stricker when he gave the order to have the lass flogged but he had no alternative having attacked a senior ship's officer. As is tradition, sir, I laid the lashes myself and was greatly relieved when she fully recovered. Alas, we have to assume she and the five other convicts perished when the *Bromley* went down. They stood no chance in the roiling sea with those ankle manacles and chain. If you have any influence, sir, I would recommend convicts both male and female are never transported in irons. The women may have otherwise survived although we shall never know."

Wilf smiled now. "I was very convincing. Mister Prosser explained the board of governors were seriously considering getting out of the transportation of convicts because there seemed to be far more lucrative contracts in cargo as England was exporting more goods every year. It was far more humane to have iron and steel products in the hold as opposed to human flesh. Mister Prosser thanked me for coming in and said the company would apply for a claim with their insurance agents. Mister Prosser asked me to give an account of the shipwreck to his secretary which I did and I returned the following morning to sign it. I would of course be compensated for my trouble and paid up for the wages they owed me." He paused to take another drink. In fact they all refreshed theirs.

"You know life is strange," Wilf continued. "For most of my life I never seemed to have any money, now all of a sudden it was almost pouring out of my ears. In addition to what they owed me for the *Bromley*'s last voyage I was given an extra twenty-five guineas for reporting the shipwreck. I returned immediately to my beloved Emily where we've been happy ever since. Oh and by the way, Fred, this is for you." He reached into an inside jacket pocket and produced an envelope which was handed to Fred. "It's your pay for the time spent on the *Bromley*. The money was included on the cheque they paid me because in all honesty I didn't know exactly where you were and the cheque could have been out of date by the time I delivered it. The cheque in the envelope is one of my own but you can be assured my credit is good, very good in fact."

The envelope was opened and a cheque removed. Fred smiled as he handed it to Sophie. "Thank you, Wilf, and in all honesty, with Cromwell's money I'd completely forgotten about my chef's pay."

"Almost a fairy story," Sophie said after kissing her husband's cheek. "We must buy Peter a gift with some of this money."

Fred clapped his hands. "I agree, perhaps a pocket watch suitably engraved as a reminder of this day. Now, as it seems we've done very well for ourselves why don't we order a bottle of champagne?"

"Aren't you forgetting Catherine and Annie?" Emily said. "We may have done very well but since they are not here I'm beginning to fear the worst. It would break my heart to think either of them have fallen foul of the law again. If they have been recaptured they'll be either wallowing in Newgate Prison, returned to Botany Bay or worse still have been hanged."

"Don't forget Ann never actually committed a crime," Wilf interjected. "However it is possible she may have failed in her attempt to get compensation through that cobbler Henry Lastman. If that's the case, who knows?"

"Of course there could be another explanation," Fred mused seriously. "Somehow or other the authorities got onto Catherine and rather than facing transportation again the pair of them decided to take their own lives. We all know how much in love they were."

"Oh, that's a horrible thought," Sophie said, burying her face in her hands.

Fred got up to give comfort. "I'm sorry I said it, my dear. Somewhere they're alright, I'm sure of that, they were both very capable and hardy. There may be circumstances we don't know about, don't forget it's two years and none of us has made contact with anybody else. Now I just suggested champagne, I still say we get a bottle and drink a toast. Please, everybody, agree."

They did and the largest bottle Peter had in stock was ordered. Fresh glasses were delivered and their waiter poured.

They all stood up and Wilf proposed the toast. "To absent friends."

"To absent friends."

"This is heartbreaking," Sophie said to Emily as they sat down again.

"I feel like I've lost part of myself," Emily added. "We were all forced together in the most regrettable of circumstances, causing us great sorrow at first only later to find immense happiness. I just hope sadness has not returned."

Wilf nodded but said nothing. What was to have been a joyous reunion had become a wake with all their achievements amounting to nothing now. Two of their number were not present and there was no way of discovering what had become of them.

The bottle of champagne was finished and they were just preparing to go to their rooms when Peter came across to Wilf, carrying a rolled sheet of parchment secured with a red ribbon.

"An express horseback courier has just delivered this, sir."

Wilf removed the ribbon and unfurled the message. In seconds his sad face became creased with a broad smile. "Listen to this, it's from Catherine and Annie," he said while standing up to read the note.

> *"To our dear friends.*
>
> *"Our coach has broken a wheel so we are delayed about four miles from Canterbury. Our driver assures us the wheel will be repaired by first light tomorrow so our journey can resume. Please wait as we dearly wish to see you all again.*
>
> *"Your shipwrecked acquaintances "*

With obvious relief Wilf beckoned Peter over to ask how far Canterbury was from Dover.

"A little under twenty miles, sir."

Wilf sat down again and made a quick calculation. "Assuming nothing else happens they should arrive well before noon. Now I suggest we all get a good night's sleep ..."

"Who wants to sleep?" Sophie said. "This news has buoyed me almost beyond belief."

Fred agreed and said, "By the tone of the note and the reference to 'our driver' they must have done very well for themselves."

"I agree," Emily replied, beaming a huge smile. "It's no use us speculating, we'll just have to wait until tomorrow. I do however agree with Sophie, who wants to sleep?"

"I was rather hoping you might say that," Wilf replied coyly.

It was a very happy and much relieved group which left the dining room, heading for their rooms. Peter too smiled, knowing he had made a handsome profit tonight from this group who were as full of mystery now as they had been on their first visit, but so long as they continued spending and paying their bills he didn't care.

* * *

The following morning they were all up and dressed well before seven. Emily and Sophie had applied extra perfume and the men took greater care shaving, not wanting to meet Catherine and Ann with razor nicks on their faces.

The dining room remained heavy with smoke from last night along with the smell of stale ale. A waiter was clearing full ashtrays away while another replaced tablecloths and yet another was refilling oil lamps. There was another young couple eating breakfast who only had eyes for themselves. To Fred's way of thinking they could be one of two things. Either they had recently been married and were on their honeymoon, or, he was married, she was not his wife but they had gone through the physical motions anyway. Either way, Fred felt happy for them.

A waiter showed them to the same table they used last night for supper. Tea, eggs and ham along with freshly baked rolls were offered and accepted. Peter entered and greeted each of them with a polite bow and a kiss on the back of the ladies' hands. He hoped they'd all had comfortable nights. They had although the men were not about to divulge what transpired between the sheets before they went to sleep.

They lingered over breakfast, hoping Catherine and Ann would arrive at any moment. Unfortunately they didn't. Time had to be killed. A stroll in the garden was suggested. As the sun was up and bright the ladies collected their parasols before venturing outside into the garden which also offered a good view of the channel and the Canterbury road. The sea air was bracing which returned memories of life at sea for Wilf and Fred. It was a little early for alcohol so they returned inside, took a table and ordered a pot of tea. Small talk was made although it was obvious the only things on their minds were Catherine and Ann. The wait was going to be frustrating yet there was nothing they could do. They imagined it was the same for their two friends.

* * *

Wilf saw it first. A magnificent maroon carriage drawn by a pair of chestnuts. It was so grand it couldn't possibly contain Catherine and Ann but when it pulled into the hotel forecourt and a footman had opened the carriage door, out stepped Ann followed by Catherine. Their faces were all smiles and despite the somewhat cumbersome skirts they rushed to meet their friends where kisses and handshakes were exchanged.

"I don't believe it," Wilf exclaimed.

"Believe it," Catherine answered.

"Believe it," Ann echoed. "We've had luck almost beyond imagination. Let's go inside. Do we have a room?"

"Yes," Fred told her. "The very best. Come, we'll show you."

A moment was taken to instruct the footman what to do with their luggage then they all went inside with Catherine's arm interlocked in Emily's and Ann's with Sophie's. Once inside they were reintroduced to Peter who remembered the pair instantly. Despite the time of day wine was ordered and would be delivered to the room. Peter saw more profit.

The new arrivals were now obviously women of considerable means and their coach reflected that. Not too many were seen like it in the Dover area. Usually even wealthy men travelled in cheaper carriages, not wishing to draw attention to themselves or the person who travelled with them because in many cases they were not related.

"Oh, it's so good to see you all again," Catherine said as she sat on one of the settees next to Ann. "Last night when the wheel on our carriage broke we were so upset. Sadly for us it was too late to get another coach as they don't run after nightfall, that was why we sent a courier. I hope our message arrived."

"It did," Wilf answered. "We were at supper and before the courier came we had started to fear the worst. We did however drink a toast in champagne to absent friends. Now though we're all together again and, need I say, we're anxious to hear your success story. Ours can come later."

"Pour us all a drink first," Emily told him.

Once they were all settled Catherine began their story.

"After leaving here we went to Canterbury and took a room to plan our strategy and buy suitable new clothes. As you know our priority was to get some form of settlement for Ann. We felt it safe to travel provided our false names were used and we took care to avoid any areas where I may have bumped into my parents, assuming of course they hadn't moved. My face was also known to the constables to whom I reported my crime in Limehouse so we gave it a very wide berth. As Ann explained the last time we were here she knew this cobbler who made high-quality boots and shoes for the king and his family. His workshop was in a tiny village called Slough so we decided to take the chance and went to see him." She paused to sip her drink so Ann continued.

"We found Henry still working in his little shop on a muddy side street of the town. His eyesight was failing yet he still recognized me and almost fell off his stool in surprise. It had been a mystery to him how I disappeared so soon after my mother's death and the hours he had grieved, but being a humble man there wasn't much he could do. Between Catherine and me, we explained my situation and Henry was genuinely sickened that people associated with the king could sink so low. I then asked him if he still made footwear for the king, he did and saw him at least six times a year now his normal sanity had returned. Together we asked Henry if he would be willing to casually explain to George one of his illegitimate daughters had fallen on hard times, was almost destitute, near to death and living rough under hedges or in barns so could he consider some form of compensation for the lass. We all assumed the king was totally unaware of what became of me and knowing he was a compassionate man before his madness Henry said he was willing to give it a try. As we said two years ago there was a good chance George would agree as he wouldn't want any form of scandal to arise now he was fully recovered and popular with the people.

"In the meantime Henry said Catherine and I could use the spare bedroom above his shop which hadn't been occupied since his lodger moved out so it would need a very thorough cleaning. He wasn't lying. We found it thick with cobwebs, the walls were mouldy and the one window was so grimy we couldn't see through it. After stripping down to our underclothing we set about cleaning the place up, looking upon it as our first real home together. There were still blankets on the well-sprung bed although they fell apart the moment we touched them. To keep our presence secret we gave Henry some money so he could buy new sheets, blankets and curtains for the window. He whitewashed the walls after we'd given them a thorough scrubbing. It was a most happy time as we acted like a married couple except for the obvious differences. Even Henry treated us like family. Of course during this period there was the anxiety about what the king's reaction would be when Henry opened discussions." She held her glass out for a refill.

Wilf obliged and topped everybody's up as Sophie asked what became of Henry's meeting with the king. Ann answered.

"Beyond our wildest expectations actually. George openly admitted to Henry some illegitimate children did exist although for obvious reasons he couldn't officially acknowledge any of them. Unofficially though, through third parties he had given the mothers money to provide food and clothing. At this point George demonstrated he had regained the full use of his faculties by telling Henry he could look forward to hearing from him in the very near future and the girl in question was not to worry." Ann looked to Catherine to continue.

"The king kept his word. Within two months a courier arrived at Henry's shop with a signed, stamped and sealed declaration that the cobbler Henry Lastman, his heirs and successors in perpetuity had been granted an annual annuity of one thousand pounds in recognition of his excellent footwear services to King George the Third. Naturally Henry realised it was meant for Ann so he began proceedings to have her recognized as his cousin and a rightful successor under the name Annie Ingol."

"Didn't you worry Ann's transportation order would be discovered?" Wilf asked.

"No, not really. Henry thought any documentation referring to Ann's fate would have been destroyed soon after the *Bromley* sailed. To be safe however a lawyer was retained to register everything under Ann's assumed name. There were no problems as it seemed it wasn't uncommon for somebody like Henry to adopt a waif. So cutting a long story short, everything was settled within six months and the payments began. Now as you will have realised we are very rich and will be forevermore with the annuity. We have bought a small cottage outside the town of High Wycombe where we live in peace and tranquillity. Since we intended to do a fair amount of travelling Ann suggested some of Cromwell's money was used to buy shares in a local carriage rental company which was advertising for financial backers so it could expand its business. We did and one of their vehicles is the one we came here in. Of course when we return it will be necessary to have words with the men who maintain them because of the wheel breaking."

"As two women didn't you meet opposition buying into the company?" Wilf asked.

"The owners did say it was most unusual," Catherine replied, "that is until they were told we had no intentions of taking an active role in the company or becoming involved in any way whatsoever. It was just our feeling since we had money to invest it would be a worthwhile venture on the assumption people had to travel either on business or pleasure."

"From that moment they took our money gladly," Ann added. "It transpired to be a good investment and is now beginning to show some returns. Of course no mention has ever been made of our regular income and we intend to keep it that way. We couldn't be more happy, could we, Catherine?"

"No. And when you think about it all this started in the smelly hold of a ship bound for Australia. I think today we shall drink rather more than we normally do. Please fill our glasses again, Wilf."

While Wilf poured Sophie had a question.

"Hasn't anybody questioned your relationship? What I mean is, two young females living together."

Ann took a breath. "Yes. If a question is asked our standard answer is that we both lost our parents in a shipwreck three years ago. It was decided as we were friends and had some money left to us we'd live together. They seem to accept it and any times we have friends in we are very careful not to display any romantic affinities. After they've gone though you should see us."

There was laughter at that statement and more drinks were poured before Wilf had a question.

"What about men? Have you never been approached, well, I think you know what I mean?"

Ann gave one of her cheeky smiles. "Yes, there have been proposals but once one of us has explained how grief stricken we are at the loss of our parents they seem to accept it. Further we have never had the urge to associate with men in any way whatsoever. Catherine was unfortunate to experience one man in her life, me none and that is how it will remain. Two virgins, although not quite."

They laughed, she winked.

"What about yourself, Catherine, hasn't anybody ever suspected you?" Emily asked.

"No. There really was no reason to as I'm known locally as Catherine Harrow. So long as I don't return to Limehouse I'm safe although there's a person there who tried to help me in my darker days, in time I'd like to meet her again. Her name is Eunice Wilson, who frequented The Grapes tavern in a capacity as a 'working girl' although she was getting a little long in the tooth. One day we may pluck up courage and visit her, for now though Ann and I are quite content."

She turned and took Ann in her arms and as they had on so many occasions kisses were exchanged with great passion. Between them there was a bond which would never be broken, everybody in the room knew that.

Another two bottles of wine were drunk before everybody agreed they needed to freshen up before lunch. Ann and Catherine especially as they'd been on the road since dawn. Yet Wilf suspected love would be exchanged before they put on fresh clothes.

He would not be wrong.

* * *

For the next two days their success stories were related over drinks and excellent meals in the dining room before retiring to one of their rooms for drinks and cigars for the men. There in more privacy they talked of old times. What a gentleman Captain Stricker had been in treating them with some respect despite their status. At the opposite end of the scale was that horrible man Hector Pimm and initially the louse Albert Brooks. Wilf and Fred heard again how terrible it had been stuck down that hold for up to fifteen hours a day and about the stench from the bilges and the constant motions of the ship. Those were the bad times of course. Then following the shipwreck the good ones, especially meeting Cromwell and his happy tribe of Myalls. Then of course there was Martha McFarlane who fed and gave them a room for the night. Sadly they never got to meet her husband Brendon, a man of dubious morals, but he was not the only person in Australia with something to hide. They tried to speculate if the four farmers on the *Bromley* had found their own pot of gold although it was assumed they would never know. Simply four ambitious people who they only knew vaguely because of the circumstances. However a toast was said to the men, hoping they had met with success. Nobody had any idea what became of Clare Hamlyn or Hector Pimm although they really didn't care.

Pleasant walks were taken around the well-kept hotel gardens which featured a goldfish pond complete with lilies. They also took strolls along the beach looking out over the English Channel where they saw ships coming and going although their points of departure or destinations were unknown. Wilf did recognize one ship as the *Lady Julian* which he knew transported convicts so they all held a moment's silence for those in the hold. They were heading for unhappiness while they themselves faced lives of pure bliss.

And of course as night descended they all returned to their own privacies. In their rooms love was exchanged in the normal manner for Fred and Wilf. For Catherine and Ann it was slightly different although the conclusions were identical. Love was made in silence and yet thunder roared within them.

* * * * *

EPILOGUE

WILF AND EMILY

FOLLOWING MUCH DISCUSSION AND FAILURE TO DISCOVER anything about Emily's heritage she and Wilf decided not to get married although all their friends and business associates assumed they were. Such was their standing in the community their daughter Caroline was accepted into the church so her life at least began on the right foot. By mutual agreement and to ease their financial burden they decided not to have any more children for two or three years. The house they were having built was costing more than the original estimate due to changes in room design and decor suggested by Emily and approved by Wilf. When finished it would be the only home Emily had ever known so it had to be perfect.

The Thompson and Malone shipyard began to prosper when they launched their first sailing ship assisted by steam-driven paddles. It was naturally named *Kilpatrick* which was Emily's maiden name although she now went under Malone. It was the shipyard's intent in the near future to only build steam-powered vessels of very high quality. Voyages across the Atlantic were becoming commonplace with crossings taking three weeks or less.

Four years after their reunion in Dover Wilf and Emily travelled to York to make Fred a proposal. It was to see if he would like to become the exclusive catering director for the Thompson Malone shipping line. Fred was of course highly flattered but refused. He was quite happy to remain with his land-based eating place chain, one he was thinking of expanding. Another thing which swayed him was Sophie's obvious reluctance to become involved with the sea again, especially as she was expecting their third child. Despite the refusal Wilf and Emily enjoyed their stay and were taken to see the Oliver Cromwell crypt in Newburgh Priory. A silent prayer was said both to the Cromwell they knew in Australia and the one in the crypt.

* * *

Quite by chance just over a year later Wilf was attending a seafaring conference in Liverpool where he met a retired captain named Gerald Mayfield who had spent years on the Australia run. Over whisky in the hotel bar the captain recounted a somewhat strange incident where he had a passenger named Pimm on the outward voyage who seemed to be carrying a grudge of some sort which always brought on severe headaches. Yet what made the incident even more strange was Pimm taking a berth on the return journey only this time he was escorting a crippled woman back to England. Wilf almost choked on his drink when realising it had to be Hector Pimm and the woman Clare Hamlyn. He asked with unusual calmness what became of the pair.

"That's the strangest part, Wilf," Captain Mayfield replied. "As the voyage progressed Pimm's headaches became more frequent so to alleviate the situation he took to the whisky bottle in a serious way. Then one morning we found him dead in his cabin. In a stupor he'd fallen and cracked his skull on an edge of the cabin bunk. The day after we buried him at sea the woman he was escorting became very distressed herself. A day later when the steward went to her cabin with breakfast she wasn't there. We searched the ship from topmast to keel but never found her. Between the doctor and myself we assumed she threw herself through the cabin window although it was never proved. All in all they were a strange couple. Still that's life at sea, isn't it?"

Wilf nodded, knowing there was much he could tell Captain Mayfield, naturally he said nothing. However it was a relief to know Pimm was dead so Ann had nothing left to fear. Before leaving the conference he hired two private couriers to take sealed notes, one to Fred and Sophie in York telling them the good news. The other went to Catherine and Ann in High Wycombe. He knew they would be highly elated and for Ann her fears could finally be put to rest. Emily too was overjoyed to hear of Pimm's demise when Wilf returned to Ireland.

* * *

Things steadily improved for Wilf and his partner. Over the years as each new ship was launched it was more luxurious than previous ones so Thompson and Malone came to enjoy great prosperity and national repute.

For Emily and Wilf though one thing was missing, another child. Then to their great joy after three mishaps Emily delivered a son in 1815 whom they named Victor. This pleased Wilf as he wanted nothing more than to bring a son into the company. As the years progressed it became obvious Victor was blessed with a great mechanical aptitude and an analytical brain. He studied engineering at Belfast university and graduated with honours. In his twenty-first year he became a full company partner. Neither Victor nor his sister Caroline were told of their mother's earlier background on the sound reasoning some things were best left unsaid. By now Wilf had attained the ripe old age of seventy-four and retired a rich man with a lifetime of memories.

In 1861 a new shipbuilding company named Harland and Wolff was formed and they bought out Thompson and Malone but took Victor on as a senior partner due to his experience in steam turbine technology. Their ships were promised to be the largest and most luxurious afloat and were to be built under the exclusive contract of The White Star Line.[5]

Newspapers described their ships as floating palaces so it became fashionable for the aristocracy and very rich to cross the Atlantic in absolute luxury and at a speed hitherto unknown. Gambling salons were also very popular aboard the largest liners as of course were the dining rooms which spared no expense, pampering to the passengers' every whim. Most ships also carried European emigrants to 'The New World' as America was being called. They travelled in what was termed 'steerage class', located at the lowest level of the ship. Conditions were very cramped and only marginally better than transportees had been subjected to. Their shipboard movements were also strictly limited although the price was right – cheap. Upon arrival in New York many émigrés were disappointed, even disillusioned, as America was not quite the country they had imagined. At home they were accustomed to neighbourly friendliness but true white Americans seemed artificial, aloof, caring only for themselves while exploiting the newcomers. Unfortunately for most their life savings had been used for the passage so they couldn't afford to go back. In fact many were never to see their homelands again as they were forced to perform the most menial tasks and work long hours for very little pay. They had no choice, there was nothing else and eastern Europe was a very long way away. Of course others with criminal intent were to make their fortunes out of gambling, liquor and

---

5   Harland and Wolff and The White Star Line are genuine companies. It should also be noted Harland and Wolff built the *Titanic* which was launched in May 1911 and we all know its fate.

prostitution. They had traversed the mighty Atlantic to do exactly what they had done in their country of origin. The mafia had gained a stranglehold in America just as it did in parts of Europe.

*　*　*

FRED AND SOPHIE

FRED'S ESTABLISHMENT BUSINESS FLOURISHED ALMOST BEYOND HIS wildest dreams. His first venture outside York was an establishment on Deansgate in Manchester, catering to the cotton merchants who were themselves making a fortune. And eventually the city was to have direct access to the sea by the Manchester Ship Canal. The next city in line was Liverpool, followed by London where the aristocracy took to Fred's gourmet fare like ducks to water. He even catered to King George III who was once again firmly in control of himself and his parliament. Fred actually met the king on one occasion yet he was very careful not to mention he knew a certain illegitimate young lady named Ann Lingos, or even one Annie Ingol.

It was Sophie who actually set her husband on his next venture when she expressed a desire to shop for French fashions, only this time actually in Paris.

"Then we shall go there, my dear, and you may shop while I search for a suitable property in which to open Cromwell's first continental eating place. It cannot fail. All I ask is you model your purchases for me in the privacy of our bedroom."

"You know I will, Fred."

So Cromwell's became international and the family couldn't be happier. Sophie delivered Fred four children whom they adored. Children who would have a far better start in life than their mother.

Their first son Peter married in 1811 and his wife Emma delivered a son one year later. The family name Pankhurst was to continue, and an Emmeline Pankhurst was born in 1858. She gave her husband two daughters, Christabel, born in 1880, and Sylvia in 1882. They founded the militant suffragette movement in 1903, demanding votes for women. It was to be a long struggle with the sisters being arrested for their marches of protest and both served time in Holloway Prison in London. However with increasing support their movement persisted and eventually women over the age of thirty were given the vote. It was a remarkable victory. The voting age was later reduced to twenty-one when the Equal Franchise Bill was passed in parliament in March 1928. It had been a long struggle.

Sophie had always been a believer in civil rights for women so she would have been very proud of the family line she and Fred started on that night they spent in the Strait of Dover Inn after their long journey home from a picturesque glade in western Australia. A glade where the rights of all its citizens were equally accepted.

* * *

CATHERINE AND ANN

N ATURALLY CATHERINE AND ANN COULDN'T GIVE EACH other children although they did the next best thing. They opened an orphanage for poor and abandoned waifs in one of the poorer districts of north London. Its full name was: The Cathann Home for Needy Children, which was to become known locally as simply The Cathann. They have a staff running it although they try to spend a few days there every month. Nobody is ever turned away and many children simply show up at the main door for a bowl of porridge or warm broth on cold winter's days. They are usually given a few pennies as well.

Catherine decided to take the bull by the horns almost ten years after they arrived back in England and visited The Grapes tavern in Limehouse with Ann. This of course under their assumed names and with Catherine's affluent appearance nobody would ever recognize her as that person most had last seen being rowed across the Thames to a waiting vessel bound for Australia.

Much to their surprise they found Eunice Wilson was now manageress of the tavern. It seemed Hilda, the bar lady, had contracted some form of disease and had died the previous year. Naturally Eunice almost fainted when Catherine announced who she was in a very discreet whisper. Ann was introduced as her lover and companion although her background wasn't explained. For old times' sake they each had an ale which Catherine admitted she enjoyed far more than that first half-pint her stepfather Patrick forced her to have. Over their drinks Catherine obviously asked after her parents. It seemed her mother had forsaken Patrick and moved to South Wales with another man shortly after the *Bromley* sailed. Patrick never fully recovered from the injury Catherine inflicted and according to Eunice he returned to his native Ireland. Nothing had been heard about him for at least five years. He was no sad loss.

After the tavern closed for the day Catherine told Eunice the full story of what transpired after she had been put aboard the *Bromley* and of meeting Annie who was already in the hold. She explained how their immediate friendship quickly transpired into the total love they enjoyed today. Tears were shed when it was explained how Annie was flogged for attacking a crew member but everything was fine now despite faint scars still remaining. Eunice simply adored Annie from the moment they met.

The next morning an offer was made for Eunice to act as a sort of consultant to the many wayward girls who walked into The Cathann home seeking help and advice. She accepted willingly. As she said, "My living was made primarily on my back or up against a wall faking satisfaction. If I can deter young women from doing similar I shall be truly satisfied and will die happy. I also know a kindly man named Mister Snekcid who I'm sure will help as well."

Eunice was very successful with her new-found station in life and The Grapes has yet to find someone to adequately replace her behind the bar.

Catherine of course realised that if there had been a place where she could have sought advice for the mental and physical abuse she received at home it might not have been necessary to assault her parents and yet by a great irony that act had given her Ann. Life sometimes weaved strange patterns.

And at night in bed they still make love with that same fervid intensity which had its origins in the hold of a ship named *Bromley* bound for a penal colony in Australia named Botany Bay..

* * * * *